Critical acclaim for bestselling author
LISA TUCKER

"A gifted writer with a wide range and a profound sense of compassion for the mysteries of the human heart."

—*Publishers Weekly*

"Brings a fresh view to the intricacies of relationships."

—*Denver Post*

"A graceful writer with an ability to create characters whose flaws help make them sympathetic and believably human."

—*The Boston Globe*

"Use[s] a winning formula: Give readers a good old-fashioned story . . . that people can't stop talking about."

—*Philadelphia Weekly*

. . . and for her poignant, impossible-to-put-down novels

THE CURE FOR MODERN LIFE

"A smart page-turner."

—*People*

"An enjoyable literary page-turner that also explores serious social issues. In crisp, lively prose, Tucker cleverly executes a series of surprising twists that make the novel as fast-paced as a thriller, but with astute and often humorous observations about the shifting morality of twenty-first-century America."

—*Publishers Weekly* (starred review)

"Tucker's book works because she knows how to limn characters, tell a story economically, and propel it at just the right allegro-vivace tempo."

—*The Philadelphia Inquirer*

"A touching and very modern relationship story with some compelling social issues. . . . Fast-paced, funny, and smart."

—*Booklist*

"Tucker deftly forces us to ponder what we'd do in this exploration of the complexity of human nature and our relationships with one another."

—*The Salt Lake Tribune*

"An emotionally satisfying page-turner."

—*Good Housekeeping*

ONCE UPON A DAY

"Tucker's graceful prose and well-crafted characters create a compelling odyssey of transfiguration."

—*People* (Critics' Choice)

"Tucker raises great questions about the nature of parental and marital responsibility."

—*Denver Post*

"Tucker's new fable is self-consciously the stuff of fairy tales . . . the book is charged with the sense that life is charmed, that chance encounters can change fate and remake them for the better."

—*San Francisco Chronicle*

"The title of Tucker's third novel sounds like a Nora Ephron movie, and on the surface the fanciful plot seems to play right along. . . . [But] another narrative strand casts a welcome emotional shadow . . . lifting *Once Upon A Day* out of the realm of romantic comedy and into the darker territory of an Old World fairy tale."

—*The New York Times*

THE SONG READER

"An engagingly intricate debut. . . . The characters become as real to the reader as they are to [the narrator]."

—*The Philadelphia Inquirer* (Editor's Choice)

"This intoxicating debut may remind [readers] of Shirley Jackson's *We Have Always Lived in the Castle* and Pat Conroy's *The Prince of Tides,* but it's not lost in their shadows."

—*Publishers Weekly* (starred review)

"A clear winner. . . . [Be] among the first to discover a brilliant new literary talent."

—*The Albuquerque Tribune*

SHOUT DOWN THE MOON

"The situations Tucker describes here in starkly lyrical prose are as chilling as if they were all derived from her own experiences."

—*People*

"Well-drawn, emotionally nuanced characters. . . . [This] compulsively readable tale deftly moves over the literary landscape, avoiding genre classification; it succeeds as a subtle romance, an incisive character study and compelling women-in-peril noir fiction."

—*Publishers Weekly*

"[Tucker's] straight-from-the-heart narration is instantly gripping."

—*Booklist*

These titles are also available as eBooks

ALSO BY LISA TUCKER

The Song Reader

Shout Down the Moon

Once Upon a Day

The Cure for Modern Life

THE PROMISED WORLD

a novel

Lisa Tucker

WASHINGTON SQUARE PRESS
New York London Toronto Sydney

Washington Square Press
A Division of Simon & Schuster, Inc.
1230 Avenue of the Americas
New York, NY 10020

First Washington Square Press trade paperback edition August 2010

Designed by Kyoko Watanabe

Manufactured in the United States of America

10 9 8 7 6 5 4 3 2 1

Library of Congress Cataloging-in-Publication Data

Tucker, Lisa.
The promised world : a novel / by Lisa Tucker.—1st Atria Books hardcover ed.
p. cm.
1. Twins—Fiction. 2. Brothers and sisters—Fiction. 3. Suicide—Fiction. 4. Psychological fiction. 5. Domestic fiction. I. Title.
PS3620.U3P76 2009
813'.6—dc22 2008055895

ISBN 978-1-4165-7538-2
ISBN 978-1-4165-7539-9 (pbk)
ISBN 978-1-4165-7574-0 (ebook)

To Billy, who will never read this,
and to Marly, Melisse, and Miles, who did.

Yes, the scenery is magical—the illusion so complete. . . . But every night when the curtain falls, truth comes in with darkness. No light shows from the mountain. To and fro I walk the piazza deck, haunted by Marianna's face, and many as real a story.

—Herman Melville, "The Piazza"

THE
PROMISED WORLD

CHAPTER ONE

While millions of people watched her brother die, Lila sat in her quiet office at the university, working on a paper about Herman Melville's later years. Someone else might have found it ironic that, on that very afternoon, she'd been thinking about Melville's son, who shot himself. Lila herself didn't make the connection until much later, and by then, she was so lost she could only see it as an obvious sign that she should have known, that she'd failed Billy when he needed her most.

Though Billy didn't shoot himself, his death was considered a suicide. Patrick, Lila's husband, had to explain it to her twice before she realized what he was saying. Her mind was working so slowly, but she finally understood that "suicide by police" happened enough that it had its own label. Billy had holed himself up inside a Center City Philadelphia hotel with a rifle, unloaded but aimed at an elementary school, so a SWAT team would have to do what he couldn't or wouldn't do to himself. As far as Lila knew, Billy had never owned a gun, but she hadn't talked to her twin much in the last two years, since he'd moved with his family to central Pennsylvania. Still, everyone knew Lila was a twin, because she talked about her brother constantly. And many of those people were probably watching as Lila's brother closed down an entire city block and sent parents and teachers and children into a terrified panic. As one of the fathers told the reporters, after the threat had been "nullified": "Of course parents are afraid of violence these days. Seems like every week, there's another nut job with an ax to grind."

Her beautiful, sensitive brother Billy—the most intelligent person she'd ever known, who taught her to climb trees and read her stories when she couldn't sleep and told her flowers were the only proof we needed that God loved us—reduced to a nut job. She wanted to scream at this father, this stranger, but the only sound she could make was a muffled cry.

Patrick hadn't wanted Lila to watch the eleven o'clock news, but she had insisted. They both knew this would still be the top story, though the city undoubtedly had murders and rapes and robberies to report that day. The elementary school was an upscale, private place, where lawyers and executives and professors like Lila dropped their children off on the way to work. Except Lila didn't have any children because, though she and Patrick were in their mid-thirties now and had been married for more than a decade, she kept begging him to wait just a little longer to start their family. What she was waiting for, Lila could never explain. She honestly didn't know.

Her brother certainly hadn't waited. When Billy showed up at her college graduation, Lila hadn't seen him in almost a year and she was giddy with the thrill of reunion. He said he was there to give her a present and handed her a large, brown box with nothing on it except a cluster of FRAGILE stickers. He told her to open it later, in her room. She thought it might be pot, since Billy always had pot, no matter how poor he was. They were both poor then (because they'd refused to take any of their stepfather's money), but Lila had gotten a full scholarship to a prestigious school while Billy had embarked on his adventure to see America, funded by a string of jobs he hated.

She took the box to the room that she was being kicked out of the next day. The dorms were already closed—classes had ended weeks ago—but Lila had gotten special permission to remain until her summer camp teaching job began. Every year it was like that: piecing together a place to stay by begging favors from people who liked Lila and sympathized with her circumstances. Her parents were dead (Billy had forged the death certificates way back, when Lila first started applying for college) and her only relative, a brother, was traveling full-time for his company. "That's true, too," Billy had said. "I'm going to be traveling for my own company—and to avoid the company of the undead."

Lila opened the box. On top, she found a baggie with three perfectly rolled joints and a note that said, "Do this in memory of me." Below that, a copy of *Highlights for Children* magazine, which Billy had probably ripped off from a doctor's office. On page twelve, at the top of the cartoon, he'd written "Billy = Gallant, Lila = Goofus." It was an old joke between them: Lila, the rule follower, had always been Gallant, and Billy, the rebel, Goofus. But in this particular comic strip, Gallant had brought a present to someone and Goofus was empty-handed.

Touché, bro, Lila thought, and smiled.

Finally, underneath an insane number of foam peanuts was a large shoe box, which he'd made into a diorama. It was so intricate, worthy of any grade school prize, except Lila and Billy had never made dioramas in grade school, not that she could remember anyway. Her memories of her childhood were so fragmented that she sometimes felt those years had disappeared from her mind even as she'd lived them. Of course, she could always ask Billy what really happened. He remembered everything.

Inside the shoe box, there were two houses made of broken Popsicle sticks in front of a multicolored landscape, complete with purple clouds and a blue sky and a pink and yellow sun. The houses had tiny toothpick mailboxes to identify them: the one on the left was Lila's, the one on the right, Billy's. In Lila's house, a clay man and woman stood watch over a clay baby inside a lumpy clay crib. In Billy's house, a clay man and woman were sitting on the floor, smoking an obscenely large joint, but a clay baby was asleep in another room, on a mattress. Billy's house was dirtier, with straw floors and very little furniture, but it was still a house and, most important, it was still next door to Lila's. They'd always planned on living next to each other when they were grown. Of course whoever Billy married would love Lila and whoever Lila married would love Billy. How could it be any other way?

Lila knew something was wrong when she saw the note Billy had attached to the bottom of the diorama: "Don't worry, I haven't lost the plot. This won't change anything." She knew what the first sentence meant since Billy had been saying this for years, but the second one was too cryptic to understand. Stranger still was how short the note was. Billy had been writing long letters from the time he could hold a crayon. He was a born writer. He'd already written dozens of stories when they were kids and he was planning to start his novel on the road trip. Lila liked to imagine him writing in seedy hotels while she learned how to interpret novels in her English courses.

She found out what he was telling her only a few days later, when he called to invite her to his wedding. He'd gotten a woman pregnant. Her name was Ashley and she was twenty-nine—eight years older than Lila and Billy. She was a waitress in a bar in Los Lunas, New Mexico. She didn't write novels or read them, but she claimed to think it was "cool" that Billy did. "He's got himself a real imagination, that boy," Ashley said, and laughed. She and Lila were sitting on barstools, waiting to drive to the justice of the peace with Billy and one of Ashley's friends. Lila tried not to hate her for that laugh, but from that point on, she couldn't help thinking of her as Trashley, though she never shared that fact with anyone, not even Patrick.

Fifteen years later, she'd forgotten about the diorama—until that night, watching Billy die on television. Then it came back to her, and she felt tears spring to her eyes because she didn't even know where it was. She told Patrick that she was going to the storage space in the basement of their building to find Billy's diorama first thing tomorrow. He gripped her hand more tightly. No doubt he thought she was in shock. Maybe she was.

The news reporter had started by announcing that the gunman, William "Billy" Cole, was in the middle of being divorced by his wife, Ashley. Patrick hadn't shared this fact with her, maybe because he didn't know it, as he'd only heard about Billy's death on the radio driving home, or maybe because he'd intuited it would upset her more. It stunned Lila, but it was the end of the broadcast that made her feel like her throat was closing up and it was becoming difficult to breathe. "Cole was thought to be depressed from the divorce and from his recent loss of visitation with his children after his wife's allegation that he'd abused their middle child, an eight-year-old boy whose name is being withheld. Earlier in the week, the district attorney had decided to bring charges against Cole for several counts of child endangerment. A warrant for his arrest had been expected today."

While Lila watched, Patrick held her tight, trying to quiet her shaking, but when she shouted an obscenity at a close-up of Trashley, he looked very surprised, and Lila heard herself barking out a hysterical laugh. It was true she never cursed and certainly never shouted. The walls of their apartment were so thin they could hear the old lady next door coughing. Normally Lila worried about this, but now she longed to hear screaming or sirens or even the room exploding: something, anything, to match the turmoil inside her mind. She repeated the obscenity she'd used, louder than before, adding, "And I don't care who hears me!"

She stormed into their bedroom, slammed the door, and collapsed to her knees. The sound that came from her was less a cry than a wail, too airless for anyone to recognize the sentences she kept moaning over and over. "It isn't real, Lila. It can't be real unless you decide that it is."

How many times had Billy said this to her? Fifty? A hundred? How could she have forgotten?

She desperately wanted to believe this, but she couldn't remember ever making any decisions about what was real and what wasn't. Billy was the one who'd told her the nightmares weren't real, the one who knew what had really happened in their past. It was Billy, too, who'd convinced her that their future would be beautiful with second chances, and then described that future so vividly it became more real to Lila than her sorrow and lost innocence. All she'd ever had to do was trust her brother, but that was the easiest thing in the world. It didn't require imagination. It didn't even require faith. Love was the only necessity. Her love for Billy, which had always been the truest thing in her life.

She used to think that without her brother she would simply

cease to exist. But now, as she heard her lungs gasping for air and felt the ache of her knees against the hardwood floor, she knew her body was stubborn; it would insist on remaining alive, even if her life no longer made sense to her. Even if she couldn't comprehend the world in which she'd found herself. It was frankly impossible, and yet this was her reality now: a world without Billy.

CHAPTER TWO

There were no words for what it was like for him, watching his wife grieve the loss of her brother. Torture wasn't strong enough, as he would have willingly undergone enormous physical pain if only Lila could have had even a few hours of relief. Though they had been married longer than most of their friends, his feelings for her hadn't diminished over the years. He loved his wife with his whole heart, in that desperate way of a man who never quite believes he deserves the love of the woman he can't live without.

Sometimes he still caught himself wondering why Lila was with him. From the first time they met, he thought she was incredibly beautiful and stunningly elegant, both soft-spoken and sharply intelligent—and completely out of his league.

It was early in the fall, at a School of Arts and Sciences mixer for graduate students preparing to go on the job market. Over wine and cheese and some gnarly meat lumps that were supposed to be sausage, everyone was talking about their fears: that they wouldn't finish their dissertations, that their advisors were out to get them, and that they would never find a teaching position anyway in this awful market. Lila was on the other side of the room, with the humanities people, but Patrick noticed her because she was standing a little apart from the fray, as though she, too, felt shy. When he screwed up the courage to walk over to her, he held up a toothpick with one of the sausages and said, "Do you think this is some kind of alien life-form?"

Lila stared at him for several uncomfortable seconds before she laughed. She confessed she'd been daydreaming, but when he asked her what about, she said Jim's return to slavery. "It's just so disturbing, and no matter how many times I teach the book, I can't get over it."

"I'm in math," Patrick said. "Sorry." And he was sorry at that moment, though being a mathematician had been his dream since he was a kid. But if only he knew what this woman was talking about, he wouldn't have to wander back to the science people, huddled over by the windows.

"Wait," she said. "I'm sure you know *Huckleberry Finn.*" When he nodded—though he didn't remember the book that well, since he'd read it years ago, in middle school—she said, "Then I can explain it to you." She looked at the wall behind him. "If you're interested, that is."

Of course he was. He loved listening to her airy voice as she explained the critical controversy about the end of Twain's novel: why Twain spent so much time sending Jim and Huck down the river, to freedom, only to have Jim freely decide to return to his owner. "I don't believe he was trying to undermine his own book," she said. "That's such a cynical way to look at it, don't you think?"

She paused. "I suppose I sound too excited. I'm a great believer in stories. I used to tell Billy I was afraid we loved stories more than real life, but he said, 'What is life but a story we don't know the meaning of yet?' "

Patrick stood up straighter. So there was a boyfriend already. Of course. By the last year of grad school, most people had paired off with someone—if they hadn't arrived with someone they'd met as an undergraduate. Why he hadn't was simple, though most people didn't understand. His mother had gotten sick. For three years, he'd spent all of his free time flying back and forth from Princeton to St. Louis to take care of her. His father was there, but his father had always ignored Patrick's mother, favoring his golf buddies and drinking buddies over his wife. At the funeral that previous summer, Patrick had decided he would never speak to his father again, though he'd already broken that vow several times. Whenever his father would call late at night, drunk, lonely, filled with regret, Patrick would soften enough to hang on the phone and listen. If he couldn't offer the forgiveness the old man wanted—this was still his father. He had to give him something.

Back at school, getting over his grief, no question he was lonely. He'd made a few friends in the math department, but he hadn't had a real girlfriend since his mom had fallen ill. The weekends were particularly hard because he wasn't teaching, though at least he always had plenty of work to get done.

Now he noticed Lila Cole's ring. It wasn't a diamond, but it was on the third finger of her left hand, probably an engagement ring. She must have seen him looking at it, because she said, "It's very unusual, isn't it?"

He nodded. "Your boyfriend must have unusual taste."

"Oh, it's not from a boyfriend. It's what Billy calls a 'twin ring.' " She held out her lovely white hand. "See the two snakes entwined together?" She laughed softly. "I told him that I'd prefer something less hostile than snakes, but he said they don't make rings with two teddy bears."

"You're a twin?" Patrick said. Trying to imagine a man who could look like this woman with pale yellow hair, eyebrows so light you could barely see them, a frame so small it seemed not only delicate but fragile, as though you could break her wrist if you grabbed it too quickly.

Another reason she was out of his league. Though she was very slight, she was also a good two inches taller than he was. He'd thought it was the shoes she was wearing, but now he saw she had on flat black shoes like ballet dancers wear. He would have to lean up to kiss her, which wouldn't have bothered him in the slightest—her bottom lip was fatter than the top and it looked so plump and kissable—but he knew it would probably bother her. He was five feet nine, not that short, but he'd been rejected by several girls in college for not being tall enough. Or so he assumed. He was never really sure why his first dates didn't lead to second dates, or why his handful of relationships just hadn't worked out. Whenever he tried to apply his mind to the problem, he never got anywhere, though at least it proved he wasn't a total geek like some of his friends. He did want to meet a woman on her own terms, even if he couldn't understand how to do that.

Obviously, he had his issues in the romance department. And sometimes when he was afraid of disappointment, he said things that were a bit stupid, as when he admitted to Lila that he was having a hard time conjuring up a male version of her.

"We don't look alike." She blinked, no doubt wondering how someone so uneducated could be at Princeton, even if he was in math. "Fraternal twins?"

He could feel himself blushing as he said, "Oh, right. Sorry," but Lila Cole waved her hand, the one with the twin ring, and said she'd just remembered something else that bothered her about

Jim's return to slavery. Before he could say he'd like to hear it, she was telling him about it. As the room started to empty, she was still talking, and he decided to ask her if she wanted to get coffee.

She nodded nonchalantly, but he was as nervous as if she'd agreed to go out on a date. And he didn't mind that she kept talking for another twenty minutes or more, long enough for them to finish their first cup. She was so passionate about her work; he liked that in a woman. Of course he cared deeply about his own, too, and he hoped at some point she would ask him what he was working on. Not because he needed to talk about it—in truth, he could barely think, he was so worried about screwing this up—but because if she didn't, it probably meant this coffee was just a chance to finish her point. She had no interest in him.

He couldn't believe his luck. She not only asked, she listened and came up with intelligent questions. They spent two hours at the café, made plans for lunch the next day, and even then, she seemed reluctant to leave. It was tempting to think that she was lonely, too, but she'd already told him she never got lonely. "Like Billy said a long time ago, there's no loneliness as long as you have stories. My books are my friends." She smiled. "Too bad I have so many friends at this point that they're threatening to take over my apartment."

So maybe she just liked him? Though Patrick had a hard time believing it, it turned out to be true. Much later, she told him what she'd been thinking at that café, the first time they were together. She numbered her thoughts with her fingers, a habit of hers that never failed to charm him. One, he was an excellent listener. Two, he seemed really fascinated by what she thought about books. Three, he was "adorable" in his white sweater and old jeans. Four, he made her understand a math conversation, which she'd thought was impossible. Five, he never once asked her that ridiculous question everyone asks about what it's like to be a twin.

Five wasn't a sign of his intuitive powers. He'd almost asked that "ridiculous question," but something she said made him forget to. He'd gotten lucky again.

Patrick didn't meet Lila's twin for almost eight months. He was nervous about the encounter, knowing that Lila had no living parents and Billy was her entire family. He'd also heard things that made him worry that no matter how hard he tried, he wouldn't like Lila's brother. At least once a week, she mentioned that Billy was "brilliant," which wouldn't have bothered him except she often added that her brother had always been the smarter twin. Lila had won prestigious scholarships, finished her PhD in four years, and already received three tenure-track job offers at excellent schools. In fact, the one she'd just accepted, in Philadelphia—where she was determined to live because Billy and his family had settled there—was at a name-brand college where Patrick would have killed to work since the teaching load was so light, allowing plenty of time for research. Patrick had one offer in Philadelphia, at a small college in the suburbs, where he would have to teach two sessions of introductory algebra for every two real courses he got to teach. But he was planning to take the job if Lila would agree to marry him, and the visit to Billy's house was his prelude to asking her. Patrick knew if he didn't get along with her fabulous brother, she'd never consider accepting his proposal.

Billy lived in a row house in a blue-collar neighborhood west of the city. Patrick knew Lila's brother had gotten married because he'd gotten a woman pregnant, but he'd never understood why they hadn't considered abortion or adoption, rather than the old-fashioned solution of marriage. Lila had said they weren't against abortion; she'd also explained that her brother was not in love with this woman, though Patrick wondered if she was wrong about this.

He knew Lila had never gotten close to her brother's wife and once or twice it occurred to him that Lila might be somehow jealous of Ashley, but he put that idea out of his mind as unfounded and probably ridiculous.

On this particular Sunday, Billy, Ashley, and their almost five-year-old daughter, Pearl, were all at home. The inside of the row house was dark and a little shabby, but it looked like it had been recently cleaned. Pearl's dolls were neatly arranged in a plastic tub, wedged behind the door. The wood floors had been swept, and the whole place smelled of lemon dusting spray. Ashley was dressed up like she'd just come from church, though her skirt was a little too short for any church Patrick had ever been in. She was pretty in an earthy kind of way: big breasts, round face, flat nose, nice green eyes. Pearl, their daughter, looked a little like what Lila must have looked like as a kid: hair so blond it was almost white, tiny as an elf, a sweet smile. Patrick smiled back at her, and Lila knelt down and gave Pearl a hug. Next, Lila hugged Ashley and spoke to her for a few minutes; only then did she finally throw her arms around her twin.

It was true: they didn't look alike. Billy was shorter, for one thing, which was odd, Patrick thought. He had long, dark hair pulled back in a ponytail, and a muscular frame more like Patrick's own. The only signs that they were related were their sparkling blue eyes and their similar gestures and expressions. No doubt they'd both picked up the latter from their parents, but for Patrick, it was disconcerting, like watching a strange man who'd memorized his girlfriend's behaviors. When Billy pulled away and stuck his hand out to him, Lila apologized for failing to introduce everyone. But she was giggling like a girl, rather than laughing the soft, sophisticated laugh Patrick was used to.

He might have felt out of place if Billy hadn't turned out to be everything Lila said he was. He told Patrick he had a few questions for him, and Patrick followed Lila's brother into the tiny dining room, fearing some kind of old-fashioned, what-are-your-intentions talk. But all over the oak table were books, mathematics books, and though they weren't at the level of Patrick's own work, they were upper-level undergraduate texts: difficult to read for all but the best majors and impossible to read for someone with no formal training like Billy. Lila's brother admitted he'd had difficulty with many of the concepts, and he'd littered each book with yellow stickies, each with a question he hoped Patrick wouldn't mind answering for him. "Lila told me your field is wavelets," he said with a humble smile. "I thought I should try to understand what you do, to the extent I can."

Patrick was impressed that he'd taken the time, especially as he knew Billy was working long hours doing carpentry to support his family, but more than that, he enjoyed talking about math with Billy. Lila's brother had a keen mind that focused in on the most interesting aspects of a topic. Of course, he couldn't work the problems, but he seemed to grasp the concepts in a way few students did. Occasionally, when Patrick would look up from the table and see Ashley and Lila getting dinner ready, he would tell Lila that he'd be glad to help, but she said they were handling it and then smiled, presumably because she was pleased he and her brother were getting along so well.

It wasn't until hours later, after they'd finished Ashley's roast and potatoes, played three games of cards with Pearl, said their good-byes and gotten in Patrick's Volkswagen to head back to Princeton, that Patrick realized no one had asked Lila about her work: not Ashley, who didn't seem to care about any of it but good-naturedly put up with what she called Billy's "hobbies," but not Billy, either.

He didn't broach the topic until they were almost home. He was worried she'd be upset with him, but she laughed. "Billy doesn't need to ask me about that. He taught me everything I know."

"Now there's a ringing endorsement of grad school."

"Okay, I don't mean literally *everything.* But he's the reason I decided to study literature. It all goes back to when we were kids, when he . . . " She glanced out the window. "It's hard to explain. Let's just say that without him, I wouldn't have the stories anymore."

Patrick didn't understand, but he didn't push her. It was part of the unspoken agreement he'd had with Lila from the moment their relationship became serious: he would never really question her about her past. It didn't occur to him that there was anything wrong with this—honestly, quite the opposite: he considered it another stroke of luck that he'd managed to fall in love with a woman who *didn't* want to share everything in her life. With other women he'd dated, what started out as a moment of sharing had usually turned into an accusation when he didn't get whatever he was supposed to out of it. Then, too, his father had been spilling his feelings all over Patrick for as long as Patrick could remember. He was frankly relieved to be with Lila, who made so few emotional demands. Their life together could be based on reason and thought, which sounded like happiness to him.

After they were married, they saw Billy's family at all the usual occasions: birthday parties for Billy and Ashley's kids, Thanksgiving dinners, Christmas Eve to swap presents, picnics on Memorial Day and the Fourth of July. When he and Lila finally had some money—and tenure—they rented a house at the Jersey Shore for a month one summer and invited Billy's family to join them. Billy couldn't get off work that long, but he agreed to come with Ashley and the kids for the first two weeks.

Patrick was desperate for this vacation. The last year had been a constant struggle to deal with the demands of teaching and the demands of his research, not to mention the never-ending drama of the political squabbles in his department. How Lila was able to keep her distance from everything unsavory about academia was something he never really understood, though he admired her for it. She kept up with the paperwork, taught her students, and went to the necessary committee meetings—all while remaining passionately engaged in her own work in American literature. One time she told him that she could read these books a thousand times and still see new meanings in them.

Did it ever bother him that Lila was so into her books? Both of them had always worked constantly, but over the last year or so he'd been struck by the fact that they weren't even having sex much anymore. To be fair, whenever he made his interest clear, she'd put aside her books and papers, take his hand, and lead him into their bedroom, but he felt vaguely uneasy that she never seemed to initiate sex or particularly miss it. But he put this out of his mind by reminding himself that his wife was good to him in so many other ways: from offering a sympathetic ear for his problems with his department to keeping in touch with his father whenever he was too busy or stressed to do it himself. After all the years they'd lived together, she still woke him up nearly every morning with a smile and a kiss and the coffee made. He continued to consider himself lucky.

And her devotion to literature was one of the things he'd never stopped loving about her. It was also one of the reasons she was so popular with her students and colleagues. Her enthusiasm was infectious. Even Patrick's coworkers in the math department knew they could never come to Lila and Patrick's apartment without leaving with an armful of books they just *had* to read. Strangely enough, these mathematicians did read a lot of Lila's suggestions. She seemed to have that effect on everyone.

Everyone, that is, except her brother and his wife. With Ashley,

Lila didn't really make an effort, but with Billy, she tried as hard as she did with anyone, and yet her brother never seemed to get around to reading any of the novels and plays she left for him. Why she read absolutely *everything* Billy suggested to her was a mystery, but then most of Lila and Billy's relationship had remained mysterious. They had lunch together alone about once a month; Lila said they spent most of their time discussing "things that happened when we were younger." He didn't ask for specifics; he assumed it had something to do with their parents dying. Lila had told him they'd died in a car accident right before she'd started college.

At the shore house they rented that summer, Lila was determined to make progress on Billy's latest obsession, a novel called *Gravity's Rainbow.* Every free moment, Lila had her nose stuck in that enormous book, including one morning when they were out on the beach, under the three umbrellas it took to shade the group: one for Lila and Patrick, one for Billy and the kids—twelve-year-old Pearl, William, who was five, and ten-month-old Maisie—and one for Ashley, who was taking a nap. The girls' names had been picked by Billy, literary names, which Ashley had agreed to because they were pretty, but she put her foot down for their son, insisting on naming him for his father rather than some imaginary person. Billy acquiesced, but insisted they call their son William, not Billy.

It would have been impossible for Billy to read at the beach while watching out for William and little Maisie. He was a good father, or at least he always seemed like a good father from Patrick's point of view. He didn't drink; he never hit his kids or even raised his voice to them. Of course, he must have grown tired of running around after them, especially at the shore, where there was always the danger of drowning or getting stung by a jellyfish or at the very least falling down and getting a mouthful of sand. So Lila's suggestion that Billy let her take care of the kids for a while should have been welcome. She was trying to help. What was wrong with that?

Over the years, Ashley had alluded to Billy having a temper, saying, "He'll get mad if we don't" about minor things like what time they would eat Thanksgiving dinner or whether they would have sparklers on the Fourth of July. Lila rolled her eyes at these claims, insisting her brother had never gotten mad about something so trivial in his life. But here he was, that day on the beach, not only angry with Lila but shouting at her.

"If you don't want to read *Gravity's Rainbow,* just say so."

"But I do want to read it. I told you it was—"

" 'Oh, I like this novel, Billy.' " His tone was sarcastic. " 'It's really good.' " He picked up William, who was small for his age; Pearl had already escaped to her mother's umbrella, lugging Maisie with her. "Why can't you keep track of what's important?" He came close to his sister and hissed, "Was it really just entertainment, Lila? Is that all it was?"

"Of course not," she said. "I don't know why you're saying this to me."

Patrick had seen his wife flinch when Billy made fun of her voice, and now he noticed that Lila was about to cry. So he stepped in, even though he was nervous, not so much about Billy turning on him—though in truth, over the years, he'd grown a little tired of Lila's brother's caustic "wit"—but about how his wife would react to him interfering in her relationship with her brother. He'd never done it before, but then he'd never felt like the situation so clearly demanded something of him.

"She was only trying to be nice," Patrick said.

"And 'nice' is so important, isn't it?" Billy flashed him a mean smile. He knelt down in the sand, placing William beside him, still clutching the silent boy by the wrist. "All hail the new God of Nice, the most important quality in the modern world—more important than goodness, more important than depth, and much, much more important than truth."

Lila was standing motionless, still watching her brother. Patrick took a breath and hoped he wasn't blushing. Had he really said anything close to what Billy was accusing him of? "I don't think being nice is more important than goodness and truth. I think it's unfair to categorize my position that way."

"Of course, because that wouldn't be nice, would it?"

Billy was staring up at him. Finally Patrick shook his head and blurted out what he was thinking. "This is beyond ridiculous."

"Aha," Billy sputtered. "So you do disappoint your god on occasion. Good to know." He waited a moment, then stood up and gave Patrick a smile that looked oddly genuine. His voice sounded normal now, too, and entirely sincere. "I knew I loved you for a reason, O brother-in-law of mine."

Patrick was thoroughly confused, but his primary reaction was relief that this hadn't escalated further. He knew if Billy ever pushed him too far, he'd have to act, but what could he do, punch Lila's brother? He'd never punched anyone in his life.

"Well, now that that's settled," Ashley said, yawning, sounding annoyed, "I'm going to take the kids back to the house for a while. Maisie is hungry and William must be, too. Pearl can help me get them some lunch."

"I'll go with you," Billy said. "I'm starving." He glanced at Lila, but his eyes settled on Patrick. "How about you guys? Are you coming along?"

"In a few minutes," Patrick said.

"Why wait?" Lila said cheerfully. "Let's all head back together." She put her right hand in Patrick's and her left hand in Billy's. As if she were trying to glue the three of them together after her brother's outburst. As if she were trying to show she didn't take sides, even if one of the "sides" was her own. Patrick was even more confused, and he tried to talk to Lila about it when they were in their room, changing out of their sandy bathing suits. She'd just gotten naked and she was shivering from the sudden blast of cold from the air-conditioner vent over by the dresser. He took her in his arms and told her it wasn't right that Billy had yelled at her.

"He wasn't yelling at me," she said, stepping back. "I know it sounded like that, but Billy has always been exuberant. It's just that he's so passionate about everything he cares about. It matters to him in a way that it doesn't to most people."

It wasn't the first time she'd explained away her brother's bad behavior by some claim that Billy was different from most people—but it was the first time that Patrick didn't buy it. This wasn't Billy's caustic wit or even just teasing. Her brother had gone off on her for no reason. It was a completely irrational way to behave.

But when he told her so, Lila insisted Billy did have a reason to be upset. That book was very important; some of her colleagues had been teaching it for years. Thomas Pynchon was one of the world's greatest authors, and *Gravity's Rainbow* was his masterpiece. Naturally, Billy cared that Lila read it as soon as possible. He wanted to discuss it with her before they went back to Philly on Saturday.

Patrick stood back and looked at his wife. "Okay, but why couldn't he have been civil about it? Why didn't he just say, 'No thanks, keep reading'?"

"Because he felt alienated from me." She threw her terry cloth robe on. "And that always hurts his feelings."

"What about your feelings?" He felt frustrated as he wondered if he even understood what had just happened. "I thought you were hurt, too?"

She thought for a moment. "I was, but I should've known he'd react that way. I was being stupid."

He hated Lila's use of the word "stupid," which she never applied to anyone but herself. He said, "You are not stupid," firmly and forcefully, too forcefully, in fact. He sounded angry. No wonder Lila fled into the bathroom. They never talked that way to each other.

He dressed in silence, dreading an awkward lunch with Billy and his family. Lila had put on the cheerful pink-and-white sundress that he loved, but as they made their way into the kitchen she was quiet and distant and clearly still upset. Thankfully Billy, who was undoubtedly perceptive, despite whatever else he was, noticed immediately and insisted on blaming himself for the problem. He not only apologized, but he thanked Patrick for bringing him to his senses. A few minutes later, while Billy and Ashley were getting the kids settled at the table, Lila walked over to Patrick and hugged him. "I'm sorry, honey," she whispered in his ear. "I didn't mean to put you in the middle of this."

"It's okay," he told her and smiled.

And it was okay now. His wife was back to herself and Billy had taken responsibility for causing the conflict. This was all Patrick wanted, or at least all he could think of to expect.

And it stayed fine the rest of the week. There were no more outbursts from Lila's brother. If anything, Billy was friendlier than usual. He went so far as to insist that he would love Patrick's take on *Gravity's Rainbow,* too, since the author had studied science and used frequent math references. "I'm sure you'll understand it on a level that I simply can't," Billy said. "Only if you have time to read it, of course. I know you're working on an important proof. Lila told me about it."

It wasn't that important, really a minor result in his field, but at least it was a result and those had been in short supply for Patrick since he'd agreed to chair the calculus committee. He did need to work on it, but he started *Gravity's Rainbow* the next morning, intending to relax a bit, too. Unfortunately the book was far from relaxing. He put it down before the vacation was over, and left it at page 57, never to pick it up again.

And the next spring, when the idea of renting a shore house came up again, Patrick surprised himself by surprising Lila with tickets to Paris instead.

Over the years they'd been together, Lila had often defended both Patrick and his profession by calling the idea that mathematicians don't have feelings a "ridiculous pop-culture cliché." He appreciated her support, though he suspected it might be true that, like himself, many mathematicians were a little uncomfortable with emotional complexity. Part of it was the job itself, which demanded that you check your feelings at the door to concentrate on a reality completely outside of yourself. One of his grad school professors had posted a sign on his wall: "Mathematics doesn't care about what you want to be true or what you think might be true but only what *is* true." Of course, discovering what that truth was could be immensely difficult, but that there *was* truth to be discovered was a given. Thousands of years of mathematics—and every single engineering and technological breakthrough—were hard to argue against.

Patrick considered his marriage to Lila to have turned out very well by and large, and not least because it had proven to be such a low-drama affair. Unlike some of his colleagues' wives and girlfriends, Lila had never once demanded that he demonstrate his love by intuiting her feelings—and a good thing, too, because even on the rare occasion when he tried to, he usually couldn't get there. His wife's relationship with her brother, especially, had continued to be mostly incomprehensible to him. This was despite the dozen or so times he'd put aside a problem he was working on to google the topic of bonds between twins. He never gained any useful information, though each time he read that twins ran in families, he found himself vaguely hoping that he and Lila would never have them.

He did want children, though, and he didn't understand why Lila kept putting it off. Most faculty couples tried to get pregnant as soon as the wife got tenure, if not before. Lila had had tenure for nearly four years when she and Patrick took a trip back to St. Louis, to visit Patrick's father and babysit Patrick's cousin Jason's kids. Jason and his wife, Doreen, had an active toddler and a three-month-old baby and they desperately needed a break. They were going on a trip to California to celebrate their fifth wedding anniversary.

Patrick had always been close to his cousins on his mother's side, and Jason had been his best friend throughout high school. The two of them had stayed close over the years. Lila liked Jason and his wife, but Patrick was still impressed and grateful when she didn't hesitate to agree to use her spring break to help them out. Admittedly, she was worried she wouldn't be able to keep a toddler and a baby happy, but Patrick understood since he felt the same way.

The first night was rough. The baby was fine, but the nineteen-month-old boy, Theo, became hysterical when he had to face bedtime without his parents. Patrick walked him back and forth for fifteen minutes, which felt like hours, but the little kid was still letting out an earsplitting wail. When it was Lila's turn to take over, Patrick had never been more relieved to get into bed and close his eyes. He knew he couldn't sleep with that sound, but he was bone tired from all the activities of toddler care: the playing and talking and laughing and distracting he and Lila had been doing all day. At one point he told her, "Why can't they stay babies forever?" The three-month-old girl had lain in her cradle or sat placidly in her bouncy chair most of the time, only needing to be fed and changed. Patrick enjoyed her big toothless grins and the odd motion she made with her legs, as if she were riding a bicycle only she could see.

He didn't expect to fall asleep, and when he woke up and the clock by Jason and Doreen's bed said 3:41, he was both surprised and a little worried. Lila had never joined him. Had she driven off into the night with Theo, hoping to calm him down with the motion of the car that had worked so well for his nap? Or had she snapped and thrown the squalling kid out the window, as Patrick had joked about doing hours ago?

He found her on the couch, with Theo lying on her, snoring softly. Lila herself was awake and stroking his cheeks lightly with her fingers. She also kissed the top of Theo's head before she noticed Patrick standing in the hallway, watching her.

"He didn't want to sleep alone," she whispered. "I didn't mind. It's been kind of nice, holding him next to me." She paused and inhaled. "He smells so good. Have you ever noticed that about babies?"

Somehow they managed to get Theo into his crib without waking him. It was no small feat, and Patrick would have been thrilled if he wasn't so tired.

It wasn't until the next day that he realized something had changed. At the first sound of Theo coming awake, Lila was out of bed and at the little boy's side—and there she remained for the next few days, almost all of the time, surprising Patrick's father, who called Lila a natural at mothering, and, of course, surprising Patrick himself. When a grateful Jason and Doreen returned, looking decidedly younger after a short time away from parenting, and asked how everything had gone, Lila said, "Perfectly. Theo is wonderful." She sounded oddly shy. After a pause, she added, "Both your children are."

It was the last thing Patrick expected: his wife had apparently become smitten with a toddler. Though Patrick himself had found parenting a lot more difficult than he'd anticipated, he still felt relieved. He wanted a family and now he felt confident Lila would, too.

He decided to wait a few days to discuss it with her. He wanted to be careful how he brought it up; he suspected she might have been embarrassed that she'd burst into tears when they'd left the little boy. Maybe he was hoping she'd bring it up herself? He wasn't sure anymore; in any case, they never had the discussion. They went back to Philadelphia and back to work, since spring break was over. And then, only three days later, her brother committed suicide.

Watching Lila's grief was so terrible that in some ways, he was glad whenever she started another rant about Ashley, though these rants also made him uncomfortable. He wanted to believe that Lila was right, and he agreed with his wife that if Ashley had no basis to accuse Billy of child abuse, then Ashley herself was the abusive one for keeping the children from their father. The operative word, though, was "if." If the charges against Billy—which, after all, had been supported by the court, though the one time he reminded Lila of this, he instantly regretted it, as she went back to bed and stayed there for hours, sobbing like her heart would break—but if those charges were really baseless, then Ashley was an abuser and yes, as Lila kept saying, an unfit mother. Someone who should not be caring for Billy's beautiful children.

Even so, he was stunned when Lila said she'd contacted a lawyer because she planned to raise those kids herself. "With your help, of course," she added slowly. Her eyes were swollen; her lovely hair was a tangled mess. "I couldn't do it without you."

He said he would help, because it was the only answer he could think of. But he did talk her into waiting a while, giving the kids time to grieve for their father before their young lives were turned upside down again. He knew if his wife still wanted custody of Billy's kids later on, they'd have to deal with it, but for now, his only focus was getting through the memorial service and the next few days.

The night before the funeral at a little after three a.m., he woke with the feeling that something was wrong. He looked over at Lila, but she was sound asleep. The room seemed cold; he got up and turned the heat up, and then he sat on the edge of the bed with his back straight and his feet on the floor, still alert, still listening for something: an intruder, a dog barking in the apartment next door, whatever it was that had woken him up. But there was no sound except Lila's breathing and the usual traffic sounds in the street below.

Patrick had never understood or respected the kind of people who claimed to believe in psychic premonitions. To him it was irrational, even ludicrous, that whenever something bad happened, apparently sane people would insist that they'd known it was going to, that they'd dreamed it a month before or seen it in a vision or read it in their horoscope. Lila used to insist that what they were really expressing was their despair at human helplessness—that deep wish within us all that if only we could have known, we could have done something to stop it, or at least had time to prepare ourselves.

In Patrick's case, though, even if he'd known what was about to happen to Lila, he wouldn't have known how to stop it or how to prepare for it. This was what kept him up that night, back in bed but lying still so he wouldn't wake her: the suspicion that he was inadequate in some essential way to what his wife needed from him now, and his fear that he might lose her for good if he couldn't figure out how to change.

CHAPTER THREE

Her brother's funeral was being held in Harrisburg, Pennsylvania, where Billy had lived with his family for the last two years. Lila thought it was grotesquely unfair that Ashley got to decide where to hold the funeral, when and where she wanted him buried, even who would be allowed to be part of the ceremony, but as Patrick pointed out, Ashley was still Billy's wife, legally, at least. Lila knew the quote-unquote *law* could not care less that Billy's wife had been responsible for his death. Why should the law care, when the law had been responsible, too, by taking Ashley's word that Billy had harmed one of his children?

She didn't plan on speaking to Ashley, but she did want to see the kids and talk to them alone, if possible. She wasn't sure what to say to them, and she was thinking about it as she and

Patrick drove down the turnpike, on the way to Harrisburg. He was holding her hand, squeezing it every once in a while. She knew her husband was worried about her, and it would have touched her if she'd been capable of feeling anything other than her grief.

Even thinking was hard for her right now, though she'd tried to present her idea of raising Billy's children to Patrick as reasonably as possible, knowing she'd need her husband's approval to go forward. The lawyer she'd consulted—while Patrick was out getting groceries—had mentioned that one of the things in Lila's favor was her long marriage. One of the only things. If it did turn out that Ashley had brainwashed any of the children against their father, "this brainwashing," the lawyer said, "or 'parental alienation syndrome' as it's sometimes called, is not always treated as child abuse by judges. It depends on who we get. We might need other evidence that she's an unfit mother, in addition to a sterling report on you and your husband. Being professors will help, but being married for eleven years is even better. Happily married. Both ready to make sacrifices to take care of these kids."

Before she hung up, the lawyer promised to get a copy of the charges against Billy—and warned Lila again that they were in for an uphill battle. "Are you sure you want to proceed? Your odds of winning aren't good unless you can prove Mrs. Cole is unfit."

Lila insisted she wanted to go forward. She had a lot of damaging information about Ashley that she could use, if it came right down to it. Billy had told her that Ashley had started drinking again. It was one of the reasons he'd taken the job in Harrisburg, to get his wife away from her drinking buddies. Apparently, she hadn't gone to a single AA meeting since Maisie was a baby, which proved she wasn't even trying to recover anymore. And she was still cutting herself; Billy mentioned this only last summer, when Lila asked if that was the reason Ashley never wore anything but long-sleeve T-shirts. And there were other things, too, things Lila didn't want to bring up but would if there was no other way.

She'd never been a fighter, but then she'd never had to be; Billy had always done the fighting for them. When they were kids, her worst fear was that he would leave her. He would usually reassure her that he wasn't going anywhere, but one time he said, "You're braver than you think." They were in the woods at the end of their neighborhood, sitting on a rotting log, plotting their escape from their parents, as always. "You'll know what to do if the time ever comes when you have to handle all this alone."

The moment had come, but her mind wasn't cooperating. She couldn't think about what to do next because she was stuck in the past, daydreaming about Billy. For so many years, she hadn't remembered most of her childhood and now was no different, but of course she remembered the things they'd talked about hundreds of times. The day Billy created the death certificates. The night he stood up to their stepfather the last time, after their stepfather tried to hurt Lila.

"My children will never be raised by another man," Billy had told her over and over when they were teenagers, and also that day in New Mexico, when he was explaining why he'd decided to marry a woman he didn't love. Ashley had waited too long to get a pregnancy test—or to tell Billy she was pregnant, Lila was never sure which. It was too late for an abortion, but Ashley was considering adoption. Or so she said, but maybe she already knew how strongly Billy felt about this.

The thought that Ashley would probably remarry someday brought Lila back to the present. She had no choice; she had to do whatever it took to save Billy's kids from being raised by a stepfather. This had always been the major theme, according to Billy: not letting it *ever* happen again.

Loss and sorrow had to take a backseat to that meaning; Billy used to tell her that constantly. "We can't afford to be weak, Lila. I've told you a hundred times that the hero is never destroyed by the bad guy, but by some weakness within himself."

As she walked into the small suburban church, she could hear him telling her to be strong. She made her way up the center aisle and managed to keep her head held high, though she could hear people whispering, probably gossiping about her and her brother. Ashley had packed the church with her friends and family. Patrick and Lila seemed to be the only ones here for Billy.

Lila had planned on sitting in the front, but the first empty place was five pews back. Patrick guided her into a spot and sat down next to her; they each flipped through the program guide celebrating the life and mourning the death of "husband, father, friend" William Cole. No mention of brother. A repeat of the "mistake" in the obituary Ashley submitted to the local paper, and another slap in the face for Lila.

She was fighting off hysteria by the time the service was over. The priest placed too much emphasis on God "forgiving brother Cole's sins" and "giving the troubled man peace," and far too little on celebrating Billy's life, as if everyone there had already tried and convicted him of this ridiculous charge. What about the years he'd supported his family, working two jobs at times, neglecting his talent to take care of Ashley and the kids? What about the night he saved Lila from their stepfather? What about all the beautiful ideas that flowed from her brother's brilliant mind?

She rushed out of the church and ran to her car, where she was still sobbing when Patrick joined her. He put his arms around her and asked if she wanted to ride in the limo behind the hearse, with the family.

"She doesn't want me," Lila sputtered.

"She suggested it," he said. When Lila didn't respond, he said,

"What about the kids? You said you wanted to see them, remember?"

She nodded and managed to get out of the car without stumbling. She walked to the family limo where, true enough, Ashley had saved room for them. Ashley's own mother was riding in the next car, along with all the other members of Ashley's big, extended family except for her sister, Trish. Trish was sitting between Ashley and William, holding both of their hands. Maisie was next to William. Only fifteen-year-old Pearl was on the other side, and she managed to take Lila's hand while her mother was weeping on Trish's shoulder.

On the drive out, Lila's eyes moved back and forth, from William to Maisie to Pearl, drinking in these children. She'd loved them all along, but now that love had turned fierce and protective, knowing they were all that was left of her brother. William looked quiet and stunned and much younger than his eight years. He'd been born prematurely and was still small for his age, and the thick glasses he'd worn since he was a toddler made him look especially vulnerable. He also looked a little neglected: his brown curls were a mess, as if nobody had thought to comb his hair for a while, and he'd missed a button on his white shirt. Pearl had obviously been crying for days; her blue eyes were as swollen as Lila's own, but there was also a naked fury in those eyes, as though life had been supremely unfair to her—a teenage reaction, to be sure, but one with which Lila wholeheartedly sympathized. Only chubby little red-haired Maisie bore any resemblance to the child she'd been last summer, the last time Lila had seen them. She was humming some kids' tune, blissfully unaware of the horrible series of events that had taken her father from her, probably even unaware that he was never coming back.

Lila hadn't seen them for almost a year because Billy had kept putting off her visits, saying only that he and Ashley were having "problems." Whenever she managed to get him on the phone, he sounded so weary and hopeless that she begged him to tell her what was going on, but he would only apologize for worrying her. Even in email, he ignored all her questions and concentrated on literature and politics and other topics that had nothing to do with his personal life. Of course Lila should have pushed harder to get through to him, but she'd always had a million excuses. She'd actually thought the paper she was writing was important, and her stupid proposal for a new class on the quest theme in American literature.

The last few emails to Billy had focused on that class. He'd said he was excited about it and suggested some novels she'd forgotten about. He hadn't said a word about being separated from Ashley or losing visitation with his kids, at least not directly. The day after he died, when she'd re-read the emails, drinking shots of scotch, trying to get her grief to quiet down, she discovered all the clues she'd missed. It wasn't the novels he proposed including, but the reasons he gave for why they belonged. *The Scarlet Letter* because, Billy wrote, "the deeper quests include betrayal, don't you agree?" *The Crying of Lot 49* because "our ability to break through the noise of our lives is gone and yet we continue the quest to speak." *The Portrait of a Lady* because "Isabel Archer has realized the truth that she was always a pawn in someone else's quest to have what she would have freely given, if only love had been a possibility."

For years, Billy had been reading American literature in this bleak way, but so had Lila. So had everyone she knew, for that matter. By and large, the classic American novels were quite dark; yet as Billy always said, this actually proved that the writers of these books were "true romantics," "incapable of detachment," "despairing to the very degree that they believed in the potential of their young country and of humanity." The literature of Europe, on the other hand, was both more sentimental and more cynical;

for what was sentiment but a cynical lack of faith in the real emotions of life?

The fact that Billy saw all these books as fitting with the quest theme wasn't unusual, either. He was right and Lila knew it, but she ended up leaving ninety percent of his suggestions off her proposed syllabus, though that was only because she knew her students would have enough trouble with more obvious quest books like *Moby-Dick.* The very idea of a quest was hard for most of her undergraduates.

The clue that something was wrong was the way Billy used the word "quest" in each and every one of his explanations. It was so unlike him to be that literal—how could Lila have missed this? Yes, she was busy, but that was no excuse. This was her brother, the person she knew best in all the world. And he'd told her a million times to pay attention to the language. Look for clues. "Life is an allegory, Lila. If you don't read it correctly, you won't see the meaning." He snapped his fingers. "*Bang,* just like that, you lose."

On the drive to the cemetery, Lila's grief was horrible but intermittent, like waves of nausea, but when they walked across the wide lawn and she saw the deep hole in the ground intended for her brother, the pain was so sudden and terrible that it would have knocked her over if Patrick hadn't been there, holding her up in his strong arms. Her husband told her later that the ceremony wasn't very long, but it seemed as long as the rest of her life without Billy, and just as terrible. The strong sunlight was an insult; the manicured lawn and blooming trees were grotesque parodies of beauty; even the other people were strangers—and frightening. Only Billy's children seemed real, but they were so far away from her, engulfed by Ashley and her family, in danger of being lost forever. Swallowed down the rabbit hole of Ashley's false interpretation of reality. Eventually forgetting everything, even that their father had—

"He loved you." She wasn't aware that she was speaking the chant that was going through her mind. "He loved all of you." She was looking at Pearl and William and Maisie, wishing this one truth would penetrate their very souls. "He loved you more than his life."

At some point, she realized that they could hear her. Everyone could. Ashley had turned her face into her sister's shoulder. William was visibly pale. Maisie put her fingers in her ears—meaning Lila was shouting? She was so dizzy suddenly, and it hit her that her nausea had become real.

She stumbled away and vomited at the base of a hickory tree. Somehow Patrick was there, holding her hair for her. Walking her over to a bench several feet away. Telling her to sit down and rest until the feeling passed.

Before he could sit down with her, she told him she was all right. "I just need a few minutes by myself," she said, glancing up at him. "I'll be back over in a little bit."

If she'd been capable of feeling anything but her grief, she would have felt sorry for her husband as he walked away hesitantly, so clearly unsure how to behave in a situation like this. Her always reasonable husband, who Billy once described as "the last American: instinctively hardworking, unfailingly decent, and blissfully naïve." Lila would have defended Patrick if she hadn't known that Billy meant this as high praise. Her brother always said that everyone was on a journey back to innocence. Billy would have said that Patrick's journey was just shorter than theirs was, because they were in a more intricate plot of hidden evil and elusive redemption.

And now she was alone in this "evil and redemption" plot that she had never understood as well as Billy had. It was the only important thing she had ever kept from her twin. No matter how hard she tried, despite all her training, she would always be too stupid to understand the plot of her and her brother's lives.

Her nausea was gone, but in its place was an emptiness so profound that it was a wonder she was breathing with nothing inside her: no stomach, no heart, no lungs, no air. She had no idea how long she'd been this way when she realized someone was next to her. She glanced over and saw Pearl, Billy's first baby, whose name he'd chosen because she was his pearl of great price, costing him all he had.

"Those are pearls that were his eyes," she mumbled, quoting the sprite Ariel from her favorite Shakespeare play, *The Tempest.* But it was true. Beautiful Pearl with the bright blue eyes, just like Billy's.

"Aunt Lila? Are you okay?"

"Of course, honey." Lila sat up straight. This was her chance to say something important. What was it she was supposed to say? That Billy loved them? She'd said that already. That their mother had killed their father? No, God, she would never hurt his children like that. She would never hurt his children, but wasn't she hurting them if she took them from their mother? Why hadn't that occurred to her before? But their mother was evil, wasn't she?

"I can't talk long," Pearl said. She sounded so angry that Lila flinched, but then she noticed the girl was looking back over her shoulder. "She's going to get pissed that I'm sitting here."

"Your mom?"

"Who else? She hates you now. She told me when Dad left that he was crazy."

"I'm sorry. She shouldn't have said that to you. It wasn't true. Your dad was brilliant and—"

"She thinks you're crazy, too. I heard her tell Aunt Trish that Dad fucked up your mind completely."

"I don't think she really believes that." Lila forced her voice to remain calm, soothing, adult. "Your dad and I were always really close and I think your mom was a little jeal—"

The girl jammed a folded-up piece of paper into Lila's hand. Before Lila could even wonder what it was, Pearl stood up and disappeared.

It was a short note, obviously written in a teenage girl's handwriting: big letters, lots of curly loops, and a large circular dot above each "i":

> *I know what my mother did, but I can't hate her for this. It's not her fault that she lacks imagination. But I have to be strong and save my brother. He told me he wished he were dead. I'm really afraid he'll kill himself if we don't get out of here. I'm writing this because I have to do whatever it takes to make sure he's all right. He needs me now so badly. I can't ever be weak again.*

CHAPTER FOUR

William was short for his age and in the dumb class at Chandler Elementary, but he wasn't a baby. He knew his father hadn't died of an accident, like his grandma said, or because his dad was "just confused," like his mom said. No one would talk to William about what had really happened, but he didn't need them to tell him that his dad had killed himself. He also knew that it was all his fault, for telling his mom about the Challenges. If only he hadn't done that, his daddy would still be alive. The guilt made him wish he was dead, too, but the letter from Daddy said he mustn't feel that way. "Please listen to me, William," the letter said. "Promise me, buddy."

William knew something that nobody else did and that made him feel older and bigger. It was his special secret—his father had left him a letter. William found it in their backyard, stuck inside the hollow part of the tree, same as all the other things his father had left for William since Daddy moved out of their house and into an apartment. Most of them were little notes, which Daddy called reminders. "Be a good boy today." "Take care of your sisters." "Don't forget to do the exercises I gave you." "Listen to your music." "Don't tell Mommy about the gun."

Daddy also left quarters and peanut butter cups and other things William liked, like stickers of robots and toy cars. But the reminders were the most important, Daddy said. "Whatever happens, you have to remember those. That's what a reminder is, something to help you remember."

William hadn't forgotten that he wasn't supposed to tell anybody about the Challenges. That was the part that made him want to slap his own face, because he'd acted like such a baby and babies only learn by being slapped. Mommy said that's why she slapped Maisie, because Maisie was too young to understand reasons. Daddy said slapping Maisie was wrong. Whenever Mommy did it, Daddy got mad and they yelled at each other so loud that Maisie cried harder than after the slap. When Daddy moved to an apartment, Pearl yelled that she hated Mommy and Mommy was a "barbarian," just like Daddy always said.

But William loved Mommy, too, and he'd felt so comfortable when she was holding him on her lap, asking him what happened that weekend. He'd been with Daddy by himself 'cause it was time for the next Challenge, which Daddy said he had to go through if he had any hope of protecting himself and his sisters when Mommy married her new friend, Kyle, who Daddy always called That Bastard. "It's just like Cub Scouts," Daddy said. "All you have to do is live in the woods for one day and then I'll come and get you. Don't be scared. Remember, you're pretending you're hiding out from a very bad guy. The woods are safe. Just keep your glasses on, that's important. You'll have a tent and enough food and all you have to do is stay put. Can you do that, buddy?"

William said yes, but he hadn't even lasted an hour before he got scared. This kid in his third grade class said there were tigers and bears in those woods. He was more afraid of bears than of people, even bad guys. When he ran out of the tent, his only thought was to find Daddy and ask if they could do the Challenge from last week instead. He liked shooting the cans, even if it was loud and he missed a lot. He liked it because Daddy was right there next to him, saying stuff like, "Good try, buddy. I'm so proud of you."

He ran and ran and he couldn't find Daddy. His legs were about to give out when the sun got lower in the sky; then he tried to go back to where his tent was and he couldn't find that place, either. He was sitting on the ground, shaking and crying, when a man and woman came up and asked if he was lost. They said they were hikers and the woman took a bottle of water from her backpack and gave it to him. Then he said he was lost and his daddy was so worried about him. He knew the last part was true 'cause his daddy was always worried about him. That's why Daddy came up with the Challenges, to keep him safe.

The hikers said they would help him find his father's tent, but then they didn't. They took him to the end of the woods and used their cell phone. A few minutes later, the police were there, but William wasn't worried. He told them what Daddy had taught him to say: that he and his father had been camping and he'd wandered off. Now he couldn't find his daddy. The police officers believed him and moved through the woods, using a loud horn thing until they found William's father. Then Daddy was crying and hugging William and it was all okay.

Mommy didn't believe it, though. She said she knew William wouldn't wander off; he'd never wandered off in his life. She said, "You're a good boy." She was stroking the top of his arm, nuzzling his head like she used to do when he was little. He liked the feeling of being in her lap. He felt his eyes closing as she told him how good he'd always been, even as a baby. But then she said, "I know if your daddy told you to stay put, you'd stay put," and he felt so guilty that he blurted out it wasn't true. He only stayed put for a little while. When the stopwatch said 1:37, he ran out, looking for Daddy.

"But you stayed put for an hour and thirty-seven minutes," his mom said. She was still stroking his arm, but her fingers were sort of fast and jerky, like the way she put grease on a cake pan. "Where was your daddy all that time?"

When he didn't answer, she hugged him and her touch was gentle again. "You were very brave to stay in the woods alone for almost two hours. You must have been so scared."

He felt his eyes stinging. "There was nothin' to be afraid of."

"Did your dad tell you that?"

William nodded. "He said he wouldn't have had me do the Challenge if there were tigers and bears in the woods."

If only his mom had asked what William meant by Challenge, he would have known not to tell her. He hadn't forgotten. He just was too dumb to realize that he *was* talking about it.

She asked how long he was supposed to stay there. He said, "For twelve hours. Daddy said he'd be back when the stopwatch said 12:00. It would be dark but not spooky dark, he said."

"It sounds hard." She kissed him on top of his head. "Were the other challenges all that hard?" She leaned her face around and smiled at him. "You must have been very brave to get through them, too!"

He smiled back. "I was brave. Daddy said I was the bravest kid ever."

"What other cool things did you do?"

"I paddled a canoe across a lake."

"Wow," she said. "And you don't even know how to swim!"

"I didn't, but I learned a couple days later so I could jump off the cliff."

"You jumped off a cliff?" She'd leaned back; he couldn't see her face. But he heard her voice get screechy. "The cliff at Hamburg?"

"I don't remember." He put his hand over his mouth. His eyes were burning again. Why couldn't he be smart like his big sister Pearl? He was so dumb for telling Mommy all this. He was such a baby for being so scared of the policeman who came to the house to ask William questions. If he hadn't been afraid of the policeman, he would have kept his hand over his mouth instead of repeating the things he told Mommy.

But he didn't tell Mommy or the policeman about the gun. He told Daddy he remembered that part, and Daddy said he was proud of him. He said it again in the letter William found after Daddy died. "You didn't do anything wrong, buddy. I was sad because I wouldn't be able to see you anymore, but it wasn't your fault I did what I did. Please listen to me, William."

William wanted to listen to Daddy, but he heard Pearl saying their mother twisted everything William said and made Daddy get arrested. So it was still William's fault for saying anything. If only he hadn't done that, Daddy would be here and they could do the rest of the Challenges together.

Now William had to do the hardest one alone, that's what Daddy said. He had to remember without the reminders. He had to not be scared and not be weak or something very bad could happen to his sisters.

"I know you love Pearl and Maisie, buddy." He did love them, but that wasn't why he was going to try to do what his father said. "Whatever happens," his daddy wrote at the end of the letter, "remember, I'll always be proud of you for trying. And remember, you'll always be my smart little man."

CHAPTER FIVE

It was mid-April, two weeks after the funeral, and Patrick had convinced himself that Lila was getting better. Yes, she still woke up crying four nights out of seven, but the other three nights, she slept through until dawn. She was still fighting for visitation with the kids, but she'd given up her plan to pursue custody after her lawyer quit, claiming it was hopeless after reading Billy's police file. Patrick hadn't seen the file, but he assumed whatever was in it had sufficiently disturbed Lila that she couldn't discuss it. She did say that her brother was innocent, but her voice wavered as she said it, and shortly after, she went into one of the trances she'd been going into since they came back from Harrisburg. Maybe the word "trance" was inaccurate. If it were anyone other than Lila, Patrick would merely assume she was thinking, but Lila didn't sit around staring at walls, thinking. She was a writer and a teacher and especially a reader. He'd never seen her go a day without picking up a book, much less the ten days it had been since she'd read anything other than Billy's police file.

Nevertheless, she was going back to work finally, which he took to be the best sign of all. Soon she would be swept up again in the progress of her students and the fascination of her research. Her grief would lose its edge with the distraction of her ordinary life.

Or so he hoped. But then, on only her second day back, at around four in the afternoon, Lila's department chairman called Patrick to come and pick her up. "She has her car," Patrick said, the first thing that had occurred to him. "Wait, was there an accident?" He heard his heart thumping in his ears. "Is she all right?"

"She wasn't in an accident," Professor Stafford said flatly. "I'll tell you everything I know when you get here." He paused. "Can you leave right away?"

Patrick had already grabbed his keys and wallet from his desk. As he walked past the math department secretary, he asked her to cancel his evening review session with his teaching assistant.

He met Professor Stafford outside Lila's office. The hall was deserted, the door was shut, but Stafford was still whispering.

"I think she's disoriented. I hope that's all this is." Then Stafford told Patrick that Lila had simply walked out of her first class this morning. "Sophomore lit. She didn't tell her students that she wouldn't be returning. After that, she failed to appear at any of her other classes and shut herself in her office."

Patrick exhaled, hoping it wasn't as bad as it sounded. On the drive over, he'd tried Lila's cell phone and her office phone to no avail. She wouldn't answer calls or emails from Henry Stafford or his secretary, Becky, either, but she had let them know that she wasn't sick and didn't need their help. Unfortunately, the way she let them know was by screaming this when Becky opened her door.

"Becky immediately apologized for the intrusion and left," Stafford said. He was nearly seventy years old; Lila said he wore the same bow tie every day and joked that he was the reincarnation of Mr. Chips. Patrick felt uncomfortable for the older man when Stafford's face turned bright red as he explained what Becky saw in Lila's office. "Your wife was under her desk. And she had her skirt off."

"I'm sorry." Patrick stood up straighter. "I appreciate you calling me."

"Obviously we would prefer to let Lila leave when she's ready." He paused. "Unless you'd like us to call campus mental health services?"

Patrick said he could handle it himself. He was anxious to get to his wife, but he waited until Stafford excused himself before opening the door. It was just as the secretary had said; Lila was under her desk, with her skirt tossed into the middle of the room. At least, she was still wearing her shirt and tights.

"I only took it off because it kept falling off." Lila must have seen Patrick looking at the skirt. "I've lost so much weight in the last few weeks."

He nodded, but he wondered why she didn't pin it on.

"I'm sure I look insane hiding under the desk." She put her arms around her knees, folding herself together, which made her look small. "But I'm so frightened."

"There's nothing to be scared of." He was simply stating the obvious; he hoped she would recognize that. He took a few steps closer. "Let's go home now."

She shook her head. "I can't . . . I'm sorry."

He noticed the files of lecture notes on her desk, along with two books she'd been planning to discuss that day: *Sister Carrie* in her sophomore class and the *Norton Anthology of American Literature,* for her freshman survey course. It all looked entirely normal, as did the rest of her office. A large window that faced the campus green. One wall of shelves filled with the books Lila loved and had been collecting since she was an undergraduate.

"Would you come sit with me instead?" she said quietly.

"You want me to get under the desk, too?"

She nodded, and after a moment, he realized that if this would calm her down, he had no choice. He crawled under with her.

"Thank you," she whispered. "I really need you right now."

It was a large desk, but it was crowded with both of them squeezed in the space between the two sets of side drawers. After only a minute or two, Patrick's neck hurt from bending down and his legs hurt from being folded up like a yogi's. Still, he waited another few minutes before he finally said, "I don't know what we're doing, Lila. There's no one in this building who would hurt you. Most of them are your friends."

"I know." She shrugged. "I guess it does seem silly."

"It's certainly not your everyday experience." He looked up slowly, careful not to whack his head. "It could be worse, though. We could be stuck under a high school desk covered with graffiti and gum."

She smiled and he could feel his shoulders loosening for the first time since he'd gotten the phone call to pick her up. He bantered about nothing for a moment or two, the easy kind of talk Lila usually enjoyed and that seemed to be relaxing her now. Finally she said, "I wonder what Mr. Chips and Becky thought of this."

"I'm not sure about Becky, but I think Stafford wanted me to know that if I couldn't get you to leave, he stood ready to have an ambulance crew pry you out."

She was still smiling right up until the last few words, when she suddenly burst into tears. Then he realized what a stupid thing he'd said. Naturally, she'd be concerned about the effect of what she'd done on her position in the department. Any faculty member would be. Hell, he was concerned for her.

"You can talk to Stafford tomorrow," he said quickly. "Explain that you weren't quite ready to go back to work. He knows what you've been going through the last few weeks." He reached for her hand. It was surprisingly cold given how warm it was in her office, especially crammed down there together. "Let's go home. We can discuss your strategy with Stafford and make sure we—"

"I don't care about Stafford." She removed her hand. When she looked at him, he noticed how long her eyelashes looked, glistening with tears. "You don't want to know what happened to me today, do you?"

"What?" He sounded surprised—and he was—but he also knew she was right: he hadn't even thought to ask this question. Partly because he assumed Lila didn't want to talk about it or she already would have, but also because, honestly, he really didn't want to know the details. Still, he managed what he thought was the necessary response, "If you want to tell me, I'll listen. Whatever you want to say."

"But you're not going to ask me?"

"No—wait, I mean, yes." He was very confused, and no wonder: Lila had never *asked him* to *ask her* to tell him something before. And she knew he wasn't good at prying things out of people. He wasn't good at any of this.

He tried asking her, but she didn't answer; maybe because he phrased the question too mechanically, just repeating, "What happened to you?" He didn't know what else she wanted him to say, what words she was waiting for.

After a long, uncomfortable silence, he said, "Look, I don't think I'm the one you should be talking to anyway." He ran his hand through his hair, scraping one of his knuckles against something on the desk that felt as sharp as a nail. "I think your friends are right. It's time to find you a good therapist."

"I already told you I can't do that. Ashley will use it against me at the visitation hearing." She had told him that. She'd also said that, at the funeral, Pearl claimed Ashley was already saying that both Billy and Lila were crazy.

"But isn't the way you're acting now even more damaging to your petition? Especially if Stafford decides he has to report this, the university will have a case file. You can see that—"

He was only stating the truth, but he instantly regretted saying this. Yes, it was entirely reasonable, but Lila was clearly beyond reasoning with. She began crying again and bolted from under the desk before he could reach her. He started to follow, but his left foot was asleep and he couldn't move very fast. "Wait, Lila, I didn't mean—"

She'd already grabbed her skirt and put it on. Before he could finish his thought, she'd snatched up her purse and left the office.

When he got to the parking lot and couldn't find her car, he cursed himself for screwing this up. How would she drive in the state she was in? What if she really had an accident now?

He rushed to their apartment to discover that she was all right; she'd made it back home. He found her in the bedroom, staring at the ceiling. When he asked if she wanted dinner, she said she wasn't hungry. When he said, "You have to eat something," she said, "Don't worry about me."

But he did worry about her for the rest of the evening. And the next morning, when she made no move to go to work, he begged her again to see a professional to talk about this.

"You need help," he said, sitting down on the bed next to her. He was already dressed, but trying not to be anxious about being late for his first class. "Do you realize you could lose your position? Even with tenure, if you don't contact the dean and—"

"Request an emergency leave of absence? Email Stafford, too, and apologize for yesterday? I'm sure they'd grant my request. I don't see the point, though."

"What does that mean?"

"I realized this yesterday when I tried to teach *Sister Carrie.*" She rolled onto her side, away from him. "The characters aren't real to me anymore. It's like they've fallen to the floor and shattered into nothing but thousands of meaningless words. It's like they died, but worse." He heard her swallowing back a sob. "It's like they never were."

He touched her shoulder, but he couldn't think of how to respond. He'd never understood Lila's intense attachment to the characters in her books. Certainly he'd never thought she'd seriously believed they were real. What was she saying?

"This is why it's over for me," she said flatly. "My career is finished."

He didn't have time to argue the point with her, but later that morning, he decided to write her dean and Stafford anyway. It had to be her grief talking. She'd worked too hard to throw away a great position at one of the most prestigious schools in the country. And she loved her work. Without it, what would she have? What would she do with her days—spend them lying in bed?

Apparently, that was her plan, at least for the time being. When Patrick returned from teaching late that afternoon, Lila was exactly as he'd left her. Still in bed, still in her robe. Hadn't even combed her hair.

When the pattern repeated for two days, on Friday morning as soon as he got to his office, he called a therapist his wife's friend had recommended and made an appointment for Lila on Monday at ten, the first available opening. Then he took a deep breath and called his former sister-in-law.

He hadn't spoken to Ashley since the funeral, but Lila had,

repeatedly. Every time, she begged to be able to speak to Pearl, but Ashley said her daughter was too busy to come to the phone. When Lila asked for William, she got the same response. And when she requested a better time to call, Ashley said she didn't know and hung up. Then a few days ago, Lila got a notice from a law firm saying that Ashley had retained counsel and that all Lila's questions about access to the children had to go through them in the future. Lila was choking back tears, but she vowed to keep at it and visit them as soon as her own lawyer gave her the go-ahead.

Unfortunately, the new lawyer Lila hired had been unable to convince Ashley's lawyer that Lila had a right to visit her nieces and nephew. "It probably won't last forever," the new lawyer said. Lila told Patrick that the guy had sounded bored. The lawyer added, "Perhaps the mother believes they need time to heal as a family first?"

But even the bored but optimistic lawyer admitted that they would probably have to have a hearing. Eventually. He wasn't willing to start the process until he gave the kids time to "heal": maybe July or August, he said.

Patrick knew his wife couldn't wait that long, and he'd made up his mind to do something about this, today. He felt like he had to take some action to help Lila and couldn't think of anything else to try. But he didn't bring up the subject with Ashley. He was never that good on the phone and he knew this would take his best effort. He merely asked if she'd be around and told her he'd like to come to Harrisburg for a little talk.

"Lila's having problems, isn't she?" Ashley said. Her tone wasn't unkind, but the question annoyed him. He said they'd talk about it when he got there.

It was a good day to take a little trip. He only had two classes to teach on Friday, and it had been easy to find a replacement. Joyce

Little was new in the department and eager to make friends. She said she'd teach for Patrick before he even told her he'd make it up to her someday. He meant he would teach her classes if she ever needed him to, but she said he could pay her back by taking her to lunch next week. He said he'd try; he was thinking that it depended on how Lila was feeling.

Joyce said, "Your wife's situation. Oh, of course. I'm sorry if that sounded insensitive."

He thanked her, but as he left, he wondered how Joyce knew, and whether his whole department knew. The thought bothered him. Patrick really liked the people he worked with, but he was a firm believer in keeping his private life private.

As he drove along the turnpike, he focused on a lecture he was giving next week. He was exhausted by the situation with Lila, and the lecture was much easier to think about. He could make the lecture better, but he couldn't make his wife better. He hated feeling so powerless.

Even though he hadn't been to Billy and Ashley's house since last summer, he had no problem finding it. It was a little stone cottage down by the river, nice actually, with a sunroom in back and a small living room with a fireplace. There was one bedroom downstairs, and two upstairs for the kids. Pearl shared the bigger room with her sister, Maisie. William had his own tiny room with spaceship wallpaper that his dad had put up when they moved in.

Ashley led him into the kitchen and asked if he wanted coffee. He said no thanks. He was already anxious about what he'd come to tell her; the last thing he needed was caffeine.

Before he could get to his point, he had to listen to Ashley talk about why she was screening all the calls that came into her house. "A lot of nuts want to talk to my kids," Ashley said. "Some father's rights guy called and cussed me out last week. They're obsessed with what they say I did to Billy. One of them said they're going to use my case to change custody laws. I said go ahead and try."

"Must be difficult," Patrick said evenly. "On you and the kids."

"The kids don't know anything about it. Me and Kyle keep our mouths shut when we're around them."

"Kyle?"

Ashley shrugged. "Yeah, he's an old friend. I went to high school with him and then didn't hear from him until a year and a half ago. We connected through one of those online things, classmates-dot-com? Ever tried that?" She smiled. "It's cool. You find out what happened to all these people you've forgotten about."

"But he's staying with you now?" Patrick tried not to sound disapproving. He'd seen a man's jacket and boots by the front door, but he'd stupidly assumed they were Billy's.

"Temporarily." She coughed. "It's kind of complicated."

That's when Patrick knew Ashley had a boyfriend, just like Lila said. Lila claimed there had to be another man because Ashley couldn't manage alone, but Patrick thought his wife was just angry. Now that he knew it was true, he wondered what kind of mother Ashley really was. Letting a boyfriend move in with her so soon? A man she hadn't seen in years?

"Where is he now?" Patrick said lightly, hoping the guy wasn't going to barge in and interrupt their conversation.

"He's out trading his car for a truck. He likes to haul things. Usual man stuff."

As Patrick had never hauled anything in his life, he couldn't comment on this. He wished the topic of Kyle hadn't come up because it flustered him. He'd always liked Ashley and found her to be reasonable enough. Truth be told, he'd thought she had her hands full with Lila's brother. He'd even felt sorry for her, living with a moody man like Billy.

Despite his discomfort, he slowly started presenting his case for why his wife should be allowed to visit the kids. He mentioned Lila's long-standing relationship with them and all the holidays and birthdays the kids had spent with their aunt. He emphasized that, though the children's father had clearly been unstable, their aunt would always be an important connection to their father's memory. She might even be crucial to their healing—a fact about the "grieving process" he'd found the night before on the internet.

He said a lot of other things and Ashley patiently listened to it all. She had a nice face; he'd always thought that. She looked like a warm, tolerant person. She was wearing a light blue sweater, faded jeans, and house slippers; her hair was pulled back in a ponytail and she wore tiny gold earrings. The very picture of a friendly suburban mom. Naturally, he thought he was getting through to her. Why wouldn't he be? He was only asking for what was right.

When he was finished, Ashley folded her hands. "Do you know what Billy did to that boy?"

"No, but Lila didn't have anything to do with—"

"It wasn't just hitting him or the things a pervert would do. That would be bad, but William could have gotten over that someday."

Patrick was trying to comprehend how she could sound so casual about child abuse, when she continued, "No, this was way worse. He could have gotten William killed."

He let her describe in great detail the risks Billy had taken with their son. He wanted to know the facts in Billy's police file, but after he'd heard it all, his first response was relief. What he'd been imagining was so much worse, actually: something along the lines of what Ashley had called "things a pervert would do." At the very least, he thought Billy had done something that had caused physical harm to William, as opposed to being only so dangerous it could have harmed the child. But "only so dangerous" didn't make sense and Patrick knew it. Billy was a parent; he'd had an absolute responsibility to keep his child safe. Ashley was right to take this to the police and he told her so, though of course he would never admit that to Lila.

It hadn't occurred to him yet to wonder why Billy had done all this. But Ashley had her own theory: Billy was crazy. And not only Billy, but his sister, too. "I know she's your wife and you don't want to think anything bad about her, but there's a lot you don't know. A lot I didn't know, either. A lot I still don't." She wiped her mouth with the back of her hand. "No need for me to find out now, but you'd better, if you don't want Lila flipping out like Billy did."

He was nervous, but he said, "Lila is fine. She just wants to see your kids, which is perfectly normal. They're all she has left of her family.

Ashley stood up and went to the kitchen counter. She reached inside a jar that said Tea and pulled out a small envelope. When she sat back down, she said, "This is a sympathy card I got the day after the funeral. Who do you think it's from?"

"No idea." He hated rhetorical questions. What was the point of asking him when he couldn't possibly know?

"It's from Billy and Lila's mother." He started to object, but she said, "Hold on, I know what you're thinking. Their mother is dead. I thought that, too. That's what he always told me."

He felt really angry then, though he tried to keep his voice steady and reasonable. "You said a lot of 'nuts' have been calling." He pointed at the envelope in her hand. "That must have been from some lunatic, too." When she didn't say anything, he added, "If the mother was still alive, don't you think she would have come to the funeral?"

"Billy's mother said she wanted to come."

He snapped, "I wish you wouldn't call her that."

"She said she wanted to meet me and her grandkids, but she couldn't come because she was afraid."

"Of course she was. Afraid of being discovered." He hoped he wasn't smirking. "Because Lila would know immediately that she was a fraud."

"No," Ashley said slowly. "Afraid *of* Lila." She handed him the envelope. "Here, see for yourself."

He pulled the card from the envelope. The woman called herself Barbara, which was Lila's mother's name. She got that part right, but so what? It wouldn't have been hard, given all the newspaper stories. She went on for a paragraph about how sorry she was for Ashley and the children before she threw in the claim that she was afraid of Lila. Which, to Patrick's mind, was exactly what he'd been saying. She was afraid of Lila denouncing her as a fake.

He was oddly calmer now that he'd seen it. It was ridiculous, and he told Ashley so.

"I thought that myself at first. So you know what I did? I wrote to the old gal. She had a return address in New Jersey, and I sat down and wrote and asked her for proof."

Ashley reached under a bowl of fruit and there was another envelope. This time she didn't hesitate before handing it to Patrick. Inside the envelope was a photograph. There was no mistaking that the two children were at least related to Lila: the girl looked like Pearl when she was younger and the boy looked uncannily like Billy. The only thing that surprised him was how much shorter the girl was than the boy, but he knew that wasn't meaningful because even though Lila had grown up to be taller than her brother, she could certainly have been smaller as a kid. On the back of the photo, someone had written: *Billy and Lila, summer 1981.*

"Maybe she found this." His hand was shaking a little. He dropped the photo on the table and crossed his arms. "It doesn't prove anything."

Ashley sounded kind, even a little sorry for him. "It sucks being lied to by the person you thought you were closer to than anybody in the whole world, doesn't it? I know how you feel."

Patrick didn't respond, though he was sure Ashley didn't know how he felt, because Ashley's mother was still alive.

Over the last twelve years, he'd tried so hard not to think about his mother's death. It was the worst thing that had ever happened to him and the only way to deal with it was to force himself not to go there. Even when he was stuck on the phone, listening to his father's memories and regrets, he always made sure he was in front of his computer, too, so he could read the news or science blogs or something, anything to distract himself.

He could feel his jaw tightening. He'd never realized until this moment how much it had always meant to him to know that he and Lila had this bond. She rarely spoke of her mother, either, but he'd always assumed this was because she, too, was trying to avoid feeling this devastating loss.

Lila's mother could not be alive. It was that simple. It was as unbelievable to him as anyone being afraid of his gentle, soft-spoken wife.

He placed his hands flat on the table. "Are you telling me you won't let your kids see their aunt because some nut claims to be scared of her?"

Ashley looked out the window behind him. "I don't know what happened to Billy and Lila when they were kids. Something did, though; I've known that for years. My husband became crazier and crazier as William got older." She shook her head. "Hell, maybe you're lucky you and Lila don't have any kids."

"Thanks," he said, without attempting to hide his sarcasm.

"She's got some problems, that wife of yours. That's what I told the lawyer. Anybody who would lie about their mom being dead to their own husband—that's somebody troubled." She lowered her voice. "All I know is that my kids aren't going to suffer another minute from the Cole curse."

Patrick laughed. " 'The Cole curse'? Come on, you sound like a superstitious idi—"

He stopped himself, but too late. She turned her back to him, but he could hear how angry she was. "Want to guess where I got that from? The *genius* himself told me that a hundred times. Too bad he's not here so you could call him an idiot."

Though Patrick apologized, it didn't matter. She told him to get out of her house. He rushed to his car, furious with himself for losing his temper and ruining whatever chance he'd had to save this. Except it couldn't have been saved anyway, he felt sure of that now. Ashley was never going to let Lila see those kids as long as she believed Lila was not only "cursed," but a liar.

Driving down the turnpike, he tried to think about the lecture he was giving, the problem he was trying to solve, the finals he needed to prepare, but nothing worked. He was back in St. Louis again, a twenty-five-year-old man listening to his mother cry from a pain no amount of morphine could help. He was back there, watching her die so slowly and horribly that he sometimes wondered if he'd ever be able to think about what either of them had been like before.

CHAPTER SIX

She fell in love with him because he wrote her a poem. How lame is that? This was before she knew that, for Billy, pretty words came as easy as finding salt in the ocean. "That boy can talk," her mother said. And then, because her mom had already been divorced twice and distrusted men: "Watch that you don't get hit in the eye when he's slinging all that bullshit."

Ashley had never gone to college, but she was twenty-nine and no dummy. She knew the difference between BS and the kind of things Billy Cole talked to her about. His dream to be a writer wasn't just pie-in-the-sky drunk talk, either, because he was never drunk and he had a briefcase full of stuff he'd already written. And he wasn't using that stuff to get laid. He wouldn't even show it to her; he said real writers never show their work until it's finished.

She was kind of relieved he felt that way, because what if he wanted her to read it and then talk about what it meant? She'd always sucked at those "deeper meaning" questions in high school.

No doubt, she had a weakness for unavailable guys, especially if they had sad puppy dog eyes like Billy Cole did. But where was the harm in hanging out with him? She knew he wasn't the type to hit a woman, and he didn't even raise hell on the weekends, like most of the guys she knew did. And it was only going to be for a little while, until he left for California or Oregon or wherever he decided to go next. Ashley's mom called him a drifter, like that was a bad thing, but Ashley herself thought it would be so cool to travel the country like that. The farthest away she'd ever been was El Paso, for her cousin Karen's wedding.

Did she ever hope Billy would ask her to leave town with him? No, because she wasn't a fool and only fools hope for things that will never happen in a million years. That he'd stayed as long as he had was good enough for her, and more than she'd expected. Yeah, he'd given her something she hadn't planned on, but she could deal with that after he was gone. She wasn't ready to be a mother and he sure as hell wasn't ready to be a father. He didn't have the money she'd need for the clinic, so why tell him about it?

And then he wrote her that damn poem and she fell in love with Billy Cole. How he figured out she was pregnant, she wasn't sure, but all those pretty words about the pretty baby she was carrying and the pretty family they would have—well, it seemed like one of those fantasies all little girls love, like Cinderella and the slipper. The guys she knew would have run if they guessed she was knocked up, but not Billy. Her mom said it was only because he was too young to get what he was in for with a kid.

Ashley took a lot of shit about Billy's age from her friends and family. She told Trish if she heard one more joke about robbing the cradle she was going to scream. Trish was the only one who thought it was romantic that Ashley was marrying Billy Cole, and it wasn't much comfort. Trish had always been kind of simple.

Still, Trish was her sister and Ashley loved her without question, the way you do with your family. This was why she thought she understood how Billy felt about his sister. Billy and Lila were twins, yeah, but how different could it be? Oh boy, was she ever stupid about that! From the moment Princess Lila blew into town, Billy rarely left her side and the two of them were always whispering in the corner of the bar where Ashley was still working, trying to make enough money for the baby. She was already five and a half months pregnant and her feet hurt from standing all night, but she tried not to bitch. At least Billy was keeping his promise to get married, finally.

They'd waited three months so Lila could finish college. Billy told Ashley he was afraid it would put too much stress on his sister if she had to come to the wedding before the end of the semester, and she might even get sick.

"Does she get sick a lot?" Ashley said, wondering why Billy had mentioned this. It seemed a weird thing to worry about with a girl Lila's age.

The question seemed to annoy Billy. "No," he said, frowning, "and I intend to keep it that way. Lila's going to graduate school to be a professor. It's what she's always wanted and I don't want anything to interrupt her plans."

Ashley's mom was the one who'd named Billy's sister Princess Lila, because she thought Lila acted like she was better than everybody else. Ashley told her mom she was being too hard on the girl, but secretly she worried her mom was right. Lila had a way of looking at Ashley like she was to blame for all this, like Ashley had tricked Billy into marrying her like one of those white-trash women on *Jerry Springer.* It wasn't until after they'd been married for a few months that Billy admitted he had told Lila something like that. Of course, this turned into a fight, the first of hundreds they would have over the years.

They were still living in Ashley's apartment, which was small to begin with and now seemed tiny with Billy always there and Ashley eight months along and big as a truck. The bed took up three quarters of the only room; the kitchen was against the back wall, just a half-refrigerator, a rusted-out sink, a hot plate, and one cabinet where the small amount of dishes Ashley had were crammed together: blackened pots under glasses, spoons and forks on top of chipped plates. The bathroom didn't even have a shower, just a peeling tub with a hose she'd connected to the faucet so she could wash her hair. Otherwise, all they had were a small TV sitting on an old dresser, and a corner desk next to the window that faced the mountains, with a stack of Billy's books arranged on the windowsill. He'd put up three pictures on the opposite wall: one of Lila, one of an old guy with a beard (it was somebody Ashley had never heard of; Billy said the guy had written one of his favorite books), and a colorful painting of triangles, circles, and zigzag lines. Over by the bed, Ashley had baby pictures of her nephews and a photo of her whole family at last year's picnic—normal pictures, not like the one Billy had of his sister, which was downright strange.

She was all by herself in some kind of spooky forest. Her blond hair was shorter then, curled around her face, which was weirdly pale, and her eyes looked big as an owl's. Her face was heart-shaped, but not soft, and her lips were locked together as firmly as if she'd decided not to talk for the rest of her life. Or maybe like she was holding back a scream? Ashley felt sure that something had scared the shit out of Lila that day, but when she'd suggested that to Billy, he'd said it was "ludicrous." One of his favorite words, as Ashley was discovering. It always made her lose track of what she was trying to say.

Ashley stared at that picture while Billy explained why he'd lied to Lila about the reason for their marriage. "She's never had a real boyfriend, Ash." Billy was still sitting at his desk. "She wouldn't understand about all this."

"So you told her it was all a trick?"

He shrugged. "It doesn't matter now, does it?"

"Did you even tell her you loved me?"

"I told her I didn't care whether I loved you or not, which was true. That I would have married you anyway because of the baby."

This was so much worse than him saying she'd tricked him into marrying her; she was stunned. She swallowed hard and stared at his back bent over his desk. His pen was moving again, like that was the end of their little chat.

She grabbed the first thing she could reach—her jean jacket—and threw it at him.

He turned around, rubbing his neck where the snap had hit him. "What?"

"You wrote me that fucking poem!"

"And?"

"You went on and on about how much you loved me and the baby."

"I said our life together would be great." He looked into her eyes. "I still believe that."

"You said a hell of a lot more than that, Jack." She went to her nightstand and yanked open the top drawer so hard the picture of her family fell forward with a clunk. "I've got it right here."

As angry as she was, she couldn't help unfolding the sheet of notebook paper gently. It was the best night of her life, wasn't it? The night Billy waited for her outside the bar and insisted on going to the rundown hotel where he was staying, rather than her place. There were hundreds of stars out that night, and she felt happy riding along in that junker Oldsmobile of his, holding his hand.

When they got inside the room, she noticed that he'd lit a few candles, picked some hyssop from the side of the road and arranged it in the plastic coffeepot—nothing fancy compared to what other women bragged about getting from their men, but it touched her. The truth was no guy had ever done anything remotely romantic for Ashley. She told herself this was because they could tell she was too tough to want this kind of crap, but deep down, she knew that none of those guys had ever loved her. They were attracted by her breasts and her ass; they liked her easy way in bed, but they didn't really care. But Billy was different, she knew that when he reached into the pocket of his faded jeans and handed her the poem. Billy saw her soft side. He knew she longed to have a family of her own. He thought their baby would be pretty. He actually wanted to marry her.

Except scanning the poem now, she knew that he'd left something out, the most important thing. The pain was so sudden and sharp that she couldn't help it; she let out a cry and let the poem drop out of her hand.

"I meant all that," he said, standing up. "Ash, what's—"

She was fighting back tears, the bitter tears of a woman so stupid it had taken her months to see what was right in front of her nose. Of course Billy Cole didn't love her. They were so different; why would he? And no man had ever managed to love her, not even her own father. Her own father hadn't seen or spoken to her in all the years since her mom had thrown his lying, drunken ass out.

"Why do you want this baby?" she said, swallowing hard. "If you don't love me, why my kid?"

"It's my kid, too, Ash."

She put her hands on her belly. "So you love it 'cause it's yours?" She was shouting. "Like these books?" She moved over to the windowsill and knocked them all off. "Like your papers?" She pushed them from the desk and watched as they fluttered to the ground.

"Like your precious twin." She tore the photo from the wall and threw it on the pile.

"That's enough." He sounded cold and angry, but she didn't care. It was over and she would never let him know how much this hurt. She would deny to him and everyone else that she had been dumb enough to believe this smart-guy writer could have actually loved Ashley Harris.

"I'm going to go so far away—" She was holding her belly again, which was cramping up something fierce. "So far away that you'll never see—" All of a sudden, the cramp got so bad it doubled her over. Then she felt the gush and saw water running down her legs, splashing drops on Billy's papers and the photograph of Lila.

If he'd gotten mad at her for ruining his things, she would have left after the baby was born. She was pretty sure about that. But instead he said, his voice full of awe, "It's time, isn't it?"

She was three weeks early, but he was right; now that her water had broken, the baby was coming. And she was terrified. Of labor. Of taking care of an infant. Of screwing up the child's life. And yeah, of living without him. Maybe that most of all.

"It's going to be fine," he whispered. He was standing right next to her. "We don't need to worry about all these details anymore." He was smiling his best Billy smile, but she hoped that wasn't why she didn't notice he'd just described not loving her as a "detail." He nodded at the picture of the bearded man on the wall. "Like he said, happy families are all alike. And that's what we're going to be, Ash. The happiest family in the world." He paused, then said something he'd said before, which she was ashamed to admit made no sense to her: "From experience to innocence, our path to redemption."

CHAPTER SEVEN

If Patrick had wanted to know what it was like, she would have told him that it felt as if pieces of her mind had simply disappeared. This was why she was afraid to even try to read now: without the characters and their voices, the words collided into each other, a cacophony of sound without meaning, a total void that reminded her of the nothingness Billy used to say was crouching right outside, threatening to swallow them up if they weren't very, very careful. "Read this," he would say, pushing another book into her hands whenever she felt the fear creeping up on her again. Then he would tell her to pretend she was Jane or Huck or Hester—whoever the main character was in the book. If she was really frightened, he would open up the book and read to her, page after page in his most expressive voice, until she was calm again, until she remembered these stories were the only truth that mattered now. "The truth with a narrative arc," as one of her undergraduate professors would call it years later. "A truth that has been shaped and molded, indeed *tortured* into a story to please the short-attention-span set known as readers."

Billy insisted that professor had to be a hack; otherwise, he would have known that writers loved stories for themselves, not only as a means to get readers. And sitting in Nancy Jamison's office, Lila knew Billy would probably call this therapist a hack, too, because Nancy said the whole topic was merely a way for Lila to avoid looking at what was *really* bothering her. As if losing her ability to read couldn't be bothering her. As if losing her life's passion couldn't possibly be an issue.

Lila was slumping in a big black chair across from Nancy, who was sitting upright in an identical chair. The therapist was older, late fifties, early sixties, Lila guessed. She had graying brown hair and hazel eyes, stylish glasses, and was extremely well groomed—in sharp contrast to Lila herself, who was wearing the only pants that would stay on her now, her sweats that tied at the waist, and whose hair was a raggedy mess since she'd needed a cut long before Billy had died.

Patrick had forced her to come here, despite how tired she was. She took sleeping pills every night and every morning, but no matter how much she slept, she never got over her exhaustion. Billy had always been the energetic one, and sometimes she felt like his death had taken away all her vitality, too. Or maybe she was suffering from depression, like Nancy claimed after only five minutes of their session. Another reason Billy would call her a hack, but then he'd always hated the diagnosis of depression, preferring the nineteenth-century word "melancholia." As he said, one could be melancholy because of the world one found oneself in, but depression ignored all the circumstances, as if life was solely about the self.

"You told me that you've always felt that books gave you a respite from loneliness," Nancy said. "Why do you think you were such a lonely child?"

"Every child is lonely." Lila believed this. Ninety percent of her students considered themselves misfits as kids—and the other ten percent were probably such misfits that they couldn't even bear to think about it or admit it.

"But you had your twin brother. Would you say you were lonely when you were with Billy?"

"No, not at all. I think that was the only time I wasn't lonely."

Nancy paused for a moment and chewed on the end of a pencil. "You said you read constantly, though. Where was your brother during that time?"

Where is Billy? I have to see him!

Oh, that Shakespearean rag, it's so elegant, so intelligent.

Quit screaming or you'll wake them up.

"Lila?"

She blinked. "I'm sorry. Could you repeat the question?" Lila was afraid to let anyone know that since she'd stopped reading, her mind kept vomiting up these strange sequences of words. Some she recognized from poems and novels; some were an expression of her own feelings; and others, she just had no idea what they meant. If only Billy were here. He knew how to interpret even the hardest texts.

"Where was your brother when you were reading as a kid?"

"He was there, too."

Lila listened halfheartedly as the therapist explained that Lila was contradicting herself by claiming that she read because she was lonely, and yet Billy was there at the time. So either she read for other reasons than loneliness or she was lonely around Billy.

Nancy suggested the latter was probably true and started a long speech about how people tend to mythologize the dead and forget everything bad in their relationship with a lost loved one. "Sibling relationships are never simple," Nancy said. "I'm sure you and your brother couldn't have gotten along well all the time. But that's normal. If you think back about a quarrel you and he had, it doesn't mean you didn't love him or that you aren't—"

"I don't remember any quarrels."

"Have you ever watched children playing, Lila? They all have squabbles, even the best of friends."

"I'm sure you're right, but as I just told you, I don't remember quarreling or squabbling or anything like that. I'm sorry, I really don't."

Nancy sat quietly for a while, and Lila wished she were home, in her own bed, away from this fruitless discussion.

"Tell me about a birthday when you were a child," Nancy said. "How about your twelfth birthday? Did you and Billy have a party? Get a lot of presents?"

"I don't see why this matters, but I'm sure we didn't have a party. My mother didn't seem to believe in parties for children."

For adults, her mother and stepfather had given parties constantly, though Lila didn't remember ever attending one. Billy said the two of them had never been allowed downstairs, and they'd often been locked in their bedrooms long before anyone arrived, as if they weren't children but savage dogs that might attack one of the guests. At least their windows were still unlocked, and most of the time Billy climbed over the roof and into Lila's room. When they were older and Lila became a better climber herself, they escaped into the woods behind their house, where they would sit for hours, talking and watching for the headlights that meant cars had begun pulling out from their circular driveway. Lila wasn't sure what their stepfather would have done if he'd come into their rooms and found them gone. Billy said they were always much too careful to get caught.

"How about your presents?" the therapist said. "What was your favorite gift that year?"

"I'm sorry, but I fail to see how this could possibly be important."

"Humor me for a few minutes."

"Probably a book. Several books."

"But you don't remember?"

"Not that particular birthday, no."

"Let's try another one. Ten is an important year for most children. What did you get then?"

"I think it was a flute. I believe that's what Billy told me."

"But again, you don't remember." Nancy paused. "All right, who was your teacher in sixth grade?"

"Mrs. Something or Other. No idea." After a few more minutes of pointless questions like these, Lila looked into Nancy's eyes. "I really don't see how this is helping me."

"I'm trying to ascertain how wide your memory gaps are."

"Why didn't you just ask? I would have told you that I don't remember most of my childhood."

Lila was prepared to hear how abnormal this was; she'd heard it many times before from friends and even colleagues. The only one who seemed fine with it was Patrick, because Patrick wasn't really interested in her past. She'd known this right away; it was part of the reason she'd felt so safe with him: he was happy to leave all that behind and live in the present. Of course, now she didn't feel safe anywhere, not even in her own mind.

Instead, Nancy looked at her. "So you wouldn't know if you quarreled with your brother, would you?"

"That's true, but I think Billy would have told me. He was a genius. He had a phenomenal memory."

"Perhaps he neglected to mention it. He might have thought it was unimportant, which it probably was."

"No, he said we never quarreled. Not about anything of substance, at least."

"Really? What was the context?"

"He was talking to his wife. An argument really. And he mentioned that he and I had never seriously disagreed."

"What was their argument about?"

Lila shrugged, but she remembered, though she hadn't thought about this in years. She and Patrick were over at Billy's house for a barbecue, and Ashley and Billy were talking about Pearl. Ashley claimed it was weird that six-year-old Pearl didn't play with the other kids at school, but Billy said it wasn't weird, it was a sign she was intelligent. Like he was. Like Lila was. Then Ashley asked if this meant Pearl had the "Cole curse." She was clearly being sarcastic, but Billy was furious. He went on and on about how Ashley had no idea what it was like to be in a true family. He said he'd never had this kind of problem with Lila and that they'd never disagreed about anything important. At which point Ashley said, "Because Lila's your puppet," and Lila got up and went outside, ostensibly to see how the steaks and hamburgers were progressing, but really because she was angry with her sister-in-law. But the whole thing had blown over by the time dinner was served. Later, when Billy asked Lila if she was upset, she said no, and she hadn't been—for herself. For him, though, she was devastated. It was Billy's worst fear: that he had inherited some kind of curse from their family. He was confident that Lila would be all right in the long run, but he was never sure about himself.

Nancy was still trying to get her to admit that she must have quarreled with her twin at some point, but she wasn't listening. She was imagining how isolated her brother must have felt during all those years, married to a woman who was capable of being sarcastic about the very thing that scared him most. If only Lila had paid more attention, she would have known something terrible was happening to him in Harrisburg. She would never forgive herself for neglecting her brother, leaving him so alone that he could see no way out.

"What are you feeling right now?" Nancy said.

Lila reached for a tissue from the box conveniently placed on the table in front of her. After a moment, she looked up. "I think you're right: I am suffering from depression. I appreciate your offer to call your colleague to prescribe medication for me. If that doesn't work we can talk more, but in the meantime, I don't think this is helping."

"Crying doesn't mean it isn't helping, Lila. You need to cry."

Nancy's tone was so gentle, it lulled Lila into admitting what she was thinking. "I don't think so. I spent a year crying once and it did nothing for me."

"When was that?"

"When I was fifteen." She sniffed. "A long time ago."

"Do you remember why you were so sad that year?"

"Because I couldn't be with Billy."

"Really? Where was he?"

"At home. But I was away at Kingston." She shrugged. "A small prep school."

"What happened? Why didn't you finish?"

"I did finish."

"In a year?"

"I think I came into the school with more than half the credits I needed."

"Still, you finished high school in two years?"

Lila nodded. She'd never spent much time thinking about it; honestly, it wasn't much of an accomplishment. She knew a woman in grad school who had finished *college* in two years. And Billy had finished high school in one year. This was why he didn't have to go to prep school, because he was already done.

"Did you start college at sixteen?"

"No." Lila hesitated, but she knew she couldn't tell the therapist the truth. Years before, Billy had made her promise to tell no one. Also, if she told Nancy Jamison, she'd have to tell Patrick, too, and she couldn't stand to do that to him, especially right now, with the end of the semester and finals looming and him having to handle everything, from driving her here this morning to their bills and the dishes and even answering all their phone calls. "My parents died that summer. A car accident. I waited a year to start college."

"And where did you and Billy stay during that year?"

"In our home," she said, forcing a shrug. "It was being sold and we didn't have any living relatives. But our neighbors popped in to make sure we were all right."

Be the white whale agent, or be the white whale principal, I will wreak that hate upon him.

My life is ruined! Don't you hear me?

Lila forced herself to speak, hoping to quiet the rattling in her brain. "It was fine, really."

Nancy went on for a while asking questions about the year Lila and Billy had spent with no parents, and Lila gave vague answers. Again, Lila wasn't sure what the therapist was getting at until Nancy said, "Do you think you're more worried about your nieces and nephews because you already know the pain of losing a parent?"

"No, I don't think so. It's really very different."

"In the way your brother died, yes, but isn't the experience of grief over losing your mother or father fairly universal?"

Lila knew she should say yes, but she couldn't make the word come out of her mouth. So Nancy asked the question three more times, rephrasing it only slightly each time, until finally Lila blurted out, "It's completely different because my brother never called any of his children 'a little shit.' "

"Are you saying your father called Billy that?"

"It was our stepfather." She looked down at her hands. "And no, it wasn't my brother, it was me."

"I'm sorry," Nancy said. She sounded genuinely sorry. "Was he cruel to you in ways other than name calling?"

"I don't know." She couldn't even remember her stepfather's voice, much less the names she knew he'd used for her: "little shit," "smart-ass," "crybaby." Billy remembered them all, including the worst one, the name her stepfather had called her on a night that was buried so far in her brain that no matter how many times Billy told her about it, nothing came to her. Not the room, not the smells, not the image of her stepfather sitting on the side of her bed and arguing with her until she sobbed agreement that she really was an "evil" girl.

"Did he hit you?"

"I think so."

"And you do remember this?"

"Some of it." The truth was, she only remembered fragments, and nothing about the worst beating her stepfather ever gave her. That happened on that same night she never could remember that turned out to be the beginning of the end.

"Where was your mother during this?"

"In the background, crying."

Nancy asked another question, but Lila didn't hear it. Her mind had wandered to something she hadn't thought about for a long time. She and Billy were in their woods, in the tree house their real father had built, so they must have been young, seven or eight? Before they got so heavy the thin board wouldn't hold them. Lila had brought her tea set and a bottle of water with her. She had poured them "tea" and they were reading a children's book; Lila didn't remember the name. But she remembered sitting close to her brother, their shoulders touching, the book spread open across their laps, and trying to read fast so she could keep up with him. After they turned the last page, Lila said she liked it. The children got saved from a bully, and afterward, they got to eat lots of ice cream. Billy said he liked it, too. Then they pretended the water in the teacups was ice cream and scooped it up with their hands, giggling as it dribbled down their chins and all over their shirts. The sun was shining through the trees into the perfectly square tree house window, making shadows dance on the tree house wall. It was a happy day, one of her very own memories. Even when Billy admitted he didn't remember it, she knew it had happened just like she said.

"Do you think your mother might have been crying because she felt helpless to stop your stepfather?"

"Give me a minute," Lila said. She was trying to remember what her tea set looked like. Pearl had had a tea set, too, a cute white one with vines of pink roses curling around the handles of the cups. When the little girl was five or six, Lila had played tea with her, but Pearl had milk in the cups instead of water. Ashley was at work and Billy let Pearl wear her best dress for the tea party and let her pour the milk herself, even though she spilled a little. Billy was speaking with a British accent and holding his pinky out every time he picked up his cup. At some point, Pearl and Lila and Billy all broke down laughing.

She looked at the clock on the table by Nancy. The hour was almost over, but she didn't want to go home. There was nowhere in the world that she wanted to be now. If only she could spend the rest of her life imagining that she was at one of those tea parties. If only she could hear Billy giggling as a boy, or laughing as a man with his own beautiful little girl. It knocked the breath out of her, knowing that she could travel the world and it wouldn't matter, she would never find her brother again.

"Lila?" Nancy said. "You still haven't told me why your mother was crying. Is this hard for you to talk about?"

She had never discussed this with anyone but Billy, but he did all the talking, skimming over all the details she couldn't remember, emphasizing only that their mother had been too weak to protect them. It struck her now that perhaps she got to remember the good things because he took responsibility for remembering all the bad. "We're living a metaphor" was the way he put it once, but he was joking that her more cheerful disposition came from her having lighter-colored hair. He never complained that he had to live his life under the shadow of always knowing what Lila couldn't bear to know. And whenever her pain got too bad, he would remind her of the second part of the plot, an elaborate story of the happy adulthood that he'd constructed out of thin air and taught her to believe in, too. The promised world; their lives, redeemed.

Nancy waited a while before suggesting, "Perhaps you don't remember why your mother was crying when your stepfather hit you? If so, it's all right, we can work on that next time. You've made good progress to—"

"But I think I do remember something," she said, and her own voice surprised her. She hadn't planned on talking about this. She'd only thought of it last night, while she was half-asleep, and this morning she'd woken up feeling like it couldn't be real. It was something Billy had never told her, not once, and it didn't seem to fit with their mother being weak. Was she losing the plot again? If only Billy were here, she would know what was happening to her. Without him, the fear was unbearable. What if she really was going crazy?

It was eleven o'clock, time for her to leave. Patrick was waiting.

Nancy stood up. Lila stood, too, but she didn't move. "I have to ask you a question," she said. "If something feels like a memory, but it didn't really happen, is that another symptom of being depressed?"

"Go ahead and tell me this memory," Nancy said. "We'll talk about what it means next week. Right now, I think you need to say it."

The phone on Nancy's desk started ringing. Probably her receptionist, letting her know that the next patient had arrived. But Nancy didn't answer it. Her eyes were encouraging.

"When you asked if my mother was crying because she was helpless to stop my stepfather . . . I think that's true. But in my head, I don't see my stepfather, I just hear her saying something while she's crying."

"What is she saying, Lila?"

"I know this didn't happen, though. And I'm really scared what this means about me. What if I'm losing my mind?"

"I think you're just afraid to tell me this. I also think you're going to feel a lot better once you do."

Lila wasn't at all sure that she would feel better, but she didn't know how she could feel much worse. So, after a moment, she took a breath and said, "My mother isn't crying because she's sad, but because she's angry. I know this even before she says the words. And then she says them over and over again, and I can't bear it, but she won't stop."

"What are the words?"

"I put my hand over my ears and beg her." Lila could feel tears standing in her eyes. " 'Please, Mother, please don't.' But she doesn't listen. She's still saying it. She says it until I can't take it any longer." Lila wanted to move to the door, to get away from the therapist, but she was glued to the spot, hearing her mother shrieking those words.

" 'I've given birth to a monster,' " Lila finally muttered. A sense of quietness descended on her, but it was an odd feeling, less like being calm than being dead. "That's what my mother was saying. About me."

And then, without waiting to see how the therapist would take this, Lila escaped from the office. Once they were in the elevator, she told Patrick that she was never coming back.

CHAPTER EIGHT

William's mother had told him a zillion times that some grown-ups didn't like kids and so you couldn't be too loud or silly in stores, even if you didn't run around and hurt anything. "Those kind of grown-ups are bad guys," Daddy said one day, after Mommy took Maisie upstairs for her nap. "That's why you can't trust any grown-up you don't know. Even if they smile and act nice, don't be fooled. They don't care about you and some of them might want to hurt you."

When the policeman came to ask him questions, after he was a stupid baby and told his mom about the camping Challenge, he did another stupid thing. He forgot what Daddy said about some grown-ups wanting to hurt you. The policeman must have been that kind of grown-up and that's why he arrested William's father, to hurt William and his sisters by taking their dad away from them. William wrote himself a reminder to be super careful around grown-ups he didn't know. And then, because he was afraid he wasn't smart enough to know when someone was tricking him, he decided not to talk to any grown-ups, even those he did know. Even his own mom.

He had to keep reminding himself of how important this was, because Mommy kept saying she was worried. He knew this was why she kept taking him to places he didn't like where another new grown-up wanted to talk to him about the Challenges, and how he felt about his daddy, and how he felt about everything. He couldn't run away because the door was closed and his mom was right outside, ready to drag him back in. "You have to talk!" Mommy said. "Please! I know you understand what I'm saying!"

Since the day after the funeral, William hadn't messed up even one time. He hadn't said a word to anybody except Pearl, and she promised she wouldn't tell that he could talk if he wanted to. At first, nobody cared too much, but after a week, his teacher got worried and called his mother in for a conference. It was the teacher's idea to take William to see all these people who wanted to talk about his feelings. But he was safe from blurting anything out now. Even Kyle, his mom's friend, couldn't get him to talk. It was just like the Challenge about being a spy that he'd done with Daddy, but now he was not only listening really good to everything around him, but never opening his mouth about anything he heard. He hoped his father could see him in heaven, because he knew Daddy would be proud.

William knew he shouldn't care how his mom felt. He'd heard Pearl and her friend Staci talking about how mean Mommy was for making them sneak around just to visit Daddy's grave, and how stupid Mommy was for falling in love with a drunken idiot like Kyle, and how it was all her fault that Daddy got killed, and William felt sort of dumb that he loved her so much. But he wasn't going to be a baby about it. He wasn't going to talk just because she sang him more songs at bedtime and made him extra snacks.

It was hard sometimes with his mother, but it was easy with the grown-ups in the ugly place. They asked all kinds of questions, but when William wouldn't answer any of them, they gave him paper and crayons and told him to draw. He liked drawing, even if he wasn't very good at it. He drew robots and cars and dinosaurs and whatever he felt like. Sometimes they told him to draw his family or himself, but he just acted like he hadn't heard and drew another robot. When it was time to go, they had William wait out in the hall and brought Mommy inside the office, but they didn't shut the door all the way and William could hear them talking sometimes. He had to put his hand over his mouth not to giggle when he heard one lady say William had drawn his daddy as a dinosaur. He told Pearl later and she laughed, too, and said, "Social workers are morons."

He only talked to Pearl when they were in Staci's car or all the way down by the edge of the creek behind their house, where nobody could hear. His big sister was so nice to him now that he could hardly remember when she used to call him a brat and tell him to get out of her room and out of her sight. He was glad he had her to talk to, because sometimes he was afraid if he kept quiet for too long, he'd forget how to speak and turn into a baby again. Pearl said that could probably happen, but it wouldn't happen to him because he wouldn't have to keep this up for much longer.

It was after school and they were down by the creek. Pearl had crooked her finger to get him to follow her. He could tell she was mad about something. He was glad it turned out to have nothing to do with him.

His sister said, "You know she's planning to make us all move to godforsaken New Mexico, right?"

William didn't know that, but he knew Mommy's family lived

in New Mexico and he knew she missed her family something awful since their dad moved out.

"What's 'godforsaken' mean?" he said.

"It means it's ugly as hell. No trees, no water, no flowers, just these shrubs that look like cauliflower and make you sneeze." Pearl flipped her hair over her shoulder. "It also means that the people who live there are illiterate barbarians. Did you know Mom's fabulous home has one of the worst education systems in the country? The lowest rate of people who go to libraries? If we move there, we can forget Princeton. We'll be lucky if we can get into community college."

William knew Daddy wanted all of them to go to Princeton for college. He also knew Aunt Lila had gone there, because Mommy said that was the only reason Daddy thought the place was so great. "Everything Lila does is sooo perfect, isn't it?" Mommy had said. Her voice was full of laughs, but they were mean-sounding. "We'll be so lucky if our kids turn out anything like Her Royal Highness."

William threw a stick in the creek. Pearl was still talking. "This is all because of that moron Kyle. Mom said maybe we would move back to Philadelphia, which would be cool because my old friends are there and it's close enough that Staci could drive up and visit and we could see Aunt Lila, but Kyle said he couldn't see himself living in 'Filthydelphia.' He wants to go home, he said. If Mom wasn't a moron, too, she'd tell him to go back to the hell he came from and leave us alone. But nooooo. Mom decides we're going with him. Without asking us! Without caring how we feel at all."

"We don't want to," William said. Though he really didn't know how he felt. He'd been to New Mexico the summer before he started kindergarten, but all he remembered was laughing and playing with Granny and Aunt Trish. He loved Aunt Trish best of all his aunts because she never made him clean his glasses and she built a Lego spaceship with him. But he didn't like Mom's friend Kyle, 'cause Kyle was always throwing beer cans in the trash and missing, and Kyle had icky breath. Plus, Kyle never did anything with him. He was always saying stuff like, "Let's play catch together this afternoon," or "We're going to go to that race on Saturday," but when afternoon or Saturday came, he was always sitting on the couch watching TV.

"Don't worry," Pearl said. "We're not moving to New Mexico. They can take Maisie with them, but they're not taking us. We're running away."

"For real?" William was a little scared, but he didn't want Pearl to know. He was so proud that she'd picked him to take with her and not Maisie.

"I have it all planned out. On Friday night, while Mom and Kyle are out on their stupid weekly 'date,' Staci is coming to get us and drive us to Aunt Lila's. Danielle is coming over to watch Maisie. All we have to do is get some stuff together beforehand." Pearl looked at William. "But just one duffel bag of clothes and things you really, really need."

"Like my boom box," William said. He never went anywhere without that. He used it to listen to all the music Daddy had been giving him since he was little. His favorite used to be Bach, back when Daddy was alive, but now he liked the guy from Russia whose name he could never pronounce, spelled S-H-O-S-T-A-K-O-V-I-C-H. Mommy said she was sick of hearing that depressing music, but Pearl said their mom had never understood classical composers. "She likes country," his sister said. "How could she?"

"Sure," Pearl said now. "But only three or four CDs. Aunt Lila will have a lot more at her house, I promise."

William thought for a moment. "Won't Mommy ask where we're going?"

Pearl frowned. "You have to pack in secret, dummy. Duh. Keep the duffel bag in your closet and cover it with your coat and some other clothes. If she opens the closet, which she won't, all she'll see is the usual mess of stuff that fell off the hangers. The worst that will happen is that she'll yell at you again to clean up the closet. But probably not, because she's too freaked out that you haven't talked for over three weeks."

She held up her hand and he raised his, too, so she could give him another slap five for keeping his mouth shut for so long. He was glad she did this, because he was feeling really bad that he was such a dummy he didn't know the duffel bag should be hidden.

He found a big rock and threw it in the creek and then watched all the ripples as it hit the water and sank. After a minute, he said, "What if Aunt Lila doesn't want us?"

"Haven't you been paying attention? She calls like every day to see us, but our wonderful mother always tells her no. Aunt Lila is on our side. She's just like Dad. She doesn't want us to live out the rest of our lives working at the DMV."

Their mother worked at the DMV. She used a machine to test people's eyes to make sure they could see good enough to drive a car. He knew Pearl thought it was a stupid job, but he wasn't sure what was wrong with it. He liked his mom's machine. It was a lot better than the one at the doctor's office where he was always being tested 'cause he was born with weak eyes.

He kicked the side of a tree for a while before he thought of something else. "What if the policeman comes and gets us?"

"I have a plan for that, too. If I tell you, you have to swear that you won't tell anybody." Pearl looked at him closely, like she was checking his face for dirt. "Not even Aunt Lila."

"I swear."

"You tell and I'll be in big, big trouble."

"Okay."

"No, forget about it."

Of course, now William really wanted to know. He begged and pleaded, but Pearl wouldn't budge; she said it was too risky. So finally he said, "I got a secret, too. I'll tell you if you tell me."

She didn't say anything. She was looking at the house. The lights were on in the living room and the kitchen, meaning Mommy was back with Maisie. Kyle was probably there, too. He didn't have a job, but he was usually gone when Pearl and William got home from school. Whenever Mommy asked Kyle what he'd done that day, he said, "Nothing much." Sometimes he lied and said he'd been home the whole time, but the one time when Pearl said it wasn't true, he said Little Missy wouldn't know because he was asleep and his truck was in the garage. "Little Missy" was what he called Pearl. She hated it. When their mom took Kyle's word over Pearl's, Pearl said Mommy was an idiot who would believe anything because she was so desperate for a man.

"My secret is BIG," he told his sister. "HUGE. I got my own plan and it's—"

"I'm sure you do, baby bro." Her voice was a smile and she called him "baby," but he didn't mind when she put her arm around him and pulled him close. He liked the way his sister's hair smelled. It was clean, like grass, but sweeter, like it wasn't really hair at all, but ropes of yellow flowers like the ones in the planter on their front porch. But when Pearl didn't let go after a minute, he felt caught, like when his granny pulled him on her lap. He could feel Pearl shaking like she was crying, but he still had to try hard not to squirm away.

Finally, his sister sniffed hard and stood up straight. "She broke Dad's heart when she went to the police. She turned him into a criminal to keep him away from us. Well, she's not going to keep us away from Aunt Lila. We belong with Dad's family. We're going to do this for him."

"Yeah," William said. And he was about to say that his secret and his plan were Dad's idea, but then Pearl said they had to go inside now for supper.

By the time supper was over, when he was back in his room, listening to S-H-O-S-T-A-K-O-V-I-C-H, he was glad he hadn't told her about the last Challenge. Daddy had said he was the only one brave enough to do what had to be done. "If it comes to that," Daddy always said, and he gave William a list of things that would help him know when the time had come. The number one thing on the list was Kyle still being with them, which made William rest easier. He wouldn't have to pack the gun or even move it from its hiding place, since Kyle wouldn't be at Aunt Lila's house for sure.

CHAPTER NINE

Patrick was halfway down the Garden State Parkway when his misgivings about what he was doing turned into full-fledged regret. He'd never believed the superstitious line that the universe punished you for making wrong choices, though it sure as hell felt like he was being punished when his car started bleeding oil. He managed to pull over to the side of the road without being killed, but that was the only good news. The bad news was that the engine of his old VW Rabbit appeared to have finally given up the ghost. And the really bad news was that his triple-A membership had lapsed sometime in the last month, another casualty of the stress of his life right now, meaning the cost to tow the car back to Philly would be astronomical. He could have it towed to the nearest town and hope he could find a mechanic who knew how to work on old

Volkswagens, but even if he was successful, the cost to replace the motor would be far more than the car was worth. He'd have to get a new car, though obviously there was no rush. Lila's Subaru was always available now. He should have taken her car today; it was nearly new and in perfect condition, but he kept thinking that as long as he left the Subaru in the apartment parking lot, there was at least a chance that Lila would get out of bed and go somewhere, anywhere, even the grocery store. That she never availed herself of this chance did nothing to his resolve to provide her with it. So he was stubborn as well as foolish.

At least she would have to drive somewhere now, though this would be awkward, too. He'd have to explain why he was halfway through New Jersey rather than holding office hours on Wednesday afternoon like he usually did. He was still thinking about what he'd say when he got out his cell and started dialing. There was no choice. He couldn't just sit on the side of the parkway for the rest of his life.

He cursed several times when he realized that he was being stupid again. He knew full well that Lila never answered the phone anymore, not even for her lawyer. She'd probably taken sleeping pills this morning. Most likely, she couldn't even hear the damn phone.

Before he put it back in his pocket, he noticed he had a text message from his colleague Joyce, thanking him for lunch yesterday and adding, "If there's anything I can do to help, call me, ok?" He might have felt guilty for talking to Joyce so extensively about his problems, but he was too busy being relieved that her number had a 609 area code. She'd mentioned something about living in New Jersey, hadn't she? She probably lived in one of the suburbs of Philly, like Cherry Hill or Mount Holly, but she was still a lot closer to where he was now than anybody else he knew. And she didn't teach on Wednesday or even come to campus; he knew this because she'd said she could have lunch any day except then. Her desire to help him seemed sincere enough, and this time he knew he could make it up to her, because she'd mentioned that she desperately needed advice on teaching the lower-level subjects. She was fresh out of grad school at Michigan, with no experience teaching the underprepared students who made up half of their student body.

He dialed Joyce and she answered on the second ring. She said she'd be glad to pick him up. He told her he would have to have the car towed somewhere, a junkyard at least, and she said no problem, she'd google his location and find the nearest place. A few minutes later, she called back and said the tow truck was on the way and so was she. She'd pick him up at the gas station that promised to take both him and his Rabbit off the highway within the next fifteen minutes.

It took more like a half hour, but the tow truck came and he only had to stand around in the gas station for another twenty minutes before Joyce arrived, too. She was wearing jeans and a short-sleeved T-shirt, and he felt bad for interrupting her day off, but she said, "Don't be silly. It's the least I can do for my only friend in the department."

Joyce was a mid-semester replacement, but Patrick hadn't known until their lunch yesterday that she'd been feeling so adrift. He told her their colleagues were actually a friendly bunch, and they must not have known that she needed their help. What he didn't say was that his department still wasn't in the twenty-first century when it came to their treatment of female professors. They were cordial enough to the handful of women teaching with them, but they didn't usually reach out to them the way they did to the other men.

"What do you think of my geek mobile?" Joyce said. The back of her Toyota had been decked out with every math and computer bumper sticker he'd ever seen and some he hadn't, like "Alcohol and Calculus Don't Mix. Never Drink and Derive."

"Nice," he said. He and Joyce had discussed being geeks at lunch yesterday. She said she'd always thought of herself that way, and they'd both agreed that their ability in math had been both a proof of and compensation for their outsider status in high school.

"Geeks rule," she said, laughing, and started the car. "So where to, Pat? Tell me where you were heading when your car breathed its last."

No one called him "Pat," but he'd already corrected her yesterday and he didn't want to embarrass her. "I was going to Cape May, but at this point I'm happy just to have a ride home."

"Is that one of the ocean towns?"

" 'Shore' they call it here, but yes. It's about a half hour down the parkway, at the bottom of New Jersey. An interesting town, actually, mostly restored Victorian homes, but—"

"It sounds great. Let's go."

He thanked her, but said he couldn't possibly let her do that. "You've done so much for me already."

"Really, it's no problem, as long as I'm home by seven to do my grading." When he still hesitated, she said, "It sounds like fun." Her voice got quieter. "I could use some of that."

He could tell she was serious, which put him in something of a quandary. If he said no again, then he was being ungrateful, given how far she'd driven to come get him and how far she would have to drive to get him back home. But how could he say yes without telling her why he was going to Cape May in the first place? She'd have to drop him off at the house of the woman who claimed to be Lila's mother. He could lie and say he was visiting an old friend, but then it might seem rude not to at least introduce Joyce to this old friend.

But on the other hand, he'd come this far and canceled his

office hours to get convincing proof that this Barbara person was not Lila's mother. If he went home now, he'd be right where he started, with nothing he could use to change Ashley's mind. Just as important, he'd be stuck where he was: desperate to dismiss the incomprehensible idea that his wife had lied to him, but unable to do so no matter how hard he tried. The last few days had been some of the worst in his marriage. He had always trusted Lila, but if her claim about losing her parents had been an outright deception . . . Well, he didn't know what he would do, but he was ninety-nine percent sure it wouldn't come to that. All he needed was enough proof to convince the other one percent.

He finally told Joyce he'd be grateful if she took him to Cape May. She put the car in gear and said, "Excellent!"

She was a very enthusiastic person; he'd noticed that about her at lunch. She also asked a lot of questions. When she asked why he'd come to New Jersey today, he decided to tell her part of the truth. He said he was looking for Lila's mother, but he left out the fact that Lila claimed her mother was dead. She seemed to be appalled that Lila was going through the loss of her twin without her mother's help. "It must be so hard on her," Joyce said. "My mother has always been my biggest supporter. She never lost faith that I would find a teaching position, and you know how much that means when you're on the job market."

"Absolutely," Patrick said.

"I'm sure your mother was the same," Joyce said. She put her window halfway down. It was warm in the car with the sun shining through the windshield. "The market must have been terrible when you graduated. Even worse than it is now."

"I don't know," he said, glad that the mother talk was already over. "Why do you think so?"

"Coming from Princeton as you did, and ending up at Dannerson College. That can't have been what you expected."

"I like Dannerson," Patrick said. "I think you'll grow to like it, too. But you're right, it wasn't what I expected. Like everybody, I expected a job at a first-rate university where I would teach the occasional class of grad students and do my research. Unfortunately, geography intruded. I had to be in the Philly area, for Lila, and Dannerson was the only place I could find."

Joyce assumed that Lila had wanted to live in Philadelphia for work reasons and mentioned how impressive it was that he'd subordinated his career to his wife's. Patrick thanked her, but said Lila's job was only part of it. The other part was Lila's brother and his family.

"Well, that's even more impressive," Joyce said. She touched his arm and turned in his direction. She was wearing sunglasses; he couldn't tell if she was looking in his eyes. "Your wife is very lucky to have you."

"Thanks," Patrick said, but he grew silent because that slight brush of her fingers on his arm had unnerved him. Colleagues usually didn't touch each other unless they were at the annual Christmas party and the wine had been pouring for a while, and even then, it was only a slap on the back that punctuated a good joke or an amusing story about the administration. And no one in the department had ever said Lila was lucky to have him. But he'd already told Joyce more, at yesterday's lunch, than he'd told anyone he worked with. He still wasn't sure how it happened; usually he was a listener, not a talker, but Joyce had seemed so interested and finally he'd found himself disclosing far more than he was comfortable with. He had no idea why she'd cared, unless she was simply trying hard to be friends.

He stayed quiet until they crossed the bridge that meant they were entering Cape May. Then he pulled out the MapQuest directions he'd printed this morning.

The house was easy to find: only a few blocks from the beach, one of the most imposing-looking places in the best neighborhood in town. "I think I may have the wrong address," he said to Joyce. He hadn't written it down, but he thought he remembered it from the envelope he'd seen at Ashley's. But this place was all wrong. It hardly looked like the kind of home a fraud would come from, and more important, whoever lived here could not be related to Lila and Billy, because they had grown up without enough money for college. This was one thing he was positive about. Lila had gotten a combination of scholarships and financial aid that never would have been awarded to someone whose mother could afford a seven- or eight-bedroom mansion like this.

"Do you want me to wait?" Joyce said. "See if it's wrong?"

"Thanks, but I'll be okay." He was positive he had the street right. If necessary, he could walk up and down knocking on doors until he found this Barbara person. "Go on to the beach. I'll call you when I'm finished."

Right before he got out of the car, he told her, again, that he appreciated her taking him here. She smiled. "I'm glad I could do it, Pat. I wish I could make this easier for you."

He wished she could, too. He was looking at the broad wooden porch and the door, realizing he hadn't thought of what he was going to say. As impossible as it seemed that the owner of this house could be trying to hook into Billy's family for whatever money they might have, if this was the right place, he wanted to make sure Barbara understood that there wasn't any money to scam. Billy's life insurance didn't cover death by suicide, much less death by violence. He'd left his family with a surprisingly large savings account, but Ashley would need every penny of that to raise three children on her salary.

He was on the porch, still thinking, when the front door opened to reveal a red-haired man in sloppy jeans and a T-shirt. Patrick must have looked startled, because the man said, "I heard you walk up."

"I'm looking for Barbara Duval." The full name on the envelope. "But I may have the wrong—"

"That's my girlfriend. Just a minute," he said and disappeared up the stairs.

Patrick felt like laughing at how stupid he'd been to doubt Lila. This man was several years younger than Patrick. He could not be dating her mother. Patrick was so sure of this that when an older woman walked down the stairs, he kept looking behind her to see who else was coming. He was still looking when she said, "I'm Barbara Duval," and stopped at the bottom of the landing.

She was wearing sweatpants and a tank top and had sweatbands on her wrists and around her head. She was wiping sweat off her neck with a towel.

"Obviously, you caught me in the middle of my morning workout," she said. He realized he was staring at her, but he couldn't make himself stop. After a moment, she said, "And you must be Patrick. Lila's husband."

Before he could respond, she turned around, but motioned for him to follow her into the spacious living room. It was decorated with dark, expensive-looking furniture; nothing like the bright colors and wicker accents of an ordinary beach house. The only sign that this house was by the ocean was an oar and netting above the fireplace.

After Barbara sat on the large gray chair next to the window, he said, "How did you know who I am?"

"How could I not know? Despite what Lila may have told you, I love my children. I've followed their lives for years."

Patrick finally sat down across from her, on one of the leather couches. But he still couldn't force himself to look away from Barbara's face. The resemblance to his wife was unmistakable: in the penetrating eyes, the high cheekbones, the almost-too-soft chin, even the blond hair, though he supposed Barbara Duval's had to be dyed. She had to be in her late fifties if not sixty, though the only wrinkles were on her neck, her arms, and her hands. The skin on her face was unlined but looked older because it seemed strangely too tight, which made him think of the dean's wife, who was notorious for her addiction to plastic surgery. Her body seemed to be in good shape: maybe plastic surgery, maybe exercise, probably a combination.

His hands were shaking as he took a glass of water the young guy—Barbara's boyfriend—offered before disappearing again.

"I gather this is a shock for you," Barbara said. "Did she tell you I was dead or just a witch? A dead witch, perhaps?"

"She never said you were a witch. She said she loved you."

"So she only said I was dead. Well, I suppose that's more efficient. She's always been quite the liar. This way she could lie about loving me and not have to act like it."

"Lila is not a liar."

"Touching, I'm sure, but as I'm alive and well and sweating in front of you, I think you might want to reassess that opinion."

He sat his glass on the coffee table. "Thanks for the water, but I have to get going. It was nice meeting—"

"Don't run off yet. You just got here."

"I really have to—"

"Will you stay if I promise not to say another disparaging word about Lila? I'd really like to know how my daughter is doing. Please."

Patrick would have kept making excuses if it hadn't been for the shift in Barbara's tone as she said the word "please." As if she really were pleading with him to stay, though he wasn't sure why.

"I suspect you're wondering how I can claim to love Lila in light of my remarks about her honesty or lack thereof?"

He sat back and crossed his arms. "It does seem inconsistent."

She shrugged. "I don't play the Hallmark card game. To me,

love demands seeing someone as they are. Myself, for example. I know I'm a sixty-one-year-old woman who is vain about her appearance, greedy about her appetites, and a variety of other less-than-flattering characteristics. But I undoubtedly love myself. I give myself everything I want: from this house to flings with the occasional younger man." She smiled and lowered her voice. "It's all right. If they're only in it for the money, I'm only it in for the sex."

Patrick felt the blood rush to his face, as though he were a child who'd overheard the secret talk of grown-ups. He flashed to a time, years ago, when Billy had called him naïve. Maybe his brother-in-law had been right about that.

He took a breath, hoping to calm down, and let his gaze wander around the room. On the sideboard over by the staircase were dozens of photographs, many of children. He pointed in that direction. "Are some of those pictures of Lila and Billy?"

She nodded. "Have a look, be my guest."

He wandered over, trying to buy time before he talked about Lila. He knew he had to say something, but he also wanted to protect his wife's privacy.

He pointed at a silver-framed photograph of Lila and Billy flanking the sides of a tree in front of a large brick house that had to be over a hundred years old. "Was this the house they grew up in?"

She nodded. "It's been in the family for generations. It was originally built for my grandfather, a brilliant judge who was seriously considered for the Supreme Court. I can't bring myself to part with it, though I don't spend much time there anymore. Being near the ocean is far preferable to being in the countryside of central Pennsylvania."

Pennsylvania? Both Lila and Billy had said they'd grown up in North Carolina. Lila had described the town she was from in great detail. She'd even told him about the summer when she and

Billy had imitated the journalists' voices on NPR, hoping to get rid of their Southern accents and sound more "cosmopolitan" before she went off to college. And she seemed to know very little about Pennsylvania when she and Patrick moved there. Why would she lie about this? But then, why would her mother? His mouth felt dry, but he managed, "How long have you been here?"

"I bought this house about ten years ago. I'd always wanted to live by the water, and I considered San Diego and several places in Florida, but in the end, I decided on Cape May." She glanced at him. "It's a lovely town, and of course, it was closer to Lila and Billy."

Before he could wonder why she would want to be close to children she never saw, he noticed another photograph in the back row. Barbara was standing next to a very unhappy-looking man. Patrick picked it up and stared at it, unable to believe what he was looking at.

"That photo was taken two years ago, the last time I saw my son."

"You saw Billy often?" He hoped his voice wasn't giving away how surprised he was. Could Lila have possibly known this and kept it a secret, too?

"Not often, no. The first time he needed money for his wife. She was in the hospital; he refused to tell me why. After that, he came back every year or two, always alone—he was adamant that I would have nothing to do with his family—and always with his hand out. He seemed to feel that I owed him and his sister, too, though Lila never asked for anything. I haven't seen her since she was a teenager."

Patrick set the picture down and came back to the couch. At least Lila wasn't keeping any visits of her own a secret, but Billy's behavior shocked him. What kind of man would ask his mother for money while simultaneously refusing her any contact with her grandchildren?

Barbara said, "So, tell me about my daughter." She settled back in her chair. "Tell me everything."

"I'll try, but there isn't a lot to say." He took a long drink of water, still stalling. "She's an English professor, specializing in American literature. She loves to teach. She's had numerous articles published and one book about Herman Melville." He paused, knowing he needed to add something a little more personal. "We'll have been married eleven years this summer. We don't have any children yet. We're happier than most people, I think." He nodded. "She's really doing fine."

Barbara waved her hand dismissively. "I know all this already. She went to grad school at Princeton. Met you there. You're from St. Louis. Your father is an aviation engineer and your mother has passed on. You're not particularly close to your father, but—unlike your wife—you do the good child thing and visit him once a year."

Patrick was very surprised, but he only said, "What do you want to know then?"

"How she is. And don't tell me 'fine' or 'happy' or any other platitude that I know is false."

He forced a shrug. "She is happy, like I said. She has a great life and good friends and—"

"Oh, please. The person she loved above all others died less than a month ago. I knew she would be devastated, but it must be even worse than I feared. Why else would you have come to see me today?"

He wanted to leave then, but he was afraid of being rude. She was still his wife's mother, despite how strange and incomprehensible she was to him.

When he didn't speak for a long, uncomfortable moment, she said, "Forgive me." Her voice had changed again. Now she sounded kind, or maybe even sorry for him? "I was under the impression that you were aware that my daughter loved her brother far more than any of the men she was involved with. You're her husband. I thought this would have been abundantly obvious to you."

Patrick felt his face grow warm. "I'd rather not discuss this."

"Most of her boyfriends realized this at some point and broke it off with her. Even Nathan What's-His-Name, the man she was engaged to right before she met you, eventually figured this out, though he was a bit dense, I think. He dropped out of med school after two years, but perhaps that wasn't an academic failure. Perhaps he just gave up once he realized that our Lila's heart had already been given away long before he came on the scene."

Now Patrick was stunned. He knew about Nathan, but Lila said they'd only dated for a few months. There was nothing about an engagement, and certainly nothing about him breaking it off with her. Lila's version was that Billy and Nathan hadn't gotten along and so she dumped Nathan. She did mention that Nathan had left medical school shortly after; he'd never thought to ask why.

Even if Barbara had some of the details wrong—and there was no way to know about that—she was right that Lila had chosen her brother over Nathan. Just as Patrick had known she would have done in his own case, if he hadn't gotten along with Billy. Why had this never struck him as wrong until this moment?

"But of course it wasn't her fault that her brother was so vastly superior to every other man she encountered. Billy was like my grandfather. He was a genius, as I'm sure Lila never tired of telling you."

Barbara was going on about Billy's IQ scores but Patrick wasn't listening. He was thinking about a discussion they'd had a few years ago, when he'd asked Lila why she was willing to listen to Billy for hours and yet she never asked Patrick questions about his research anymore. She said that math was outside her area of expertise, but as he pointed out, she could have at least asked about the basic ideas. He didn't remember how the discussion ended, but he was positive it wasn't with Lila saying that he, Patrick, was a genius. She'd never said that in all the time they'd been together. Apparently, she didn't believe it.

"However," Barbara was saying, "he hardly made use of his brain in the life he chose to live. No doubt he blamed me for that when he wasn't blaming the poor white-trash woman he married only because he didn't believe he would ever really fall in love with anyone."

"Ashley is not white trash. That's an unfair assessment."

"Perhaps you're right. I suppose I'll find out myself soon enough, now that Billy isn't here to keep me from her and his children." She paused. "I wonder if he was afraid I would tell his wife that the only woman he ever really loved was his sister. Of course, I would never say such a thing, but he—"

"It's not true," Patrick said. Though he wasn't sure about this. He wasn't sure about anything at that moment.

"No, sadly enough, it is. He couldn't love anyone but Lila, I'm afraid. The truth is my children had a most unnatural bond from before they were teenagers." Barbara smiled. "Emphasis on the unnatural."

It took him a minute to realize what she was implying, and when he did, he stood up. He no longer cared about being rude; he had to get outside, where he could breathe. This was becoming a revolting conversation, and if that opinion made him naïve, so be it. He would rather be the most naïve person in the world than someone who could talk as casually about this as Barbara Duval did.

He made it to the door, but before he could turn the knob, she was there, talking again. "You think I'm hinting that Lila and Billy had an affair? I don't doubt that they wanted to, especially Lila, but—"

"Enough," he hissed. The admonition was intended for her, but also for his own mind, which was bombarding him with the sudden relevance of the fact that his wife never seemed to want to have sex with him. But it wasn't relevant. Of course it wasn't. This was all a bizarre nightmare.

"What kind of mother do you take me for, that I would allow my children to do such a thing? Believe me, I tried everything to control my daughter. I'm sure she seems quite innocent now, but as a child—oh my god—she was the proverbial bad seed. You can't imagine the havoc that girl wreaked on my—"

He managed to turn the knob, finally, and he raced outside and down the porch steps like he was escaping a fire. If Barbara said good-bye or anything else, he didn't hear it. He was down the block before he realized he could stop now; she hadn't followed him. At least he should slow down before somebody saw him running in panic like he'd just left the scene of a robbery.

He did manage to slow down, but not by much. He was still walking so fast that before he'd had a chance to catch his breath, he was at the beach. The sight of the ocean normally calmed him, but even the ocean couldn't compete with the garbage that woman had spewed into his head. He wanted to cry or scream or break something, but instead he wandered up to the boardwalk and kept walking, trying to think his way out of what he felt, the way he always had before.

He wasn't worried that Lila and Billy had ever done anything physical with each other. The thought nauseated him, but even their mother admitted it hadn't happened. And he'd watched them together for years; they were very affectionate, but in an entirely innocent way.

But what about all the rest? What about the things he'd always known, but never understood the meaning of? That Lila wouldn't have married him if Billy hadn't approved. That Lila seemed to enjoy spending time with Billy more than with him. That Lila talked to Billy and laughed with Billy and obviously confided in Billy in ways she'd never done with him. And yes, that Lila loved

Billy more than she had ever loved him. If she'd loved him at all. Even of that, he was no longer sure.

He didn't really know his own wife. That was the other thing that kept stabbing him in the heart. She'd lied to him numerous times: about Nathan, about where she grew up, and of course about her mother being alive. That was still the worst lie, the one he couldn't imagine ever forgiving her for.

He kept walking, and with each step, he felt like everything he'd believed about his marriage to Lila was coming unraveled, until all he could see were the losses. The children he'd wanted and they'd never had. The countless times he'd ached for her and kept it to himself, so she could keep working. The research he would have done if he hadn't given up his own dreams so she could have her dream of living by Billy.

He wasn't sure how far he'd wandered when he noticed Joyce sitting on the beach with her shoes off and her pants rolled up to her knees. She was bent over, writing something, probably lecture notes for tomorrow. That's when he realized that it was already late afternoon; the sun was hanging low in the sky. By the time they got through Philly's rush hour, she'd be lucky to be home by eight.

When he walked up behind her, he noticed she was writing a proof. He apologized for being gone so long and shrugged off her question about how it had gone with Lila's mother with a quick "Okay." He took a deep breath and forced his voice to sound light. "Working hard or hardly working?"

"I'm trying to prove Stone-Weierstrass," she said, smiling. "I'm sure it's trivial to you, but it's not going well. I think I've forgotten too much from my courses in real analysis."

"You're a number theorist. Why are you bothering with that anyway?"

She stood up, brushing sand off her jeans. "No reason," she said, but she sounded unaccountably shy. He didn't understand what was going on until a sudden gust of wind blew her papers all over the sand. He leaned down to help her pick them up and that's when he found a copy of his own latest article. She'd either xeroxed it from the obscure journal or downloaded it from their even more obscure website.

A few weeks before, one of the older secretaries had teased him that the "new girl professor" had a crush on him. At the time he hadn't given it a moment's thought because no one ever got a crush on him, not even his most impressionable students. He just wasn't the type of man women had crushes on. And even holding the evidence in his hand, he still thought that perhaps Joyce just had an odd interest in the topic of his paper. She wouldn't have to re-prove Stone-Weierstrass unless she wanted to understand it as completely as he did, but maybe she worked that way. He wasn't like that himself, but he didn't have time to be anymore.

But then he asked her why she was reading this, and she said, "It's fascinating." He knew she meant it, but he also knew it wasn't true. His paper couldn't be fascinating to someone with her background. It wasn't even fascinating to anyone in his field, which was why it ended up in such a little-known journal. It was a minor result, and sure, he was proud of it, but it didn't mean much in the scheme of mathematics.

He was so surprised he was speechless. And maybe he was blushing. And maybe he wanted her to do what she did next. Maybe that's why he came a little too close to her when he was handing back her papers.

Still, even as she kissed him, he knew he would feel guilty later on. But right then, it seemed like the simplest, most normal thing in the world. Though most people would consider Joyce entirely ordinary—short and a little chubby, with a nose that was a little too big and a mouth that was a little too small—Patrick found her smart and incredibly easy to be with. She also had one thing his gorgeous wife didn't. She actually wanted to spend time with him. She wanted to talk to him and listen to him and even kiss him. Such ordinary stuff, but it felt like the upending of all he'd believed about relationships.

He knew it couldn't continue, but at that moment, he thought if only he could stay here forever, listening to the clean, normal sound of the waves breaking on the beach while she held him in her arms, as though he were worth holding, as though he were a person someone was capable of wanting most of all.

CHAPTER TEN

Even Ashley's mother had to admit that Billy was turning out to be an amazing father. Her mom didn't like that they named the child Pearl—she thought it sounded like an old lady's name—but she said Ashley had obviously done the right thing letting Billy pick the name, because look how close that man was to that baby! It was a sight to see, especially as most men couldn't care less about their kids until they were old enough to do things with. Even then, the things most men wanted to do, like hunting and fishing and throwing a ball, meant they were never as close to their girls as their boys. But not Billy Cole, or, as Ashley's mom was now calling him, Super Dad. The name was partly tongue in cheek, but there was real affection, too, and not only from her mom, but from the rest of her family, who'd decided Billy Cole was all right. A real keeper.

By the time Pearl was two years old, Ashley's mom seemed to be damn near in love with the man. On Saturday mornings, when Ashley and her mom went to the grocery store together, the same way they had for years, Ashley would listen as her mom went on and on about what a great provider Billy was—for getting a job and keeping it—what a great husband he was—for not cheating and not leaving—and what a great all-around catch he was for Ashley—smart and funny and good-looking to boot. Sometimes Ashley tried to hint that things weren't as wonderful as they appeared, but the hints went nowhere. If she said, "I wish I was happier," her mom would say, "Don't we all?" When she tried, "I wonder sometimes if he loves me," her mom said, "Welcome to marriage." When she mentioned, "We never go out like we used to," her mom snorted and said, "You got a child now. What did you expect?"

What did she expect? Not much, actually. If someone had told her, before she met Billy, that she'd end up with a man who *would* cheat or quit his job and stay home all day, drunk on his ass, she'd have been mad as hell, but deep down, she'd have known it was probably true. She never, ever expected to marry a man who would dance around in the living room with their daughter before he left to work at a dirty construction site for eight- or nine-hour days, sometimes longer if they were doing inside work. She never expected to marry a man who came home from work all smiles, asking how his "two favorite girls" were doing today.

It was only when Pearl went to bed that everything changed, almost like a curtain dropped and the perfect father was replaced by a completely different guy—not the Billy she'd known before their daughter was born, but another person who was quiet and strange and damn near impossible for Ashley to understand. Yeah, he was tired from working all day and Ashley was tired, too, from running around after little Pearl, who was always a real handful when her dad wasn't around. "Daddy" had been Pearl's first word, and by two, she was already saying whole sentences, many of which were screams as Billy left in the morning. "Don't want you. I want Daddy!" "Don't weave, Daddy!" "Play wif Pearl, Daddy!" Billy would respond with a smile and a kiss and a promise to come back as soon as he could. For Ashley, it was harder, because once Pearl heard Billy driving away, the little girl would throw a full-fledged tantrum, complete with fists pounding on the floor and earsplitting screams at her mother. And then Pearl would demand that Mommy play "moonbeam" or "catch the air people" or some other bizarre-o game that Billy had invented, and inevitably get mad when the game wasn't "right." It took Ashley months to figure out that these games were really nothing but Billy pretending that something exciting was going on, and it was his excitement that their little girl was missing, not some rule Ashley wasn't following. No matter how often Ashley opened her hand and showed their daughter that she had caught one of the "air people," Pearl insisted her mommy's hand had nothing in it. Daddy, though, could catch them anytime. Daddy could even catch the air people queen!

At night when Pearl was in bed, Ashley tried to talk to the stranger Billy about the way their daughter acted when he wasn't home, but he shrugged it off as no big deal. Her mother did the same, saying all little girls have a thing for their daddies.

"I don't remember being that way," Ashley said.

Her mom rolled her eyes. "You were the worst of all my girls. You followed that loser everywhere, even when he yelled at you to go bug Mommy." She looked at Ashley. "You got a husband that doesn't yell or hit your child. What are you complaining about?"

She wasn't complaining; she was just trying to figure out why she felt like an outsider in her own family. Sometimes on the weekends, when Pearl was happily playing with Billy, Ashley would go for long drives alone in the mountains outside Albuquerque, wondering who would care if she never came back. Trish would, for sure. Her mom, too, even though they weren't close like they used to be. Billy, she had no idea, but it wasn't him who bothered her most; it was her daughter. Would Pearl even notice that her mommy was gone? Would she remember anything good about her mom, or only the fights that had gotten so out of hand lately that Ashley was afraid to tell anyone about them?

Everyone in Ashley's family believed in spanking. She'd been spanked herself many times, and it hadn't caused her any harm. But what she was doing with Pearl, though it had started out as spanking, ended up being something that Ashley was deeply ashamed of. Because Pearl didn't react like a normal kid when she was taken over her mother's knee and swatted a few times. She didn't cry and she certainly didn't calm down. If anything, she was madder than before, flailing her chubby arms, kicking Ashley in the stomach and on the legs, even biting Ashley on the knee so hard it drew blood. It was the bite that caused Ashley to slap Pearl in the face. Ashley's own mother believed in biting toddlers back, but Ashley couldn't bring herself to do that; plus honestly, she was afraid of what Billy would say if he discovered marks on the little girl. So she slapped Pearl instead, not hard, but hard enough to make Ashley burst into tears at what she'd done. She was about to tell Pearl she was sorry, but the little girl was too furious to listen. She elbowed Ashley in the nose and proceeded to hit her mother again and again, all the while screaming that she wanted to go "back." "Back" meant the tiny backyard they had now that they were living in a rental house a few miles from Ashley's mother. But when Ashley took her daughter outside, Pearl immediately ran over to the hole in the coyote fence, squeezed herself through it, and took off toward the arroyo that led to the highway where she saw Billy disappear each day on the way to work. Ashley managed to grab her little girl before she got far enough to be in real danger, but when she picked up Pearl, hugged her to her chest, and said, "You scared Mommy," her daughter looked right at her and said what sounded like "hate you." Ashley was never sure about this—or at least she wasn't until Pearl started saying it all the time, even when Ashley managed to keep her cool, even when she and her daughter hadn't had any fights for days. Unfortunately, the "hate you" would often cause Ashley to blow it all over again.

For as long as she lived, she would never forget those horrible battles with her two-year-old. Pearl fought her mother like her life depended on it, and too often, Ashley fought back. She slapped her child, she shoved Pearl away when she was hitting or kicking, and once or twice, she knocked Pearl down. She was just lucky that none of those shoves landed Pearl into the corner of a table or a sharp object. She would never have forgiven herself if she'd bruised her baby, much less seriously harmed her.

Thank God, by the time Pearl was three, the fights had completely stopped. At the pediatrician's office, Ashley had discovered a booklet about disciplining a child without spanking using timeouts. She was surprised how much it helped. Using timeouts, she only had to slap Pearl's hands occasionally, when the little girl was reaching for something dangerous, like a pot on the stove, or breakable, like her father's computer. But Pearl still said "I hate you" to her mother just as much as ever, until Ashley thought she really meant it.

Her own family was no help. They all doted on Pearl, especially Ashley's mom, who said her granddaughter was "cute as a pixie and sharp as a tack." They were amazed that Pearl could read and write words at only three years old. Ashley's mom told Billy, "That must be from your side of the family, 'cause none of the Harris line could do that. Hell, some of us don't read that well now!" Billy said something humble and kind, as he usually did—to them—and

Ashley's mom loved him more than ever. It was all just so perfect, from where Ashley's family sat, that if Pearl hated her mother, it had to be a harmless phase.

In the end, it was Billy who fixed the problem, though he didn't mean to and wasn't even aware of it, really. Or maybe he was. Ashley was never sure what he was thinking during those nights when he would sit quietly staring out the window of their kitchen, or writing on the computer that Lila had given him for his twenty-second birthday. He was polite enough, answering any question Ashley put to him, discussing any problem they had with their bills or the house or the car, but he never said much about how he was doing beyond "tired," "worn-out," and the worst one: "empty." He did seem empty, like he wasn't even there when Pearl was asleep. Even when they made love, he went through the motions, and they were always finished before the news came on. Billy didn't watch TV, but Ashley did. She had to do something to pass the time and lift her spirits a little.

Then one Saturday night Ashley got drunk with some friends from high school. Billy had told her to go out and have fun, but it was hard to have any fun, given the strong feeling she had that her husband was relieved to be rid of her. As she told her friend Deb, "He barely talks to me except about stupid crap like, 'Should I do the dishes or are you going to?' I don't think he cares about me at all." Deb got stuck on the fact that Billy was willing to do the dishes; she said her husband was a pig who wouldn't lift a finger to help with housework or either of their two kids. "You're lucky," Deb said, and Ashley ordered another Captain Morgan and soda. And another. And another. Pretty soon, she was having fun, all right. And she was feeling so bold that, by the time she got home, she was determined to have it out with Billy. Force him to cut whatever *this was* the hell out.

He was sitting at his computer, as usual. He said Pearl had gone down to bed at eight. "I saved you some leftovers," he said without looking up. "We had beef and noodles."

"Well, I'm not hungry," she said, plopping down across from him at the kitchen table. His desk was in the living room, but he always sat in here, closer to the hall that led to the bedrooms, so he could hear Pearl if she woke. "And I want you to tell me what you're writing there."

She'd asked him before, countless times, and he always said, "Nothing important" or "Just some ideas." He tried a vague answer this time, too, but she slammed her hand on the table and said, "No."

He looked up, finally, but he didn't say anything. His eyes were unreadable.

"You're not going to get away with this. Not this time. I want to know what my husband is doing. I think I have a right to know!"

"You're drunk." His voice was mild—or empty—as always.

"Irrelevant." It was one of his favorite words, and she let out a laugh that she'd used it right. "Tell me what's on that screen. What is it, a bunch of bitching about your stupid wife? Letters to another woman?"

He sat still for a moment. Maybe he thought, since she was already getting loud, Pearl would eventually hear her and wake up. Or maybe he'd really wanted to show her all along, but she'd never asked forcefully enough. Who knew, but he turned the heavy computer monitor around and said, "Be my guest."

Ashley had no idea what she expected, but it sure wasn't this. She was stunned to realize that he was writing about their family—and not just Pearl, but her, too. He wrote about them going out to breakfast at the diner that morning and what they'd talked about and what a "lovely scene" it had been. He wrote about Ashley buying Pearl a new pink jacket last week, which he called the "continuous grace of the mundane." He wrote about the three of them going to the family center the evening before, how Ashley had swum laps, while he and Pearl were in the children's pool, and said this was "more evidence of the surprising beauty of the ordinary." Then he wrote a question: "Why has the ordinary been overlooked or actively denigrated by our greatest writers?"

She read screen after screen, and it was all the same: good things that had happened to them and comments by Billy that she didn't really get but could tell weren't bitches or complaints. Finally she turned the monitor back around and looked at him. Her voice was quieter, a little shy. "Why are you writing all this?"

"Because it's true."

"But there's lots of true stuff. Why write about the stuff we did?"

"I've told you, our family is the most important thing to me." He folded his hands. "I'm not interested in writing about anything else right now."

She was still too drunk to make sense of what he was saying. His tone was as hollow as ever. He sure as hell didn't sound like someone who would write about all these happy things they'd done.

"You know what I think?" she said. "I think you're just pretending. Making everybody think you're this happy family guy." She forced a smirk, hoping it wasn't true even as she said it. "That's why you have to write it all down every night. It's like you'll forget your act if you don't."

"It's not an act," he said softly. "It's who I'm trying to be."

"But you have to try. You don't really feel it."

He frowned. "I shouldn't have expected you to see any nobility in effort."

She wasn't sure what he was saying, but she was actually glad he frowned. This was the old Billy, the one she could talk to—or at least fight with—until she understood him. And that's what she did.

She asked him why he had to try about a dozen times before he finally cut the vague horseshit and got mad. "Because I'm not happy," he hissed. "And if you understood me at all, you would know why."

She didn't understand him, but she wanted to. "Is it because you have to work and can't write your book?"

"I obviously could write my novel if I wanted to." He rubbed his forehead like he had a headache. "I have over four hundred pages of observations about our lives."

Four hundred pages? He must have been doing this for a long time, maybe even since Pearl was born. After a few minutes of awkward silence, she stood up and went to him. Now that she knew he was sad, it felt like a whole different ball game. She was sad, too. Maybe they could come up with something new, together, that would work for both of them.

"What is it then?" she said, and knelt down beside him and put her hand on his knee. She was wearing a sexy black blouse, unbuttoned to highlight her cleavage; she hoped he didn't think it looked cheap. She hoped she didn't smell too much like booze. Maybe if she could show him she cared, he would kiss her the slow way he used to.

He didn't shrug her off, but he didn't look at her. "New Mexico is your home, Ashley. I would never ask you to give that up. But this isn't my home and never has been."

"You want to move back east? Is that it?"

"No. I wish I could go back, but I don't see—"

"Fine. Let's go to North Carolina."

He finally turned around and looked at her. "Are you serious?"

"I love you." She felt the tears coming, meaning the booze was wearing off. But it was true and she'd wanted to say it for so long. "I would do anything to make you happy, baby."

"What about your mother and your sisters and your aunts and uncles? Are you saying you won't miss them?"

"Sure I will. But I've missed you a hell of a lot more."

He thought about this for a moment. Then he pulled her up to him and kissed her. It wasn't particularly passionate, but it was grateful—and so was she when he led her into the bedroom. At some point while he was undressing her, he whispered, "I love you too, Ash," and she started crying again, but softly. She didn't want him to lose interest in what they were about to do.

A few days later, he told Ashley that he'd thought it out and he did want to move. But not to North Carolina, to Pennsylvania. A big city: Philadelphia. He said he picked it because, though it wasn't that close to home, it was a lot closer than he was now and at least on the same side of the country. Plus, he knew he could get a job there; he'd read about a boom in construction. He also said it was close to where his sister was, and of course she was his only family left anyway.

Ashley immediately said yes, but it took her a week or two before she understood that being near Lila was always the point. Why Billy hadn't mentioned this right off, she didn't know. Ashley didn't dislike Lila anymore; in fact, she was looking forward to getting closer to her. Billy's sister seemed nice enough. She'd come to visit for a few weeks every summer, and she sent Pearl little presents all the time: books, mainly, but also dolls and dress-up clothes and even a pretty tea set.

And the best part of all, whenever Lila visited, Billy hung out and talked with his twin so much that Pearl lost interest in her wonderful father and happily glued herself to her mother's side. So even as Ashley cried about leaving her family, she secretly hoped that moving would prove to be just the ticket for solving all her problems with her daughter. And Billy, too, of course. She hoped this faraway place would give all three of them a fresh start.

Still, she was nothing less than shocked when it worked. She was no fool. A good outcome was always the last thing she expected.

In Philadelphia, Billy was his old self again, talking to Ashley about all kinds of things, most of which she didn't understand. Pearl no longer hated her, or at least she stopped saying the words. Maybe it had been a phase, but it seemed to Ashley that their new city was magic. She loved the old houses and the rain and even the crowds of people everywhere. She wrote her mom about the Italian market and the Liberty Bell and the first big snowstorm, which thrilled her—and meant Billy got to stay home with them for days.

They didn't see Lila that much, but when they did, it was all right. Billy said Lila was working hard in her last year of graduate school, and she only had time for an occasional lunch and it had to be in Princeton. He drove there alone every once in a while, and Ashley was glad for him. He was always so much happier after he'd seen his twin.

Naturally, Ashley still had complaints: Pearl wasn't sleeping that well; Billy was boring sometimes; Ashley was often lonely without her friends and family. But compared to before, it was damn good. And compared to what happened after, it was heaven.

That first year in Philadelphia would turn out to be the only truly good year in her marriage. Even years later, Ashley would remember it that way. She was never sure why it changed, though she knew when it did: when Pearl was four and a half, and Ashley was diagnosed with cervical cancer.

They cured it so easily, only surgery to remove part of the cervix and the surrounding lymph nodes: no hysterectomy, no chemotherapy, no radiation. They even said she might be able to have more kids, which turned out to be true. In the scheme of things, it really wasn't that bad, but Billy didn't see it that way. He kept repeating, "This is the first appearance of the snake in the garden," until finally Ashley went back and read the first part of the Bible, hoping to understand what the hell he was talking about. She didn't understand, and the explanation he gave spooked her. He told her he had been cursed all his life and now that "Cole curse" was affecting his family, too.

"There's no way out," he said. Ashley would never forget the look on his face; he was not only dead serious, he actually seemed afraid. "I was a fool to think I could ever escape this."

CHAPTER ELEVEN

When Patrick came home from work on Wednesday, Lila expected him to be pleased that she'd showered and washed her hair without any prompting from him. Not only that, she was in their living room, sitting in her usual chair by the bookshelves, rather than lying in bed. She was still wearing pajamas, but they were the relatively new white-and-gray–striped flannel pants—no holes, not faded—and the purple Henley shirt that he liked so much when she got it last year that he'd told her it wasn't really pajamas at all and she could wear it anywhere.

She'd been inspired to do all this at six-thirty, when Patrick was already an hour and a half late coming home. She imagined him having a hideous day, with lines of students outside his office, all of them anxious for help before finals. He walked in the door at 9:52, and it was even worse than she feared. He was so worn-out that he didn't even look in her direction, but instead marched down the hall toward their bedroom, saying, "Get up, Lila," in a tone that was so aggravated, she was relieved she'd thought to get up on her own, so he could relax and not deal with her tonight.

"I'm in here." When he came into the living room, she forced a smile. "I've already eaten, too. I even answered the phone when your dad called. Not much of an accomplishment, I know, but I'm glad I talked to him. I didn't realize how worried he'd been that he couldn't get through to us."

He nodded, but he didn't smile back. His expression was so strange that Lila instantly knew something very bad had happened to him today. Her first thought was that one of his students had cheated. He always took that very badly. She told Billy it was one of the first things she'd loved about Patrick: he was a fair, honest person who believed in a fair, honest world.

He dropped his backpack on the floor and fell into the overstuffed chair across the room, farthest away from her. He sat with his eyes closed for several minutes, long enough for Lila to wonder if he'd fallen asleep. She wasn't sleepy herself, but she knew she would be very soon; she'd broken down and taken her sedative only minutes before Patrick arrived. She was planning to write him a note before she hit the bed: a friendly apology for not waiting up, a cheerful explanation that, this time, he didn't need to drag her into the shower or force food down her throat, but nothing about the reason she'd given up and taken the sedative, nothing about the last four hours, when she'd been fully awake—and obsessing over something that she knew was meaningless, even trivial.

It started with the conversation she'd had with the therapist about Kingston, the prep school she'd attended when she was fifteen. The therapist had thought it was odd that Lila graduated in two years, but Lila knew it was true because she'd seen her transcript many times, though not for over a decade. This evening after her shower, while she was waiting for Patrick, she'd looked through box after box of old files and finally unearthed the Kingston transcript, which clearly stated that she'd graduated in June 1988, when she was still fifteen. Close to sixteen, though. Her and Billy's birthday was July 12.

So she was right that she'd left Kingston because she was finished with high school, but something else was bothering her. The transcript included credits from her hometown high school in North Carolina: just a listing, no grades, because Kingston, like most private schools, didn't calculate grades from other schools in its GPA. The listing included all the usual subjects and the courses she'd tested out of, but it also included two classes in theater, one in the fall, one in the spring. That Lila didn't remember taking theater wasn't a problem—she didn't remember taking half these courses and those she did remember weren't necessarily her own real memories, since they were all classes she and Billy had taken together and he'd talked about with her over the years. The problem was that Lila knew she'd been way too shy, at fourteen years old, to take drama or chorus or anything that would have required her to do more than sit in the corner and listen to the teacher. She'd never even had any friends, not that she could remember anyway. This was why Billy had been the one who took theater, not Lila. She was absolutely positive about this because they'd talked about it only a few years ago, when Pearl tried out for her middle school play. She didn't get the part, but Billy was proud of her for trying. He mentioned loving drama when he was in school and something about believing that Pearl could be good at it if she wanted to. Then Lila said, "I'm glad she's not too afraid like I was." And Billy said, "William is more like you. He's so quiet; I'm sure he'll never take theater, but it won't matter. He'll be doing genius-level work by the time he's in high school."

Billy had a bedrock belief that all his children were brilliant, including William, despite what his teachers said about him being slow. He wanted William moved out of that elementary school and put in a better school where his talents would be appreciated. They didn't have the money, or at least Ashley said they didn't. Billy thought they should make their son's schooling a higher priority. Lila knew it was one of the many things they'd argued about.

Obviously it wasn't important anymore what Lila had or had not taken in high school. She'd graduated college summa cum laude and finished her PhD; no one would ever ask to see her high school transcript now. But still, if that transcript was wrong about her taking two semesters of theater, why? And was it wrong about the other courses, too? Had she really finished so many classes in her first year of high school? This would have required her skipping study hall and skipping lunch, too, which was what she'd always thought she'd done, but only because she'd believed the transcript. Didn't she remember eating lunch with Billy that year? He'd tested out of a lot more courses than she had, and he'd never been opposed to skipping a class, but she had been. This was one of the reasons Billy always called her Gallant, because she was too law-abiding to break any rules.

She was still trying to remember if she'd really eaten lunch with Billy or just imagined she had, when Patrick finally opened his eyes.

"Your mother is still alive, isn't she?"

"What?"

"You heard me, Lila." He wasn't looking at her, but at the wall of books behind her. He sounded furious. "Answer the question."

She pulled her legs up and put her arms around them, curling herself into a ball. Her voice became small, too. "Why are you talking to me this way?"

"Because I know you lied to me about this."

She wondered how he knew, but she was afraid to press him when he was already so angry. "Then why ask me?" she said slowly.

"Because I've realized I deserve to hear the truth."

"The truth is . . . I don't know if she's alive." She hugged her legs tighter. "I haven't seen her since I was teenager. When I told you she was dead, it was because she was dead—to me and Billy. We had to do that or—"

He raised his hand palm out like a stop sign. "I only want to hear why you lied about it to me."

She felt light-headed suddenly, but she managed, "Because I promised Billy I wouldn't talk about this to anyone. He was afraid if—"

"So you didn't tell your *husband* because your *brother* didn't want you to. Of course. How could I have forgotten that a promise to Billy could never be broken?"

"Are you being sarcastic?" Patrick had almost never been sarcastic in all the years she'd known him. And the look on his face was so bitter; she was actually a little frightened.

He didn't answer. He stood up and walked across the room toward her, and then over to the window, and then to the doorway that led to the kitchen, and then down the hall, and then back to the chair where he'd been sitting. But he didn't sit down; instead, he continued pacing around the room, circling their apartment like a predator circles its prey. Or like a man who is so hurt that he doesn't know how to talk to his wife about his feelings? Lila felt like prey, but she forced herself to think about what her husband must be going through. She knew from talking to his father that his mother's death had devastated him. If he felt as though Lila no longer understood that loss, he would feel both betrayed and horribly alienated.

"Patrick." When he didn't stop pacing or look at her, she

swallowed hard. "I know how this must seem to you, but I do understand the agony of losing a parent."

"Of course you do. Even though your mother is alive and living in New Jersey, while mine has been dead and buried for twelve years. But you and Billy *pretended* your mother was dead. And pretend is all that matters, right?" He shook his head. "The stories are just like reality. You've said so a hundred times."

Lila's stomach lurched at the news that her mother was not only alive, but living so close to them. New Jersey? What was her mother doing there? And how could Patrick know this? She pulled the blanket off the back of the chair and wrapped it around herself as she wondered if it was possible he was wrong.

After a moment, she forced herself to concentrate on her husband. The light from the living room lamps seemed dimmer, the first sign that her pill was taking effect. But she opened her eyes wider, determined to stay awake and tell Patrick the truth. "I really do understand because my father died. When I was eight years old."

Patrick finally stopped pacing, which Lila took as a good sign. But then he said, his voice shaking with anger, "So you lied about that, too?"

"What do you mean? I never talked about this with you before."

"Yes, you did. Can't you even keep track of your lies? You told me he died in the same car accident as your mother did when you were—"

"No, that was my stepfather. My real father died when I was a child, and I missed him every day." This wasn't completely right. Billy missed him every day, but Lila didn't remember him well enough to miss him with such intensity. But she knew he was a good man, nothing like their stepfather. He built them a tree house. He taught them to swim. He gave them bear hugs when he came home from work. She could still hear him asking, "What have my twins been up to today?"

"So the guy who worked at the bank was your stepfather," Patrick snapped. "Thanks for telling me this now, eleven years too late. What did your real father do? I'd appreciate the truth for a change."

Lila hesitated. It wasn't that she didn't want Patrick to know, but that she didn't want to say the words aloud. She'd tried so hard not to think about this since Billy's death. She was sure it was meaningful somehow, but she wasn't ready to face that meaning yet—if she ever would be.

"Fine, don't tell me. Why should I know? I'm only your husband."

"He was a police officer," Lila whispered, hearing the words "suicide by police" for the thousandth time. "His name was William. He was killed in the line of duty."

"Are you saying if I look up records, I'll find an officer named William Cole who died in the line of duty? Because I can't stand any more lies, Lila."

She said yes and pulled the blanket up to her neck. Her father was the truest part of her history, the part before all the bad things happened. His name was William Cole. She remembered his shiny badge, the gun he always put on in the morning before he left for work. She even vaguely remembered that day in November when he went to work and never came back. She wasn't sure exactly how old she and Billy were when they were adopted by their stepfather and forced to use his last name, Duval. Billy changed their name back to Cole when he forged the documents. "The first step toward our freedom," he'd said. "Obliterating the evidence that we ever had anything to do with Harold Duval."

Patrick finally sat down on the other end of the couch. He was looking straight at her. His gaze made her nervous, but she didn't look away. After a long, uncomfortable silence, he said, "Did you ever love me, Lila?"

"Of course." She felt tears spring to her eyes. Why was he asking her this? What was happening? "I still love you. I'm just not doing very well. I'm sorry."

He ran his hands through his hair. "Then why didn't you ever tell me this before?"

"I wanted to, I really did. But at the same time, I was trying to put all that behind me, so I could have a new life with you. Billy said it was the best way, because—"

"Billy said, Billy said, Billy said. Christ, did you ever do anything he disagreed with?"

Lila was stunned that he sounded so angry saying Billy's name, as if he'd completely forgotten what had happened to her brother, as if he'd even forgotten what was happening to Lila herself since Billy died. Or was it that he didn't care anymore?

Love is a familiar. Love is a devil. There is no evil angel but Love.

You're nothing but a stupid little mouse.

She shook herself to stop the drowsiness that was creeping into her body and her brain, to focus only on her husband and what was happening here. But it was as if the Patrick she'd always known had disappeared and in his place was a man who didn't love her or even like her. She pushed her fingers against her eyelids, willing the tears not to fall. Finally she said, "What difference does it make now?"

"It makes a difference to me. I want to know if you ever told me anything that he didn't want you to." Patrick exhaled. "Even one time will do."

She could tell this was crucially important to him, though she couldn't understand why. Billy had never told her what to say to Patrick, unless it involved their past. And yes, she knew it might seem strange—from the outside—that she'd gone along with Billy on this, but she'd always thought her husband understood that Billy wasn't just her brother; he was a part of herself. Of course she trusted Billy. She also needed his advice because he was the one who remembered everything and understood what it all meant and, most important of all, knew how they could overcome it and be happy. It was Billy who'd convinced her that they were doing nothing wrong, that Americans had always left their pasts behind to set out for new lives. Billy said it was not only the central theme of American literature, but also the promise of the American dream—that we can reinvent ourselves however we want. True, most of these reinventions failed spectacularly, at least in American lit, but Billy said it would be different in their case. They would live so well as adults that their past would no longer matter, or as Billy said, quoting Emerson: "All history becomes subjective; in other words, there is properly no history, only biography."

When Lila didn't answer, Patrick said, "Just tell me one time when you chose me over him. One time, and I'll let this go."

The way he'd rephrased his request was so odd that Lila just stared. Her mind felt heavy and stupid from the sedative, but didn't Patrick already know there had been dozens of times that she'd done what he'd wanted rather than what Billy had? Their trip to Europe, to give only one example, had put her in the position of having to explain to her brother that they couldn't spend their vacation together at the shore, even though Billy wanted this so badly he'd saved up to pay for the house rental himself that year. Billy had been disappointed, but he'd said he understood that her husband's plans came first. Patrick even knew about that conversation, because he was there when she got off the phone with Billy.

She was thinking about that summer when it suddenly dawned on her that it had been the last chance she'd had to spend a full week with her brother and his family. This was right after he moved to

Harrisburg. Maybe if they'd gone with Billy instead of to Europe, she would have known something was wrong and been able to help him. Maybe he'd still be alive.

She was crying softly when Patrick stood up and went into the bedroom. She would have felt panicked if the sedative hadn't been dulling her reactions. Something terrible was happening. What had she done wrong? If only she weren't too tired to figure it out.

But as she stumbled down the hall, she heard him crying, too, and she thought she knew why he left the room. Her husband almost never cried and when he did, it always embarrassed him. She came into the bedroom, ready to hold him, though she knew she probably couldn't say anything that would be comforting. She needed to sleep and forget about everything. Tomorrow, she would try again to find out what was upsetting Patrick.

When she saw their suitcase lying open on the bed, her first stupid thought was that he was going to a math conference. After it dawned on her he wouldn't be doing that in the middle of the week before finals, she slumped down on the bed, thoroughly confused, and took one of his shirts out of the suitcase, his blue-and-yellow plaid button-down. He'd bought it last September when they were shopping in Center City. Every year, they went shopping before the fall semester started. It was their annual ritual, and something they'd joked about, saying if students got new school clothes, teachers should, too.

She hugged the shirt to her chest and watched as he packed a few pairs of pants, three other shirts, a handful of underwear and socks. When he went into the bathroom and came back with his small toiletry case, he'd stopped crying. He put it in the bag and zipped up the suitcase without asking for the blue-and-yellow plaid shirt back.

"I'm going to check into the Marriott across the street from Dannerson. I'll leave you their phone number."

She was so tired now that his words seemed to come to her from underwater. "The Marriott?" she mumbled. Patrick liked individually owned hotels, not chains. Maybe this wasn't real? It felt so real, though. The shirt she was holding smelled like the light starch Patrick always asked for at the dry cleaner's. She associated this clean smell with him.

"I've put up with a lot, Lila. The last month has been unbelievably stressful. You can't go to work. You won't let any of your friends help you. You've refused therapy. You won't even drive your car or answer the phone. I've tried so hard to help you through this, and I would keep trying forever. But it doesn't seem to make a damn bit of difference to you."

"It does," she said, into the shirt. She was lying down now; the shirt was pressed against her face. The lights were bothering her. It was so hard to keep her eyes open.

"In what way? Tell me one thing that's different with me here."

She wanted to say that his breathing next to her at night gave her a reason not to kill herself, but she couldn't form the words, and she wouldn't have said that anyway, for fear he'd have her hospitalized. The therapist had told them both that if Lila expressed any suicidal impulses, she should be taken to the ER and admitted to the psych ward immediately. While she was thinking how to answer, she fell asleep for a second or two, but then she forced herself to sit up and tried to smile, hoping to show him that she wasn't crazy; she was a normal person, with all the normal needs. She even raised her finger the way he liked, to indicate she was making a point he couldn't disagree with. "You bring me food."

He flinched and she vaguely sensed she'd done something wrong. But what did he want her to say? She'd already told him she loved him. "I love you," she said again, but her voice wasn't cooperating. It was so quiet. Or maybe he wasn't listening?

"I'll order groceries in for you. Unless you decide you can drive your car. Though mine is destroyed, I'm going to leave yours here and take a cab."

"The Rabbit? What—"

"I have to go. I still have a stack of homework to grade and two finals to prepare." He looked at her. She was lying down again. She didn't want to, but her head was so heavy, she couldn't hold it up anymore. "And you obviously took your sedative sometime in the last half hour, when I was begging you to be honest with me."

She wanted to tell him that he was wrong, that she'd taken the sedative before he'd gotten home, but all she could manage was, "Not then."

"But it's not your fault, Lila." He sounded so calm suddenly, like his usual self. Her eyes were closed, but she reached out her arm for him, hoping he would come back to the bed and lie down with her. They could sleep until morning, when she would realize this had been another bad dream. Like the dream she kept having about the deafening explosion and Billy screaming and her being frozen with fear, unable to get to him. There was blood all over the place, but she just stood there: not crying, not yelling for help, not saying anything. When she woke in the morning, she knew it wasn't real because she hadn't even been there. She couldn't have helped her brother.

She heard her husband's voice but it was so far away, like he was talking from another country. Or from New Jersey, where her mother was alive? That was the part that made her suddenly sure none of this could be real. Patrick had nothing to do with her mother. He was the most important part of the better life Billy had always promised her. He was kind and brilliant and completely ignorant of all the terror of her past. She had always protected him from knowing. It was the right thing to do, so he could stay just as he was: a beautiful soul.

"I hate leaving you like this," Patrick said. "If I honestly thought that my being here was doing anything for you, I'd stay. But the person you really loved is dead and I can't bring him back. It's not your fault that it was never me."

"Patrick isn't dead," she whispered into her pillow. "It's just a bad dream."

Then she fell asleep so deeply that she didn't hear her husband leave and she barely cried out when the gun exploded and Billy was screaming and screaming for her to do something, but she couldn't do anything because she was so worried she was going to get in trouble for ruining her special dress, the one she was supposed to wear to her daddy's funeral that her mother said made her look like an ugly little mouse.

CHAPTER TWELVE

All day on Friday, William was as nervous as that morning in the tent, when Daddy left him alone as part of the Challenge, but this time he was not going to mess up. When the teacher said they had to study for their spelling test on Monday, he opened his book and wrote the list of words, even though he knew he wouldn't have to take this dumb test because he wouldn't be here on Monday or ever again. Pearl had told him that at Aunt Lila's, they would go to private school, where everybody was rich and they gave you great hot food for lunch every day, even french fries, his favorite. Plus, she said, some private schools don't even have grades, which wouldn't matter for Pearl because she got straight As, but would be great for William, since he got mostly Us for unsatisfactory. The only subject he was good at was math, but Pearl reminded him that Uncle Patrick was a mathematician and maybe he could work it out so William could take a lot more math and a lot less spelling and writing. Spelling was the thing he hated most, but he forced himself not to grin when the teacher said he'd have to study at home a lot if he expected to pass this test without having his book available as a crutch.

By the time he got off the bus, he was clearing his throat every few seconds, which his mom called his tic. She hated the tic, but the more she talked about how bad it sounded, the more William found himself doing it, except now he was doing it with nobody around but Pearl, and she wasn't griping at him. She did give him a glass of water and tell him to drink it, but a minute later, he was at it again. It felt like a piece of food was stuck in the back of his throat, and even though he knew it wasn't real, he couldn't stop acting like it was. Finally, Pearl gave him a big package of gum and told him to chew instead. When it worked, he was surprised nobody else ever thought of this, even Daddy. Pearl was really, really smart.

He was chomping away on his fourteenth piece of gum when his mom came home with Maisie. She told him he was going to rot his teeth with sugar, but after he held up the package of sugarless gum, she frowned. He knew she was hoping that he'd mess up and answer her questions with words; she was always trying to trick him into talking. Finally, she said, "I miss your sweet voice, baby," which made him feel sad, but he stuck another piece of gum in his mouth and went back to clicking Legos together. When his mom went upstairs to get ready for her date with Kyle, she told him to watch Maisie, but that was easy because Maisie was just sitting on the couch, watching *SpongeBob* on TV and sucking on frozen peas. She liked frozen peas better than anything, which normally William thought was really weird, but now he wondered if he'd miss his sister whenever he saw a bag of frozen peas, or even cooked peas. He sort of wished they were taking Maisie with them and Mommy, too, but that was a dumb wish and he knew it. Maisie would cry for Mommy until his ears hurt, and if Mommy herself was going to Philadelphia, they wouldn't have to go sneaking off to Aunt Lila's in the first place.

He'd been thinking about Aunt Lila's apartment all afternoon. He didn't remember it that well, but he thought it was really small and he knew it was on the ninth floor of a super tall building. The ninth floor was bad—he was still afraid of heights, even though he'd finished the Challenge where he jumped off a cliff —but worse was the small part. Pearl said Aunt Lila had three bedrooms, the same as their own house, but one was for her and Uncle Patrick, and one was like their office, so that only left one for him and Pearl to share. She said they'd work something out, but William liked having his very own bedroom with the rocket ship wallpaper Daddy had hung up. He didn't want to undress around his big sister. He was also worried about burping or picking his nose or something that would make Pearl decide that he wasn't her friend anymore, but just a dirty little boy like she used to call him before Daddy died.

He wished he knew for sure whether Pearl was right about Aunt Lila really wanting them. She almost never played with him like his aunts and uncles on his mom's side, and even at the funeral, she stared at him with those freaky big eyes of hers and didn't say much at all. In his whole life, he couldn't remember ever doing anything with Aunt Lila all by herself.

His mother and Kyle finally left, and Pearl gave William another slap five and said it was time to do their plan. She called Staci and then she called her other friend Danielle, who was always babysitting for lots of money but was going to take care of Maisie for free because Danielle knew how mean Mommy was, trying to make them move to godforsaken New Mexico, thousands of miles away from their father's twin. Both Staci and Danielle were there in like ten minutes, and then, before William could even pick up his Legos or give Maisie more peas, their duffel bags were loaded in Staci's trunk and they were pulling out of the driveway.

"Good-bye," Staci said, "and screw you!" She was giving their house the finger and laughing.

"Don't do that," Pearl said. "That was my dad's house, too."

Staci said sorry, but William's stomach hurt, remembering how much his father had loved this place. He would walk around outside, throwing seed on the ground for the birds and showing William stuff like the little vines that grew on the side brick wall or the frogs that had moved into their tiny pond. That's how they discovered the big hole in the oak tree, where Daddy decided to hide the reminders and other cool stuff, just for William. Daddy said he wanted to buy this house someday, rather than just renting it, 'cause then they could stay there forever. "Maybe you'll live here with your children," Daddy said. "Would you like that, buddy?" William said yes, even though he didn't know if he'd ever have children, since he didn't like girls at all, especially Sophie Peterson, who called him dumbo and laughed whenever he missed the ball at recess.

Now that his father was dead because he and his mom had fought so much and he had to leave the house and not see the kids anymore, William knew he'd never, ever get married. Aunt Trish had never gotten married and she was the happiest of all his aunts. Mommy said Trish was simple, that's why she was always happy. William wished he was simple, too, so he could be happy rather than worried all the time.

"I've never driven in Philly before," Staci said. "I'm kind of psyched to try driving in all that traffic."

They were on the highway already. William knew a rest stop was coming up that had great doughnuts, but Pearl had already told him they were going to hurry to Aunt Lila's, just in case something went wrong on Mom and Kyle's date.

"It'll be all right," Pearl said. "My aunt's high-rise is on the very edge of the city, close to the river. We can get off on the South Street exit, and then it's just a few blocks and we're there."

"How do we know she's home?" William said.

"We don't, but I couldn't call her." Pearl looked at Staci. "My mom's lawyer is such an asshole. He'd probably have Aunt Lila arrested if she agreed to let us come there."

Staci nodded, but she said, "I don't get it. If the guy's that big of a dick, won't he have your aunt arrested after you're there?"

"Sure, he'll try. But he won't get away with it. Trust me on that."

William could tell from Pearl's low voice that she was talking about her big secret plan. Whatever it was. He was dying to know, but he knew she wouldn't tell him. It was okay, because when she'd asked why he was bringing Daddy's toolbox, which was heavy and so big it took up a lot of space in his duffel bag, William had said, "That's MY secret." Pearl laughed, but he didn't feel bad. He'd been kind of worried she'd force him to take off the padlock and then she'd see the gun inside and he'd have to tell her everything.

At the last minute, he'd remembered his father telling him that no matter how nice and easy things looked, he had to always be prepared. William didn't think Kyle would show up at Aunt Lila's and do all the other things on Daddy's list for the last Challenge, but what if he was just too dumb to see how it could happen? His father had said the point of the Challenges was to teach William how to be ready for every possibility. "I know you won't have to jump off a cliff," Daddy said. "But you will have to do things you're afraid of. This will teach you how to feel the fear and do it anyway."

It was a good thing Daddy had made him jump off a cliff,

because he was right: William was already having to do something he was afraid of by running away. His teachers said William was the best-behaved boy, 'cause he didn't break any rules or cause trouble like a lot of the other kids at Chandler Elementary. His mother said he'd always been like this, that he was born good. Even when he was just a baby, cruising around the house in his walker, he wouldn't go near the DVD player or Daddy's computer or the stove, and if he did get near them accidentally, he would shake his head no and hurry off the other way. "You were my angel baby," Mommy said. And if Pearl was in the room, Mommy laughed and said, "And Pearl was my devil." It was only a joke, and Pearl laughed, too—until Daddy moved out. Then Mommy said the same thing and Pearl just stared at her and so Mommy never talked about angels or devils again. William was glad because he thought being an angel was like being a girl, since angels all wore dresses.

He was glad he was breaking a rule now, too. He'd been teased at school for being chicken, but nobody would think he was chicken when they heard he'd run away. If only he wasn't so worried about everything. It was getting dark and every time a car came up behind them, he squinted out the back window, trying to see if it was his mom's Ford or, even worse, a police car. He was out of new gum and the old piece in his mouth was getting small and dry and yucky, but he couldn't spit it out or his tic would come back worse than ever because he was so thirsty.

By the time they got to Philadelphia, William had to go to the bathroom, and he was listening to music on his boom box to distract himself. Staci was talking about this creepy neighbor of hers and asked why Pearl had been standing in his yard, talking to him, but Pearl said she wasn't really talking, and then she changed the subject to something about their school that William didn't even try to follow.

Staci said, "Can't you get him to turn that thing off?"

"He's just nervous," Pearl said. William thought she sounded nervous, too. "We're almost there anyway. Let him play his music if he wants." She turned around to William. "I bet you can get Aunt Lila to buy you an iPod, even though Mom wouldn't buy you one for Christmas. Then you can listen to anything as loud as you like."

William smiled because he wanted an iPod, but most of all he wanted to get to Aunt Lila's, fast. "Almost there" didn't mean what he thought it meant, though, and by the time they pulled in front of Aunt Lila's building, he had to pee so bad he was dying. He was glad Staci decided not to try to find a parking space, but he wished it wasn't taking so long for Pearl and Staci to hug each other goodbye. Before they went into the building, Pearl asked why he was fidgeting so much and he said he really had to go to the bathroom. She leaned over and whispered, "Do you think you could cry about it? Because if Aunt Lila isn't home, I want you to cry as hard as you ever have in your life. Think about Dad if you have to. Otherwise, we'll have to walk all over the city in the dark and even then, we might not find a bathroom for you. City people don't like letting kids use their bathrooms."

William said he would try. Finally, they dragged their duffel bags through the glass door and inside the lobby and Pearl told the man standing there who they'd come to visit. He picked up a phone and held it to his ear, but didn't say anything. He told Pearl that Lila Cole wasn't answering. "I'm sorry, but she doesn't appear to be home."

At which point, William did just what Pearl wanted: he started bawling like a big fat baby. He felt stupid, but it wasn't that hard. He was scared, he was hungry, he was thirsty, and he was sure he was going to pee his pants if he didn't get into Aunt Lila's apartment right away.

"What's wrong with the little guy?" the man said.

"We've been traveling all day to visit our aunt," Pearl said. "She's our father's twin sister and my brother loves her so much." She knelt down and put her arm around William. "It's really been hard on him since our father died last month. Aunt Lila is all we have left of him now."

"Aw, the poor little guy," the man said. "What is he, about six? I have a boy his age." He looked at William. "I'm sure she'll be back in an hour or so. She never goes out anymore."

William looked at Pearl and she nodded, which was good because it felt easier now to keep crying than to stop. The man guessing he was six years old was bad enough, but saying it might be an hour? He knew he'd never make it that long and then he'd pee all over the floor and this man would yell at him and call the police and he'd have to go to jail. His mom had told him peeing in pubic was illegal after they saw this homeless guy do it down by the river one time.

"Okay, okay," the man said. "If you're sure Ms. Cole is expecting you, I guess I can let you wait upstairs for her."

"She is," Pearl said. "We've been talking about this visit for weeks. I bet she's just out buying some of William's favorite foods." She sighed. "He's always been her favorite."

"Will you stop crying if I let you wait upstairs?" the man said, smiling.

William nodded. Then the man took a big ring with zillions of keys out of a desk drawer, and they all headed to the elevator.

He pushed up his glasses and wiped his eyes with the sleeve of his jacket; he was still sniffing and coughing, but he was excited by all the lights in the elevator. The man let him push the button for floor nine; then the metal box shook a little and up they went.

Aunt Lila's apartment number was 909. The man knocked three times before he opened the door, and even then he said,

"Ms. Cole?" and waited a minute before he stepped back and let them inside.

"Thank you," Pearl said, smiling a weird, fakey smile. "My aunt being away was problematic, but you've solved the situation. I'm sure my aunt will thank you, too."

As soon as the man nodded and left, Pearl took William down the hall to the bathroom and a few minutes later, he was fine again. His sister was in the living room, standing by the duffel bags, texting on her cell phone. When she clicked it shut, she said, "Danielle said they aren't home yet. Good." Then she came over and hugged William. "You were great with that doorman. The crying was brilliant." She leaned back and smiled. "You're a lot smarter than they give you credit for."

He shrugged, but he felt warm and happy inside. Other than Daddy, nobody had ever called him smart before.

"I bet you're hungry, aren't you?" Pearl said. When he nodded, she said, "Okay, we'll look for something to eat, but first let's figure out where to put these duffel bags. We don't want Aunt Lila to walk in the door and stumble over them. Plus, it looks like we're planning on staying for a while."

"We are," William said.

"Of course, dummy," Pearl said, lifting her bag. "But I want to explain that to her first."

He wished he'd kept his mouth shut so he wouldn't have switched back to "dummy" so soon. He was too short to lift his bag, but he scooted it along the wood floor, out of the living room, past the bathroom, past Aunt Lila and Uncle Patrick's office, to where the two bedrooms faced each other on opposite sides of the hall. Pearl started into the one on the left and he was following so close that he ran into his sister when she suddenly stopped.

"Aunt Lila?" Pearl said.

William dropped the handles of his bag and moved to where his sister was standing, and sure enough, there was Aunt Lila, asleep in bed.

"Aunt Lila," Pearl said louder, moving a little closer. She repeated this four times, each time getting closer, until finally both Pearl and William were standing right by the bed, looking at their aunt's face.

"She's super tired," William said.

Pearl wasn't listening. She was shaking Aunt Lila and saying "wake up" really loudly.

"She's going to be mad," William said. He was thinking of their mom, who yelled if they woke her up when she was super tired. Unless they were sick and going to vomit. Then it was okay to wake her up.

"There's something wrong with her," Pearl said. She was pulling on Aunt Lila's arms. She finally managed to lift her up but as soon as she let go, Aunt Lila flopped back down again.

"Is she dead?" William whispered.

"No, she's breathing," Pearl said. She looked at the bedside table and picked up a pill bottle. She read the label and said, "Shit."

"She forgot her medicine?" William said.

"I've heard of this stuff; some girl at school offered it to me after Dad died. It's supposed to be a *serious* sleeping pill. Now she'll never wake up until tomorrow morning!" Pearl shook her head so hard pieces of her blond hair were flopping against her back. "Which means we have a big problem!"

"Why?"

She ignored William and walked out of the bedroom. He followed her. When they got into the living room, she said, "Where the hell is Uncle Patrick anyway?"

"Maybe he's at a bar like Mommy and Kyle."

"No way. Haven't you heard Mom talk about how Aunt Lila and Uncle Patrick never do anything fun? She thinks they live like they're a hundred years old. Mom and Dad used to fight about it. He said they lived a life of the mind, but Mom couldn't understand that. Mom never understood anything about Dad or Lila. Or me." Pearl crossed her arms and started tapping her foot on the floor. "There has to be some way to reach him. He has a cell phone, right?"

William didn't know, but Pearl wasn't really asking him, he could tell.

"I'm hungry," he finally said, to remind her, but also to get her to be calm like she was before.

She frowned. "Okay, okay, Jesus! I'll get you something to eat." She took him into the kitchen and handed him a bag of bagels. After that she went crazy looking all over the apartment for Uncle Patrick's cell phone number. She never did find it, so finally she decided to call a number under a magnet on the refrigerator. It said "Marriott," which she said was a hotel. "It can't be him, but maybe whoever it is knows how to reach him. If we don't find him tonight, we're fucked."

"Will the policeman arrest us?" William was eating his second bagel, sitting on the couch, looking at a boring magazine called *The New Yorker.* He was getting a little sleepy—or at least he had been, until Pearl said that curse word, which Mommy said was the worst curse word of all.

"No, dummy. But we'll have to go home."

"Oh." He felt a little guilty as she was dialing but he wasn't sure he cared if this Marriott person knew where Uncle Patrick was. His own bed sounded good right now, but he didn't want to ruin Pearl's plan of running away.

He heard Pearl talking, then waiting, and talking again. "Please tell him that his niece Pearl called and there's an emergency at his house. Ask him to come home right away. Thank you."

After she shut her cell phone, she sat down next to him and

ripped off a big chunk from the bagel in his hand. He wasn't going to gripe, but she pointed at the bag like he already had. "There are three more. You're not going to starve." She chewed for a while before she said, "Uncle Patrick is staying at that hotel. Must be some college thing. I left a message with the hotel front desk and on the room voicemail. They said the hotel isn't very far from here. If he doesn't come in the next two hours, I'll try that number again."

"Can we turn on the TV till he gets here?"

"Do you see a television?"

He didn't, but he knew sometimes people hid their TVs behind wood doors. A lot of his friends had their TVs hidden like that. But Aunt Lila and Uncle Patrick didn't have one of those cabinets with wood doors. All they had were rows and rows of bookshelves.

Pearl had her cell phone out again, texting someone. He asked if he could listen to his music now and she said not yet. When he asked her what he should do, she shrugged.

So he sat and looked at the pictures in one boring magazine after another, until he finished the stack on the coffee table. It didn't take him long. Most of the magazines didn't have many pictures. When Pearl was still on the phone, talking to Staci, he closed his eyes. He must have fallen asleep, because the next thing he knew, Uncle Patrick was bursting through the door.

"Where's Lila?"

"She's asleep," Pearl said. "It's not—"

William yawned and watched as Uncle Patrick rushed down the hall and peeked into the bedroom. The bedroom light was still on. He flicked off the switch before slowly walking back.

He looked at Pearl. "What's the emergency?"

"It's complicated." She cleared her throat like she'd caught William's tic. "That's why I wanted to talk to you about it."

Uncle Patrick sat down in a dark green chair. He rubbed his

face, which was all stubbly like Kyle's got when he wouldn't listen to Mommy and shave. Finally he said, "What are you kids doing here?"

"Nothing," Pearl said. "We just came to be with you and Aunt Lila."

"Really?"

His eyebrows were raised like Mommy's always were when she thought someone was lying. So William said, "Pearl isn't lying! We runned away tonight to be with you guys."

He knew he'd messed up when Pearl elbowed him in the ribs, hard. He felt like crying, but instead he started clearing his throat again. Nobody seemed to notice so maybe the tic wasn't that loud.

"All right," Uncle Patrick said. "Unfortunately, it's illegal for you to be here without your mother's permission. I'm sorry, I'm going to have to call her, and I'm sure she'll demand that I bring you back immediately."

"But we can't go back," Pearl said. "That's what I have to tell you. There's a good reason."

Uncle Patrick stared at nothing for a minute. "Why didn't you talk to your aunt about this? Why call me instead of waking her up?"

"I tried," Pearl said. "I think she took sleeping pills, because I said her name and shook her and even tried to drag her by the arms."

"Oh my God," Patrick said. And then he was running down the hall again. Pearl got up, too, and William followed his sister. They found Patrick standing by the bed, holding the pill bottle. He grabbed the phone and said some stuff really quickly that William couldn't follow. When he hung up, things were so confusing that William sat on the floor and held his head in his hands. His tic had gotten so bad it was making his throat hurt.

Pearl and Patrick were both talking at once. They were both crying, too, which made William so scared.

"I thought she was just asleep," Pearl said. "I'm so sorry."

"They'll be here soon." Uncle Patrick was talking to Aunt Lila, holding her up in his arms. He sounded as upset as Mommy when the police came to tell her Daddy died. "Any minute. Hang on."

"I'm so sorry," Pearl repeated. "I didn't know you could still wake up if you take sleeping pills." She was twisting her hands together like she was cold. "Is Aunt Lila going to die?"

"I never should have left you," Uncle Patrick said. "Oh my God."

Then there was a banging on the door, and Pearl ran to open it, and after that there were two men and a woman standing over Aunt Lila and behind them, a policeman. William scooted into a corner and stayed very quiet, so nobody would notice him. He watched as Aunt Lila was taken out of the room on a rolling bed, still asleep, even though all these people were doing things to her and Uncle Patrick was shouting, "Is she going to be all right? Please, just tell me what's going on!"

The policeman told Uncle Patrick he could ride with his wife in the ambulance, but not the kids. Uncle Patrick nodded, but he said quickly, "Their mother needs to be called. They ran away to come here." Then he was following the rolling bed down the hall and out of the apartment. William knew they were all gone because it got so quiet. Only he and Pearl and the policeman were left in Aunt Lila's bedroom.

"What's your mother's phone number?" the policeman said.

Pearl leaned against the dresser and kept crying. She didn't say anything.

He asked for the number two more times. Then he said, "Do you understand that running away is a serious matter?"

"I don't care," Pearl said, coughing. "I'm not going back. I love my aunt. She's my dad's twin. She understands who I am. I want to live here with her."

"Even if your mom agreed, this isn't the right time." The policeman sounded sort of nice all of a sudden. "Let me take you home and maybe you can come back when your aunt is feeling better."

"I know my aunt tried to kill herself, but I know why she did it, too. She misses my dad, and my mother wouldn't even let her talk to us." Pearl rubbed her arm across her eyes, but she couldn't stop crying. William was crying, too, now, because he finally understood what had happened. Aunt Lila had tried to do the same thing Daddy did. She might die, too.

"Your little brother is tired," the policeman said. "Just tell me the number and we can get you both home and get him in bed."

When Pearl didn't answer, the policeman turned to William. "Do you know your phone number, little fellow?"

"Yeah," William cried. He was so insulted by everyone assuming he was a baby just because he was so small for his age. And how dumb would he have to be not to know the phone number? He was good with numbers. But he wasn't going to let himself be tricked again. He put his hand over his mouth and decided not to say another word to this policeman.

The policeman shrugged and said he could find out the number with or without their help. He was just about to call the police station when Pearl said, "If you take us back, he'll hurt me again."

"Who?"

"My mother's boyfriend." Pearl sounded strange and the look on her face was like nothing William had ever seen. She looked as blank as the chalkboard looked in the morning at school.

The policeman said something William didn't follow and Pearl said, "If you don't believe me, look!" She spun around and raised her shirt up over her back. William saw the strap of her bra, which made him feel embarrassed, but he also saw the purple and blue bruises all over her, from her shoulders to the top of her jeans.

"Kyle hit you?" he gasped, and Pearl nodded in his direction before turning back to the policeman, who wasn't dialing the phone but instead putting it back in his pocket. He asked Pearl if they could go into the living room to talk for a minute, alone.

William knew "alone" meant he wasn't supposed to follow them, but he couldn't if he wanted to. His legs felt like noodles and his stomach felt like he'd swallowed the biggest rock by the creek. He didn't have Daddy's list with him, but he knew for sure that this was on it. He even remembered the words Daddy used: "That Bastard hitting you or Maisie or Pearl for any reason whatsoever." He'd had to look up the word "whatsoever," and though he still couldn't define it in his own words, the way his teacher always said to, he'd figured out what it meant in the sentence. It meant Kyle could never hit them, not even if they mouthed off or bugged him while he was watching the game, not even if they broke the window on his truck by accident or even on purpose.

And this was way down at the bottom of Daddy's list, with the other stuff his father had drawn an arrow next to. William knew what that arrow meant, because Daddy had talked to him about the arrow every day they were doing the Challenges. The arrow meant the time had come to save his sisters.

As he sat on the floor of Aunt Lila's bedroom, clearing his throat like he really had tried to swallow a boulder, he could hear Daddy saying, "You have to feel the fear and do it anyway. I know it's hard, but you're smart, buddy. You'll figure out that's the only secret to being brave."

CHAPTER THIRTEEN

For more than a half hour, Patrick had been stuck in the ER admissions department, filling out forms and answering questions. The intake clerk wasn't completely heartless; she'd waited to trap him until after the attending physician said that Lila was going to live. His wife was lucky, apparently, that she'd only taken her sleeping pills and not mixed them with alcohol or other drugs. She was also lucky that she'd been taking so many sedatives in the last month, day and night, that she'd built up a tolerance. They pumped her stomach and gave her another drug that worked to counteract the sleeping pills. The doctor said she was already physically alert—groaning, responding to reflex tests, and the like—and she'd probably be mentally alert within the hour. Patrick had told the clerk that he should be there when his wife woke up, but the clerk insisted this paperwork had to be completed first. At the moment, she was on hold with his insurance company, waiting for preauthorization for a psych admit.

Which gave him time to think about the last several hours. Even if he hadn't been with Joyce when his niece had left a message at the Marriott, he still would have felt this was unreal, but as it was, he felt feverish and light-headed, as though he was literally sickened by what had happened.

He'd spent Wednesday night alone and Thursday night, too. He could have gone out anytime he wanted—he had a rental car, a brand-new Mazda—but the only place he wanted to be was back home. He kept thinking Lila would call, even just to say that she needed food or soap or a prescription refilled, but the only phone calls he got were from Joyce, making sure he was all right. Offering to help in any way she could. Worrying that he was spending too much time by himself.

By Friday night, he knew he needed to get out of his tiny hotel room, so he agreed to go to dinner with Joyce, but he kept his cell phone with him, just in case. Joyce picked him up at seven and they went to a steak place near campus. He had two beers; she had a few glasses of wine. While they were eating, Joyce asked him if their kiss was the reason he'd left his wife.

"Oh boy, I can't believe I just asked you that," she said. "What I meant was that I hope what happened between us didn't cause you any problems at home." She paused. "I'd hate to think I'd hurt you. I'd never want to do that."

"Please don't worry about it. It's not your fault." He waited a moment. "My guess is this has been coming for a long time."

He'd said "guess" because that's just what it felt like: as though he were some unprepared student throwing out an answer that might well be ridiculous. Only a few days ago, the idea that he would ever leave his wife was not only absurd but unthinkable. And yet here he was.

A moment later, he heard himself saying, "I don't think she ever loved me." But was this close to the truth? He certainly believed that Lila wouldn't have lied to him over and over if she really loved him; yet he had *felt* loved by her, hadn't he? Did he even know what love was?

Joyce reached for his hand, but to her credit she said, "She married you. She must have loved you at one time."

He thought about moving his hand, but didn't. "You could be right." He shrugged. "I just don't understand it." After a minute, he changed the topic to the dean's latest annoying faculty memo.

Another beer, another glass of wine, and somehow Joyce was sitting on his side of the booth, pressing her leg against his. She admitted that she'd had a crush on him for a while. He admitted that he really enjoyed her company and was glad she'd pushed him to come out tonight. After they finished dessert and split the check, they were back in her geek mobile, heading to the Marriott. Her hand was on his thigh. She was kissing him at every red light. She obviously assumed, as he did, that they were going back to his room together. He hadn't had sex in a long time: not since Billy died, of course, and only once or twice in the months before, because Lila was always busy, working on an important paper. He couldn't remember Lila ever wanting him with the passion that Joyce quite obviously did. He was incredibly excited as they drove into the hotel parking lot.

They were already out of Joyce's car, sharing another kiss, when it finally struck him that he couldn't go through with it. He was still a married man. No matter how much he wanted Joyce, he took his commitments seriously, including his promise to be faithful. He could tell she was disappointed, as he was, but as he walked back into the hotel alone, he was relieved that he'd managed to do the right thing.

That would turn out to be the last clear-cut moment of the night—the rest was a blur of terror and guilt and panic and other feelings he couldn't even identify. Yet he knew the doctor was right: it could have been much worse. If Patrick had stayed out an hour longer, if the kids hadn't shown up, if Pearl hadn't thought to call him when she did, Lila could have aspirated vomit and damaged her lungs, or stopped breathing and damaged her brain, or even died.

When the intake clerk finally said he could go, he ignored a fleeting desire to run in the other direction rather than back to the room where they'd taken his wife. He pushed back the curtain and found a nurse sitting with Lila. His wife was crying, but the nurse said that was normal. The stomach pumping, or "gastric lavage" as she called it, had involved an endotracheal tube that was "more than uncomfortable" and the drug to counteract the sedative might have caused some agitation and withdrawal. "But she'll be all right soon," the nurse said. "A doctor will be coming to talk to her. He should be down shortly." Then she patted Lila's arm, stood up to check his wife's IV pole, and told Patrick to buzz the nursing station if they needed anything.

"I have to get out of here," Lila said as soon as the nurse walked away. Tears were streaming down her face, but it couldn't be normal crying, because she wasn't making any crying sounds. "I know I haven't been a very good wife. I thought about this a lot yesterday." She was speaking quickly, as though she was afraid he'd interrupt. "I don't blame you for wanting to leave me, but could you just pretend that you're going to take me home? That way, they'll think someone is watching out for me and let me go."

He sat down next to her and took her hand. The doctor had already told Patrick that, unfortunately, he wouldn't be allowed to just take Lila home. There were laws involved when someone attempted suicide. He told her he would do his best, but then he explained what the doctor said. Or he started to. He told her there would be a psychiatrist coming down to talk to her, but before he got to the strong probability that she would have to stay in the hospital for a few days, just to make sure she was no longer a threat to herself, somehow Lila already knew what was coming. She jerked her hand away and yelled, "No! Don't you understand? I can't stay here. I just can't!"

Patrick braced himself for medical personnel rushing in and tying Lila down or giving her a sedative, something. But when nobody came, he lowered his voice, hoping Lila would take the hint and lower hers. "Don't worry, babe, they won't keep you for long." He forced a smile. "Our insurance will make sure of that."

"They will keep me. They'll say they won't, but they will. And I won't be able to see you. They won't even let you visit." At least she wasn't yelling anymore. He was trying to stay calm, thinking about how to reassure her, until she added, "They won't let me see Billy, either, no matter what they promise."

What he felt then was so entirely physical that he didn't even realize that his mind had shut down. It was like he was a child again playing ball and he'd had the ball kicked right into his stomach. Except it was worse: it felt like the air hadn't just been knocked out of his lungs, but out of his entire body. He couldn't feel his legs or his arms. The room looked shimmery and strange, as though his eyes had lost their ability to focus.

"Wait, I know Billy can't come here." Lila was looking at the ceiling, speaking slowly. "He died, didn't he?"

"Yes." He inhaled, hoping her initial confusion was normal after a trauma. He was grateful that she'd already come back to the present, but he was more alert now, afraid there might be other things she would say that would shock him. The monitors attached to Lila seemed louder; the fluorescent lights harsher and more annoying. Even the hospital smell, which he thought he was used to from all the times he'd visited his mother, was suddenly obnoxious and vaguely nauseating. He wanted to get out of here every bit as badly as Lila did.

When she didn't say anything for a while, he said the only thing he could think of. "I'm sorry."

"You didn't hurt Billy." She was still looking at the ceiling. Her odd tears had stopped, but her expression was blank, unreadable. "I don't think you were even there when Harold shot him, but I don't know. I may be losing the plot again."

"Harold?" The name of the policeman who shot Lila's brother had never made it into any of the news reports. Patrick thought this was because they didn't know exactly whose bullet had killed Billy. He'd been shot multiple times by the SWAT team when he'd refused their demand that he move away from the window and drop the rifle he'd aimed at the second floor of the elementary school.

"I don't think you know him," she said quietly, as though she was talking to herself, working out the details. "You weren't invited to any of the parties, were you?"

He was wondering what the hell she was talking about when he heard the screech of the metal rings as the curtain opened again. A man introduced himself as Dr. Samuels. He looked like all the other doctors Patrick had seen so far: younger than expected and unmistakably tired. He said he needed to talk to Lila for a few minutes, and turned to Patrick. "If you wouldn't mind waiting outside. Someone will come and get you when the discussion is over. If we decide to move your wife to another room, you can go with her and help her get settled."

He'd already stood up when Lila begged, "Don't leave me. Please."

"He'll be right down the hall," the doctor said. Then he looked at Patrick and nodded in the direction of the waiting room.

Patrick reassured Lila he'd be back soon and walked away. Even after he closed the curtain, he could hear her repeated pleas that he stay with her.

He made it to the waiting room, went into the bathroom to wash his face, and sat back down by the window, where the sun was already turning the horizon a pale orange. It took him a minute to realize it was Saturday now, almost morning. He wasn't tired, at least his mind wasn't, but his body ached a protest that he hadn't slept in twenty-four hours.

He wasn't sure how long he'd been sitting there when the psychiatrist came out to talk to him. The sun was up; it looked like it was turning into a beautiful spring day, very few clouds. As expected, Dr. Samuels said that Lila was going to be held over the weekend and possibly longer. He said this would give them a chance to examine her and more aggressively treat her. He also admitted that Lila was very upset about this, but that was common enough for survivors of suicide attempts. Especially in a situation like hers. When Patrick asked what the last part meant, the doctor said, "From what your wife said, my guess is this isn't her first encounter with the mental health system."

He nodded. "She went to a therapist, but didn't feel it helped."

"I'm talking about as an inpatient. Do you know of any previous hospitalizations?"

"No. Absolutely not. And I've known her for twelve years."

"Perhaps when she was younger? In college? Before?"

Patrick wanted to say this was impossible, too, but he couldn't. He had no way to know if this was another thing she'd lied to him about. "I don't see how this is relevant," he insisted. "She's depressed because her twin brother committed suicide."

Dr. Samuels got out his notes. "Her brother Billy?" Patrick

nodded, and the doctor said, "The one who got shot when she was fifteen?"

He felt his throat constricting, but he managed, "Her brother died barely a month ago. I think whatever you gave my wife to wake her up has left her very confused."

"That's possible," Samuels said mildly. "She did say several times that she'd 'lost the plot.' Is that her way of saying she feels disoriented?"

Patrick said yes before he realized he honestly didn't know what Lila meant by that phrase. She'd been using it for years, but not often, and usually after she'd spent time talking to her brother. He'd always assumed it was one of Billy's idiosyncratic expressions that needlessly complicated the situation. Whereas most people would say they couldn't remember something, only Billy would say he'd "lost the plot." Was that what it meant, that Lila couldn't remember? Or did it mean she was confused?

"She's an English professor," Patrick said, looking at the psychiatrist. "She tends to think in terms of plots and stories."

"Ah, I see," Dr. Samuels said, though what he saw Patrick couldn't say. He didn't understand himself why he'd shared that. He had no idea what relevance it had.

Finally, the doctor stood up. He told Patrick to wait there and they would come get him after they ran a few more tests and were ready to move Lila to the psychiatric unit. "It won't be too long," Samuels said before walking away.

Patrick closed his eyes, desperate to relax, but his mind kept circling back through all the horrors of last night: the moment he realized his wife had overdosed, the terrifying ride in the ambulance, the life-and-death struggle he'd just witnessed in the ER. The guilt he felt for not being there for Lila was overwhelming, but the more he recoiled from what he'd seen, the more he couldn't deny that he was also angry—and not simply with himself, but also with his wife. What she'd tried to do to herself was simply unfathomable to him. Right now, in this very hospital, there were hundreds of people struggling to get well, desperate to extend their lives another year or even another week. Innocent people who would have done absolutely anything for a chance at the life Lila wanted to throw away.

That his own mother had been one of those people was not lost on him. It seemed both ironic and sad that the biggest reason his mother had wanted to live was to meet Patrick's wife and hold his children, her grandchildren.

He opened his eyes when someone came into the waiting room. The policeman was about Patrick's age, but at least a hundred pounds heavier and several inches taller; he looked immense staring down at Patrick. When the officer said he needed to question him, Patrick assumed he wanted to know about Lila's suicide attempt, and he asked if he could call the guy later. "I'm really not up to talking about it right now."

"I'm sorry, but this can't wait." He introduced himself. His name was Officer Curran. He looked around the waiting room, which was deserted at this early hour. Only the TV in the corner was still going, showing some kind of infomercial. "I need to know if you're aware of any problems with your niece's home life."

"You mean because she ran away?" Patrick looked at the ER doors through which Samuels had disappeared. It had been almost an hour. Maybe the doc had forgotten about him? "I really don't see the urgency. "

"She's made some allegations." Curran eased himself down in the blue plastic chair next to Patrick. "I'm hoping you have information that could help our investigation."

"Her father was arrested for child abuse, is that what you mean? But as he died a month ago, I see no point in finishing the investigation into—"

"What do you know about Kyle Eaton?"

"Who?" Patrick said, but then he remembered. Ashley's new boyfriend. "I've never met him."

"Anything you've heard about the guy? You never know what could be important."

He hesitated, but he shared with Curran that he didn't think Ashley knew her boyfriend very well, since she'd found him on a website that connected old high school friends. "But that's really it. I'm sorry."

Curran wrote something down; then he asked if Patrick had any reason to think Ashley would look the other way if her child were being harmed. When Patrick didn't answer, the officer said, "Let me put this as plainly as I can. Do you have any reason to believe she's an unfit mother?"

A month ago, the answer would have been an unequivocal no. Even now, if he hadn't felt angry with Lila—and desperate to find some way out of this feeling—he would have kept his mouth closed. But instead, he found himself telling Curran the things Lila had been ranting about for the last month as though they were facts. That Ashley was an alcoholic. That Ashley was prone to self-mutilating behavior, including cutting her arms and thighs. That Ashley had beaten Pearl when the little girl was just a baby.

He might have felt nervous that he was violating his principles about truth and evidence if he hadn't felt more furious with Ashley with each revelation. After all, she'd started this, hadn't she? She had Billy arrested after she began her online relationship with Kyle Eaton, maybe even because of that relationship. She was responsible for destroying her family and possibly Patrick's as well.

Whatever minor qualms he had about what he'd said disappeared when the policeman said that Ashley's boyfriend was being investigated for physically assaulting Pearl. Then he remembered what Lila told him about Ashley being unable to live without a man, any man, and he repeated this, too. He also shared his own reaction that he was shocked Ashley had let a virtual stranger move in with her children.

Finally, the officer was satisfied that Patrick had told him everything he knew. He said he appreciated the cooperation, adding, "I hope your wife gets better."

"Thank you."

Curran stood up. "Your niece told us what your wife has been through since her brother passed. It sounds like she's had a tough time."

When the man walked away, it was 9:47. Patrick asked the front desk clerk how much longer it would be before Lila was moved. He desperately wanted to get Lila settled so he could head home and get a few hours of sleep. He was so tired his eyes were burning and simply lifting his arm was like lifting a fifty-pound weight. If only he could sleep, maybe he could face up to everything that had happened—and figure out what to do next.

CHAPTER FOURTEEN

Anyone but Billy would have called it a string of bad luck and that's how Ashley saw it, though at some point she stopped trying to convince her husband, knowing he'd just look at her like she was a moron. He'd told her a hundred times that it was her prerogative not to examine her life. Then he'd quote some dead guy named Socrates to explain why he wouldn't do the same: "The unexamined life is not worth living."

Well, the examined life was sure as hell not worth living, either, at least not the way Billy did it. Yeah, he put everything into a pattern and he threw in a bunch of fancy quotes from books to make it sound better, but the upshot was as simple as it was shitty: her cancer, his job loss, both car accidents, even Pearl's problems at school—it was all because of the Cole curse. They weren't just dealing with a lot of rotten crap; they were doomed.

Later, she would see it as kind of pathetic, how hard she tried to cheer him up even though most of the bad stuff happened to her. She was the one who got cancer, after all. She was the one who was rear-ended twice: once down the street, just a fender bender, but once on the highway, leaving her with back pain for months. She was even the one who had to find another school for Pearl, after their daughter's bizarre behavior in kindergarten got her thrown out of the public school.

Even when Billy got laid off, it was Ashley who had to deal with the problem of making ends meet. She went back to work waiting tables and did all the scrimping and saving so they could keep paying their bills and the tuition at Pearl's new Catholic school. After a few months, he got another job that paid better than the one he'd had before, but he wasn't happy about that, either, except he was relieved they could afford to move Pearl from St. Peter's to a private school just for smart kids, where Billy believed she'd always belonged. Just as well, as the nuns were threatening to throw Pearl out, too, since none of their punishments seemed to do a damn thing to change Pearl's attitude problem. That was what they called it. Billy said she was just too smart to sit and act interested when they forced her to listen to some simple-minded book she could have read to herself two years ago.

He turned out to be sort of right. At Pearl's new private school, the teachers never called to complain that she'd thrown her crayons on the floor or told them they were stupid. But she didn't talk much at all at the new school, and that was another thing to worry about. She had no friends in kindergarten and by first grade she never even mentioned the other kids in her class, as though she'd decided it didn't matter who they were or what they thought of her. And she sure wasn't happy, Ashley was positive about that—

except when her father was around. Then she smiled and laughed and played like a normal kid, even if Billy wasn't playing with her. Sometimes Ashley thought Pearl was trying to cheer her father up, which would have made her worry more if she wasn't doing the very same thing. Like mother, like daughter. Every night, she and Pearl sat at the dinner table listening to Billy blather on about something or other that had nothing to do with anything real. At the end of it all, Pearl got a big smile and a pep talk about how smart she was. Ashley's only reward was peace and quiet while she did the dishes.

So why did she keep loving him? As stupid as it sounds, she would let herself forget all about the bad times whenever Billy was in a good mood. Only Billy could turn an ordinary Saturday into a wild adventure, dragging Ashley and Pearl all over the city: down to Penn's Landing to count the ships, over to South Street to look for cool, cheap things for the house, up to the museum to find which painting had the most purple or a head shaped like a triangle or some other funny thing that he'd decided to turn into a contest for her and Pearl, with the winner deciding whether to eat vendor hot dogs or Chinese. After one of these days, Ashley felt like Billy was the smartest, most exciting man she would ever meet in her life. He could also be so kind—sitting up with Pearl when she had nightmares, even if he had to be up early for work; bringing home little gifts for Ashley, like the lavender candles she loved and her favorite painted locket that he bought from a street artist; writing sweet poems for both Ashley and Pearl on their birthdays and Christmas and sometimes for no reason at all other than he'd been thinking about them. The problem was that Ashley could never figure out what changed him from kind and exciting to gloomy and withdrawn, and so she drove herself nuts trying to figure out how to get him to change back.

She really didn't understand how much work it was, being with

Billy, until years later when she went online and started talking to Kyle Eaton, who'd been her very first crush in high school. It shocked her that Kyle not only asked her things like "How is your day going?" but actually seemed interested in her answers. Billy thought small talk like that was an utter waste of time. And time was the one thing they didn't have anymore, as he always said, with that note of fear in his voice that never failed to make Ashley a little afraid, too.

Because she was the only one he shared his darkest stuff with, she figured he had to love her, too, at least a little bit. Pearl was a kid, so naturally he didn't tell her when he "realized," somehow, that he wouldn't live to be forty. But he didn't tell Lila, either. With his twin, he always kept up the bullshit that everything was fine, no matter what they were going through. When he lost his job the day before Lila and her husband Patrick came to dinner, Billy didn't even mention it and insisted on having expensive steaks so Lila wouldn't worry. Too much stress could be bad for her, he said—like it wasn't already bad for *them.*

Whenever Ashley asked him why he treated his sister like this, he didn't get mad; if anything, he was more patient than usual as he explained how determined he was that Lila escape the Cole destiny, which was his usual way of talking about the curse. He said the same thing about Pearl, though he worried constantly that their daughter was so close to him that he'd have to work hard to make sure she escaped. Lila was easier, now that she was safely married to an "innocent" man like Patrick.

"She's going to have a good life," Billy would conclude. "It's the one thing I can give her after what we went through."

Usually Ashley let it drop here, but one time she couldn't resist asking, "But why do you have to give her anything? Why are you always so damn protective of Lila?"

They were sitting on the front porch: Ashley on the swing, Billy on the steps, facing away from her. It was just getting dark, but it was a school night and Pearl was already in bed. Ashley was hoping Billy would open up about the rotten childhood he'd hinted at but never explained. She'd figured out that his stepfather was some kind of bastard, but she honestly didn't know why that was such a big deal. She'd known a lot of people who had asshole stepfathers or stepmothers. It sucked, but it didn't mean the rest of their lives were doomed.

When he didn't answer, Ashley said, "She's your sister, not your daughter. Hell, you're even the same age."

"That's true if you use the most simplistic metric of chronological age."

"And what metric do you use?" She knew what he meant by metric: not the metric system like they taught kids in school, but just a way of measuring something. He used this word all the time.

"Mental age. And before you ask, I don't mean that Lila has a lower IQ. I think IQ is meaningless, because—"

"I know." She couldn't help interrupting, anything to avoid hearing his rant about this again. "So what do you mean?"

"She's had fewer life experiences than I have." He paused. "In a very real sense, she's always been younger."

"Well, how about me?" Ashley was staring at him, willing him to turn around and look at her. "I've had a lot of experiences, so I guess we're kind of the same."

She was desperate, as usual, to prove a connection with him. This must have been why she didn't pay attention to the obvious fact that Lila and Billy had grown up in the same house, with the same mother and stepfather, so how could Lila *always* have been younger, experience-wise?

When he said, "Maybe that's true," she was beaming. Until he continued, "But if it is, that's another reason you and I shouldn't have more children. As I've said a hundred times, I know my life is not going to turn out well. As long as you're with me, yours won't, either. We can't put anyone else at risk."

He had said this a hundred times, but this time was different. She'd been waiting for the right moment to tell him that her gynecologist had confirmed what she'd known for weeks. She was pregnant. A high-risk pregnancy, the doctor said, because of her age and her cancer, but he didn't expect any problems. The baby would be born a few weeks after Ashley's thirty-sixth birthday.

When she'd gone off birth control, she hadn't told Billy, which she knew was wrong, but she figured she had plenty of time to deal with it later. The gynecologist said most women who stopped taking pills couldn't get pregnant right away, and her case was trickier, since even if she did get pregnant, she might miscarry before she even knew. But she was eleven weeks pregnant without even any spotting, so everything was okay so far. The doctor would monitor her closely. Worst case, he said, she might have to spend the last part of her pregnancy in bed.

She took a deep breath and told Billy what she'd done. There was no choice; she was already getting thicker around the middle and tired of explaining away her occasional vomiting as "something I ate" or a "touch of flu." Even Pearl knew something was up, because Ashley kept falling asleep right after dinner. She told her daughter that Mommy was just tired from working, but Pearl was too smart to buy that. She knew Ashley had been working for more than a year and recently she'd actually cut her hours down to take Pearl to dancing classes (Ashley's choice) and chess club (Billy's), still hoping the little girl would make a friend. Pearl had asked, "Are you sick?" so many times that Ashley felt horrible for worrying her daughter. It was time to let both her and her father know the wonderful truth.

But when she was finished telling Billy, all he said was, "Fine."

"Fine?" she sputtered. "That's it?"

"Oh, I'm sorry." His tone was clearly sarcastic. "I forgot to add congratulations."

She stood up and moved to the porch steps. "Billy, please." She sat down next to him. "I want another baby so bad. And Pearl will have a little brother or sister."

"If the child doesn't die, she will. If you don't die giving birth to it."

"What a horrible thing to say!"

"No. The horrible thing is what's going to happen." His voice was quiet, hopeless. "The fact that you don't see this is because you still don't understand what I've been telling you for the last two years."

She put her hand on his arm. "But remember what you said before Pearl was born? About us being a happy family?"

"I was quoting Tolstoy: 'Happy families are all alike.' " He looked at the sky, though it was too cloudy to see the moon or any stars. "I wanted that for us, but the universe wouldn't allow it. I've accepted that. I'll never be free of the past."

She didn't know what the past had to do with it, but she was afraid of getting sucked into the bad way he was looking at this. "Maybe this new baby will change our luck. Have you thought of that? Maybe we'll be—"

"Saved?" He laughed harshly. "The baby-as-messiah motif?"

The whole conversation had hurt her, but his laughter was the final straw. "Whether you like it or not," she said, "I'm having this baby. Better get used to it." Then she went into the house and up to their bedroom, where she spent the next hour facedown on the bed, too depressed even to cry.

The next few days were awful, with Billy barely speaking and Pearl working harder than ever to get her father to smile or laugh or at least talk to her about chess or books or something he liked. But on Sunday morning, he woke up and told Ashley he'd decided she was right. Maybe the new baby could be a chance for their family to regain their happiness. "Another shot at redemption," he said. "Why not?" His voice changed the way it always did when he was quoting some dead guy: " 'Remember to the last that while there is life there is hope.' " Then he said, "Charles Dickens," though she hadn't asked.

From that day on, he treated her more gently than he ever had when she was pregnant before: making sure she rested and took her vitamins and ate good food, even going to the doctor with her several times. He said he was "throwing his weight against reality," which she didn't exactly get, but she was glad he was being so nice. Pearl was thrilled that she would have a sister or brother, and she liked the name Ashley picked out, too, after the ultrasound confirmed it was a boy. The little girl would put her mouth up to Ashley's belly and say, "Hi William," at least once a day. It was like they really were a normal family again, and Ashley was sure that another kid was just what they'd needed all along. Three people was too lonely, especially when one of them was moody, like Billy.

It honestly never crossed her mind that something would go wrong. With Pearl, she worried constantly that the baby would be born without all her fingers or toes or even would be stillborn, but with William, she was so sure he was going to be fine that she never even had those weird nightmares that her mom had told her were normal in pregnancy. It was almost like Billy had taken on the worry for both of them, or maybe she was so determined to believe he was wrong that her mind wouldn't even go there. Sure, she tried to stay healthy and do everything right, and she really intended to stay in bed for the last four months, like the doctor said she had to, or she might go into premature labor. It was a pain in the ass, but she would do it. If nothing else, Billy would freak out completely if she didn't. "Don't tempt fate," he said, over and over. He even had Pearl trained to report if Ashley spent too much time standing in the shower or snuck downstairs to the kitchen for a drink or a sandwich.

But it was all sort of sweet, and Ashley wasn't afraid of Billy. He never got mad at her during the pregnancy, and he didn't even get mad when she ruined everything. He told her it wasn't her fault, and she knew he believed it. It was the Cole curse again, "visited on another generation." He sounded as sad and empty as a ghost as he looked through the clear plastic box in the newborn intensive care unit where two-and-a-half-pound William was locked away from them, hooked up to monitors to breathe for him and feed him and keep him alive. "The sins of the father visited on the son."

It was Ashley's sin though, not Billy's, because she had gotten out of bed to pick up Pearl at day camp. She'd tried to call Billy when Pearl got sick, but his foreman said he'd have to page him and it would be a few minutes. When ten minutes went by, she decided to get Pearl herself. The day camp was only a mile and a half away; she could go and be back before Billy called home. She was anxious to get to her daughter, who was throwing up, but yeah, she was also dying to get out of the house. She'd been lying in that bed for a month. She felt like she would go crazy if she didn't get a breath of fresh air.

But the real reason was that she was so sure nothing would go wrong. Billy never blamed her for that, but he did say she was "tragically mistaken" when she kept sobbing that it had been such a perfect summer day. He quoted a passage from some book. The singsong voice he used for the first person talking made the speaker sound as stupid as Ashley had been: "But the past is passed; why moralize upon it? Forget it. See, yon bright sun has forgotten it all, and the blue sea, and the blue sky; these have turned over new leaves."

"Because they have no memory," Billy answered, in his own depressed voice. "Because they are not human."

Her husband never blamed her, but Ashley never stopped blaming herself. Not during the days she waited to hear if William would live or the weeks she waited to take him home. Not during the months she watched him in his crib, knowing his brain hadn't developed right and he might die without the oxygen tank. Not during the year and a half while she waited to find out if his spine and hips would be deformed or his hearing damaged or something else so bad she couldn't even let herself think about it; not during the three years while she charted his progress—so much slower than Pearl's in every way it was heartbreaking—hoping he was only developmentally delayed, but fearing he was permanently retarded.

Their family was doomed; she believed that now. They would never be happy and she would always be guilty for not listening to Billy's warnings. For being too stupid to understand what one moment of carelessness could do to her son.

By the time she found out that William was going to be all right—a little slow compared to the other kids his age, but nothing he couldn't make up in time; no permanent issue except his poor eyesight, which was correctable with glasses, and which might have been a problem even if he hadn't been premature—it was too late for Ashley. Her self-blame had led to a self-hatred that she was always drinking to escape. She didn't go back to work; she let her friends drift away; she wouldn't even talk to her mother or her sisters. Billy had said he knew he was going to die before he was forty; Ashley went to bed most nights hoping she would die before tomorrow, so she wouldn't have to face another day of who she'd become.

At some point, she also had to face the fact that her husband looked down on her for being too weak to live under the curse he'd dealt with his whole life. "Poor Ashley," he would say. His voice was cold as death. "Forget about what your self-destruction is doing to Pearl and William. It's all about you now, isn't it?"

She knew he was right, and she finally made herself go to AA. It helped more than she expected, but it was still a struggle: she would quit drinking for months at a time, then slip up for a weekend, then climb back on the wagon. William was three and a half when she discovered she was pregnant again, an accident, of course, and she vowed she wouldn't touch a drop for the whole nine months. She made it, but only by cutting herself when the fear got too bad. Though the amnio and all the tests showed the baby was okay, she wouldn't let herself believe everything could work out until Maisie was born, perfectly normal; then she was so grateful she started attending Catholic church for the first time since she was a teenager. She went alone, early in the morning while Billy and the kids were still asleep, letting them think she was meeting a friend for coffee, wishing she didn't have to lie, but afraid to start an argument with Billy. He believed in God, but he always said religion was the "opiate of the masses." She had no idea he was quoting Karl Marx, but she knew he was wrong. The church was the place you went to fight off stuff like curses and destiny and doom. And she was fighting for all of them—and praying she would have the strength to be a good mother.

By the time Billy left, she felt like she was becoming the kind of mom her kids deserved. Yeah, it was hard for them to deal with the breakup of their parents, but she'd finally decided Billy was right when he used to insist that the Cole curse would only affect her and the kids if they were with him. He'd gotten crazier and crazier over the years, ranting to Pearl and William the way he used to do with Lila, for hours, on all his favorite subjects: the dumbing down of America, the terrible school system, the evils of watching TV, the corrupt government that relied on ignorant voters to keep power. But the really weird thing was how he was always telling stories to Pearl or William about something or other that had happened when they were younger *that never happened.* His stories sounded so real, that was the weirdest part. Ashley caught herself more than once almost believing Billy's bullshit; no wonder the kids had trouble figuring it out. When he told Pearl that, at six years old, she'd not only claimed she wanted to live in New York but kept a journal with pictures and stuff she'd written about the city, Pearl spent hours in the basement looking for a journal that didn't exist. When he told William that when he was only three, he could already add dozens of numbers in his head, William beamed, then switched to sheepish embarrassment as he admitted he could only do sixteen numbers now. "That happens," Billy said sadly. "If a child's natural ability isn't fostered in school, it atrophies a little. But don't worry, your innate brain power hasn't changed. Once we get you in the right school, you'll be living up to your potential."

They didn't have the money for a private school and Billy knew it. For a few minutes, Ashley felt bad, thinking they were letting their son down, but then she remembered the truth that William could barely speak when he was three. Pearl had never mentioned she wanted to live in New York until she was a teenager. And Pearl's first word had been "daddy," not "problematic," like Billy claimed in another long story about his daughter's amazing vocabulary. William had torn apart the Rubik's Cube he'd gotten for his fifth birthday—after trying to solve it for about a minute—and Billy's "memory" of how proud he was that day was nothing but another sign that he was going over the edge.

Even visiting his father turned out to be dangerous for William. Ashley had been shocked by the things Billy was forcing that child to do, but she'd stepped up and protected her son when it mattered. Sure, she felt bad for Billy, but what choice did she have? Her husband was losing it. The police officer told her something even worse was probably coming, and he turned out to be right. No matter how bad she felt when Billy went berserk and got himself killed—and God, the pain was damn near unbearable—she tried to be a good mother and focus on comforting her kids.

Sometimes she wondered if she'd made a mistake, letting Kyle live with them so soon after Billy moved out, but she hoped Kyle would actually make things better. The poor kids had never known a normal life with parents who did things for fun, like bowling and baseball games. Kyle could help her teach the kids that everyday stuff was all right. You didn't have to be reading constantly like Pearl or listening to classical music night and day like William to have a good time. Most important, they didn't have to please their father anymore. They could goof off and watch TV and Kyle would never say they were "wasting their minds." Kyle would never tell them what to do, period—that was part of the deal before Ashley told him he could move in with them. She didn't want any man thinking he had the right to discipline her kids.

Of course, Kyle was also sweet to her, and that was a big part of the reason she was glad he'd come to Pennsylvania. She was forty-four years old and she'd never had a guy really care what she had to say. It was freaky at first, but now she wondered how she'd ever put up with any guy who didn't.

On the Friday that turned out to be their last date, she told Kyle a little more about her life with Billy, the way she always did, and he listened and sympathized, as usual. When she said it was time to change the topic, he said okay, but then he shook his head. "You've had some real shit luck. That's one thing I know for sure."

He was a little drunk, but Ashley had stuck to ginger ale all night. Still, she laughed like she was tipsy and he said, "What's so funny?"

"Nothing," she said, and put her arm around him. He was a little heavy, but she liked that. He felt like a big, warm bear. She'd told him about the curse, but she didn't expect him or anyone to understand why "shit luck" to describe her life would feel like such a relief to her.

"Well, it's over now," he said, grinning. "Stick with me, baby, and it'll be smooth sailing from here on out."

She smiled, though she didn't believe it would all be smooth sailing. Bad things happened to everybody, like her mom always said. But sure, she felt like she was due some good luck for a change. Maybe she'd wake up tomorrow and William would be talking again. Pearl would smile at her like she used to. Hell, come to think of it, that was all she really wanted right now anyway. The other thing she'd always hoped for—that Billy would change, that Billy would stop being crazy, that Billy would love her the way she'd never stopped loving him—well, there was no point in thinking about that anymore. Now it was all about her kids. If only they were okay again, she'd be sitting on that pile of good luck she'd been waiting for for years.

CHAPTER FIFTEEN

In Lila's dreams, Billy told her how the story had to end. The two of them would be running through narrow corridors or up an unending flight of stairs or across a field that seemed to stretch out as far as the sky, trying to escape something horrible that Lila could never see. Billy saw it, though, and he would pull Lila's arm until it ached to get her to move faster, to hurry before it destroyed them. "We have to win," he would say, panting and out of breath. "It's the only way any of this makes sense."

Lila always woke up before they got away. This was true when she was a teenager, and it was still true through all the years she'd had these running dreams. It was her most common kind of dream, and sometimes the sole dream she'd had—or at least that she'd remembered the next morning—for months and months. She used to tell Patrick she wasn't the dreaming type. She wondered if she simply read so much that her imagination didn't need the usual nightly exercise.

After Billy died, she dreamed more, but still far less than she would in the hospital—if dreaming was even the correct word for what was happening to her. Lila thought so, but she wasn't aware that the doctors had given her heavy doses of drugs when they couldn't get her to stop thrashing and screaming at them to let her go. She couldn't know that the drugs were powerful enough to calm and subdue her, but not powerful enough to keep her asleep for very long. All she knew was that every time she gave up struggling and closed her eyes, she found her brother. This was enough to keep her lying still, hour after hour.

In one dream, she and Billy were sitting on cardboard boxes in a moldy basement, with spiderwebs draping every lightbulb and windowsill. He was holding her shoulders, looking right into her eyes, telling her that their mother wasn't real. "What you see is what she's become because of him. She's weak, Lila. She doesn't mean to do this." The next minute—or the next dream?—they were in the bright white kitchen, sitting on wooden stools, eating pretzels, and Lila heard her stepfather whistling "Fly Me to the Moon." "I'm not hungry," she said, dropping a handful of pretzels back in the bag. But it was too late; she saw Harold's shadow as he rounded the corner, holding that silver golf club.

Then she was outside in the woods behind their house, and she had a chess piece clutched in her fist. Billy was trying to talk her into giving it to him. "It will be worse if you wait." Lila was sitting on a rock; Billy was standing above her. The sun made his head look like it was ringed by a halo. "It'll be all right. I'll convince her you're sorry."

She'd just handed over the ivory chess piece—and seen Billy

smile—when she came out of the dream to hear Patrick asking how this could possibly help his wife. He sounded angry, or was it guilty? "Christ, she's done nothing but lie in bed at home for weeks. How is this any different?"

Another man said something long-winded that Lila didn't catch, though she heard the words "agitation" and "antidepressants" and sleepily wondered if it was possible that every word he'd said had started with "a." Then she heard Billy talking again.

"Every story needs a villain."

They were in the basement—so many of the dreams took place in the basement or outside in the woods, even Lila's dreaming mind noticed this and vaguely wondered why. Billy was explaining some book to her. Or was it a story he'd written? He was always writing stories. Lila was so jealous of his talent, even though she knew he wrote most of them for her, to keep her from being sad.

"Think about it," Billy continued. "The villain shows the amount of good in everyone else. They are judged by how close or far they are from him."

She nodded but didn't say anything. She was eating the most delicious apple that Billy had brought down to her.

"What else do you want?" he said. "Mom just went to the store."

Before Lila could answer, she heard her mother calling for Billy.

"I'll come back later," he said.

"No." Lila reached to grab her brother's arm, but he was already standing. She could feel tears welling in her eyes as he walked slowly up the stairs. Then she climbed up on the table by the basement window, maneuvered herself through the narrow opening, and ran into the woods, still choking back tears. There she met a woman in a white bridal gown, and Lila wondered who would get married in this forlorn place. "It's almost over," the woman said, but her voice was strange, like it was coming from the radio. "You'll know when it's time." Then the woman ascended to the sky, like Genevieve, Lila's patron saint—or was it only the Virgin Mary who had ascended?

And indeed there will be time, Lila thought, waking up when a nurse walked into the room. It was a line from a T. S. Eliot poem. She continued reciting the poem in her mind until it finally hit her that she'd really had a patron saint named Genevieve. That part was true. They'd been Catholic before her mother remarried. How could she have forgotten that?

She fell asleep again and saw a man ice-skating, but when she got closer, she realized it wasn't Billy or her stepfather; it was Patrick. Patrick, who'd never skated in his life as far as she knew, was jumping in the air and spinning to a landing, like the skaters in the Olympics. Every time he came close, she asked him, "How did you learn this?" but all he would do was wink and smile. He wasn't the kind of guy to wink in real life, but Lila forgot that and thought he was so much more himself.

"Minor characters matter," Billy told her.

"Patrick isn't minor," she mumbled, and then she realized Billy couldn't hear her. He was still talking about *Huckleberry Finn.* "You can't understand Huck without seeing him with all the people he meets."

Was she still asleep? This seemed like a memory, not a dream. She and her brother really had read *Huck Finn* at least a half dozen times. Billy insisted, because he said this book would be a variation of their own plot. The reasons were obvious: Huck had to escape his cruel father. "But stepfather is so much more believable," Billy said harshly. "Aren't we lucky to have it work out like that? . . . Of course, the big question has to be why. In Huck's case, his father is an alcoholic. That's the nineteenth century for you: bad parents are either drunk or poor or both. In the twentieth century, we use psychology, but to me the truly modern answer is no one knows. Because there are alcoholics who aren't assholes, right? There are abused children who don't abuse their kids. So we might as well call it old-fashioned evil as long as we understand that evil means nothing more than the howling emptiness of a soul with nothing to give."

She thought she must be awake, when suddenly they were running up a hill and Billy was laughing and calling himself "Man of Steel." They were young, maybe six or seven. Lila wanted a superhero name, too, and she picked "Grass Girl." When Billy asked her what Grass Girl did, she said, "She can roll down hills faster than anyone." It was the one thing she was better at than her brother: rolling down hills. She loved doing it, too, even though she always got dandelions and puffballs caught in her long hair.

Then the scene changed again. It was dark outside and her mother was crying loudly in another room, while Lila was slapping herself in the face. Billy was crying, too, but he walked over and grabbed Lila's hands. "You didn't do it."

"I'm sorry," Lila said. Her voice was still a child's, like Grass Girl's. But nothing about her was a child anymore. Even her room looked wrong to her now, with the pink bed covered with stuffed animals and the little white bookshelf where her dolls sat in a neat little row. The bears and elephants and dolls all looked at her as though they were waiting for her to come back and play with them. She picked up one of the dolls and ripped its head off and said, "No!"

It was the night her father died; Lila opened her eyes and was suddenly sure of that. Except Billy had never told her she'd destroyed all her dolls, but she felt sure of that, too. Why had he never talked about that night?

She wanted to keep thinking about what this meant, but she couldn't. She was already feeling so drowsy that she had to close her eyes.

The next thing she knew, they were in church; her mother was with a man but he didn't look like Harold. He was a short, bald guy with a sweet smile, and Lila liked him because he always gave her pennies. "A little girl can never know when she'll need to make a wish."

Lila was holding Billy's hand as they walked out of the pew. Her mother smiled at the unnamed guy and whispered, "Don't my babies look adorable?"

Billy's hand was sweating. They were never allowed to touch each other in front of their mother, but she'd told them this time was different. This time she wanted them to hold hands and act like "normal" children. "Do you think you can manage that?" their mother had said, looking straight at Lila. "It should be easy enough, assuming you're not still trying to ruin my life."

A statue of the Virgin Mary was above them, weeping. The prayer raced across Lila's mind as if it were too frightened to pause long enough to become words: *HolyMaryMotherOfGodPray-ForUsSinnersNowAndAtTheHourOfOurDeathAmen.*

At the door of the church, a priest said to Lila, "We were worried about you." He smiled. "We all prayed you'd recover, and look, here you are."

She felt her face turning red. What was wrong with her that she didn't know what he was talking about?

"You're not crazy." How many times had Billy told her that? He used to say it all the time; she was sure. But the voice speaking now was her own. She'd woken herself up, telling herself she wasn't crazy. Which struck her as more than a little funny, given where she was. She couldn't laugh, though. Her mouth felt as dry as if she'd been eating dust.

Then she was yelling, "Billy, Billy," and he was downstairs with her, holding her in his skinny child's arms. She told him about the man in the shiny silver truck who was coming to kill her. "It's not real," he said, shivering. It was always cold in the winter down here, despite the white cube with the hot red face that Lila was never supposed to touch.

A space heater, she thought now. It was right by the cot where she slept whenever she was being punished.

"You're okay." He sounded sleepy, but he said, "Do you need to hear a story?" She stammered out yes, and he said, "Once upon a time, there was a blond-haired baby who toddled off and got lost in a land of ugly trolls . . ."

She woke up shaking, as though the cold in her dream had followed her into the hospital. All at once, she realized she knew that story about the baby and the trolls. She remembered when Billy used to call her Baby Lila. She used to get so mad at him about that.

She managed to stay awake for several minutes this time, thinking. They were probably only ten when Billy came up with the story—no wonder the symbolism was so obvious. She was the baby, and her mother and stepfather were the trolls. Billy himself wasn't in the story. He was just the one who'd created it.

The cot was real, too. She could see it so clearly, in the middle of the basement, surrounded by beige garment bags that looked like an army of faceless monsters when she was a child. She had her own room, but she was always being sent to the basement. Maybe Billy was, too? She couldn't remember.

Lila fell asleep wondering why Billy was always comforting her and she was never comforting him. Maybe that was why her next dream was of a fight they'd had. They were in the woods and she was yelling, "Shut up! Shut up!"

She was older then, thirteen or so; it was after the growth spurt that left her taller than Billy. She didn't have a coat on, but it wasn't warm. The leaves were turning; the forest looked like an explosion of red and yellow.

"What do you want me to say?" His brown curls looked messy in the wind. "You know it never happens when they aren't here. How could she be right about—"

"I don't believe you." She was still yelling. "I'm going in. I'll ask her myself."

"Okay, but you know what will—"

Then she was running past the tree house her father built and down the hill, into the house. Her mother was home, for a change. Lila hadn't seen her in what felt like weeks.

"Look who's here," her mother said. She was standing in the kitchen, but it didn't look anything like the kitchen had looked before. It was all brand-new—again? Even the toaster was so shiny, reflected in the sun, that Lila blinked when she glanced at it.

She was afraid to speak. She'd told Billy she was going to ask her mother, but now that she was here, she couldn't do it.

"Are you feeling better now?" her mother said. Her arms were crossed. The look on her face was so different than Lila remembered. If she remembered her mother's expressions, which she wasn't sure of at all.

She crossed her own arms, feigning defiance. "I want to play chess."

"Oh, well, come on then," her mother said, laughing. "Has your brother been coaching you?"

"No," Lila said, because it was true; she and Billy never played chess. He hated chess, even though he played with their mother constantly.

But didn't he teach his children chess? Lila thought, and wondered again if she was awake. If she was awake, she should be able to speak. But when she opened her mouth to say her husband's name, it got swallowed up in the dream and came out as, "Where?"

"You poor thing, you haven't even seen the new living room, have you?" Her mother crooked her finger and led Lila down a hall into what had been the guest room. Now a wall was missing and the living room was enormous. One corner was dedicated to her mother's passion: chess. Along the wall were all the trophies her mother had won playing the game.

The chessboard was new and so were the ivory pieces. Lila gasped at how beautiful it was, and her mother smiled. "I'm glad you have the aesthetic sense to appreciate this. I consider that a good sign, if a relatively minor one."

After she sat down, her mother said, "Are you sure you're up to this?"

"I'm fine," Lila said, though she didn't feel fine. She felt like screaming. She knew she would lose again, and nothing would change. But she was smart, too, wasn't she? Billy always said she was. He said there was nothing wrong with her, that Harold had made it all up.

But Billy was wrong. By the ninth move, she'd lost her queen. Her mother made that "tsk, tsk" sound that meant the game was over.

Lila felt tears standing in her eyes. They were so salty they burned, and she remembered again that she was dying of thirst.

"Why am I like this?" Lila finally said. Her mother was sitting back, looking at her as though examining a vaguely boring sculpture. But at least Lila had asked the question Billy kept refusing to answer. "Like what?" he always said, as though the question made no sense.

"I assure you, I don't know. They told me you would grow out of it." Her mother sounded like she was swallowing a laugh, but Lila wasn't sure. That was the problem. She could never tell what was clearly outside of her and what was only in her head. "I wish you had; then I wouldn't have to keep punishing you."

She stood up to go back to Billy, but then she heard herself talking: "I felt a funeral, in my brain, And mourners, to and fro, Kept treading—treading—till it seemed, That sense was breaking through—"

"You're reading Emily Dickinson!" her mother said, clapping, then standing, too. She was so much taller than Lila. Beautiful, tall, and brilliant. Billy said she could have married any man in the world, but instead she picked that bastard Harold. They met during one of her many trips, to cities all around the country, for chess tournaments. She'd never taken Lila on these trips, but she always took Billy. When Lila was younger, she would cry for days, alone in the big house, but now she read from the time she woke up in the morning until she went to bed. She read while she was eating cheese out of the package and running a bath for herself at night. When her brother returned, he would tell her wonderful stories about all the things he'd seen and all the marvelous places they could go when they were grown. They also talked about the books Lila had read, but nothing about what either of them had felt while he was gone. He said as long as they didn't speak of that, it could never become real.

Now Lila nodded, suddenly shy. Had she been trying to impress her mother? She wasn't aware of it, but since she had, she wondered if she should recite the rest of the poem. Maybe her mother would see that—

"I think poetry is a very good idea for you. After all, memorizing is a kind of thinking. A lower kind, perhaps, but still useful for developing your brain and moving away from your instincts."

Her mother was laughing. Lila felt so humiliated that she reached for the chessboard and knocked it over and watched as all the lovely pieces spilled onto the rich gold carpet. She ignored her mother hissing at her to pick it up and shrugged off her mother's promise that she would be punished for this. As she ran up the hill and back to Billy, her mind kept repeating a quote he had given her: "Art still has truth, take refuge there."

Then she woke up in the hospital, and the nurse was changing her IV bag, thank God. If only she could ask for a drink of water, but her voice wouldn't cooperate.

She watched the nurse, thinking about Billy's quote. It was from Matthew Arnold, a nineteenth-century writer, who claimed that this was what the German poet Goethe had believed. The first time Billy told her this she was young, maybe eleven or twelve? He said that reading not only offered truth but was *safe.* Nothing in her books would ever hurt her, Billy promised. And years later, when she was a professor, she kept Billy's quote on her desk, along with one of her own by Melville: "Those whom books will hurt will not be proof against events. Events, not books, should be forbid."

She'd never cared that she couldn't remember most of her real life before the age of sixteen. It didn't matter because she could remember all the stories and poems. In college and grad school, her professors said she had an extraordinary recall for quotes and scenes and characters.

But the dream was so disturbing. She was absolutely certain that something had been wrong with her when she was a child. She could feel the familiar sense of being profoundly flawed. She could also feel Billy throwing himself against this with all his childish force, as though his life depended on saving Lila from knowing whatever *this* was.

Then she was sitting in her bedroom, at the white vanity desk with the mirror she hated. She was looking at Harold, who was standing in the doorway. He was a giant man with huge shoulders and what Billy called a perpetual sneer.

He said, "Planning to grace us with your presence at dinner tonight?"

Lila was trying to stop eating. A girl in one of her books said it was easy to do. The girl had done it to lose weight, but Lila liked it because it made it hard to sleep. She needed to stay awake and focus her mind to prove to her mother that she could go to school, too, like Billy. And if she didn't sleep, she wouldn't have so many nightmares.

"You know you'll end up in the hospital if you keep going with this," Harold said. "Do you want to put your mother through that after everything else?"

Lila stood to go downstairs, as Harold knew she would. He was always threatening to put her in a hospital, and though her mother had resisted so far, Lila was terrified that someday Harold would win, and she would be taken away from her brother for good.

Billy was already sitting at the table, reading Kafka. He nodded his head very slightly—and Lila knew he was signaling her that it was starting again.

Her stomach tightened, but she forced herself to eat a little steak and asparagus. She nibbled on the crust of bread. And she tried to focus her mind on the most recent poem she'd memorized, like Billy told her to, instead of on what her mother and Harold were saying. But she still heard enough of it to make her feel like a dirty, abnormal girl.

"Lila hasn't had a fit all week," her mother was saying. "It's been positively calm around here."

Whose woods these are I think I know, his house is in the village though, he will not see me stopping here, to watch his woods fill up with snow.

"That must be a new record for her," Harold said, but he didn't look like he'd looked upstairs. He seemed smaller and younger, and he'd even grown a beard. She was so confused, but she knew it had to be Harold because of his sneering tone. He was holding his fork up, emphasizing his point with a jab at the air. "Although she still managed to cause trouble. She seems to have a talent for that."

Lila knew what he was referring to. A few days before, she'd been helping Billy rehearse his part in the high school play, *My Fair Lady.* They were doing the scene where Higgins kisses Eliza Doolittle, a scene they'd done a dozen times without acting out that part, but this time Lila impulsively leaned over and kissed her brother on the lips. It was a horribly wrong thing to do, and Lila knew it even before she realized her mother had walked into the room. She wanted to apologize like Billy told her to do, but when the time came, her mouth refused to cooperate and Harold had beaten her on the legs. Only ten strokes from his belt, and she didn't have many bruises, but still, why hadn't she said she was sorry? She was so stubborn. It was one of many things she disliked about herself.

My little horse must think it queer, to stop without a farmhouse near, between the woods and frozen lake, the darkest evening of the year.

"It's really quite understandable," her mother said. She sounded surprisingly kind. "One of the problems with Lila is that she's not a thinker. She uses her body to express herself, unlike the rest of us."

Lila had heard this so many times, but it always upset her. Billy had warned her repeatedly that it would only get worse if she defended herself, but each and every stupid time, she blurted out something that annoyed Harold. Unfortunately, this time was no exception. The beautiful Robert Frost poem had disappeared; in its place was her own loud voice. She was always too loud at the dinner table. "I wouldn't call hitting someone with a belt using your mind. I would call it barbaric!"

"Very clever." Her stepfather tilted his head in her direction; his mouth was moving, but the voice sounded like her mother's. "I suppose you would have us reason with a barbarian, too? Say if we encountered Attila the Hun?"

"I'm not Attila the Hun."

"Did I say you were? Stick to the argument."

"No," she stammered, looking down at her plate of uneaten food. Both Harold and her mother believed in using "logic" at all times. Billy never screwed it up, but Lila did constantly.

Harold took a drink of his scotch. "The incest taboo has been around for centuries. I think it's safe to say that only a barbarian wouldn't understand that and comply."

"Come on," Billy said mildly. "It was an innocent—"

"Though that, too, is probably understandable," Lila's mother said to Harold. "The two of them have been together since they were in the womb. Perhaps it's natural that she desires him. The real question is how to teach her to act from what she knows to be right rather than her instincts." She was looking at her husband. "I promise I don't know the answer to that."

This isn't a dream, Lila thought. She could see herself. You never see yourself in dreams.

She tried to think about Patrick, but her face was on fire. She was that girl again, the one who had to listen to a litany of her faults whenever Harold returned. Since he was an executive at an international bank, his job required him to travel all over the world, but he always came home eventually. And when he did, he would invariably have to assess Lila's development. The older she got, the more Harold and her mother felt like she was a danger to Billy. They never said it that way, but they always looked at Lila when they were talking about this embarrassing "incest taboo" topic. As though they could see things inside her that she couldn't see.

And now that she'd kissed Billy, she felt condemned and so guilty. She did love her brother, but she didn't really know any other boys because she was always at home. Yet shouldn't she have a crush on someone, if she was a normal girl? What was wrong with her that she had sort of liked kissing her twin?

Billy had said that kiss had meant nothing. He said only a

pervert like Harold would think it did, but Billy couldn't see inside of Lila. He didn't even know about the "moral assessments" with Harold and her mother. Lila was afraid to tell, because her brother already hated Harold so much that he told Lila someday he would kill him.

She had to be awake now; she could see her psych ward room. Maybe she had told the nurse she was thirsty, because there was a cup of water by her bed, and she reached for it and drank it down in one gulp. It helped a little, but she still felt dry and shaky, like she was recovering from the flu.

She lay in her bed, looking out the window at the wispy clouds floating across the sky, a beautiful spring day. She disliked this place, but it wasn't as bad as the other one. And there had been another one; she was suddenly and absolutely sure about this. She even knew the name of the other place: the Westwood Psychiatric Hospital.

She wasn't there very long, maybe a few weeks, but it felt like a year. By the time he came to save her, she was disoriented and half-crazy with grief.

Of all the things Lila remembered—asleep, awake, or somewhere in between—this was the one that made her cry: Billy, appearing out of nowhere, like an answered prayer, the proof of a merciful God. He had money and train tickets and he said he was taking her home. He also said their mother had left them for good, finally.

The attendants were distracted by another screaming girl. Billy was able to lead Lila out of the hospital yard without anyone trying to stop them. They were already down the hill and running up toward the train station when she thought to ask about Harold.

Billy seemed surprised by the question, but he didn't flinch when he answered. "He won't be a problem for us anymore. He's dead, Lila. I shot him."

"When?"

"It's not important now." He took her hand as they rushed to catch the train that was already there, as though it were waiting just for them. "This is the end of that story. Now begins the new era, into the world I always promised you, where we write our own lives."

CHAPTER SIXTEEN

When William found out they weren't going home, he smiled to let the social worker know he was glad. She said, "Are you afraid of your mom's boyfriend?" and he nodded, like Pearl had told him to do. It wasn't exactly a lie 'cause he was very afraid of seeing Kyle and having to do the last Challenge. Pearl said if everything went as she planned, they'd never have to see Kyle again. He hoped she was right about that.

They were in a police department, which he didn't like, but Pearl said they wouldn't be here for long. They'd already had to spend the night on cots in a little room with a coffee machine and William had woken up like a hundred times, whenever a police officer came in to get coffee. The social worker had talked to them early in the morning, and since then, they'd been stuck sitting on a wooden bench. At first, Pearl was really happy 'cause the social worker said Aunt Lila wasn't going to die, she'd just have to stay in the hospital for a while. William was happy about that, too, but after a while, they both got so bored from sitting there that they stopped talking about Aunt Lila or anything. Pearl was half-asleep and William was multiplying numbers in his head when their mom showed up.

The social worker was walking with her, but their mom broke out running when she saw them and grabbed them in her arms.

"My babies," she said, and she was crying, which made William feel so bad for her. He patted her back the way she always patted his when he cried, but he didn't say anything. Pearl had already told him, last night, to go back to the not-speaking thing. "Just until I work this out," she said. Since he wasn't sure what she was working out, he was too confused to know what to say anyway.

His sister pulled away from Mommy and sat back with her arms crossed. "I don't want to talk to you."

"Sweetie, please—"

"You always take his side about everything. You believe him when he says he's home all day or he isn't drinking or he cleaned up the house, when it was really me. You always take his word over mine."

"Once I get you home, I'll make it up—"

The social worker put her hand on their mother's shoulder. "We're jumping the gun a bit. As I said, this meeting is to give you a chance to talk to your daughter and have us all explore together what the next step will be."

Whatever they were going to talk about didn't include William. They got up and walked into a room with a glass door, after telling William to stay on the bench where the secretary would be looking out for him.

The secretary asked if he wanted a hard candy and he took one. It smelled like furniture polish. He sucked as slowly as possible, but his candy was long gone AND he'd had three drinks from the water fountain AND he'd done a hundred and twenty-seven multiplications before his mom and sister came out. The social worker sat down next to him first. She said his mommy and Pearl both thought it would be a good idea if he stayed at his grandma's for a while. "How do you feel about that?"

He smiled as big as he could to let her know it sounded perfect to him. Aunt Trish lived with Grandma. He could play with her all day instead of going to school.

But then as he was listening to them talk, he realized something was wrong. The social worker said it was an unusual situation, since they didn't know their grandmother, but as the state's policy was to look for kinship foster care possibilities first, and their mother was in favor of it, they would stay there while the home study was being done. Of course, they would have to be monitored. Someone from CPS would be checking on them every few days.

William noticed Pearl was staring at him, warning him not to say anything. So he didn't, even though he was totally confused. A few minutes later, when the social worker took Mommy back in the glass room, his sister whispered, "I took Dad's mother's phone number before we left and I called her this morning. Trust me, if we can't be with Aunt Lila, this is where we want to go."

His mouth dropped open. Daddy had told them many times that his mom and dad were dead.

"She wants to see us," Pearl went on, "that's obvious, since she was the one who called Mom and persuaded her to let us stay there. She even said she'd pay for Mom to hire a better lawyer, which was weird, but I think she's just trying to get on Mom's good side." Pearl stopped and messed with the ring she had on a chain around her neck. It was their father's, and the only ring William had ever thought was cool, 'cause it had snakes instead of being some boring circle. His sister had worn it every day since Daddy died. "I knew she had money, but she must be really rich to just do that for somebody she barely knows."

Now he was even more confused. How did his sister know anything about this grandma who was supposed to be dead? But when he asked her, she only said, "I found something in the basement."

"What?"

She didn't answer.

"What?" he repeated, shaking her arm.

She pried herself loose and frowned. "Cool out. It's just something Dad wrote. A long time ago."

"Like a story?" William knew their father had written hundreds of stories. They were all in boxes stacked like blocks along the wall across from the washer and dryer. Daddy had told William that he could read them when he was older, if he wanted. But if he didn't, that was all right, too. "The experience of writing them was enough for me," Daddy said. "Art is its own reward, buddy. You don't need anyone to tell you whether what you've done is good or bad. Remember that."

Pearl answered, "Yes, like a story," but he could tell she didn't mean it. "Now, stop worrying. Kyle has already been arrested. If Mom gets rid of him for good, we'll be home soon enough."

William didn't want to make Pearl mad, but he said it anyway. "I don't like this. I want to go home now."

"Not an option. Even Maisie can't be there until this is over. Mom said she's staying with Libby. The CPS people have to approve her, too."

Libby was Maisie's preschool teacher. He didn't know what CPS was, but it made him nervous, thinking that Maisie was stuck at school night and day now. He wished he could listen to his S-H-O-S-T-A-K-O-V-I-C-H and just go to sleep. He felt like something was stuck in his throat, a piece of that icky candy, and he was trying to think of something else so his tic wouldn't start up, when their mom came back.

"I'm going to get this straightened out as quick as I can," she said. "It's all a horrible mistake." She was sniffing again and William felt so sorry for her, he touched her face. She kissed his hand. "You know I love you guys, right?" She was looking back and forth from Pearl to William. "I would never do anything to hurt you."

William nodded, but Pearl made her face look all blank and stonelike. She lowered her voice so nobody but them could hear. "You already did. You got Dad killed."

Mommy burst into tears and William knew for sure that she'd never meant for that to happen. Even if it was her fault, like Pearl always said, it was a mistake. Like what William had done when he told about the Challenges. He put his arms around Mommy and whispered, "It's okay."

He had to say it. Daddy used to tell him that everybody needs reminders sometimes that are just for encouragement. Like "I Am So Proud of You" or "It's Okay." She smiled through her tears, but she didn't make a big deal about him speaking. It was like she knew it would embarrass him or even get him in trouble with his sister. There wasn't a lot of time anyway, because their new grandma had just arrived to pick them up. She came into the room like she was the school principal and everybody had to stop what they were doing and pay attention to what she said.

William was instantly afraid of her because he was still thinking of her as sort of dead, even though he knew that was dumb. But Pearl let New Grandma hug her. So William had to, too. New Grandma smelled really good, but her face was sharp and pinched and her voice was kind of icky, like the smile Sophie always gave him at school right before she hit him in the stomach with a dodge ball.

She didn't look like Daddy. Not that William could see anyway.

But William didn't look like his mom, either, so maybe that didn't mean anything.

"I've wanted to meet you for a very long time," she said when she let William go. "You're my son's only son."

She was looking at him so hard, like she wanted to have a staring contest, which always made him start blinking like mad. He pushed on the nose of his glasses. His eyes were watering, too. He always lost those staring contests.

"You're eight years old now, aren't you?" she said. "In third grade."

He nodded, but he was swinging his legs, listening to his sneakers squeak on the shiny tile floor.

What happened after that was another meeting of Mom, New Grandma, Pearl, and the social worker behind the glass doors. It took so long that William bunched up his jacket to use as a pillow and fell asleep on the hard wood bench. When he woke up, Mommy was kissing him good-bye and then he and New Grandma and Pearl were going downstairs to get their bags from the room where they'd put them last night, by the front desk of the police station. A few minutes later, they were in New Grandma's big white car: Pearl in the front with her, and William all alone in the back.

He was clearing his throat like crazy. He didn't like this plan of Pearl's at all. And it wasn't just New Grandma and his creepy feeling that she was some kind of ghost; it was the way Pearl sounded talking to her. Like New Grandma was the doorman at Aunt Lila's building, and Pearl was just being fake-friendly, like she was even trying to trick New Grandma or something.

His sister said she'd looked forward to being with Grandma for a long time, which he knew for sure was a big fat lie. It had to be, because if Pearl had known New Grandma wasn't dead before, she would have asked Daddy about it.

"You can talk, too, now if you want," Pearl said, turning around to look at him. She'd been smiling so long it was like her face was stuck that way, but William knew for sure she wasn't really happy. He could tell by her eyes, which looked every bit as mad as the day he'd spilled water on her cell phone. He even felt guilty like he had then, though he hadn't done anything.

"I don't want to," he finally said, and Pearl laughed a fakey laugh.

"He'll warm up to me soon enough," New Grandma said. "Everybody seems to. Your father was the same way. I used to tell him he could charm anyone if he put his mind to it."

"What about Aunt Lila?" Pearl said.

"Oh, Lila was nothing like Billy and me. But that's a story for another time. Right now I want to hear all about you."

She was like every grown-up in the world, asking all these questions, but she didn't ask Pearl if she liked school or what she wanted to be when she grew up, like most grown-ups did. She asked what books she'd read recently, what she thought about the election, a bunch of other stuff that William didn't really understand or care about. Pearl answered each question in a tone so bright it sounded like somebody had stuck a flashlight in her face. He wished she would stop acting this way. He wondered how long it would be before they could get out of this car.

"As I told your mother and the social worker, I own property in the area so you won't have to change schools," New Grandma said. William recognized this highway. It was on the way to their house in Harrisburg. "My grandfather—your great-grandfather—left me this house when he died."

Pearl said something William didn't hear, and New Grandma said, "Yes, it's only about twenty miles from your house. I wondered if your father moved to Harrisburg to be closer to this place. He knew I was living in New Jersey, but the house has always been maintained. He came here several times in the last year, as a matter of fact." She shook her head. "I don't suppose he mentioned any of this to you kids."

"No." Pearl sounded really upset all of a sudden. "But I'm sure he had a good reason."

"Oh, I'm sure he did," New Grandma said.

William didn't say anything; he was staring out the window, watching as they turned down one familiar road after another. Long before New Grandma turned into the enormous driveway, he had a bad feeling about where they were going. But he didn't tell Pearl or New Grandma that he'd been here before. He didn't want anyone to know that he'd seen every part of this creepy place.

It was during one of the last Challenges. His father had brought him here on a Sunday morning so early that he was trying not to yawn as Daddy explained that this Challenge was about learning to escape. Daddy had made a bunch of drawings that showed all the rooms and halls of this big house. William was going to have to figure out a way to get outside from every room. He would have been really scared, except that Daddy said he'd do it all with him. He would never have to be alone in this spooky-looking house.

"Who lives here?" William asked, looking up at the windows reflecting the sun. He was worried that the people would come home and be mad that he and Daddy were using their house like this.

"No one. That's why we're using it, even though you won't ever have to escape from any place that's half as complicated as this. It's good practice, though, and we can take all the time we need."

But when they went inside, it wasn't lonely and deserted like the empty house at the end of their neighborhood. It had rooms full of furniture and even wood by the fireplace.

Now, as he forced himself to walk through the huge front door, he felt like crying, remembering how much better it was to come here with his father than with New Grandma. Pearl seemed excited;

she said, "What a great house" over and over as New Grandma showed them the wall of books in the den and the humongous white kitchen and the view of the woods in back. There were deer in the backyard, just standing around like they had nothing to be afraid of.

But William stayed super quiet. In his head, he was listening to Daddy telling him that he could always escape, even if a house had confusing halls and bedroom doors that locked from the outside and bars on all the windows in the basement. Like this one did, which his father called a "deceptively beautiful prison."

He asked what "deceptively" meant, and Daddy said, "It's all a lie. It looks entirely normal, but the grown-ups who lived here were very bad. The children were like Hansel and Gretel."

William was horrified. The Hansel and Gretel story was his least favorite in the fairy-tale book, because it was so weird. "They tried to eat the kids?"

"Worse," Daddy said. "They tried to destroy their souls."

"Wow," William said. He didn't know exactly where the soul was, but he knew it was the most important thing, since his father always said so. He said, "But the kids won in the end, right?" The kids always won in Daddy's stories. That was the point of the Challenges: to make sure William would be a brave kid who could win, too, no matter what. To make sure he would always, always be safe.

But this time his father shocked him. "No," Daddy said. "Gretel escaped, but Hansel didn't."

They were standing in the front hall. Daddy was looking up at the long wooden staircase that went up and turned and went up some more. "Hansel died here?" William breathed.

"You could say that." Daddy's voice was all hollowed out and empty, like the tree in their backyard. "Even if he didn't accept it at the time."

Just the thought of that dead boy made William start to tremble and clear his throat. What if Hansel's ghost was about to come down those stairs right now? What if the ghost even wanted revenge and took it out on him?

After a long, awful minute, his father leaned down and took William in his arms; then he held him against his chest and said he was sorry for scaring him. "You don't ever have to worry about Hansel, I promise."

"Why not?" William said, when he'd calmed down enough to speak.

"Because he doesn't matter now. He was a coward who, over time, became everything he hated." Daddy shrugged. "Let's just say he wasn't worth saving."

CHAPTER SEVENTEEN

Patrick was incredibly frustrated that the hospital hadn't figured out how to make Lila better. She'd been there for almost two weeks, and they hadn't even decided on a diagnosis yet. Not that this had stopped them from treating her with a cocktail of heavy-duty medicines that made Patrick's head spin when he googled them. No wonder Lila could barely function, given that every one of the meds had drowsiness and lethargy listed as side effects. She was awake more often now, but she couldn't seem to do much beyond lying in her hospital room. He kissed her each time he arrived and again before he left. That was the extent of their communication beyond his random comments about such fascinating topics as what was on TV or the weather.

He felt guilty for turning on the TV in her room when he

came to visit her, but he couldn't think of what else to do to pass the time. He'd offered to read to her, but she'd said no. The books he'd brought to the hospital, many of her favorites, were on the windowsill, exactly where he'd left them. The doctor said she probably wouldn't feel like reading for a while. When Patrick asked if she would ever feel like reading again, the doctor said he assumed she would, but then the doctor didn't believe Lila's decision to leave her career was that strange. "Depression often causes people to lose interest in their jobs and their hobbies," he said. "Sometimes they even lose interest in their children."

"Are you saying that my wife is depressed? That's the official diagnosis now?"

"It certainly seems likely," the doc said. "We'll know more after we've given the medicines a chance to work."

In other words, if the depression drugs worked, then Lila had been depressed. The logic seemed backward to Patrick, and it angered him when they refused to admit it, but then everything seemed to anger him right now. Luckily, he was done with his finals and he'd turned in his grades, so he didn't have to deal with anyone in his department. He didn't even have to talk to anyone on the phone, which was a good thing after what had happened with Ashley, though of course it was probably worse with her, since he continued to blame her for starting all this.

She'd called a week ago Tuesday, ostensibly to speak to his wife, but when Patrick said Lila was in the hospital, Ashley didn't ask why. He assumed Pearl or the police or both had told Ashley what had happened, but he wasn't sure how much she knew and he was relieved she didn't expect him to discuss it. As it turned out, the only thing she wanted to talk about, or more precisely, rant about, was what had happened with her children and how unfair it was. She said the people from Child Protective Services were treating her like a monster. They acted like she was guilty of not only fostering an environment of child abuse—the main charge for which she was being investigated—but also of abusing the kids herself. They didn't just take away Pearl; they took Maisie and William, too, "for no reason." They wouldn't even say whether she'd be allowed to visit her kids while the home study was being done.

She skipped over his question about where CPS had taken the children, saying only that they were fine and he didn't need to worry about it. "But I can't visit my own kids?" she barked. "Isn't it supposed to be innocent until proven guilty in this country?"

Her attitude seemed so ridiculously inconsistent—not to mention hypocritical—that he couldn't resist pointing out that the same thing had happened to Billy.

"No," she sputtered, "it's not the same at all. Billy could have gotten William killed! It figures you wouldn't get it."

"You're right. I don't see the distinction. If anything, I think this is worse. Billy was the children's father, while your boyfriend is nothing to them." He paused but he couldn't resist finishing his thought. "Perhaps you should consider that you brought this on yourself when you didn't hesitate to introduce a virtual stranger into their lives."

"Kyle didn't do it," Ashley hissed. "Not that you care."

It was Patrick's turn to be incredulous. "You're actually defending that guy?"

"No. I can't afford to do that, not if I want my kids home. I'll let him rot if they'll just give me back Pearl and William and Maisie. But I'm just telling you, he didn't do it." He heard her inhale audibly and wondered if she was smoking again. "Maybe all that shit you told the cops about me is true, but that isn't."

He might have felt a little guilty if she hadn't slammed the phone down so hard it hurt his ear. Instead, he walked away wondering what was wrong with her that she was more willing to believe her boyfriend than her own daughter. And if the things he'd told the police officer *were* true, thank god CPS was investigating her, before the children got seriously hurt.

That afternoon when he was visiting Lila, he considered telling her that she'd been vindicated, but decided to wait. Before she could get the custody she wanted or even visitation, she would have to be mentally stable—and she was a long way from that now. And even if she did get well, would he be able to stand up in court with her, as though he believed she'd be a good influence on the kids? How could he know that, when he didn't really know Lila?

If that hadn't been clear to him before, it certainly became obvious the next Friday afternoon, when Dr. Kutchins, the psychologist working with Lila, asked for Patrick's help. She looked to be about thirty, maybe even a researcher fresh from grad school, with an overworked grad student's disheveled appearance. Her long black hair was coming out of her ponytail, and her clothes were as wrinkled as if she'd been sleeping in them for days. But of course he agreed to help in any way he could. Lila had been there for exactly three weeks and he was desperate to do something.

The psychologist led him to her office on the other side of the elevators from the patients' rooms. It was smaller than he expected, and the desk was cluttered with notebooks, articles, and open books piled on top of each other. He took the only seat available, across from her. After she told him to call her Marti, he said, "Why? Is that your name?"

It was meant to be a joke, but he'd forgotten that only Lila seemed to understand why he always thought it was funny to take statements at their literal value. With everyone else, he had to explain what was already a lame attempt at humor. He watched the psychologist blink as he pointed out that she hadn't said her name was Marti, she'd just said to call her that.

"My name is Marti," she said blandly. "Now, are there any other questions before we proceed?"

He said no and decided not to confess that he'd only made the stupid joke because he was nervous. He was here to help Lila. He didn't want anyone psychoanalyzing *his* feelings.

Dr. Kutchins—Marti—began by saying she just wanted information about Lila's background. She opened a notebook where he could see a long list of questions. He hoped they weren't all for him.

He wasn't sure what he expected, but he stumbled on her very first request. "Do you know if your wife ever suffered a head injury as a child? The neurologist noticed an old skull fracture on her MRI and wondered about the cause."

"Can't you talk to Lila about that?"

"I could, but I haven't wanted to bring it up in her therapy yet." She paused. "I take it you don't know the answer?"

When Patrick admitted he didn't, she said it probably wasn't important. The next question, she said, was much more critical. "Lila has frequently alluded to a violent incident involving her stepfather. Would you mind filling in the details?"

This time he was even more surprised. A violent incident? What the hell did that mean? Dr. Kutchins must have taken his silence as reluctance to divulge personal information, because she quickly explained that there was no confidentiality issue; Lila had signed a waiver saying they could discuss any aspect of her case with her husband. "She obviously trusts you," the psychologist said.

Kutchins clearly meant that, but Patrick suspected she'd have to reassess her opinion after she discovered that he not only couldn't answer this question, but also couldn't say much of anything about the kind of home Lila had grown up in or whether she'd had difficulties in school or whether she'd gotten in any trouble as a teenager and so on. Indeed, by the time she'd finished her list of questions, Kutchins seemed positively perplexed, and even more so when Patrick admitted that Lila's childhood wasn't the only thing he and his wife had never really discussed; they'd also never talked about his.

Since the doc had already said something about survivors of childhood abuse being reluctant to speak about their pasts—and Patrick had swallowed his objection at Lila being described as an abuse survivor—Patrick hastened to add that his own parents had not been abusive. He was relieved when Kutchins said this session wasn't about him so he needn't worry; he wouldn't have to volunteer any information about his life unless he chose to. "But I wonder if you have an opinion about why Lila hasn't shown more curiosity about your experiences as a child?"

"Actually, she has. Whenever we visit my father in St. Louis, she spends at least an hour going through another photograph album or watching another home video. And she asks my father a lot of questions. I'm fairly sure she's not merely being polite."

He found himself thinking about the last time they were in St. Louis, to take care of Jason and Doreen's kids. Not only did Lila spend all of Theo's nap watching a video on the fascinating theme of Patrick's first bicycle, but she juggled the grumpy post-nap toddler in her arms as she listened to his father's long, rambling account of the summer when nine-year-old Patrick had flown off his bike and broken his ankle. Patrick was only half-heartedly paying attention, but he was surprised his father knew so much about this. In most of his memories of that summer—and all of the other summers, too—his mother was with him and his father was at work.

"So Lila asks your father about you," the psychologist said.

It wasn't a question, but she paused so long that he finally realized what she was waiting for. He sat back. "You mean instead of asking me?"

"Well, yes. I suppose it could be a defense mechanism, to keep you from asking her questions, but it's not what we usually encounter with abuse survivors. More typically, they are eager to hear stories from their spouse's childhood, as long as that childhood seems 'normal' in a way theirs was not."

He felt put on the spot because the truth was, especially when they were first together, Lila *had* asked him questions about what he was like when he was a boy, but his answers had always been too short to satisfy her. Usually, he told her it wasn't interesting, and it wasn't—to him. But if Dr. Kutchins was right, he'd been selfish to deny Lila these "normal" childhood stories because she had so few of her own. The operative word, though, was "if."

"I'm not sure why you keep calling Lila an abuse survivor." He knew he sounded irritated, so he took a breath. "I mean, we don't know that that's true, right?"

"Not with scientific certainty, no. She could be lying about the things she's told me, but I hardly think that's likely. Her memories are so fragmented that she would have to be a very skilled liar to parcel them out this way—and to what end? To convince me of something she won't even admit to herself yet: that her mother was cruel?"

He could have mentioned that Lila had lied to him many times, but he didn't want to personally attack his wife's honesty, even to her therapist. Yet he did feel he had to address one point. "I'm not sure if this is relevant," he said slowly, "but I got the distinct impression from Lila's mother that Lila does believe her mother was cruel."

He was thinking of Barbara Duval's claim that Lila thought of her as a witch, but the psychologist didn't ask him for an explanation. Instead, she said, clearly surprised, "You've spoken with her mother?"

"Yes. She's not dead, despite what Lila told you."

"Lila never told me that her mother was dead." Dr. Kutchins gave him a long look. "If I sounded incredulous, it's merely because you didn't bring this up before. You do have some information about her childhood then? At least her mother's version of it?"

He admitted he'd only seen her mother once, and only for an hour or less at that; he didn't really have much information. But the psychologist insisted that whatever he had could be useful, so finally he told her. He didn't leave anything out, even the part about the "unnatural bond" with Billy, though he emphasized that Barbara Duval maintained she had not let her children have an affair.

For the first time, Dr. Kutchins seemed like a thirty-year-old recent grad named Marti rather than a hospital staff psychologist. She blurted out that Barbara Duval sounded "horrible," and then she looked in his eyes. "Are you telling me you seriously wonder if Lila was abused after hearing all this?"

He ran his hands through his hair, wondering what she was getting at. What had he just said that proved Lila was abused? "Wait," he said, "I love my wife, but how would I know what happened when she was—"

"First this woman acts seductively with her own daughter's husband by telling you about her sex life, and then she calls her daughter a bad seed?" Marti laughed. "I'm sorry, but in all the literature I've read and all the patients I've seen, I've never come across a child that could reasonably be described that way. It has about as much credibility as thinking a child is demon possessed."

"I'm sure she didn't mean it as a diagnosis," he said before wondering why he was defending Barbara Duval. The truth was he'd thought she was horrible, too, but then he'd let her get to him, hadn't he? He'd let her twist his mind to the point that he'd kissed another woman and even walked out on his wife. Which led to Lila's suicide attempt. Which led to this moment, sitting in the office, still trying to justify himself by bringing up the example of . . . Columbine?

"Those Colorado teenagers who shot up the school were clearly not victims. There *are* bad kids out there, right?" He grew quieter, already feeling embarrassed. "Not that I'm saying Lila killed anyone."

"But you suspect your wife was one of these so-called bad kids?"

He saw her then: Lila, kneeling down to help Maisie dress her doll, holding little Theo against her chest, smiling as she sang "Happy Birthday" to his father, laughing with her grad students at the party she gave for them last year. He thought of the way she felt, too, and not only when they were making love, but when she was kissing the back of his neck, nestling her feet against his feet in bed, resting her hands on his face as she asked "What's up, honey?" whenever he seemed sad or sick or just unusually quiet. Of course he didn't think his gentle wife had been a bad child. He wasn't even sure if he believed in bad children, despite what he'd just said.

He said no, and then he did something ridiculous. He started to cry.

Dr. Kutchins handed him a tissue. He blew his nose and wiped his eyes as he finally admitted that there was only one thing he really suspected Lila of. "I don't think she loves me."

"You're wrong about that."

"I know she says she does, but I don't think she means it."

"Would you feel differently if you knew that she says your name whenever she's afraid?"

"She does?"

Kutchins nodded. "She thinks of you as the safest, best part of her life." The psychologist paused for a moment or two. "Look, I know we agreed at the outset that this session wasn't about you, but I have something that just may help." She turned around to her file cabinet and took out a workbook and handed it to him. "This is for families who are dealing with suicide attempts. I think if you read this, you'll find all your feelings right now are normal: the guilt, the anger, the feeling that she wouldn't have done this if she really loved you."

He didn't say anything, but he clutched the workbook in his hands.

"The truth is that your wife is ill, just as if she had cancer. We need to get her better, but in the meantime, you need to forgive her, and yourself."

He thanked her and quickly stood up to leave. He was deeply ashamed of breaking down and taking over a session that was supposed to be about Lila, but as he left the hospital, he realized he was also calm in a way he hadn't been since that day in New Jersey. The therapist had helped him; there was no denying it. If only he'd been able to help her help Lila.

By the next morning, he'd decided there was something he could try. He could spend some time trying to track down the basic facts of Lila's childhood. If he couldn't make up for not knowing before—honestly, for not even wanting to know before—it was the least he could do now.

He headed out to the hall and took the elevator down to the storage area in the basement of their building. It was a dusty crate made of wood, crammed halfway to the ceiling with their things. He took off the padlock and started moving boxes. It took him a while to get past all the stuff from graduate school that he and Lila had kept: notebooks from all their important classes, dissertation copies, graded papers and tests. There was also the usual assortment of junk that they foolishly thought might be useful someday: a futon cover, even though they no longer had a futon; a lamp that had broken a few years ago, but which they planned to have fixed; several trash bags of clothes that Lila hoped would come back in style. Finally, wedged behind the Christmas ornaments and their tax files, he found the light blue Rubbermaid tub, unmarked, where Lila kept all their important records. She'd insisted on the plastic tub in case the basement ever flooded, which it never had according to the landlord, and probably never would, since their building was built on top of a small hill.

He'd seen this tub a dozen times, but he'd never gone through it before. As he knelt down and popped open the lid, he felt a little nervous, like he was spying on his wife. It was true that she kept all her treasures in here, too: the diorama she'd been so desperate to have when Billy died; the few letters Patrick had written her when they'd just gotten engaged and he was overseas at a conference; a half-finished baby sweater that she'd planned to give to Pearl until she discovered how time-consuming knitting was. And sprinkled all over everything were dried flowers, the dozens of bouquets that Patrick had given her over the years, all of which she'd put in the tub as soon as they were dried-out enough to pose no threat to the papers underneath.

The papers were the critical part for Patrick, and yet he spent time examining everything else, too. This was their life together, a fast-forward version, and though some of it depressed him, considering all that had happened, he found other parts comforting. Years ago, before Lila completely trusted her computer, she'd kept printed copies of her email correspondence, not only with Billy, but also with Patrick's father, and as he read these emails, he was surprised how much she and his father had talked about how Patrick was doing. Inside were notes about his struggles with the department, his dedication to his students, even his headaches, which weren't serious, but which his father had apparently worried about because his own father had had migraines and died of a brain tumor. He knew his dad had changed over the years, primarily because he'd spent so much time alone with his regrets, but he was surprised at how close his father had been with Lila so early on. And that Lila had been so *aware* of everything that was going on in his life; that was the biggest surprise. She talked a lot about what he'd given up to her marry her—a better job, where he could do the research he loved—and she'd asked both his father and Billy what she should do to make up for it. If Billy answered the question, Patrick couldn't find it, but his father wrote: "My son can be content anywhere. He's like his mother in that way. Make him sausage spaghetti once a week and pancakes on Saturday, go with him to a few baseball games, and tell him you love him every time you think of it. Don't worry, he'll be fine."

The funny part was that Lila had done all this for the first few years, and his father was right: it did make him feel content. He'd never realized why until he read this—Lila had been imitating his mother. When he was a kid, his mom had made his favorite sausage spaghetti on Thursday nights and pancakes every Saturday. She'd taken him to the baseball games his father was always too busy to attend. And she'd constantly said she loved him. He'd been lucky that way, even if he hadn't realized it at the time.

But apparently, his wife hadn't been so lucky. He still couldn't get his mind around the fact that her therapist thought Lila was a child abuse survivor, but if it was true, then all the more reason for him to help if he could. He grabbed the four folders of papers and, after moving all the boxes back and locking the crate, took them upstairs.

It only took him fifteen minutes to locate all the relevant documents, but immediately, he knew they might not be as official as they seemed. Lila's mother's death certificate in the first folder, though it looked as real as his own mother's, could not, of course, be real. Was Lila's birth certificate also forged? It said she was born in North Carolina, not Pennsylvania. There were no elementary school records, but there were copies of transcripts from two different high schools: one from a prep school in Virginia that listed a home address in Grayten, North Carolina, and the other from a high school *in* Grayten, North Carolina, the town where Lila had always said she'd grown up.

He turned to the web to find the North Carolina address, but it didn't come up in the phone listings, and the street on MapQuest told him nothing other than that it was on the outskirts of a little town, which was how Lila had described the place. He tried to look up her birth certificate through one of those people-find sites and, after paying $59.95, discovered that the only publicly available records for his wife were dated after she began college, and most of those were already familiar to him: their marriage certificate, their credit report, their addresses going back to Princeton. He was just thinking about paying another $59.95 to look up Billy when the phone rang.

The caller ID showed his father, who'd called at least five times in the last few weeks, leaving friendly messages for Lila asking how she was feeling. Patrick felt bad that he hadn't even told his dad Lila was in the hospital. He picked up the phone and attempted to dispense with the basics of the situation quickly, like ripping off a bandage, but it didn't work. His dad was upset; he wanted to talk about why she'd tried to kill herself. He was adamant that it couldn't be just her sadness over Billy.

"Lila has too much to live for," the old man said. "Hell, I just talked to her myself—what—two days before this happened? You said it was a Friday night . . . I know I talked to her on Wednesday because I had a doctor's appointment that morning." He went on about the doctor's appointment for a while, and Patrick listened enough to know that it was just a routine checkup for blood pressure and cholesterol. Then his dad said, "She told me she was doing better. I remember this now. She was waiting for you to come home from work. She made a joke about surprising you by being out of bed and dressed for a change."

"I don't know, Dad," he tried. But his father wouldn't let it go. He wanted to speculate about what *might* have happened, what *might* have upset her, what *might* have made her lose hope, until finally Patrick relented and told his father that he'd left Lila that same night, Wednesday, and gone to a hotel. "So that's what happened, all right? It's my fault."

His dad was quiet for a while; then he started on a long, rambling explanation of his own failings as a husband. Patrick was looking at his computer, as usual, reading a site on obtaining North Carolina birth certificates. He'd heard all this before a hundred times. But at some point, it struck him that this was, in fact, beginning to be relevant. And when his father asked, "Do you see where I'm going with this, Son?" he knew the answer—though he didn't like it.

"You didn't know how to be close to Mom," Patrick said, and exhaled. "You're saying I'm the same way with Lila. Well, I'm sorry, but I disagree. Let's leave it at that."

Patrick had always prided himself on being different from his father. He didn't stay at the office until all hours; he didn't go out drinking with the guys from work to blow off steam; he didn't even know how to play golf or poker or any of the other "man" games. Instead, he was always home with his wife, the same way he'd been with his mother when she was dying. There was simply no comparison.

"I'm not saying it's the same," his father admitted. "I was a shitty husband. You're a good man and you're trying, but you don't know how to really talk to Lila. That's all I'm saying. Because I didn't show you how a husband should talk to his wife."

Before Patrick could defend himself, his dad said he had to go because his dog was barking and something about the neighbors that Patrick didn't catch. After he hung up, he poured himself a cup of coffee and sat very still, thinking about something he hadn't thought about for years.

"I want to talk about what will happen to you," Patrick's mother said, out of the blue, one afternoon when she was in the hospital. It was early spring, his second year at Princeton. He was sitting in the chair next to her, pretending this was an ordinary conversation, though his mom was hooked up to IV lines, a chemotherapy pump, a catheter, and numerous monitors.

"Happen to me? I'll probably go into debt, like everyone else I know." He rolled his eyes. "Grad school has a way of doing that."

"You know what I mean. When I die."

"You're not going to die for a long time." He forced a shrug. "This is a premature conversation."

His mother started coughing. He poured her a cup of water and stood next to her, holding the cup at an angle so she could take sips. Her throat was always dry now from the chemo, but if she took a full drink she gagged.

After he sat down again, his mom said, "It's important to me. Please, listen."

A nurse came in to check the bandages from his mom's surgery to remove the lymph nodes under her arms. His mom waited until the nurse left; then she said, "I want you to make up with your father."

"Why?"

She gave a string of reasons, none of which convinced him. Finally she said, "Because he loves you. He just doesn't know how to show it."

Patrick couldn't remember exactly what he'd said to that, probably some vague promise to consider her request and then a quick change of topic. She'd made this claim before, and every time, he'd thought the same thing. If he can't show it, how do I know it's there? Am I supposed to take this love as an article of faith? What good is his love if it can't give me anything I really need?

He snapped out of his reverie when he looked at his watch and realized he needed to get going or he would be late to the hospital. Unfortunately, he hadn't found anything useful to give to Dr. Kutchins, but he'd have to look again later. He prided himself on always arriving at the beginning of visiting hours, whether Lila noticed or not.

When he got to her room, he was surprised to see her sitting on the bed, fully dressed. The books on her windowsill were gone, packed in the side pouch of the bag of pajamas and toiletries he'd brought her last week. The bag was on the floor at the end of the bed.

His first thought was that she was being transferred somewhere else, somewhere worse. "What's going on?" he said, hoping he didn't sound afraid.

"You were right about our insurance," she said softly. "It only pays for psychiatric hospitalization if you're certifiably dangerous." She paused. "When the doctor told them I probably wasn't going to kill myself, the insurance company decided I have to be seen as an outpatient from now on."

Probably? He sat down on the bed next to her. "Are you going to do the outpatient treatment?"

"I have to." She lowered her eyes. "I don't know what's wrong with me, but something is."

She sounded so sad that he didn't know what to say. The truth was he'd never known what to say when Lila was unhappy. So, who knew, maybe his father was right about him. This was his chance to change, but all he could think of were concrete things he could do for her. Take her out to lunch on the way home. Read aloud from one of her favorite books. Stop and get her a double latte or a cinnamon pastry or any of the other things she usually enjoyed. But these ideas seemed so lame that finally, in desperation, he blurted out, "Is there anything you need me to do? I'll do it, whatever it is."

"There is something." She took his hand and placed it between her own. "I know it sounds strange, but if you're not too busy, could you drive me to North Carolina?"

While he certainly hadn't expected this, he wasn't exactly surprised, either. He could feel that there was a perfectly logical reason behind her request, a reason he almost grasped. It was the same sensation he often had right before he solved a proof: like a glimmer of possibility was about to turn into an idea that would not only end his confusion, but make that confusion look ridiculous in hindsight.

And then, suddenly, he thought he had it. "You're not sure if you're really from North Carolina?"

He had no idea how this could be true, but still, he felt oddly relieved. This could be the missing piece that would make it all consistent—the Lila he knew and the Lila he'd thought was a liar.

"If I'm not," she said slowly, looking down at her knees, "then I must be crazy, right?"

He didn't know the answer to this, but he forced a smile. "It doesn't matter. You told me yourself that geniuses are always a little crazy."

"That's a myth. Look at you. You're not crazy."

He was stupidly grateful, but that wasn't the reason he lifted her face and kissed her. He wanted to comfort her, but that wasn't the only reason, either. She looked so beautiful to him. After eleven years together, he guessed she always would.

They agreed that they would go to North Carolina, together, that night. As they were walking to accounting to settle their bill, he said that perhaps this trip would help her figure out what she needed to know about her past. "Every problem has a solution," he said, repeating the first part of what he always told his graduate students. The rest he kept to himself, hoping it wouldn't apply in this situation: Some of those solutions won't be found by us, however. Some may not be found by anyone for a thousand years.

CHAPTER EIGHTEEN

The trip to Grayten, North Carolina, took longer than Patrick had estimated, and Lila felt bad for him. Each time she woke up, she told him how sorry she was that she couldn't help with the drive. "It's not your fault," he said, before reminding her that drowsiness was a side effect of her medicines. Sometimes she got confused and thought she was on the train with Billy, going home after he'd freed her from the hospital—or at the end of the year she'd spent at prep school; she wasn't sure which. She'd slept most of that trip, too, or at least she thought she had. That would explain why she didn't remember anything about that journey years ago other than arriving at the house, which was completely different from the house in her mind. Even the rooms were in different places, but Billy said their mother had done extensive remodeling and redecorated again. A moment later, she heard some woman start crying. Her name was Maria, and Billy said she was there to help them. Lila assumed she was a cleaner—their mother had always hired cleaners—and it turned out to be true, but Maria was different because, though she did keep house and cook for them, she lived with them all the time, night and day, until she died from a heart attack a few months later. After that, they had the house to themselves for a full year, until the fall after they turned seventeen, when Lila went off to college and her brother set out to travel and become a real writer. Sometime during that year alone with Billy, Lila began to have real, continuous memories, the way the people in her books did, the way she'd always suspected all normal people did. And so she had no trouble recognizing Grayten, North Carolina, when Patrick pulled into the town on Sunday morning, right after dawn.

It was still a tiny town with only one stoplight at the intersection of Johnson and Main. As they made their way down Main, she opened the window and held her face out to smell the familiar scents of pine trees, azaleas, and manure from the surrounding farms. The breeze helped her stay alert so she could point out to Patrick the local grocery store where she and Billy had bought a mix of healthy foods and the candy they were addicted to: Hershey's bars, Good & Plenty, and especially bags of Reese's Pieces, which they usually consumed on the long walk home. The memory was so real to her, she could feel those sweet, crunchy candies in her teeth. In the same strip mall as the grocery store, there used to be a doctor's office and a pharmacy, a video rental place, and a small Sears that relied on catalog orders for everything but basic clothing and housewares. The Sears had grown; the video store was now a Blockbuster; and the doctor's office had changed into a bank, but Lila told Patrick the way it had been and explained that she and Billy had gone in every place but the video rental, since they didn't own a TV.

Lila knew full well that the only thing this proved was that she'd lived here for a year and a few months as a teenager. The much more important question was whether she'd actually grown up in Grayten. She'd always believed that she had—until the past week, when her psychologist, Dr. Kutchins, had worked hard to convince Lila that the vivid "memories" she'd been having in the hospital were at least reflective of reality, even if some of the details were off. But if those memories were in any sense real, then the place where she'd grown up was definitely north of here, with winters more like New York's or Pennsylvania's than like North Carolina's. She'd come up with the idea for this trip hoping to find out for sure, though she was reluctant to find out, too, for fear her life would make even less sense than it did now.

Still, she was more relaxed, just driving through this town that was exactly as she remembered. Her husband also seemed more relaxed, but maybe he was simply relieved to be able to stop driving and have breakfast. The old diner at the entrance to the highway was gone, replaced by a Denny's, but as Patrick pointed out, at least the place was open. He said the streets were as deserted as if the whole town was still asleep, but Lila said that everybody was probably getting ready for Sunday morning church.

"There's a big church only a mile or so from where we lived," Lila said. The waitress had seated them and handed them large plastic menus that felt a little sticky. "Billy and I could hear the bells on Sunday morning, and we always headed outside, to what he called God's church, to pray to the trees and the flowers and the sky."

"Your parents never made you go to church?"

"I think my mother did. I remembered something in the hospital about being Catholic before she married my stepfather."

"It's a Catholic church then?"

"I'm not sure," Lila said.

"This town seems too small to have two churches," he said. The waitress returned, ready to take their order. They both chose pancakes, and after the waitress left, Patrick joked that the stickiness of the menu must have subliminally predisposed them to think of syrup.

They ate quickly, because they were starving, but also because Lila had told Patrick she was anxious to go out on Route 6 and see the house. She was hoping whoever lived there now would let them in, but worst case, they would be able to examine the property. She didn't remember ever going beyond the backyard with Billy when the two of them lived there alone, but she wanted to confirm that all the other things from childhood she'd "dreamed" in the hospital had not happened here. That there wasn't a woods backing up against the lawn, or a steep hill she and her brother had liked to roll down, or especially that tree house their father had made for them: the one thing she knew had to be real, as she'd always remembered sitting in it with Billy, reading that children's book about heroes and ice cream.

She knew exactly how to get to the place from the grocery store, so they went back to Main and then Patrick followed her directions until they reached Route 6. Everything looked vaguely familiar until they got to the spot where the house should have been—where the house *had* been, Lila was sure, because she recognized the farmhouse on the other side of the road, set about an acre back, surrounded by tobacco fields. She remembered sitting in the rocking chair Maria had moved into her bedroom and looking at that farm from her window, though she and Billy had never met the family who'd lived there. Not during the year she could remember, anyway.

"It used to be right there," she whispered, pointing at a large rectangular space bounded by trees. Patrick insisted on driving a little farther, but she knew it wouldn't make a difference. The house of her happiest memories with Billy was gone, disappeared from the face of the earth, just like her brother.

She felt like crying, but she asked her husband to double back and pull over on the road. She was determined to walk to the line of tall trees at the far edge of the empty field, to see what was on the other side. She was overwhelmed by a sudden, desperate hope that she really had grown up here. If only she could stand in the woods where she and her twin had spent so much of their time as children, then maybe she would experience a flood of memories that could comfort her by bringing her brother close again, even if it was only in the past.

As she got out of the car, she heard the church bells ringing, which she took to be a good sign. But when she rushed across the field and through the trees, she found nothing but another farm. No hill, no woods, nothing that even resembled what she'd imagined in the hospital. Of course, it had been twenty years, but she knew instinctively that this was not the same place, and she was so disheartened that she slumped onto the ground.

"What's wrong?" Patrick said, kneeling beside her.

"This isn't the right town."

"It has to be. You knew the strip mall, knew the way to get here, knew about—"

"I did live here, but only for a year or so, when I was sixteen."

"But both of your high school transcripts list this as your home."

She looked at him, surprised he knew this. Then she said that her brother must have forged those transcripts, the same way he'd forged her parents' death certificates. She only meant that Billy had changed the address on the transcripts, but she was immediately gripped by the possibility that he'd forged it all: both of her transcripts and even the recommendation letters she'd used to get into college. Her brother was good enough to pull it off, and he would have done it without hesitating if he'd decided she needed fake records, but why would she have needed them? Was the real situation closer to what she'd imagined in the hospital: that her mother hadn't ever let her go to school, and the only train trip she and Billy had taken "home" was when he'd freed her from Westwood Psychiatric Hospital?

"But if your brother did that, you would know." Patrick swatted a fly off his jeans. He sounded as confused as she felt. "This doesn't make any sense."

"I don't understand it, either." She paused. "Will you just hold me for a while?"

He sat down and stretched his legs out; then he pulled her to him, so her head was leaning against his chest. She listened to the reassuring sound of her husband's heartbeat as she tried to think about what all this could mean. If the memory of Billy freeing her from Westwood was real—and she'd been wide awake when she'd remembered that, as Dr. Kutchins had repeatedly emphasized—then her brother had let her enter college and spend her adult life with no conscious knowledge of ever having been in a psychiatric hospital. He'd never mentioned a word about it, though this didn't explain why she herself hadn't known. Even Dr. Kutchins hadn't come up with an answer for that, though she said they'd continue to explore it on an outpatient basis—after Lila's insurance company had refused the psychologist's petition to keep Lila in the hospital for at least another week.

Billy always said Lila's lack of memories wasn't that abnormal, given what they'd gone through with Harold, and she'd believed him. She'd believed what he'd told her about her formal schooling, too, especially as he'd told the same stories a hundred times. He said she'd cried through most of the year at prep school, because she didn't like being away from home. She'd never made many friends, because she was too shy. She'd gotten all As. She'd been a perfect rule follower, a Gallant, while he was busy getting into trouble like the Goofus he'd always been.

She told Dr. Kutchins that Billy probably came up with the Goofus/Gallant comparison to keep Lila from remembering that her parents seemed to view her and her twin precisely the opposite. It was an innocent story, Lila insisted—and she was still holding on to that. Even if Billy had made up their entire lives, his only motive had been to protect her; of this she was positive. This was why he'd rehearsed the past with her constantly and told her she was losing the plot whenever she forgot any of the details. He was trying to protect her from something, just like when they were children. She missed him more for this, even as she felt determined to discover, finally, what that something was.

Lila looked up at Patrick. "I want to go to church."

"Now?"

"The service has to be still going on. The bells didn't ring that long ago."

He didn't ask why, for which she was grateful. They stood up and she squeezed his hand as they walked back to her Subaru. "I'm glad you're with me," she said, and it was true. Though there was so much she couldn't find words to express, simply having her husband there made all this doable. Dr. Kutchins had told her that it might help to train herself to think of the past as over and unable to hurt her now, but she knew this instinctively as long as Patrick was at her side.

She wanted to go to church to talk to the minister. She knew it was a long shot that he would have information that could help her, but it was Sunday and the county records office was obviously closed. The minister would know more people in town than anybody else, so at least he might know whose house she and Billy had lived in when they were sixteen. The house had to have belonged to somebody.

When she walked into church though, her face fell. The minister was way too young, maybe right out of seminary; it was very unlikely that he would know what the town was like twenty years ago. She thought about leaving, but everybody was already staring at her and Patrick because the door had banged shut behind them, and she felt so worn out that she relished the idea of sitting quietly while she figured out what to do next. She guided her husband to the last pew.

The service was over and the congregation was filing out; Patrick had just whispered, "What now?" when an old woman stopped in the aisle next to them. She was leaning on a cane; at first Lila thought she was only pausing to get her bearings, but then she realized the woman was openly staring at her. The possibility that this woman recognized her only crossed her mind a moment before the woman said, "I thought you was somebody else."

"My name is Lila. My brother's name was Billy." She thought about using a last name, but wasn't sure which one they would have used in town and didn't want to confuse the woman. "Are you sure you don't know me? We lived here in the late eighties for about—"

"Naw, the person I was thinking of hasn't lived here since the seventies. And she'd be a heck of a lot older than you." The woman shrugged. "My eyes ain't as good as they used to be."

"Oh," Lila said. "Sorry to bother you."

Lila must have sounded disappointed, because the old woman's voice became kinder. "Maybe you're kin, though? Her name's Beth Andrew."

"No, I'm afraid not."

"Well, have a blessed day," the woman said. "Praise God."

"Praise God," Lila repeated.

After the old woman walked on, Patrick whispered, "Praise God?"

The shock on his face made her suddenly feel like laughing, and she kissed him on the nose. "I was only being friendly," she said. "But thanks for cheering me up. Now I can face the minister. Should I ask him to marry us? We've never been married in a church. Maybe it's time."

"You can't be serious."

"No, but you're so cute when you look stunned that I couldn't resist."

He smirked, but he took her hand. She felt glad again that he was with her. Even if the minister was no help, she could handle this. She led her husband to the door, where everyone had disappeared except the minister and the last of the congregation: the same old lady with the cane, who was probably waiting for her ride.

They were only talking about whether it would rain; still, Lila didn't want to interrupt. But the old woman saw her hovering a few feet away and gestured with her free hand to come near. After the woman introduced the minister as "Reverend Tom," Lila introduced herself and Patrick, and they both shook his hand.

The woman was staring again. "What did you say your last name was?"

"Cole," Lila said. "Though my stepfather's last name was—"

"Oh my goodness, seem like you *are* kin to Beth Andrew. Her name before she got married was Cole. Ain't that funny?"

Lila felt her heart in her throat, though she still thought it had to be an odd coincidence. Even as the old lady asked who her father was, Lila was preparing for the woman to say she'd been wrong. And she did, but she added something that took Lila's breath away. "Beth's brother's name was William, but he didn't have no kids. Died too young, I guess." She shook her head. "It was written up in the papers here. He was a policeman. Shot in a robbery up north a long time ago." She frowned. "Too bad he didn't stay put. Too much crime up north."

Reverend Tom looked at Patrick. "Are y'all new to the area?"

Patrick must have sensed something was wrong because he'd put his arm around Lila and he kept glancing at her face. But he sounded calm. "No, my wife lived here a long time ago. Out on Route 6. Apparently, the house isn't there anymore."

"Now this here is getting downright spooky," the old lady said. "'Cause you know what? Beth Andrew's mama lived on Route 6." She looked down at the concrete steps. "What in the world was her name? Something Italian-sounding."

"Maria?" Lila said, though her voice came out so strangled and strange she barely recognized it.

"That's it! After she died, I guess some relatives sold the place. I didn't hear much about that, but I know the house was leveled way back when Reagan was still president." She adjusted her weight on her cane. "Last good president, if you ask me."

The woman went on about politics for a while until finally Lila managed, "Could you tell me who might know the family?" She looked back and forth from the minister to the old woman. "Anybody?"

"No," the old lady said. "Beth moved away, too, years ago. She was younger than you when she worked at the Kroger. That's how I knew her. We used to gab while she rang up my groceries."

Reverend Tom looked closely at Lila. "I might be able to find out for you."

Patrick said, "We would really appreciate it."

"Hold on a minute. I'll call my father. He was the preacher here for thirty-five years."

"Best darned preacher, too," the woman said. "Why he retired last Christmas I'll never know 'cause he was still a spring chicken if you ask me." She laughed a hoarse laugh. "'Course, everybody under seventy's a spring chicken to me."

Reverend Tom disappeared into the church. While he was gone,

Patrick attempted to make small talk with the woman, which Lila appreciated, knowing how much her husband hated small talk, especially when it was about politics and even worse when it was peppered with the old lady's praise of people like Jesse Helms. Lila would have helped him out if she hadn't been struck dumb by two completely opposed thoughts: that William Cole had not been their father or that Maria Cole, the "housekeeper," had really been her grandmother. And that Billy had obviously known the truth, whatever it was, or he would not have brought her to this town.

The reverend handed Patrick a piece of paper with a name, phone number, and address. He said this woman had been Maria's friend, but he couldn't say how close they were. "My father said the Coles were Catholic, so he doesn't know as much about them as most families in town. I'm sorry. Hope this helps."

"Who is it?" the old woman asked. "I might know her or her kin."

"Eunice Lewis," the preacher said.

"Naw, don't know any of them. She lives in the colored part of Grayten, east side of Johnson. Never even been there myself, but it ain't far."

When they got back in the Subaru, Patrick talked about the old lady as though she'd just admitted she was the founder of the KKK. Lila listened, but she couldn't really drum up any outrage; she was too nervous.

It only took about fifteen minutes to get to the address the minister had written on the piece of paper. The house was a small green ranch with a carport and a garden of roses surrounding a dogwood tree right in front.

"Maybe we should have called first," Patrick said when they were getting out of the car.

"I wouldn't know what to say," Lila whispered. The problem was she still didn't as Patrick rang the doorbell.

Eunice Lewis was an old woman, too, at least seventy, more likely eighty or more, and she came to the door pushing a walker. Her face was friendly, though, and she gave a large grin when Lila got out the name Maria Cole and explained that she wanted some information because she might be Mrs. Cole's relative. Mrs. Lewis invited them in and insisted on giving them lemonade, despite the effort it took for her to bring the glasses and hold on to her walker. But it was only when Lila said her own name, after she and Patrick had sat down on the bright yellow sofa and Mrs. Lewis had settled herself into an old checkered recliner, that the old woman said, "Well, glory be, I knew it was you!"

Lila didn't want to be rude and admit that she didn't recognize Mrs. Lewis, but luckily, Mrs. Lewis seemed eager to talk about how she knew Lila. They'd met several times, apparently, at Maria Cole's house, before Maria died. Mrs. Lewis went on for a while about what a great friend Maria had been before Lila finally took advantage of a pause to mention that she was confused about something.

"A woman at church told me William Cole didn't have any children." Lila sounded as timid as she felt. "Is that true?"

" 'Course he had kids." Mrs. Lewis laughed. "Had you and your brother, didn't he?" She took a drink of her lemonade. "Most folks in town don't know, being as how Willie and your mama had already moved up north to live in the house her grandpa left to her."

"They both grew up here, then? My father and my mother?"

"Your daddy was born in Grayten and probably would've died in Grayten if he hadn't run into Barbara. But your ma wasn't from anywhere, far as I could tell. She called herself 'cosmopolitan,' I guess 'cause her parents moved around a lot." Mrs. Lewis shrugged. "She was driving up north after some party in Florida when her car broke down on the highway outside town. Your daddy was already a policeman and he stopped and helped her. That's how they met."

It struck Lila as romantic—at least more romantic than she expected. "Did they get married here?"

"Naw, and that's the other reason folks in town don't know Willie had kids. They never did get married. Maria said he asked her to all the time, but she wouldn't 'cause he wasn't her notion of a husband, on account of he didn't make a lot of money and her family was rich."

Patrick surprised Lila by saying, "That sounds like Barbara Duval."

Mrs. Lewis nodded. "She named Billy after his dad, but Willie wanted y'all to have his last name, too. No sir, she wouldn't have it. But he stayed with her anyway, hoping she'd change her mind. Maria used to wonder what he saw in that girl."

Lila thought about when her brother forged the documents, when he told her he was changing their last name *back* to Cole. Yet if her parents had never married—and her mother had refused to let them have their father's name—then Billy had made this part up, too. But why? Did he believe this fact somehow diminished the reality of their father's love?

A phone was ringing. Mrs. Lewis reached into a calico pouch hanging from the arm of her walker and pulled out a cell. After she told whoever it was that she'd call back, she continued right where she left off. " 'Course, he thought his twin babies hung the moon. He sent Maria pictures of y'all every couple of months, and he wanted to bring you down to Grayten for a visit, but I gather your mama wasn't for it. Maria was just itching to see you and she would have gone up north herself if the doctor hadn't said she was too frail to travel. She had two heart attacks before the one which killed her, and a couple of bouts with cancer, but she never complained. Your granny was a tough old gal."

Lila looked out the window that faced the backyard. There was a large swing set, probably for Mrs. Lewis's great-grandkids. She thought about Maria, a short woman who always wore dresses and what she called her "sturdy shoes." She had long gray hair that she wore in a loose braid that hung down to her waist. Her face was soft with laugh lines and wrinkles around her eyes that made her look sympathetic. She was always worried, that's what Lila remembered most.

After a moment, she admitted, "I didn't even realize Maria was my grandmother." Lila was careful not to look at Patrick. She knew how strange this must sound to him. "That probably seems impossible, but—"

"No, it don't. You were such a sick little girl, honey. Your granny didn't want to say anything that could make you more confused than you already was. And Lord Almighty, was it touch and go for a while. You didn't even speak more than a couple of words for weeks and weeks. And you couldn't touch no food other than them biscuits Maria made for you, anything stronger you just brought right back up. The doctor said this would go on until them drugs were all out of your system. Maria sat by you, night and day, to make sure you didn't have no seizures. That was the big thing your granny and your brother were worried about, 'cause the doctor said a seizure could mean you'd have to go back to taking all them bad pills."

"What pills?" Lila said. She hoped she didn't sound hysterical—or crazy. "I'm sorry, but I don't remember anything about this, either."

" 'Course you don't," Mrs. Lewis said. "The doctor said them drugs had hurt your memory." She looked at the nearly empty glasses still sweating on her coffee table and started to reach for her walker. "Y'all want some more lemonade?"

Patrick stood up. "I'll get it. You just relax. Please."

After he walked to the kitchen, Mrs. Lewis said, "He seems like a nice fellow. You know, your brother always told your granny that you'd have a good life if they could just get you all better. My goodness, I've never seen a brother do for a sister like your brother did for you. He was just a kid himself, but oh, did he take on responsibility." Patrick returned with the lemonade pitcher. As he filled up the glasses, Mrs. Lewis said, "How is Billy doing these days? Did he ever get around to writing that book he told Maria about?"

At this, Lila's eyes welled up with tears, leaving Patrick to explain that Billy was dead. Mrs. Lewis got tears in her eyes, too, when she heard how he died, and Lila wished her husband had left that out, but she understood that if he had, there might have been questions that would have made the whole thing last even longer.

"Oh my Lord," Mrs. Lewis said, several times. "It pains me to hear that." She looked at Lila. "Your family's had so much trouble. First Willie, then Beth. I guess it's lucky Maria don't have to know about this."

"Beth died, too?" Lila had always thought she didn't have any aunts or uncles or cousins, as her mother was an only child. Now she'd discovered an aunt, only to find she was already gone.

Mrs. Lewis nodded. "Had a car accident right after she and her husband got transferred to the navy base in Florida. You and your brother were all that was left of Maria's family. That's why she never stopped writing them letters to your mama, begging to see you. Well, least she got to have her grandbabies with her when she died. That had to be a comfort to her."

They all drank their lemonade in silence. Lila was wondering if they should go and leave this woman in peace when Mrs. Lewis said, "Wanna see a real nice picture of your daddy?" Lila nodded and Mrs. Lewis reached under the coffee table for a photo album. She flipped through it and held up a photo of two teenagers. "That handsome boy there is my son Darnell." She smiled. "He and Willie were best buddies in high school. Your daddy was a good boy and he grew up to be a mighty good man. Believe you me, he never would have left your side if he hadn't been killed."

Lila had always remembered her father's sweetness in a vague way, like the glow of a happy book for which she could no longer recall the plot. In the hospital, whenever she'd tried to think about him—urged on by the psychologist, who hoped Lila would remember more—she was never able to get past her sudden panic, as though if she thought about him too much something terrible would happen. And now, sitting in Eunice Lewis's sunny living room, she was feeling the panic again. She was hearing words, too, those random phrases that had plagued her since she quit reading, though they seemed to have disappeared while she was in the hospital. Except these words weren't random, were they? At least some of them seemed to be variations of what Mrs. Lewis had just said. *He was a good man. He never would have left that way if you hadn't told him. Don't you see what you did? He was a good man and I loved him. I loved him, you stupid little—*

The voice, though, was nothing like Mrs. Lewis's kind southern drawl. It was her mother's voice, Lila knew this even before she saw her mother standing in front of her, as real as anything in the room—more real, because she made everything else disappear.

Her mother was standing in the hall outside Lila's bedroom screaming because Lila had opened her big mouth and told her father about Richard. And Lila knew *full well* that she wasn't supposed to talk about Richard because her mother had said Richard was her mother's *secret friend* a million times. And now her father was dead: shot when he wasn't paying attention because he was so upset when he left for work.

Lila was sure she hadn't told her father the secret, but the only thing she could say was, "I'm sorry, Mommy." As she sat on her bed, pulling the ends of her hair so hard her scalp ached, she kept reminding herself that "dead" meant Daddy couldn't walk in the door and scoop her up in his arms and call her pretty pumpkin. "Dead" meant she couldn't give him the pencil holder she was making for his Christmas present from twigs she'd gathered in the backyard. "Dead" meant he was white like a sheet and scared because he was going to be put in a box in the ground.

What kind of little girl would do such a horrible thing? You did this on purpose, didn't you? You wanted to ruin my life!

"It's a nice photo," Patrick said. "Where is your son now?"

Lila glanced at her husband and then at Mrs. Lewis, who was answering Patrick's question. They were both exactly as they had been, and no wonder, as this felt like it had come to her all at once. It was less like a dream than like a thought. She wouldn't have been surprised if it had all happened in the time it took for a single breath. It felt like a revelation, but also, strangely, like something she'd always known, but had just been too afraid to think about.

Now she understood why she'd destroyed all her dolls that night. It wasn't just the loss of her father; it was the loss of her innocence. Because she was to blame, at least in her mother's eyes. But had her father really been killed because he was upset and distracted? Had she really slipped up and told her mother's secret? She felt guilty even thinking about it, though she also knew she'd been eight years old, the age of Billy's little boy. Even Ashley at her worst would never say that to any of her children, Lila was sure. And Billy had been there, and he'd never blamed Lila. That same night, after her mother had taken to her bed wailing and howling, her brother had told her it wasn't her fault and held her hands to stop her from slapping herself in the face.

The phone rang again and this time Mrs. Lewis talked for a moment, obviously confirming plans for the afternoon. When she hung up, Lila said they really should get going now, and Patrick agreed. They both thanked Mrs. Lewis for all her help, but before Patrick could stand up, Lila said, "I do have one more question before we go." She inhaled. "It won't take long. It's just . . . you mentioned a lot of medicines I was taking. Can you tell me what they were for?"

The old woman looked into Lila's eyes. "I'm surprised you don't know this, honey. Your brother knew all about it. Didn't y'all ever talk on this?"

"No," Lila admitted. She felt her chest constricting as though her heart literally hurt, thinking of all the things her twin kept from her—and that she would never be able to ask him why.

"Well now, it's been a long time so I don't remember what the doctor told Maria all them medicines did. Lots of it was for sicknesses I'd never heard of, but I remember the thing about seizures 'cause that was what Maria talked about the most. There were two or three drugs to keep you from having those seizures, and lots of other stuff that Billy said had no purpose at all but to make you behave." She frowned. "I couldn't understand giving any child medicines for that."

Lila must have looked as stricken as she felt, because Mrs. Lewis shook her head sadly. "Your mama had problems, honey. It wasn't anything you did."

"Thank you," Lila said, but she admitted she was too confused to make sense of any of this.

"Before you go," Mrs. Lewis said, "let me tell you a little story about your mama. Maybe it will help."

Lila nodded and hoped Patrick didn't mind waiting another minute.

"This happened a long time ago," Mrs. Lewis said, "back when Barbara and Willie were still here, but I'll never forget it as long as I live. We were all over at Maria's having dinner: the two of them and Beth and me. Maria was trying to get closer to your mama, 'cause Barbara had stayed in town so long and Maria knew Willie was falling in love with her. So Maria decided to make a special dinner, used her good china, had me over to help 'cause she was so nervous that it all be perfect. I remember Willie was just beaming 'cause he was so glad to have his family and his girlfriend together and things going so well. And he hugged Maria and his sister a lot, 'cause that was his way."

Lila smiled at this description of her father, which reminded her of Billy. Her brother had been so affectionate. Sometimes she woke herself up weeping that she would never feel his arms around her again.

"Now, I thought Barbara looked a little strange whenever he gave one of those hugs, almost like she was jealous, but I figured I was in no position to judge, not knowing her very well. But later on, when Maria was in the backyard giving scraps to her collie, I walked back in the living room just in time to hear Barbara telling Willie that Maria had insulted her. 'She called me spoiled and said I needed to work for a living like everybody else,' Barbara said. Then she let out a kind of phony-sounding cry and threw herself in Willie's arms. 'I love your mother, but she doesn't like me.' "

Mrs. Lewis sighed. "Naturally, Willie got very upset—so upset that Barbara ended up telling him not to worry, that she would go and talk to his mom and try to work things out. I don't know where Beth was, but Maria was back in the kitchen, running water over the plates. Willie slumped down in a chair and I kind of followed a few steps behind Barbara, not trying to be nosy, just wondering what on earth was going on. Barbara came up to Maria and smiled just as sweet as she could be. Then she said, 'I know you think I'm spoiled and I need to work for a living like everybody else. I'm sorry you feel that way. Unfortunately, this means that Willie and I can't stay here any longer.' She smiled again. 'Thank you for the delicious meal.' "

Mrs. Lewis paused to take a drink of her lemonade, and Lila glanced at her husband. He was leaning forward, as though he was riveted by this story. So was she, but she was afraid of it, too, so she concentrated on the willow tree in the backyard, swaying in the breeze.

"Now, the thing you have to understand is your granny was the kind of woman who would have torn out her own tongue before she insulted anybody invited to her house. I watched as she stood there, struck dumb with horror that Barbara had figured out her private thoughts. 'Cause the truth is, Maria did think it was kind of odd that Barbara didn't work. Everybody in town thought that. Everybody thought she was kind of spoiled, too, 'cause it was true, she was.

"Somehow by the time Barbara went back to Willie, she'd worked up a flood of tears that just melted him with worry. They ended up leaving a few minutes later, before Maria could figure out how to fix this or even serve the coconut pie she'd made for dessert. And it was only a few days later that Barbara convinced Willie to move to her grandpa's house up north. Naturally, Maria was just heartbroken and she blamed herself for hurting that girl, even though she hadn't done a thing. She told Willie she was sorry and he forgave her, but they never really talked like they had before, 'cause Willie thought his mama didn't like his girlfriend, and Maria thought his girlfriend didn't want anything to do with her."

Patrick said, "But why did she do it?"

Mrs. Lewis was silent for a moment. "I puzzled on that for a long time. Heck, it took me a while just to get how she did it. You see, there was this little piece of dinner table talk about how hard Maria had worked all her life. Barbara must have taken this talk as meaning that Maria wouldn't approve of her—and that's how she turned it into a lie that was kind of true, too. See, she was really smart, Barbara was, but it was like she used all her smarts to mess with other people, which I couldn't understand." Mrs. Lewis nodded at Patrick. "As to why, my guess is she wanted Willie all to herself, but that still don't explain why she didn't even seem to feel bad being so mean to Maria. But that's the way meanness is sometimes. There's no more reason to it than why a snake bites you if you get close to it."

Mrs. Lewis clasped her hands together; they were gnarled and covered with thick veins, but Lila wished she could hold them. She wished her own granny were still alive. Someone who could make this all right. Patrick was there, and he'd listened to everything as intently as she had, which she was grateful for, though she wished she'd thought to take him to a hotel first. All of this had to seem like an intractable mess to him, and he'd always hated intractable messes, especially when they were disturbing.

After they'd thanked Mrs. Lewis again and both been given one-arm hugs as she steadied herself on her walker, Lila and Patrick made their way to the Subaru in silence. He started the car and turned on the air conditioner; it wasn't that hot, but it was extremely humid. As he headed down the street, he said, "Where to now? Do you still want to stay here until tomorrow as we planned?"

"It's not necessary," she said evenly. "I know you need to get back to work. If you don't get started soon, you won't have a result by the end of the summer. The woods are lovely, dark and deep, but we have promises to keep."

For years, she'd been using this line from Frost's poem with her husband: just her way of acknowledging that they didn't have time for something or other. But it felt strange to be saying this now that she'd remembered the night she'd tried to use that same Frost poem to block out the things her mother and stepfather were saying about her at the dinner table. No wonder Billy was always telling her to read and keep reading, and helping her memorize lines by incessantly repeating them. Because art would never hurt her, he said, but also because she'd had some kind of memory problem, obviously. She vaguely remembered taking the pills that were supposed to have caused this memory problem—if they really had—but her brother had always said they were like vitamins that she had to take because she got sick so often. Her mother hadn't said anything about them, not that Lila could remember anyway.

"My work can wait," Patrick said. "All I care about right now is you." They were at a red light; he turned to face her. He took a breath and his eyes fluttered shut for a second, the way they always did when he was thinking hard about some problem. "I realized today that your life has been unimaginable to me . . . but I want to understand it." He took another breath, and then he said something she never expected. "You can talk to me, Lila. And I promise, whatever you tell me, I won't change the subject. I won't turn away."

She was deeply touched, but it wasn't until they were on the highway, headed back home, that she finally felt brave enough to take him up on his offer. It must have been hard for him to drive and listen to her sobbing out the only part of the story that mattered now. She would never know the truth about her life. She'd lost the plot for good, but she couldn't find reality, either. And everywhere she looked, she found more sorrow and confusion.

"I'm like a person without a past," she cried, "without a self . . . with nothing I can hold on to to keep me on this earth." She gulped when she realized how the last part sounded, and she quickly added that she didn't mean it; she wasn't going to try to harm herself again. "I'm sorry," she said, and then she cried harder, knowing what that night must have done to him.

Through it all, her husband kept his promise. He never seemed afraid or nervous, and he never tried to change the subject. He just held her hand and listened so well that eventually she no longer felt like crying. Even in her gloom, she saw it as a great gift that Patrick truly seemed to want to stand with her in this.

She slept for a while, and when she woke up, they were on I-95, about two hours from Philadelphia. Now she was ready to think again, and to try to understand. She went round and round but she kept coming back to the same place. If only Billy were here, he could tell her what all this meant.

She wasn't sure if Patrick was still paying close attention—it was late and dark and he had to be tired from all this driving—but then he said, "What about the things your brother wrote? You've told me writers always use their lives in some way. Maybe he did and you could interpret it."

Lila hadn't forgotten about all the novels and journals Billy had been working on since he was a teenager. She'd seen a lot of pages over the years, but Billy had never denied that there were hundreds, maybe thousands more he wouldn't show her or anyone. "Call it a writer's need for privacy," he'd said, and Lila hadn't pushed him, knowing writers often felt shy about showing things they thought weren't as good or were merely unfinished. A few days after the funeral, Lila had called Ashley and asked if she could have the boxes of Billy's writings and copies of whatever was on his computer, but her sister-in-law had refused. "That stuff is for my kids," she'd said. "When they're older. If they want it."

At the time, Lila had been too upset to argue, but now she would just have to beg and plead until Ashley relented. All she wanted was a look at everything her twin had written; she could promise to give it all back when she was finished. Or she would give enough of it back that her sister-in-law wouldn't know the difference, since Ashley had no idea what was in any of those boxes, Lila was sure.

They were right outside of Baltimore when she asked Patrick how he would feel about stopping by Harrisburg. "We can turn off on Highway 83 and get there by nine, nine-thirty at the latest. I'm sure Ashley and Pearl will be up, even if William and Maisie are in bed." She waited a moment. "I need to apologize to Pearl anyway."

When she'd discovered that her niece and nephew had been the ones to find her unconscious, her guilt had been so immense that she'd told Dr. Kutchins she almost wished she'd never woken up, so she didn't have to feel this. She'd done a horrible thing to those children—a fact the psychologist didn't deny. "Suicide is incredibly hard on survivors. It's hard on survivors when the attempt fails, and immeasurably harder when the attempt succeeds." Dr. Kutchins had already said many times that Billy's suicide had hurt both his family and Lila in ways Lila wasn't admitting. She was always asking Lila why she couldn't seem to get angry with her twin about anything, but Lila couldn't answer because she really didn't know.

It was too dark to see Patrick's face, but when he didn't respond, Lila said, "We can stay in a hotel there tonight so you won't have to drive home until the morning." She touched his shoulder. "I'm sorry to ask this, but it would really mean a lot to me."

"I don't mind driving, but I need to tell you something. I probably should have told you before." He paused. "I think I made a mistake."

"It's all right," she said, even though she was very nervous. Patrick sounded so strange. And he never kept things from her. True, she hadn't been herself for the last few weeks, but she still wasn't. Whatever it was would have to be very important for him to say it now.

And that's when he told her what had happened to Pearl. Before he was even finished with the details, she started trembling so violently that her husband decided to pull over on the side of the interstate. As he held Lila in his arms, he stressed that the children were perfectly fine. Their mother's boyfriend had no access to them, and neither did she. They were probably staying with friends, but even if they were in foster care, they were all right. If Ashley had thought otherwise, she would have complained, Patrick said. She certainly complained about everything else.

Lila appreciated her husband's efforts to calm her, even if they didn't work. She couldn't explain why she couldn't stop shaking.

It made no sense, but she felt as though she'd been transported to the past, to a night she'd only recently remembered, when she was twelve or thirteen and she'd tried to run away from home.

It was close to Christmas, maybe Christmas Eve, and the ground was covered in snow; Lila kept slipping as she tried to make her way up the hill in her patent-leather shoes with the little straps. There was no moon, and as she hurried through the thick woods, she had to keep one of her arms straight out so she wouldn't run into a tree or have a branch stab her in the eye. But the worst part of all was the cold. It stung her cheeks and made her lungs ache every time she took a breath. It numbed her fingers and made her feet feel like concrete blocks she was dragging along with her. By the time Billy found her, she was crouched down on the ground, too frozen to move or scream. He said he had no choice, the way he always did, and then he grabbed her arm to drag her back home.

CHAPTER NINETEEN

Ashley left the TV on night and day, but it didn't help. With her kids gone, the silence of the house seemed louder than even the most blaring commercial. And the whole place felt so weirdly empty with all their toys and clothes and things put away in dressers and closets. According to the social worker, keeping the house clean was an important part of showing that Ashley was a decent mother. Never mind that a house with kids in it would never be this clean. A house with kids could never stay the same for an hour, much less for day after silent, empty day.

At first, she had her anger at CPS to distract her. That and Kyle, who'd somehow managed to make bail and was staying with some guy he'd met at the truck mechanic's shop—and calling Ashley constantly to beg her to see him. He knew if she agreed she would jeopardize her case, but he kept saying, "I'm innocent," as though that was the only thing that mattered. Usually she just repeated that she couldn't risk it, but after a few more talks like this, she got annoyed and asked him what would happen to her kids if the court didn't figure that out. "They will, baby," he said. "They have to or they're a bunch of lying bastards."

"You sound like you don't even know there are tons of lying bastards in this world. What, were you born yesterday?"

"I know all about liars." His voice was low and mean and she knew he meant Pearl. "I know more than I ever wanted to know about liars."

She couldn't really blame him for being angry if he was innocent, which she honestly believed he was—and not because he kept saying so. It was Pearl's statement to the police that was the problem. It sounded way too much like one of Billy's stories about Lila.

What made it particularly strange was that as far as Ashley could remember, Billy had only told this story once, during the last month before he'd moved out, when he'd already started telling those whoppers about their kids' past. For all Ashley knew, this Lila "memory" was no more real than Billy's bullshit about William solving the Rubik's Cube when he was five. Then too, she didn't think Pearl had even been in the room as Billy described the night fifteen-year-old Lila had been forced to lie facedown on her bed without her shirt on while her stepfather struck her back and shoulders repeatedly with his belt. Lila's only crime, Billy insisted, was questioning that bastard, and for that his twin had been beaten so badly she couldn't lean against a chair or lie on her back for weeks. The rest of the story involved Billy's mother, who didn't know anything about it, Billy said, and something about him and Lila running away shortly after it happened.

There was nothing about trying to have his stepfather punished or put in jail, but everything else in Pearl's story was a perfect match: from her lying facedown on the bed to Kyle's having done it because she questioned him. Of course, the cops would never believe that Pearl had copied the whole idea from her dad; they would think Ashley was just making up shit to protect her boyfriend. Especially since, as that hag social worker pointed out, Ashley had now lived with *two* men accused of endangering her children. They all probably thought of her like one of those trashy women who would do anything to please a guy, even sacrifice her own kids.

Why Pearl had done this was the big mystery, but Ashley tried to understand. She also tried repeatedly to explain to Kyle that her daughter had been going through a tough time. "It isn't fair to you, I know," she said after his whine about Pearl being a liar. "But she's only a kid in a lot of ways. And what happened to her daddy hit her really hard. I don't know why she did it, but I—"

"You wanna know what I think?"

She didn't, but she said, "What?"

"I think she's a spoiled little bitch who always gets—"

"You're calling my daughter a bitch? Who the hell do you think you are?"

He backed down immediately, saying he was sorry but he just missed Ashley so much he was going crazy. "I love you, baby," he said several times. Still, Ashley was mad enough that she would have stopped talking to him forever if she hadn't been worried he'd try to get back at her by making up lies to the cops about what kind of mother she'd been. But she took fewer and fewer of his calls as he got more whiny and obnoxious. And when she finally told him he couldn't keep bothering her at work, he snapped and started screaming about how unfair this was and how it was all Pearl's fault. She could feel her heart beating faster, but she didn't slam the phone down until he snarled that somebody needed to "teach Little Missy a lesson."

She immediately called the detective who'd arrested him. The detective said he'd investigate, and "if the situation warrants, we'll revoke his bail." But he added, "I really wouldn't worry. There's already a restraining order to keep him from getting near your daughter. As long as *you* keep him away from her, she should be fine."

She felt like she'd been slapped, but she called her social worker, Mrs. Pritzel, hoping she would take this seriously. Mrs. Pritzel said she would call the office of the judge who'd granted bail. She also threw in that it was probably good that the court hadn't agreed yet that Ashley could be told the exact address where the kids were residing. "This way he can't get it out of you," she said, as though she, too, believed that Ashley would actually help that creep find her child.

Kyle called again that night around eight o'clock, and when Ashley didn't answer, he kept calling every few minutes all night long. She was afraid to turn off the phone in case the kids needed her—they were allowed to call her, though they hadn't done it yet, but she couldn't call them for fear she would pressure them in some way. She didn't sleep at all and she was a wreck at work the next day, thinking Kyle would show up at her office or even try to hunt down Pearl. But the day after that, they finally issued a warrant to have Kyle picked up again and his bail revoked. Not because of what Ashley said, but because the detective had done his job and found that Kyle had a record in New Mexico. When Ashley heard that her former boyfriend had been in prison before, once for theft and once for *domestic assault,* she felt like she couldn't breathe. Mrs. Pritzel said, "This is why a woman with children has to do her homework before she gets involved with a man." Ashley wondered how she could have found out about a criminal record, but she had no desire to defend herself. It was just like her brother-in-law said: she'd brought a virtual stranger into her kids' lives, and her excuses at the time seemed pathetic now. She'd been chatting on the internet with an old friend from high school when he showed up at her door one day to "surprise" her. He claimed he was between jobs and needed a place to stay. He gave her some sob story about his hard life, and since she'd always been a sucker for stray dogs, she fell for it. One night on the couch turned into a week and soon he was in her bed, her boyfriend. She'd been a gullible fool—and a bad mother. Again.

Kyle had stopped calling, but Ashley couldn't relax for a minute. She wanted to hear that he was behind bars. Her expensive lawyer said that the cops had started a countywide manhunt after Kyle wasn't found at the address he'd given to the court. But there was nothing but silence until Monday, when Mrs. Pritzel told her the police had determined that Kyle had fled the state to avoid prosecution. She was too relieved to care that Kyle had already made it to Albuquerque, which, Mrs. Pritzel said, would make the extradition process more difficult. Even if he made it to Mexico, where they could never prosecute him, Ashley didn't care as long as he stayed far away from her children.

Later that day, her lawyer, Mr. G. Christopher Lynch, called to see if she'd heard that Kyle had left town. He blabbed about that for a few minutes; then he asked a bunch of questions about how Ashley's home study was going, though he didn't seem to care about her answers. He didn't seem to do much of anything, though Barbara Duval had sworn he was the best in the state when she convinced Ashley to hire him and promised to pay all his hefty fees.

For the next day or so, Ashley continued feeling jittery, but by Wednesday night, she was calm enough to feel extremely depressed that she still hadn't talked to Pearl and William. Maisie had begged to see her mom, and Ashley had had supervised visitation with her baby at the preschool several times. All of the other mothers had stared at her, which wasn't a surprise since Kyle's arrest had been in the papers, but it still hurt like hell. Yet that pain was nothing compared to what it was like to know her oldest kids continued to be unwilling even to speak to her. She'd never gone this long without talking to them, and sure, she could always call Mrs. Pritzel for an update—and hear again that her kids were doing as well as could be expected at Barbara Duval's house, no need to worry—but it wasn't the same. She was desperate to tell Pearl how sorry she was, because whether Kyle had hit Pearl or not, and Ashley didn't know anymore, he was still a bad guy who never should have been allowed to speak to her daughter, much less sarcastically call her beautiful Pearl "Little Missy." And her sweet little boy, she was dying just to hear his voice. It had been a month and a half since she'd really heard him speak, and his quick whisper in the police station had only made her long to hear him say something, anything else.

But she knew she deserved all this horrible crap that was happening. Every day that went by, she thought of another reason why she'd been an idiot. Even her mom hadn't approved of her letting Kyle move in so soon after Billy had moved out—hell, her mom hadn't approved of Kyle, period. "You need to work this out with your husband," her mom had said. "Bringing in some loser now is just stupid, and you ain't stupid, are you, Ashley?"

As it turned out, yeah, she was. She was stupid enough to think a man who was nice to her had to be a decent guy. She was stupid enough to think that if she separated from Billy, she would be free from the damn curse or the shit luck or whatever it was that had messed up her whole life. And she was stupid, for sure, to think that any guy could come in and make her forget about Billy.

By the time the weekend rolled around, another weekend without her kids, she was reduced to spending most of her time in bed. She and Billy had bought this bed years ago, before William was born, on one of those days when Billy woke up normal, better than normal, really: Ashley remembered him telling her some quote that he translated to mean he was thrilled just to be alive. He spent more than an hour picking out the perfect quilt for their new queen-size bed. He said he wanted a pattern that said "permanence" and "family." "We might have this forever, Ash. Think of that. This quilt could literally be the fabric of our memories."

She'd put the quilt away when Kyle moved in, but on Sunday morning, she got it back out. That night, she was lying in a fetal position, using her finger to trace the quilt's rich gold and green rings, tan and pink squares, and center orange stars. That she was also talking to her dead husband was weird and she knew it, but she no longer cared how weird she was, except when she was being inspected by Mrs. Pritzel or one of the others from CPS.

She'd believed in angels since her grandma died when she was a little girl. Her mom had told her Grandma was an angel, and it made sense to Ashley since Grandma had been so gentle, almost like an angel when she was alive. Her mom also said you could pray to angels to talk to God for you, and so she decided to pray to Grandma, because Grandma already knew her and would understand what Ashley meant.

If Billy was in heaven, he might be an angel, too. Her priest had told her the old rule wasn't true anymore—that someone couldn't be in heaven if they killed themselves and didn't receive the last rites. God is love, the priest said. God is forgiveness. If your husband was sorry for his sins, the priest said, that was what mattered—and Ashley knew Billy was sorry because he'd told her so.

When he'd called, it was a Tuesday night in March, a little after eight o'clock; Ashley was trying to finish the dishes and trying to keep Maisie from falling apart before she could get her in the bathtub. Kyle was watching some sports thing on TV. William had his boom box blasting upstairs, and Pearl was freaking out about a book she couldn't find that she needed for a homework paper.

They'd been fighting for so long she didn't know how to talk to Billy without yelling, but this time he didn't give her a chance to say her usual "Dammit, why are you calling here?" or "What the hell do you want?" As soon as she said hello, he said, "I'm sorry."

"For what?" She turned off the faucet and wished she had something that would record his answer. The cops had said to let them know immediately if her estranged husband said anything new about what had happened with William. They'd already arranged to have Billy charged with seven counts of child endangerment, but that number could always be increased.

"Everything," he said. "What I've done to our family. And to you."

She was surprised, but she didn't buy it for a minute. Was he trying to soften her up to help his case? It wouldn't work, that was for sure.

Pearl was going through the giant stack of papers on the counter, still looking for that book. Ashley turned to her. "Take Maisie upstairs." The little girl was tearing apart a plastic sponge and screaming that she wanted to watch cartoons. "Run her bath and keep an eye on her."

"Mom, I have homework!"

"Just do what I told you to do!"

Pearl picked up Maisie, but she gave her mother a dirty look. Nothing new there. Ashley expected Billy to give her shit about the yelling he must have overheard, but he didn't call her a barbarian or any of his usual put-downs. He didn't say anything other than repeat that he was sorry.

"I never became the man I wanted to be." He sounded incredibly sad; Ashley could hear that now that she was alone in the kitchen. "I just couldn't escape."

"Are you talking about the curse? 'Cause I don't believe in that anymore." She'd told him this several times during their fights, but he never listened.

"No, Ash. I'm talking about myself."

He hadn't called her "Ash" for months and months, maybe even a year. She slumped down at the table and started picking at a juice stain with her fingernail. She wasn't sure what he meant by escaping himself, but she couldn't help it; she felt sorry for him and blurted out that he could still get his life together. "You'll probably have to see a shrink to figure out why you did all that dangerous crap with William. The cops told me that's the first step, and it won't—"

"It's too late. I've been this way since I was William's age. I never had enough courage."

"What do you mean?" Her voice rose, thinking about all the shit he'd made William do, shit her son still believed showed he was brave. She wished Kyle would talk to William and convince him that jumping off cliffs wasn't brave, it was dumb. She hoped maybe Kyle could make her son understand that being a man was about more than taking stupid risks with your life.

"I never had the courage to do what was right." Billy paused. "I still don't. I'm sorry."

Upstairs, Maisie was screaming like Pearl was drowning her. Kyle's sports show and William's boom box were still going strong. It was way too loud for her to figure out why Billy was telling her all this. She said she had to go now, and before she could offer to call him back later, he was already gone. So she'd walked away feeling like a fool because he'd hung up on her without even saying good-bye.

But now, lying under the quilt, talking to angel Billy, Ashley hoped he would ask God to forgive her for not paying better attention to her husband's cry for help. "You know I'm not that smart," Ashley said. "I just didn't put two and two together."

How many times had Billy told her that if he knew he was immoral and he couldn't change, he'd kill himself? More than a few. And yet she really hadn't understood that that was what he was saying that night, which turned out to be the last night of his life. Maybe she still wouldn't have figured this out if she hadn't had so much time on her hands without the kids. Then she could have lived forever without feeling like God was punishing her for not trying harder to stop her children's father from committing suicide.

It was like an eye for an eye. The kids had lost Billy, the most important person to them—at least the most important to Pearl and William—and Ashley had lost the kids, the most important people to her. She knew she deserved this, but she hoped Billy could fix it. "If not for my sake," she prayed, "for theirs. They didn't do anything wrong. Does God want to punish them, too? Why?"

She traced another ring in the quilt, wondering if the kids felt like they were being punished. What if Pearl and William were actually better off with their grandma? She was rich; she probably had a big house and all kinds of cool stuff. Maybe they were having the time of their lives and that was why they hadn't bothered to call her.

Billy had never said anything bad about his mother, and he wouldn't tell her what was going on now at Barbara Duval's house. She didn't expect him to; she wasn't crazy; she knew prayers weren't answered like telephones. He couldn't tell her how the kids were, and he couldn't make her feel better when she got paranoid that somehow Barbara Duval was going to trick her and try to get custody of her kids. She'd only gone along with Barbara Duval's plan because she'd heard foster care was awful and Pearl and William had to stay somewhere. They weren't close to any of their teachers like Maisie was with the head of her preschool. Ashley's own family wasn't in the state. The only choice other than Billy's mom would have been Lila and Patrick, and the court would never have gone for that after what Lila did, even if Ashley had asked them to.

It was probably dumb to be afraid that Barbara Duval was scheming against her, but Ashley had time for all kinds of dumb fears. She had time to think about each and every nightmare: from the one where William was screaming for her and she couldn't find him, to the one where Kyle had kidnapped Pearl and was torturing her for lying.

Talking to Billy, even if he wasn't an angel, was the only way she could calm herself down. He'd always cared about the kids, too; she knew that even when he was acting too crazy to be allowed to see them. Now that he was dead, she imagined him forever his best self, and she wished he were there to help her figure this out.

When the doorbell rang, for one stupid second she imagined her wish had come true. Or maybe it was the kids themselves? It was almost ten o'clock on Sunday night; no one from CPS and no neighbor would come over this late. No one she knew from work or any of her friends would come over without calling.

She grabbed the baseball bat under her bed when it hit her that it had to be Kyle. Sure he'd left town, but what if he was back? As she crept into the dark living room, she thought about calling the police, but she was worried that would make it worse for her somehow. Kyle could tell them she invited him here. He could lie about anything and that dumb detective might think she didn't care about protecting her kid.

At the front door, she checked the chain to see if it was on tight; then she slowly opened the door a crack and yelled, "I'm calling the cops if you don't leave right now."

"We just want to talk." It was her sister-in-law.

"But we're going," Patrick said. "No need to call the police."

She was so relieved that she took the chain off and opened the door before she thought about whether she wanted those two in her house. Then she stood back when she realized that, as pathetic as it seemed, she was dying to hear any voice but her own.

But when she realized why they were there, she immediately regretted having let them in and insisting on making them hot chocolate. She was trying to be nice; Patrick was rubbing his hands together, and Lila's bare arms had goose bumps, and no wonder, as it had dropped almost thirty degrees in the last few hours, a freak cold snap in the middle of May that had obviously caught Patrick and Lila by surprise—and without jackets or even long sleeves. Yet as soon as she set the steaming mugs in front of them, they made it clear that they hadn't come to see her at all; they only wanted Billy's papers from the basement. She told them the truth, that she'd promised Pearl she could have all of that. And when Lila said she'd give everything back in a few days, Ashley snorted. "I'm not as stupid as you think. How would I know you didn't keep the best stuff?" She shook her head. "Let's just wait for Pearl to get back. If she says she doesn't mind, it's okay by me."

"Can't you call her?" Patrick said. "Ask her how she feels?"

"Not without checking with my caseworker first." Ashley gave him a long look and he lowered his eyes.

"We can wait until tomorrow," Lila said. Her voice was always soft, but there was something else in it now, too, something pitiful. "Before we leave, though, could you at least tell us where the kids are? I'm really worried about them."

"I told you they're fine," she said, turning back to Patrick. "Nothing to worry about."

It was one of Barbara Duval's conditions for taking the kids and paying Ashley's legal fees: Ashley was not to discuss any of this with Lila or her husband. Billy's mother said she and Lila hadn't spoken for years and it was none of Lila's business. She also hinted that Lila would be very upset to learn that any of Barbara's money was going to Ashley and her children rather than to Lila herself. At the time,

Ashley had found this strange, because she'd always thought Lila never cared much about material things, but she'd decided not to question it. She would never have believed that Patrick would tell the cops she was an unfit mother, either. There were probably a lot of things she didn't know about her sister- and brother-in-law.

"If you don't want to tell me because you're afraid I'll try to visit them, I promise you I won't." Lila wrapped her arms around herself. "I no longer think I would be a good influence on them. I did a horrible thing . . . a very selfish thing." She lowered her eyes. "I wish it weren't true, but it seems you were right to try to keep them away from me."

Ashley was both surprised and really impressed that her sister-in-law had admitted this, especially since Lila knew that Ashley had obviously done a crap job of protecting her kids when it came to Kyle. Was it possible that Lila wasn't judging her for that?

"Well, we all make mistakes," she offered. "Me as much as anybody, I guess." She took a sip of her hot chocolate and waited to see if Patrick or Lila would jump on the chance to bitch about Ashley's screwups. When they didn't—and her sister-in-law's lips were quivering like she might cry—she said, "Hell, Lila, you know I don't know what I'm doing. I mean, look at me. I've been wearing this same pair of jeans and this same T-shirt since Friday night." She smirked. "I haven't even showered or combed my hair 'cause I'm too busy praying to your brother."

"I talk to Billy, too," Lila whispered. "In the hospital, I woke myself up more than once speaking to him."

Patrick crossed his arms. He looked like he wanted to say something, but didn't. He probably thought all this talking to Billy stuff was a crock, and maybe it was, but it still made Ashley feel much closer to her sister-in-law. Certainly a hell of a lot closer than she felt to Billy's mother, who, come to think of it, had never even said she missed her dead son. Of course, Lila and Billy had both treated

Barbara Duval like she was already dead. Barbara said they'd had a "falling out," but Ashley wondered what kind of family feud could possibly end up like that.

She was suddenly nervous. Nobody was talking. Lila was staring down at the table, and Patrick's eyes were red with exhaustion. She didn't really decide to tell them where her kids were, but once the words were out of her mouth, she knew why she had. If this screwed her future relationship with Barbara Duval, including an inheritance the old lady hinted at, she didn't care. She didn't even care about the fancy do-nothing lawyer Barbara was paying for. She needed to hear that the kids would be okay at Barbara's house. If Billy couldn't tell her that, she would have to trust his twin.

Patrick responded first. He sounded confused. "They're in New Jersey?"

She told him no; Barbara Duval had another house about twenty miles from here. "The social worker says it's a nice place," she said, looking at Lila. "I guess your mom is looking out for them, right?"

Her sister-in-law's normally pale face had turned ashen. She looked so strange that Ashley wondered if she was going to be sick.

"I didn't know what else to do," Ashley sputtered. She felt frozen in Lila's bizarre gaze. "Pearl called her first. I don't know how she got Barbara's number."

"I'm sure they're fine." Patrick looked at his wife. "Let's not panic."

Ashley pushed back from the table like she was going to run, but there was no escaping this feeling. "Oh God," she stammered. "I knew this wasn't a good idea."

And the weird part was, she had known. She'd ignored her instincts with Barbara Duval just like she'd ignored the feeling that Kyle was lying to her about his past, about looking for work, about how much he liked her kids. Just like she'd ignored the voice inside her head that had told her, year after year, that Billy's dream of a happy life was never going to happen, that no matter how bad he wanted it, it just wasn't in him.

Then it hit her that she also knew what had driven Pearl to run to Lila's house, and even to call Barbara Duval. It was so clear now she was angry at herself for not getting it before. The night Billy died, Pearl had gone into the basement and come up with one of his manuscripts, bound in a blue cover. An old one, written when he still used a typewriter, before Ashley had even known him. Pearl shut herself in her room and read that thing constantly whenever she didn't have chores or homework. Her daughter never said what it was about, and Ashley didn't think to take a closer look. She did notice that Billy had scribbled on a title—and recently, too, since he'd used one of Maisie's stickers to write it on—but she didn't think about what that title meant.

"For LEC: Truth Comes in with Darkness." Now it seemed obvious. "LEC" was Lila's initials. The rest was a quote from one of Lila's favorite books, the one she wrote about in graduate school. Billy didn't say it constantly like some quotes, but Ashley remembered it because he told her it came from the most heartbreaking story he'd ever read.

He must have given Pearl that sticker and told her which manuscript to put it on. But Maisie hadn't even gotten those stickers until a few weeks before Billy died. Did he already know he was going to kill himself when he wrote this? Ashley felt sure he did. And he wanted Lila to have whatever he'd written all those years ago, but instead his daughter took it on herself to read it at least once and maybe several times. And this was why she stomped into Ashley's room one night, when Kyle was watching TV, and said, "You never understood him, but I'm going to. He was my father and he deserved to have someone who wanted to know what the fuck happened to him!"

Ashley told Pearl to watch her mouth. She was folding clothes and she thought she didn't have time to deal with her daughter's anger. Were Pearl's eyes red? Probably. She was always upset about her father. Why hadn't Ashley paid more attention to this? Why had she only given Pearl hugs and repeated that same old crap about time healing all wounds, which she didn't even believe?

Now Ashley felt like crying, thinking of what her little girl was up to. She'd gone to Billy's sister, and when that didn't work out, she'd arranged to be with Billy's mother. Because she missed her father so badly she'd convinced herself that understanding him would make it hurt less. Even though he wasn't there, she was still running to her crazy, magical daddy. The only one who could catch the air people queen.

CHAPTER TWENTY

The first few days at New Grandma's house were mostly boring, except the ride back and forth to Chandler Elementary. That part was awful, just William and Grandma in the big white car, driving for what felt like hours instead of fifteen minutes like it had been on the bus from his real house. He used to hate that bus because Sophie Peterson liked to grab his backpack and dump everything out on the floor, but now he knew there were worse things than crawling under seats to catch pencils and markers before they rolled away.

New Grandma talked more than anybody in the entire world. That's what William whispered to Pearl, and she held her hand across her mouth to keep her laugh inside so New Grandma wouldn't say, "What's so funny?" Wherever they went in the whole huge house, they were never really sure they were alone 'cause their grandma might just appear out of nowhere, like some ghost who could walk through walls.

If Pearl had been in the big white car, too, it might not have been so bad, but she got to stay home all day. After she told the social worker she was afraid to go to school 'cause of what Kyle did to her, her teachers said since she already had an A+ for everything this year and high school was almost over, she could just come in to take the finals in a few weeks. So she wasn't there when William was squeezing himself against the passenger door and trying so hard not to cry that his stomach hurt and then feeling dumb that he was such a baby that he kept wanting to cry when New Grandma hadn't hit him or yelled or done anything but talk and talk and talk.

"I've made an observation about you, William," she said one afternoon before they were even out of the school parking lot. "You want everyone to think you're not very smart because it allows you to get away with more. Very clever."

At first, he thought New Grandma was about to punish him. He knew trying to get away with things was bad, like trying to get out of doing the dishes. And clever wasn't always good, because sometimes his father had said "how clever" when he and his mom were fighting and his mom would scream louder or even cry. But when he said he hadn't done anything wrong, New Grandma smiled.

"Ah, you're doing it with me, too. Touché. However, I do hope at some point you'll realize you don't have to bother. Nothing you could say would shock me. It's one of the advantages of refusing to play the game."

New Grandma talked about The Game constantly, but it wasn't a normal game like Monopoly or baseball. William figured this out, though he wasn't sure what it did mean 'cause she said it so many ways, like anything could be a game, even being a grandma. On Wednesday morning when they were late to school, before she came inside to say she was sorry to William's teacher, she winked at William. "It's time to play the grandma game. Don't worry, I've always been very good at handling peons."

When he got home, William remembered to ask Pearl what a "peon" was. His sister said it meant worker, like a foot soldier. He asked Pearl if a peon could be in a game and she said sure. "Pawns are peons. Dad used to call them peasants, remember?"

He did remember, but he didn't see what any of this had to do with being late for school. Maybe he would've if he were better at playing chess, like Pearl was, but then he might be stuck playing with New Grandma all the time, like his sister. Grandma had a whole shelf of silver and gold trophies that she won playing chess, though William remembered what Daddy said about them. The trophies were one of the first things William had noticed when his father brought him to this house for the escape Challenge, 'cause they were so shiny and cool-looking, way better than the stuff they gave out at school for the spelling bee. But Daddy said they were "worthless" and then took William upstairs, where he taught him how to pick a lock, in case he ever got locked inside a room somewhere and needed to get free.

Staying in this house, William missed Daddy worse than ever. Somehow New Grandma figured that out—it was another of those things she called her "observations." And William hadn't said one word about Daddy to New Grandma, 'cause Pearl had warned him not to. So how could New Grandma know? He wasn't going to ask, but she told him anyway. She said she could read his mind!

"And now you're afraid, aren't you?" She laughed. "And you're more afraid that I knew you were afraid."

She was right, he was really scared and clearing his throat like crazy. Since she'd never said anything about his tic, he didn't even try to control himself. He figured maybe grandmas were too old to hear stuff like tics unless they had one of those brown microphone things in their ears, like his grandma in New Mexico had.

"I could always tell what your father was thinking, too." She touched William's shoulder. "We were so close. I think I can safely say that for most of his childhood, he considered me his best friend."

William knew this wasn't true. Daddy had said a thousand times that Aunt Lila was his best friend when he was a kid. But before he could say one word, New Grandma had figured out what he was thinking again! It was so creepy. She also said he was wrong 'cause Daddy and Lila weren't that close. "Oh, your father liked to pretend that he and his sister had some mystical twin bond, but the truth was, he was far more like my side of the family than Lila ever was. Until they were teenagers, your father was only kind to poor Lila out of guilt. Then she bewitched him, but I can't blame him for that. Whatever problems she may have had, Lila was a beautiful girl."

New Grandma was smiling, but it looked wrong somehow. Later, when William was trying to explain all this to Pearl, he kept messing up the parts he didn't understand, but he did know New Grandma's smile looked like she just ate a spoonful of pepper. Pearl whispered, "I told you not to talk to her about Dad and that goes for Aunt Lila, too. She can't—"

"What's the secret?" New Grandma said. She was standing in the doorway of the kitchen when one second before she'd been upstairs in the bathroom. William had heard the water running with his own ears. He felt the hair rise on the back of his neck.

Pearl's eyes were darting around, but she didn't sound scared or nervous when she came up with a big fat lie. "I was just telling him I hope we don't have leftover mushroom ravioli for dinner because I really didn't like it. I'm sorry I didn't tell you this before. I didn't want to be rude."

"And so we'll have something else," Grandma said. "Your candor is refreshing, Pearl. Most children would have made something up."

Their grandma looked happy, which William didn't get at all since she'd said she'd spent hours making that ravioli while he was at school. Plus, she winked at him when Pearl wasn't looking, like she knew Pearl was lying about the secret. Later that night, when New Grandma was on the phone, he tried to warn Pearl, but his sister gave him a dirty look and hissed, "I already told you she can't know what we're thinking. She may be smart, but she's not Santa Claus."

Every day, Pearl seemed to get grumpier and grumpier, but William figured it was because she never went anywhere or saw her friends or did anything but hang around New Grandma, who kept beating her at chess. So far, Pearl had lost every game and Grandma said she would continue to lose until she thought about the game differently. This was on Friday afternoon, when William was already feeling happier 'cause he knew he wouldn't have to ride with New Grandma for the next two days. Then she told William that someday he would be a much better chess player than his sister, and he couldn't help feeling a little proud. Nobody had ever said that to him, not even Daddy. But when New Grandma asked him if he liked chess, he said, "It's okay."

"Nicely done," she said. "It's always best to keep your true feelings to yourself. This is why your sister is failing. She shows all her disappointments to her opponent. Even when she believes she's hiding her motivations, she goes too far the other way to be convincing."

Grandma went on about Pearl and chess until William lost interest, but he couldn't do much besides look out the window. This was the problem with New Grandma's talking and talking and talking: he couldn't multiply numbers in his head or think about Daddy's reminders or even daydream 'cause her voice was so sharp, the words felt like pokes in the ribs.

"For instance," New Grandma said, "look how hard Pearl is working to hide the fact that she doesn't like me."

Maybe he was kind of daydreaming. He thought she was talking about chess. He could feel her looking at him and his face felt as hot as when he was a kindergartner and he got sunburned at the shore.

"Ah," she said, "so I am right about that."

He knew she was reading his mind again, but this time it was worse than ever 'cause he didn't even know he was thinking Pearl didn't like New Grandma until New Grandma said that. He was so scared, he yelled, "It's not true. Pearl wanted to come stay here! It was her idea and everything!"

"Poor boy, are you worried I'll tell her about this? I know your sister would be angry with you, and even if she wasn't, she would undoubtedly consider you stupid for admitting this, when we both know you are at least as smart as she is." She turned into the long driveway. "This can stay our little secret, agreed?"

He spit out "yeah" 'cause he didn't want his sister to be mad at him and he really didn't want her to think he was stupid. But he felt so nervous that he ran into his room and shut the door without even saying hi to Pearl, even though he hated his room more than any other part of the whole house. Grandma called it the "brown guest room," but the curtains and the sheets and the comforter weren't really brown; they were like a swirly pattern of brown and white and black that made William think of dead animals. The bed was gigantic, but it was a lot harder than his bed at home and so high up that he couldn't move away from the center for fear he'd fall out. The only good thing was he had his own bathroom and it was just boring brown, not the dead animal pattern. He spent a lot of time in the bathroom, looking out the window, wondering if he could walk all the way home before New Grandma or the social worker caught him and made him come back. He was pretty sure he knew the way, but he hated the idea of being out there alone on the little road through the woods. If only he hadn't chickened out when Daddy wanted him to stay in the woods by himself, maybe he'd be brave now.

He was lying on his bed, chewing up little balls of paper because his throat hurt, and thinking about his mom. Every time the social worker came to check up on them, she said Pearl and William could call their mom anytime. But Pearl told him he couldn't 'cause it would mess up her plan and she made him swear he wouldn't without checking with her first. He was worried about Mommy, but he knew she'd still be sad even if he did call, 'cause she couldn't be with him and Pearl. Daddy had killed himself 'cause he couldn't see them, even though Daddy got to talk to them on the phone all the time.

William had swallowed dozens of spitballs, but he didn't feel any better. He couldn't think about Mommy without being scared she'd kill herself. He couldn't think about Daddy without crying like a stupid baby. He didn't want to think at all 'cause it made him nervous, but there was nothing else to do. This place didn't have any TV or Nintendo or even any toys other than the ones he'd packed, and he'd played with them a zillion times. He could have listened to his boom box, but he felt too embarrassed after what New Grandma had said yesterday. "Your musical selection suits you. It's from the romantic period, very emotional. And you're certainly not a normal boy."

He knew "romantic" was some kind of love thing. That was bad enough, but the part about him not being a normal boy made him feel like a stupid sissy. He could never run as fast or hit the ball as good as the other boys. Everyone made fun of him 'cause he was so short for his age and he had to wear those glasses all the time.

But he'd always thought music like S-H-O-S-T-A-K-O-V-I-C-H was not just for girls. Why hadn't Daddy ever told him it was this dumb romantic thing?

He was looking out the window, watching a squirrel darting up and around a tree, when he was finally so bored he closed his eyes. The next thing he knew, someone was knocking on his door, hard, and then Pearl was in the room. He was confused at first. He thought she was waking him up to go to school. But the clock by the bed said 5:17, and he remembered he hadn't even eaten dinner yet. Plus, she was yelling at him to pay attention because she was only going to say this once.

"Shhh," he said and pointed at the hall.

"She's at the store," Pearl said loudly. "And who cares anyway, when you've already done the stupidest fucking thing you could possibly do!"

His sister was pacing back and forth from the bed to the window. She was as mad as he'd ever seen her, way madder than when he spilled water on her cell phone.

"What?" he said, sitting up. He felt kind of guilty, but he didn't remember why. He'd been dreaming about Daddy being in a bike race with some stranger man. In the dream, William was down at the finish line, holding a flag, hoping Daddy won.

"You told her I didn't like her! And don't give me that bull about her reading your mind!"

"But she did. She even said so."

"She told me it was only a joke. A JOKE, just like I told you it had to be. And how could you believe something like that? Don't you remember the millions of times Dad told us to use our reason, not superstition? What do you think he meant, huh?"

William had never been sure what his father meant by that. Daddy told him it was like the difference between really understanding numbers and just believing some numbers were lucky and could win you the lottery. "But you can still like six best," Daddy said, and smiled. Six had always been William's favorite number.

He was swallowing hard, hoping he could stop himself from saying something dumb and making Pearl even madder. He was so thirsty. He wished he hadn't chewed up that paper. Mommy had told him over and over that it was bad for him.

"And then you just came up here and fell asleep like nothing happened." Pearl leaned against the big dresser with the giant mirror. Her face looked like she hated him, but in the mirror, he could see the back of her head and the yellow ropes of her hair that smelled like flowers. "Why didn't you at least tell me about this?"

"I'm sorry." He looked down at the dead animal blanket. "Grandma said it was a secret and—"

"Perfect. Just fucking perfect." Pearl stomped to the door. She sounded like she was spitting. "I never thought my own brother would keep secrets about *me*!"

And then she was gone. William jumped off the bed to follow her. He ran to the opposite end of the staircase, to the blue guest room where Pearl was staying, but she wasn't there. He rushed all over the top floor and ran downstairs; he checked the kitchen and the dining room and the giant book room and the exercise room and the special chess room and even New Grandma's bedroom, but just to peek in, because he was afraid to walk all the way inside. He was yelling his sister's name at the top of his lungs and starting to cry, too, as he went from the front yard to the backyard, and then up the big hill where Pearl liked to walk. At the top of the hill he still couldn't see Pearl anyplace so he kept going into the forest, even though it scared him. He yelled his sister's name over and over until his throat was on fire. The sun was shining orange on the trees and he was about to go back when he looked up and saw something that was so surprising, he forgot about crying. It was a beautiful tree house, just sitting in the sky.

He'd always wanted a tree house, but his daddy had said no, it was too dangerous, and Kyle was too busy watching TV to build one, even though he kept saying he would. And now one had just appeared, like it was a gift for him. He might have been too scared to climb up if the tree hadn't had all these wooden steps nailed in the bark, like a built-in ladder. It only took him a few minutes and then he was sitting in that tree house all by himself, on top of the world.

It had the coolest window, just big enough for his face to squeeze through, like he was the lookout on a pirate ship. He didn't see Pearl anywhere, but he did notice the big white car heading toward their house, meaning New Grandma was coming back.

He stayed in the tree house for a long time, pretending he was a robot on a spaceship, and then Batman in the bat cave, and then a spy who was hiding out from all the evil government bad guys like Daddy used to talk about. He pretended New Grandma was one of those bad guys as he watched her cooking in the bright white kitchen. He took a crumbling branch from the tree house floor and stuck it out the window, like it was a telescope to see her better, but then it turned into a gun and he shot her, *bang, bang, bang,* so Pearl would like him again.

He felt sort of guilty for shooting New Grandma, but even worse when he realized it was getting too dark and he had to climb down for dinner.

After Grandma told him Pearl was going to be eating in her room, he rushed upstairs to make sure his sister was really there and hadn't run away or disappeared. He opened her door without knocking and saw her sitting on her bed, reading and eating from a tray made of wood. He felt better, until she yelled at him to go away.

Then he was all alone, and he walked back down to the dining room as slow as a turtle. He sat down to a plate of stinky fish he'd never seen before and eggplant, which he hated. He asked

Grandma if Pearl was being punished and she said no. "But I do expect a certain level of civility."

He wasn't sure what she meant, but he was glad Pearl wasn't in trouble. And he liked the idea of eating in his own room, but when he asked if he could, too, Grandma laughed. "You're very civil, William. I can't imagine you ever saying the cruel things your sister said to me this afternoon. I can't imagine you screaming at her the way she just screamed at you."

"She was mad 'cause—"

"Please don't make excuses for her. She needs to understand that in this house, everyone is expected to be rational. Healthy disagreement is wonderful, unreasonableness is not."

He listened to a lot more talk like this while he moved the eggplant around his plate and cut the fish into little tiny pieces that didn't smell as bad. Then he remembered to ask New Grandma why she told Pearl the secret.

"It wasn't your fault. Please remember that, no matter what your sister accuses you of."

"But why'd you tell her?"

"Because I care about my son's children." She smiled. "Why else?"

He didn't know what to say to that, so he kept swallowing the fish and wishing Pearl would come downstairs. But she didn't, and when dinner was over, New Grandma told him she was going to teach him more about chess. He said he didn't really want to learn, but Grandma said, "Of course you do. You're a smart boy. What would your father say if you didn't try?"

Daddy always said trying was super important, so he was trapped. New Grandma even made him clean his glasses. It was an awful night, except when Grandma said he had a "talent with bishops." The bishop was his favorite of all the chess pieces 'cause he liked diagonal lines.

The next morning started out bad, too. As soon as he came downstairs, New Grandma reminded him that the housekeeper was coming on Monday, so he had to make sure his things were put away. "She's going to clean your room from top to bottom," Grandma said, "including your closet." Then she gave him that weird wink-smile, like she was saying, "You can't hide anything from me."

He'd woken up determined to remember that New Grandma couldn't read his mind. Pearl said it was impossible and Pearl was really, really smart. Somehow New Grandma was tricking him, but he couldn't think about that now; he was too worried she'd find the gun. Daddy had told him not to let anybody know about it, and even though it was in the toolbox, the housekeeper person might wonder what was in there and then she and Grandma might break open the lock.

He went back in his room to think about where to hide it, and then he thought of the perfect place. His new tree house. New Grandma was way too old to climb up there, even if she did figure out where it was, which she couldn't anyway, 'cause she really couldn't read his mind. He moved it while Grandma was on her exercise machine and Pearl was still asleep. Nobody saw him take it out of the toolbox, he was sure. He wrapped it in the extra pillowcase with the dead animal pattern, stuck it under his shirt, and crept up the hill and into the woods. He didn't stay in the tree house very long, 'cause it was so cloudy, like it could burst out raining any second. He just left it in the corner, under a bunch of old boards with rusty nails sticking out, and on the top board, he wrote in magic marker: Stay Away Or Else.

By the time he got back, Pearl was downstairs making waffles with New Grandma and talking like nothing was wrong. And they were talking about Lila, which Pearl had told him never to do. Pearl was smiling but not that fakey-friendly smile, her real smile.

She even smiled at William when she said, "Grandma has decided to give me Aunt Lila's clothes. Isn't that cool?"

It seemed like a weird thing to care about, some old clothes, but Pearl was excited when they all went down to the basement to get the things. There were only three boxes, which William was glad about 'cause it meant they didn't have to go back and forth, lugging up stuff. He wanted to get out of this spooky basement as fast as possible. Even Daddy had said the basement was creepy. Grandma kept all the boxes up on wood squares; she said the basement got wet when it rained. William saw little trickles of water coming down on the wall in back, which seemed so sad, like the stones were crying.

Grandma and Pearl went up to Pearl's room to go through everything, and William sat on a chair by the giant bookshelf, counting the rows of books. For a while, everything was calm and sort of boring, but then New Grandma showed up, right when he was ready to count the sixth row (his favorite), and told him he had to do something for his sister. "Go upstairs and tell her she doesn't look too skinny in that dress."

He wasn't sure why he had to do this instead of Grandma, but he stood up and headed upstairs. He could hear Pearl crying before he got halfway up. He felt so bad for his sister that he ran the rest of the way. She was standing in the middle of the room in a violet dress that looked softer than anything he'd ever seen. "You look nice," he said, 'cause she did and 'cause he wanted her to stop crying.

She peered into his face and sniffed. "You really think so?"

He nodded and she sniffed a few more times, looking at herself in a mirror on the closet door. She turned to the right and the left, and the soft dress sort of whirled around like a spinning top. Then he remembered what he was supposed to say.

"You don't look too skinny."

She let out a wail so loud it hurt his ears. He told her he'd only said that 'cause Grandma had asked him to, but that didn't make her stop crying. He could barely make out what she was saying. "How could you do this to me?"

He didn't know what he'd done, but he tried to make her feel better. He went over and threw his arms around her waist and said, "It's okay," the way he always did when Mommy was sad. The dress was just as soft as it looked, but a shiny kind of soft. He wished he had a blanket like this.

She pulled his hands off and jumped back like he was dirty, even though he'd washed off all the syrup on his fingers right after breakfast. "If Grandma told you to hit me," she sobbed, "would you do that, too?"

He was confused and horrified. He never hit anybody, not even mean kids at school. "No." He shook his head. "No."

"But it's perfectly fucking fine to tell me I look fat? Because *she* told you to?"

"Language, Pearl." Grandma was standing in the doorway. "Please calm down. It's hardly a tragedy that one dress doesn't flatter you. Try some of the others. Several of Lila's things were loose on her. Perhaps those would—"

"Just stop it!" Pearl was still crying and her voice came out all squeaky, like one of Maisie's baby toys. "Leave me alone!"

Grandma turned to him. "William, will you wait in your room?"

"No." He stomped his heel and stared right at Grandma. "I wanna stay with Pearl."

"I don't think that's appropriate." She nodded in Pearl's direction. "Your sister is going to be changing clothes."

Pearl already had the dress unzipped and halfway over her head. He saw his sister's pink underpants and he was so embarrassed that he turned away and headed for his own room.

He could hear Pearl yelling all the way down the hall. His tic was going crazy and he decided to make a fort out of that stupid dead animal blanket. He hadn't made a fort for a long time, but he didn't care if it was babyish. He needed someplace to hide from the feeling he'd hurt his sister without even knowing how.

He took the heavy gold bookends from the desk to fasten the blanket on the windowsill side and pulled the desk chair up on the bed to hold down the other side. Then he crouched down under it and took off his glasses, so everything would go blurry. He held his knees to his chest and listened to the wind rattling the glass and then, a little while later, raindrops tapping on the window. He liked the sound of rain best of all the sounds in the world.

He wished he could stay in this fort until it was time to go home, but he knew he couldn't. He had to have lunch; he had to have dinner; he had to come when New Grandma called him for chess lessons and anything else. And all day, stuff kept happening between Grandma and Pearl that he didn't understand and made him so nervous he thought his heart would burst. His sister cried so often it was like she wasn't even the normal Pearl anymore, but some sad alien who took over her body. He was so scared by nighttime that he couldn't fall asleep and he lay in bed for hours before he decided to creep down the hall and see if his sister was awake, too.

She wasn't, but he sat down on her bed 'cause he felt better just being in her room. The sound of her normal breathing was so nice that before long he was under the covers, lying next to her. He knew Pearl didn't like it when he crawled into bed with her, but she always let him anyway if he had a bad dream. He figured he'd tell her in the morning that he had a bad dream, which wasn't a big lie, since this was as scary as a bad dream for sure.

It was all his idea, but New Grandma didn't care. The next morning, she was in Pearl's room, standing with her arms crossed, saying Pearl should know better than to sleep with her brother.

"It's simply inappropriate," Grandma said. "At your age, you know exactly what I'm talking about."

Pearl was sitting on the edge of the bed in her sleep shorts and the MOBYlives T-shirt that used to be Daddy's but shrunk in the wash so Daddy gave it to her. She looked super upset, but at least she wasn't crying. She said she was sorry a bunch of times and she kept saying stuff like, "I didn't mean it," and "I won't do it again."

William was rubbing his eyes, trying to talk but nobody would listen. After a while, he went back into his own room. He wanted his mom so bad, worse than he ever had in his life.

The rest of Sunday turned out to be even more awful than Saturday. Pearl was like the invisible person in the house and New Grandma wouldn't leave William alone long enough for him to sneak out to the tree house or do anything fun. Even when she took him shopping to buy him any toy he wanted, he couldn't stop wondering why Pearl couldn't come, too. New Grandma told him because he was a wonderful boy, but he sure didn't feel like one. He got this huge Lego model he'd always wanted that cost more than a hundred dollars and he was kind of excited, but then Grandma told him to build it downstairs, with her. While he clicked the blocks together, she did her yoga and listened to weird music and talked so much that he could still hear her voice that night when he closed his eyes to try to sleep.

By the time he got home from school on Monday, everything was a zillion times weirder. Pearl was sitting in the big book room and New Grandma sat down with her and they started talking about what Pearl was going to eat and not eat and how many hours she would spend on Grandma's exercise machine and all this other stuff that Pearl had to do, but nobody would tell William why. Even after he got his sister to come outside with him, so New Grandma couldn't hear, Pearl just shook her head when he asked what was going on.

"It's not fair," he said. "You like muffins, and Grandma has that good cinnamon kind." Muffins were on that list of foods Pearl couldn't eat.

"You wouldn't understand," Pearl said, swallowing hard. "It's part of my diet, to prepare myself to be competitive. Also I have to lose ten pounds before I can fit into Aunt Lila's clothes."

They were walking on the hill and the sun was shining on her yellow hair. Her face and her hair were the regular Pearl, but she was wearing these ugly black pants he'd never seen before and a shirt that looked like it was made for a giant.

"Mommy says diets are bad."

Pearl shrugged. "Mom eats junk food and never exercises. I think Grandma knows more about keeping in shape than Mom does. I'm glad she wants to help me."

His sister didn't sound glad at all. Her voice was like a zombie's and her eyes looked sort of red, like she'd been crying again while he was at school. For the first time, he felt lucky that he was only stuck with New Grandma in the car, not all day like Pearl was. He knew they played chess a lot, but he didn't know what else they did. Whatever it was, he knew it wasn't any fun.

"You got to call Staci. She'll be nice to you. You can go somewhere with her in her car and then—"

"I can't. Staci's so thin." Pearl lowered her eyes. "I can't face any of my friends now that I know what I look like."

He threw his arms around Pearl. "I hate Grandma!" he said, 'cause he really did all of a sudden. He knew it was bad to hate anybody, but he couldn't help it.

"It's all my fault," Pearl whispered. She didn't push him away, but she felt like Maisie's doll, all floppy. "I guess I'm not as smart as I thought."

"You are so! You're smart like Daddy!"

"I wish I was." He could feel her shaking. "I always thought I was like Dad and Lila. Dad always said I could do anything, but I don't think it's true."

He wanted to drop his arms, 'cause he felt weird hugging his sister, but he was worried she'd fall over or start crying so hard she wouldn't be able to breathe and then she'd die. "I'm gonna call Mommy."

She pulled away. "You can't do that. You promised!" She knelt down in the grass and looked at him. "Please, William. I'm begging you."

Her face was covered in streaky tears. He felt so sorry for her that he said okay, but then he asked why.

"Because I still don't know what happened to Dad. And even if I'm too stupid to understand, I have to keep trying." She stood up and held her arms out, like she was praying to the sky. "Oh, Daddy," she stammered. "Daddy."

Pearl never called their father Daddy and it scared William. It scared him so bad he couldn't sleep that night. His sister was awake, too; he could hear her walking up and down the hall like a nervous ghost, but he knew he'd get her in trouble if he came out and said anything. New Grandma had told him at dinner that Pearl needed to be left alone, to think about what kind of person she wanted to be. William didn't understand at all, but he didn't understand any of this. He didn't understand why Pearl couldn't eat anything but salads and why she had to read all these big boring chess books and why Grandma talked about his sister like Pearl was in the dumb class at school, when William *was* in the dumb class and Grandma kept saying he was so smart.

And day after day, it got worse and worse and worse, like Pearl was a toy and her battery was dying. But she kept telling him nothing was wrong and she didn't want to see her friends or go anywhere and it wasn't Grandma's fault and he couldn't call Mom or tell the social worker and don't worry about it. He was so confused his head hurt whenever he wasn't in school. And when he was at school, he worried about his sister so much that his teacher said if he didn't pay attention, he'd be spending next year in third grade, too.

He knew for sure now that New Grandma couldn't read his mind, 'cause she still talked in the car like he was a good boy. Even when she said, "I know you're upset about your sister," she didn't really know how he felt or she'd be super mad.

He spent most of Saturday in the tree house and he snuck out there again on Sunday morning, after Pearl told him to mind his own business when New Grandma was laughing at Pearl while they were playing chess. "You'll never win unless you learn to control yourself," Grandma said, and then ha, ha, ha, like a witch. He was so mad that he didn't come down when it was time for lunch, even though he was hungry. His plan was to stay in the tree house forever, but then Pearl came and found him before dinner and said if he didn't come down right now, she'd come up and get him.

He didn't notice Pearl's arm was hanging all weird until they were walking back down the hill. He asked if she hurt herself and she said yes, but he could tell she was lying. Then he knew for sure that New Grandma had hit Pearl, but Pearl said, "It's no big deal. She was trying to teach me an opening any serious player should know and I kept being too stupid to get it. She just twisted my arm a little to get me to pay attention." Pearl smiled, but it was a nervous smile, like the kind you give a mean teacher. "It worked, too. I almost won, and Grandma says I'm just about ready for my first tournament now. She said if I work really hard, I can try out for the teenage team in Philadelphia next week." Pearl was walking quickly, but she was holding the busted arm by the elbow. She looked past William. "Dad was on the team when he was nine years old. I'm six years late, but better late than never."

"Daddy said chess trophies are worthless. Worthless means—"

"I know what it means. And Dad only said that because he quit playing chess when he got older, because he was angry with Grandma about something that happened with Aunt Lila."

He ran up to her. "What?"

"You're too young to understand. I don't blame Dad. But it wasn't Grandma's fault, either, I know that now. She couldn't stop Aunt Lila from hurting him."

His head was throbbing and his stomach felt like it had moved up to his throat. Daddy loved Aunt Lila. This didn't make any sense. "Grandma hit you and made you cry. I don't like her. I wanna—"

"It didn't hurt, okay? It was nothing compared to letting that freak who lives next to Staci take his belt and . . ." She mumbled something else, but before he could ask what she was talking about, she said, "And it's all for my own good. She's trying to help me, just like she helped Dad." Pearl went to push her hair out of her eyes, but her face crinkled up like she was in pain and she dropped her elbow back onto her hand. "She wants me to be a champion. She said she'd pay for me to go to Princeton if I just try harder. That's what Dad wanted for me, and I think he'd be proud that I'm willing to work to get it." Pearl looked back at the trees. "I don't want to be lazy anymore."

"You're not lazy," he mumbled. 'Cause she wasn't. Pearl worked hard in school and helped around the house and did everything right. Even her plan to run away was all neat and perfect 'cause she thought of all the stuff they needed to pack.

He followed her back to the house for dinner. But before Pearl could sit down and eat, she had to change into those ugly black pants that didn't fit her and the giant shirt. Pearl said these clothes were to get her to be careful about food, or she'd end up wearing this size for real. New Grandma had given her a little scale and everything she ate had to be weighed like fruit in the grocery store. It was all part of her training, Grandma said, and Pearl nodded like she didn't mind eating nothing but a bunch of lettuce leaves and four bites of chicken.

William didn't eat much, either, 'cause he was thinking about the last Challenge, and what he was supposed to do if Kyle hurt them. He'd forgotten some of the stuff on the list, but he remembered Daddy saying that if Kyle went away and a new person showed up, William should just scratch out Kyle and put in the new person's name. But New Grandma couldn't be the new person, 'cause she was Daddy's own mom. But she'd hit Pearl and a bunch of other stuff William knew was bad, even if he couldn't say what.

All through dinner, he could hear Daddy talking to him, not like Daddy was a ghost, but like Daddy was reminding him of stuff. Like when New Grandma was smiling at Pearl, William heard Daddy warning him not to trust grown-ups he didn't know. "Even if they smile and act nice, don't be fooled. They don't care about you and some of them might want to hurt you." And when New Grandma was wondering why Pearl always wore that ring around her neck, the cool snakes one, and Grandma said a bunch of stuff about Aunt Lila he didn't understand that made Pearl take off the necklace and set it next to her napkin, like it was some icky piece of food she couldn't chew, William heard Daddy saying, "Words can be like arrows. You can't see them, and that's why they're so dangerous. With an ordinary arrow, if you get hit, you know you have to remove it from your body. With words, you can never pull them out once they get stuck in your mind."

But he didn't get scared until New Grandma was talking about how cold it was going to be tonight; so cold the newsman had issued a frost warning, meaning the flowers might die. He knew it wasn't supposed to be cold like this in the middle of May, but that wasn't the part that scared him. New Grandma said something about the house always staying warm no matter what the weather and then she said, "And I've lived here for many, many years." Then he remembered Daddy telling him that the grown-ups who lived here before were very bad. They tried to destroy the souls of the kids, that's what Daddy said. And the worst part of all—they won. They killed a boy like Hansel in this creepy, awful house.

William pretended he had to pee and snuck upstairs to his own bathroom, where he sat on the edge of the tub, looking out the window, with his hands stuck under his legs. He knew his father wanted him to be brave. Daddy always said William HAD to win, no matter what. And he had to protect his sisters. It was the last thing Daddy said in the special letter just for William.

"I know you love Pearl and Maisie, buddy."

He did love his sisters, more than ever now. He missed Maisie bad, but he missed Pearl, too. The Pearl downstairs listening to Grandma was like a crushed-up piece of paper or a toy someone had stepped on. She had to hold her fork all weird-like, so her arm wouldn't hurt. Even her voice was so much quieter it made him want to cry.

He was so scared he felt like his heart was going to explode and make a mess all over the bathroom tile, but that was okay. All he had to do was try his best, like Daddy wrote in the letter. "Whatever happens, remember, I'll always be proud of you for trying. And remember, you'll always be my smart little man."

CHAPTER TWENTY-ONE

Lila wanted to believe that the children were all right. She wanted to feel reassured—as her sister-in-law and her husband did—after Ashley talked to the social worker and Pearl. Not surprisingly, Mrs. Pritzel had been annoyed that Ashley had looked up her home phone number and bothered her on a Sunday night, but she said she'd visited Pearl and William last week and just spoken to them on Friday and they were doing very well. The social worker also said that, now that it had been three weeks, it was time to start supervised visitation with Ashley, and she would set up a meeting between the children and their mother on Tuesday evening, Wednesday at the latest.

This was good news, Ashley said, as it was the first step toward bringing the kids home. She was also happy that the social worker agreed that she could call Pearl's cell phone number, if she was really concerned, just to check in. Unfortunately, Pearl was still angry with her mother, or, as Ashley put it, "She sounded like I was bothering her even though all I told her was I loved her and was worried. She said, 'But you weren't worried when you had *him* living there, were you? You weren't worried when you cut our own father out of our lives.' "

Lila didn't know how to respond, but she couldn't judge Ashley as harshly as she had before, and not only because her sister-in-law was near tears. She felt ashamed and embarrassed that when Ashley had asked Pearl if she wanted to talk to her aunt for a minute, Pearl had said no. "Are you sure, honey?" Ashley said. "She's sitting right here and she's worried, too." Ashley hadn't shared Pearl's response—until Lila stupidly insisted on hearing it. "It was just some crazy crap about you causing Billy's death." Ashley sighed. "She's trying to find somebody to blame. Me, you, doesn't matter, as long as it isn't her daddy's fault."

During these phone calls, Patrick was busy using Ashley's computer to track down Barbara Duval's address in Pennsylvania. He said it was surprisingly easy to find, and he'd printed the directions, in case they needed to head out there tonight. But when he heard what had happened, he said they should wait until morning to decide what to do, and Ashley agreed. She was afraid of causing trouble with Mrs. Pritzel and losing her chance to see the kids this week and maybe even get them back.

After they talked for another half hour or so, Patrick and Lila went upstairs to Pearl and Maisie's room. Ashley had insisted they stay over, and Patrick had gratefully accepted. He crashed on one of the twin beds while Lila took the other. Within a few minutes, her husband was snoring softly. No wonder, he had to be exhausted from all that driving.

It was after midnight. Lila expected to fall asleep quickly herself, but the drowsiness side effect of her medicine must have worn off. If anything, she grew more awake as the minutes ticked by—and as she thought about what Pearl had said about Lila causing Billy's suicide. Her first reaction was to feel intensely guilty, as though she was responsible in some way she hadn't accepted. But when she realized this was the same feeling she'd had when her mother screamed that she'd caused her father's death, she was suddenly positive that her mother was behind this, too. Somehow she'd manipulated Pearl into believing Lila had done something awful to Billy.

If this was the only thing her mother had managed to convince Pearl of, it would be sad, but not an emergency. But what if Lila's mother also convinced Pearl to turn on Ashley? Or William? What if she even convinced Pearl to turn on herself?

Dr. Kutchins had told Lila that her mother was very dangerous. "You keep defending her because she didn't beat you like your stepfather. Ignoring the fact that she allowed him to do this, you still have to consider that her cruelty was as bad, if not worse, because it was so covert. Research has shown time and time again that a parent can destroy a child without ever landing a blow."

Pearl wasn't a young child, but since her father died, she was clearly vulnerable, and possibly more profoundly troubled than any of them knew. While they were downstairs, Ashley had confided that—though Kyle was undoubtedly bad news—she had a "strong hunch" that he hadn't actually beaten her daughter. Her sister-in-law didn't elaborate, but Lila was disturbed at the mere possibility that Ashley could be right. If Pearl had staged this, if she'd actually allowed someone to beat her until she was bruised . . . Lila kept wondering if something frightening was going on within Pearl, something that might lead her to harm herself in other ways. And even if Pearl was fine, what about William, who was only eight and had already been through the police investigation that had led to his father's suicide?

Maybe Lila would have talked herself out of doing anything if she hadn't remembered all the times her brother had said, "My children will never go through what we did." As she got up and threw her clothes on, her only thought was that she owed it to Billy to make sure his precious kids were safe.

She stopped at the other twin bed and looked down at her husband, sleeping flat on his back, his fists curled against his sides like a baby. He'd done so much for her in North Carolina, and she wanted him with her now, badly, but she was also afraid of him seeing her mother again. Billy had always said that they had to protect everyone else from the terror of their past—and look what happened when Patrick got close to that past before. Somehow her mother had managed to change her sweet husband into an angry man who came home to Lila talking as though he didn't know her or even like her. After spending only an hour with her mother in New Jersey, her husband had actually walked out on her—for the first time, the only time, in eleven years.

Even if her mother hadn't caused that, she could have, Lila was sure. Because her mother knew something no one else knew: some secret about Lila. This was her deepest fear that nothing in therapy had been able to diminish. Despite Dr. Kutchins and even Mrs. Lewis insisting it wasn't Lila's fault that her mother was cruel to her, some part of Lila could never believe it. Because her mother knew something they didn't know. Something that could drive anyone, even Patrick, away from her for good.

Before she left Ashley's, she took Patrick's directions off the kitchen table and a blue jacket from the hook by the door. It was 1:42 according to the clock in the Subaru when she headed for her mother's house. She turned on the heater full blast. The wind was blowing so fiercely that the little car seemed to be working hard to stay in the lane on the highway.

She knew this house could turn out to be where she and her

brother had grown up, though the right house could be in New Jersey or any other area where it snowed. But when she came to the last street listed on Patrick's printout, at 2:17, there was no more doubt. The name of the road was Jennigan, and she remembered trying to write that word when she and Billy were four or five years old. She was pushing down hard on the crayon, trying to write it as well as her twin could. The crayon was purple. She could see it so clearly.

She forced herself to concentrate only on the road, which was a maze of curves until she reached the top of a hill. There it straightened and narrowed significantly. It looked like it had been cut out of a forest hundreds of years ago; there were so many trees that they made a canopy over the street, blocking out the moon and the stars. Every half mile or so a house would appear on the right or the left, always with a lamp or a porch light left on, but then the road would go back to utter darkness. She was following the mailbox numbers, but also following her instincts. Her body told her when she found the right house.

It didn't look that distinct. Several homes she'd passed had had circular driveways, and many of them were large, historical brick homes, like this one. Yet only this place made her start trembling so hard that she had to turn into the driveway with one hand, because her other hand was cupped against her chin to stop her teeth from chattering.

Now that she was here, she realized why she hadn't thought it was insane to drive over in the middle of the night. Several of the lights were on downstairs. Their mother had always been a night person, according to Billy. He said she used to wake him up sometimes to play chess, and apparently she'd done the same thing with Pearl. The curtains were drawn back; Lila could see them sitting in the front room, but she'd cut her engine and turned off her headlights so she could roll to a stop without them seeing her.

As she sat in the Subaru, she concentrated on her brother, hoping he would give her courage. When that didn't work, she thought about her husband innocently sleeping back at Ashley's, but this just made her wish she were back there with him. Somehow she propelled herself out of the car and up the first few steps of the walkway. Before she made it onto the front porch, though, she turned and rushed around to the side of the house, where she crouched down against the bushes, trying to catch her breath. It was so cold she was shivering, and she pulled Ashley's jacket tighter around her. When she felt well enough to stand, she walked back, climbed up to the porch, and pulled the heavy door knocker, all the while forcing her mind to focus on nothing but Billy's children—his pearl of great price and the little boy who'd been named after Lila and Billy's gentle father.

Her mother opened the door and said, "Hello Lila" without any perceptible surprise in her voice, as though she'd known her daughter was coming. As though nothing had changed in twenty years.

For her part, Lila was surprised how different her mother looked. Her hair was still blond, but her face was so much thinner. She seemed shorter, too, or at least she was shorter now than Lila. Only her smile hadn't changed; it was still ambiguous, apparently genuine but not matching her eyes, which were either angry or laughing or both, Lila had never been able to tell.

"I can't tell you how glad I am you've come. I thought I might die before seeing you again, but here you are." She clapped her hands. "A veritable prodigal daughter."

Her mother reached out to hug Lila then, and Lila couldn't think fast enough to deflect her. She didn't want to be reminded of those old days when she used to long for a hug or kiss from her mother, when she'd stubbornly held on to the hopeless desire that someday her mother would love her, too.

It was the theme of her earliest memory, according to Dr. Kutchins, who had pushed and pushed Lila to talk about this and acknowledge how it had made her feel. She and her brother were four or five years old; they'd been playing in the backyard when they came across a beehive. They knew better than to touch it, but they still got too close and both of them got stung a few times on the legs. They ran back inside the house, wailing from the pain and the shock that something like this had happened to them and Mommy didn't even know. Their mother looked at their legs and sprayed some cold stuff from a can that helped, but they were both still sputtering and crying, so Mommy told Lila she could have a Popsicle; then she picked up Billy. She carried him around, hugging and kissing him, while Lila ate her Popsicle. When Lila said it was her turn for Mommy to pick her up, Mommy said she wasn't strong enough to hold her and her brother. "My turn, Mommy," Lila repeated, holding up her arms. "That's why I gave you a Popsicle," Mommy had said. "If you wanted to be held, you shouldn't have eaten it. You can't have both."

Now when her mother dropped her arms and took a slight step back, Lila looked past her, distracted by the house. She didn't expect to remember any of this, and yet the front hall was so familiar it took her breath away. On the right was the ancient mirror framed in mahogany and flanked by two flower stands that Lila used to think were giant candlesticks. On the left was the long bench with the carved back that looked like it belonged in church. The walls were painted pale yellow, which she didn't remember, but the thick planks of the wood floor were still gleaming, reflecting dozens of lights from the chandelier above. And at the end of the hall was the wide staircase that led up to the landing and a window seat where she and Billy used to read when it was raining. It used to have rows of black and white pillows; she could see them in her mind perfectly.

When Dr. Kutchins had asked her about this house, she hadn't been able to describe a single room except the basement and her own bedroom, and even those descriptions were sketchy. What she knew best was the surrounding land: the hill and the woods and the tree house. She wished she could run back there now to escape her mother, who was already trying to confuse her.

"I heard you're an English professor. How wonderful! Billy told me when you were doing your dissertation that you'd chosen American literature, which suits you, I think. Melville is an interesting choice for a woman, though I'm sure it makes you unusual in your field."

She knew Billy had not told her mother anything because Billy hadn't even seen her mother. Either Patrick told her or, more likely, she looked up Lila's faculty page on the internet. Lila took a deep breath and walked past her mother and through the doorway that led to the front room, where Pearl was still sitting in one of the stiff leather armchairs next to the pedestal table that held the chessboard. Her mother was right behind her. "I think you should go to bed now, Pearl. We can continue this game in the morning. It's late and I'd like to talk to my daughter."

"But I need to talk to her," Lila said. "I came here because—" Pearl was already standing and Lila walked over to her. "Wait, I know you're upset with me but—"

"I have to go upstairs now." Her voice was quiet and depressed, nothing like the way she usually sounded. And she was wearing stretch pants and a button-down shirt that seemed utterly wrong for a teenager, in addition to looking at least four sizes too big.

"Just for a few minutes," Lila said, trying and failing to catch her eye. When Pearl started to walk away, Lila said, "Please," and reached for her niece's elbow.

"Let go! You're hurting me!"

Lila dropped her arm and gasped, "I'm sorry." She'd thought she was barely touching her niece, and the idea that she'd hurt Pearl brought tears to her eyes.

"Go on, now," her mother said. "I want to talk to your aunt."

Pearl left, but not before she glanced back at Lila. Her niece's expression was still angry, but Lila thought she saw confusion as well.

She told her mother she wasn't leaving until she got a chance to talk to Billy's children.

"I assume you'll be staying until morning, then," her mother said brightly. "How nice. We'll have a chance for a good, old-fashioned mother-daughter chat. Have a seat. I'll make tea."

"No thanks," Lila said, but her mother was already gone.

She found it too oppressive, standing in this dreary room, faced with the ivory chessboard, surrounded by her mother's trophies. She walked to the front hall, and while she was considering whether to follow her mother to the kitchen or find another room, she heard a noise above her head in the room that used to be Billy's. It sounded like someone crying, though she knew that might be her imagination conjuring up all the cries she'd heard in this house years ago.

As she rushed up the stairs, she kept her eyes straight ahead, unwilling to be distracted by the window seat on the landing or anything else. She was determined to find out what was going on before her mother could stop her. When she got to the door, the pitiful sound was louder: it was unmistakably real, coming from a little boy. Then she noticed the button on the knob was pushed in, and she instantly knew what had happened to William.

She turned the button and flung open the door. The bedside lamp was on, but he wasn't in bed; he was pushing on the window latch, trying to get it open.

"Daddy did it last time," he stammered. "I thought I knew how, but I can't."

She had no idea what he was talking about, but it didn't matter. He was crying so hard that nothing mattered but gathering him in her arms. He felt hot and limp, as though he'd been sobbing for hours. He didn't resist when she picked him up and carried him to the chair across from the bed, to hold him in her lap. His hands were clasped tightly behind her neck.

After a moment or two, he said, "I didn't do nothing bad." He swallowed hard. "I didn't—"

"Come on now, William." Her mother was standing in the doorway. "Tell your aunt the truth."

"I don't care what he did. Locking children in their rooms is horrible." Lila stood up, shifting William's weight to her hip. She walked to the doorway holding the shaking little boy, and her mother stepped out of the way, thank God. Lila didn't want to stay in this room another minute, for fear her mother would lock them both in.

"It's past his bedtime." Her mother sounded eerily calm. "I know you've never taken care of children, but surely even you can see that a child needs sleep."

Lila looked down the long, dark hallway before turning the other way, to the light and the stairs. She carried William down very slowly, making sure her foot was firmly in the middle of each step. Though small for his age, he was still very heavy for her. When they got to the bottom, she walked into the first room and sat down on a beige love seat, hoping to catch her breath.

If the chess room was Lila's least favorite room in this house, this one she'd always liked because of the wall of books her mother owned, including several first editions going back to the early nineteenth century. She liked that the books remained even when her mother changed everything else, from the furniture, none of which she recognized now, to the mantel on the fireplace, which Lila thought had been brick before or maybe white, but which now looked like marble. She felt better just sitting in this room, and William was calming down, too, even though her mother had followed them and was standing a few feet away, lecturing Lila about how tired William was going to be tomorrow when he had to go to school.

"I'm taking him with me," Lila finally said. "I'm taking him and his sister home."

"I'm afraid that's not possible. Their mother is still under investigation, and I don't think social services will look kindly on you as a guardian, given your history . . . not to mention your recent behavior."

Lila winced, but her voice stayed firm. "We'll see about that."

"Can I get my toys?" William said, looking at Lila. He sounded like his usual sweet self now. He was even smiling shyly.

She was a little uneasy, but she said, "Sure, honey, if it's really important to you." He must have felt it was, because before she could stand up to carry him back to his room, he'd jumped off her lap, and he was halfway to the front hall when it hit her that he didn't intend for her to go with him. She didn't force the issue; she knew he would be all right as long as her mother was down here, haranguing her. But she couldn't resist telling him to hurry. "And let your sister know what's going on. Tell her as soon as you guys are ready, we're leaving."

"I won't let you do this," Lila's mother said. "You shouldn't even be driving. It's not safe."

"What?" Lila forced a laugh even though she was intimidated by the way her mother was looking down on her with unmistakable condescension. "I'm a very good driver. I've never had an accident in my life."

"Perhaps, but I'm sure you're aware that your brother did not want you driving with his children in the car." She crossed her arms and smiled slightly. "I'd think you'd want to honor his wishes."

If only she could have shot back that this was absolutely false. Instead, she felt her face get warm as she realized that she'd never driven Billy's children anywhere. But wasn't this just a coincidence? Whenever the two families went out together, either Patrick was driving or Billy and Ashley had the kids. She did remember discussing this with Billy once, a long time ago, when Pearl was four and Lila was going to take her to get an ice-cream cone. She'd just started to back out of the driveway when her brother came running out without his shoes on, saying he wanted to come, too. "Scoot over," he said. "I'll drive."

She did as he requested, though she found it a little strange, knowing Billy disliked driving and let Ashley take the wheel nine times out of ten. "In case you've forgotten," she said, "I do know how to drive. You taught me how. Remember?"

"And I did a good job, if I do say so myself."

"So what's the problem?"

"There's no problem. I just wanted to test out your brand-new car." Her "brand-new car" was a beat-up Datsun that she'd bought for nine hundred dollars, all she could afford on her grad school stipend. "And I love ice cream." He turned around to Pearl. "Tell your aunt how much I like ice cream."

"He likes the icky coffee kind!"

"All right," Lila said, "but you better not be turning into one of those macho guys who never lets his sister drive."

"Quién es más macho?" he said, holding up his arm and flexing his muscle. At which point Lila smiled, but Pearl cracked up as if it was the funniest thing in the world, which made Lila and Billy laugh, too. Before long, the conversation had turned to other things, and the subject never came up again.

Now Lila was swallowing hard, trying to remember that her mother was dangerous. "She wanted to hurt you," Dr. Kutchins said. "It made her feel powerful to hurt a defenseless child." And she wants to hurt me now, Lila thought. She wants me to ask her why Billy wouldn't let me drive with his children.

"I'm a good driver," Lila said. "You're making this up."

"Oh, you poor thing, he never told you, did he? Does that mean you're no longer taking your medicines? I think that's risky, but if your doctor feels it's no longer necessary . . . I assume he's a specialist. I would hope so, given the stakes here."

She thought of Mrs. Lewis saying some of the drugs were to keep her from having seizures. One of Lila's students had epilepsy and couldn't drive. Was that what her mother was talking about?

Oddly enough, she felt as if she knew exactly what having a seizure was like, but she'd always thought this was because of Billy's story. She didn't remember the title; he'd written it years ago, while she was still in college. The main character was a lonely young girl who feared she was going mad. The girl saw herself throw things in anger, heard herself scream from frustration and nightmares, but inside her mind was another child: quiet, calm, reasonable, good. The way Billy framed the story, the seizures seemed like a metaphor for the painfully harsh criticism the girl constantly leveled against herself. But the onset of each one was described so vividly that Lila felt like she'd experienced them right along with the character—she remembered the intense dread, the sudden brightness of the room, the sense that the objects around her were melting, the pervasive scent she could only describe as the smell of the color yellow.

Her voice was trembling, but she forced herself to look straight at her mother. "I don't have epilepsy anymore, if I ever did. And I think most of those medicines you gave me were to control me."

"Not most, but some of them, yes. You had violent outbursts, but the doctor said you would grow out of it in time." She shrugged. "Perhaps you finally have."

She felt like her mother had slapped her. Before she could stop herself, she said, "What are you talking about?"

"The doctor said the seizures and all the rest were a direct result of the skull fracture and the damage to your brain."

Her mother's face was a mask of concern, but her eyes weren't cooperating. They were laughing at Lila, mocking her for not remembering any of this. Mocking her the way they always had for being too stupid to win at chess.

But Lila couldn't say anything because she was feeling the truth that had been left out of Billy's story. She was tumbling, flying, flailing, falling. She tried to grab the rail, but she was going too fast and the sharp corners of the steps kept coming up to hit her in the face and arms. Though she would never remember the end of it all, when her head slammed into the concrete floor of the basement, she knew exactly what it felt like to fall into the darkness that had ended her childhood. The strange part was that she hadn't really even been afraid, except that she would get in trouble for ruining her special black dress.

CHAPTER TWENTY-TWO

Before he packed up his toys and stuff, William ran down the hall to tell Pearl that they were going home right now. Aunt Lila had come to save them!

He hadn't seen Pearl at all since New Grandma had locked him in his room 'cause he tried to do what Daddy wanted and protect his sister. It was after his bedtime, but he thought he heard Pearl crying so he'd snuck back downstairs. They were in the chess room, and he crouched down by the doorway in the dining room where he could see and hear everything.

"You believed he married her because he loved her? Oh, my poor girl. I thought I was simply stating a fact."

Pearl didn't say anything. She was sniffing and gulping and staring at the chessboard.

"Your father was a complicated man. Very few people knew who he really was." New Grandma moved her queen and said, "Check." Then she hit the button on the chess clock.

Pearl looked at the board for a moment before she knocked her king over to resign. She turned away from New Grandma, toward the window. "I really thought I did."

William could see his sister's reflection in the window. She looked so sad that he stood up and walked over to her and patted her face. He had to do it 'cause it was like New Grandma was trying to squish Pearl's feelings like a bug.

He knew he would get in trouble for not being in bed, but he didn't care. When Grandma told him to go back to his room, he decided it was time to be super-duper brave. He said no and then he said, "You stop being mean to Pearl."

She laughed. "Why, William, I can't believe you would say such a thing."

"It's not funny. You're making her sad. You hurt her arm."

She stood up and put her hands on her hip bones, which stuck out like knives. Her skinny elbows were bent out like paper clips.

"I think you're making a mistake," she said, staring into his face. "If so, I assume you'd like to apologize."

He was blinking like mad and clearing his throat, too, but he said it again. "You're mean to my sister. YOU should say sorry!"

"Go on, buddy. I'm okay." Pearl's voice was still the flat pancake, but she called him "buddy," which made his eyes start itching.

"Your concern for your sister is quite touching," New Grandma said. "But I'm afraid this is getting tiring." She leaned down and said in his ear, "If you don't go to your room right now, I'll have to ask Pearl to carry you there. Do you want that?"

He felt trapped. It would be so embarrassing to be carried to his room like a baby. Plus Pearl's arm would hurt a whole lot worse if she did.

He said he would go upstairs, but before he left he said to New Grandma, "Don't hurt my sister anymore or I'm gonna call Mommy and the social worker. I'll tell my teacher, too!"

"Stop it," Pearl said. Now she sounded mad at him. "I told you she didn't hurt me."

"Obviously, I've completely misjudged you, William." New Grandma's face was red as a ham. "You're nothing like your father. You're no different from every other American boy." She snapped her fingers and pointed to the stairs.

He ran away, 'cause he was scared of her ham face. But when he got in his room, he felt kind of proud. She said he was nothing like Daddy, but he didn't believe that. Daddy always said being an American was a good thing. Even if the government was evil, Daddy said, the people were good and the American books showed that. Plus, being a boy was a whole lot better than that romance thing.

He figured New Grandma had to be sort of scared, too, 'cause now she knew she would get in big trouble if she kept hurting his sister.

He fell asleep for a while, and he woke up and the clock by the bed said it was 1:55, the middle of the night. He'd heard a loud noise, like something falling over, but he couldn't run downstairs to make sure Pearl was okay and he couldn't get to the phone to tell on Grandma 'cause she'd snuck upstairs and locked him in the bedroom. It had to be Grandma 'cause Pearl wouldn't do this to him and there was nobody else there. He was so scared, but he knew he had to think hard and not cry. This was just like the escape Challenge and Daddy had told him there were two ways out. He could pick the lock or he could climb out the window and crawl down to the kitchen roof and then hold the big pipe until he got to the ground. First he tried to pick the lock with a Lego, 'cause he didn't have a credit card like Daddy had used. He forgot he was supposed to keep one of Mommy's dead credit cards with him all the time. He pushed against the door hard with his shoulder and that didn't work, either. So he had to do the window, which was a lot worse, 'cause sliding down that pipe made his hands burn. Plus he'd have to go outside in the dark.

Daddy had showed him how the window latches worked, but now that he had to do it, he wasn't sure he remembered. He tried pushing and pulling and squeezing until his fingers hurt. Then he sat on the bed for a while, crying and being mad at himself. Then he tried the door again and the window again and the window in the bathroom, which had the same kind of latches and didn't work, either. He was crying loud now 'cause he was starting to feel like maybe he would never get out of here and he'd die and be a ghost like Hansel. Then there'd be nobody to help Pearl and New Grandma would flatten her for good. After a while, he was crying so hard he couldn't even call for Mommy or Daddy anymore 'cause his breathing was all messed up like a goldfish that jumped out of the tank. And that's when the door just opened, like magic. Except it was better than magic 'cause it was Aunt Lila and she was so nice to him; she picked him up and carried him around almost like she wasn't Aunt Lila anymore but Daddy. He thought about them being twins and that made him feel less embarrassed that he was acting like a baby in front of her. When Aunt Lila told New Grandma it was wrong to lock him in no matter what he'd done, he was like, Ha, ha, ha, you old Wicked Witch of the West. The Good Witch is here and everything will be okay.

And now they were going home to Mommy and he was so happy he skipped down the hall and opened Pearl's door. She was sitting up really straight on the edge of the bed. Her hands were in her lap, and all of her was real still, like she was getting her picture taken.

He told her the good news and she didn't smile or move. So he came closer until he was right in front of her and told her again. When she still didn't move, he said, "Pearl, you got to listen to me!"

"I heard." She was staring so hard at something that he looked to see what it was, but there was nothing but the blank wall.

He figured maybe she didn't believe New Grandma would really let them go. Or maybe the flat pancake thing would take a while to go away. But then she said, "I don't know what to believe anymore. Aunt Lila seems gentle, you know? Like Dad."

"Yeah." Even Aunt Lila's big eyes weren't weird to him now, just kinda sad. But he was confused why his sister was saying this. Then he thought maybe it was the bad stuff with the pills that had happened at Aunt Lila's house. He sat on the bed next to Pearl. "I'm glad she didn't die."

His sister was quiet for a minute. "Sometimes I want to die."

He cleared his throat like a hundred times; then he said, "'Cause of Daddy?"

"Remember how he used to tell us all the time that the world is beautiful? He'd say stuff like, 'God is in every tree, every flower, every child, every kiss, every heartbreak.' But you know what's strange? Dad hated himself. It was like he believed all of the world was beautiful except him."

William was still trying to figure out what she meant when she stood up and said, "I guess Aunt Lila is waiting."

"You going to pack now?" he said.

She nodded. "Go get your stuff."

He was about to run off when he thought of Daddy saying everyone needs encouragement. He looked at Pearl. "I'm glad you're my sister."

"I love you, buddy. Remember that." Her voice was so weird, like she was floating in the sky, so far away. "I'm sorry. Now go on and pack up your duffel bag."

"You didn't do nothing," he mumbled, but he turned and walked down the hall.

When he got to his room, he started shoving his toys and clothes into the duffel bag. He didn't care if all his clothes were wrinkled; he just wanted to get out of here quick. But when he had almost everything packed up, he saw the toolbox and remembered his big problem.

He knew he couldn't just leave Daddy's gun. Even if he didn't need it anymore, 'cause Kyle was gone, he had to keep it with him. Daddy said to never, ever let anybody get their hands on it. "You would never shoot anyone unless you had to, to protect your family. Other people aren't as trustworthy."

But he was so scared to go to the tree house at night. His tic was going nuts just thinking about walking into that spooky forest.

He put on his jacket with the hood and tiptoed past Pearl's room before heading down the back stairs that they never used 'cause they led nowhere, just to the laundry room and the door to the walkway behind the garage. He forced himself to open that door and walk into the backyard. It wasn't too bad at first, 'cause he could still see the lights from the house. But when he got to the hill, the wind was howling and shaking the trees, and the moon was making monster shadows on the ground. He was so cold and he kept feeling like some bear was creeping up behind him, ready to eat him alive, so he took off running, and he ran and ran, deeper into the forest. He didn't stop when his side started hurting, and when he tripped on a dead branch, he jumped right up and kept going. A few times he was worried he was getting lost, but then he'd see something familiar, lit up by the moon, and he knew he was on the right path, the way he always went to the tree house. Finally, when he was panting and out of breath and even his glasses were steamed up, he made it.

He felt sort of proud as he started climbing the steps. He was really scared, but he'd done it anyway, and Daddy said that was the meaning of brave.

When he got to the top, he felt a little bad, thinking he'd never be in a cool tree house like this again. But it was still too dark and spooky to rest, so he rushed to the corner and moved all the boards from the place he'd hidden the gun.

It took him a long time to accept that it wasn't there. He got a zillion splinters, feeling all around the corner and the whole tree house floor. While he was doing this, he was talking to himself about how dumb it was to put the gun here, where anybody could find it. Maybe some person who didn't understand, like he did, that shooting a person wasn't like in cartoons. Shooting a person was the worst thing in the whole world, 'cause then their family would cry and miss them and worry all the time that they might forget what their daddy was like.

CHAPTER TWENTY-THREE

Lila wished she could get closer to her niece, but Pearl had already told her not to move. They were still in the room with the wall of books; she was sitting on the same beige love seat where she'd held William in her lap, and her mother was sitting in the leather wing chair. At least her mother had sat down when Pearl had walked in threatening to kill herself if they didn't tell her the truth. She'd made some cruel quip about her granddaughter having a flair for drama, but she hadn't walked away and for that Lila was grateful. Because Pearl was serious, Lila had no doubt. Her niece sounded utterly despondent, as if she'd already made up her mind how this would end. And even if she wouldn't feel this way tomorrow or an hour from now, it didn't matter. The gun she was holding against her temple meant a decision of the moment could never be erased.

Had her mother really been so reckless as to leave a gun lying around with children in the house? And where was William? Pearl had said he went outside, but nothing about when or why. Lila worried about him wandering around in the dark, especially on a chilly night like this, though she was glad he wasn't here to see what was happening with his sister.

She was standing over by the fireplace; the gun was in her right hand and her left hand was outstretched as though she was imploring them. "All I want is the truth. Maybe you're right," she said, nodding at her grandmother. "Maybe I didn't know my dad, but I tried to. I tried as hard as I could, but I failed."

Lila couldn't fathom why her mother would've told this grieving girl that she hadn't known her father, but she told Pearl it wasn't true. "Honey, listen to me. You lived with him for fifteen years. She hasn't even seen him since he was a teenager. You know a lot more—"

"No more lies! I saw the pictures myself. She showed them to me. He was visiting her while he was telling me she was dead."

"Your aunt isn't lying, Pearl. Billy kept his visits from her, as well." Her mother's smile was barely perceptible, but Lila noticed it and shuddered. "I think he was afraid she wouldn't approve."

Lila felt like the wind had been knocked out of her, but she refused to feel what this meant. "I don't know why your dad didn't tell me," she said slowly, looking straight at her niece. "But I still believe that I knew him, and you did, too." Pearl reached up to rub her right elbow, as though it was bothering her. This was the same elbow Lila had touched earlier. "I'm sorry again about your arm," she said gently. "I never meant—"

"You didn't. It was my fault. But this has nothing to do with what I want to talk about," Pearl said, her voice rising. "I want to know why Dad hated himself enough to do what he did. And don't tell me it's because of what happened with William and losing custody. I know that's not true. He said it started when he lived here, in this house."

"I already told you my thoughts on this," Lila's mother said, sounding like a petulant four-year-old. "Apparently, you didn't appreciate my answer."

Lila was surprised. "Billy told you he hated himself when he was a child?"

"Here it comes." Her mother frowned at Lila. "You're going to blame me. I'm the horrid mother who made her poor children so unhappy." Her voice was dripping with sarcasm. "No doubt you blame me for Pearl's instability, as well, based on nothing other than that she's been staying here for the past three weeks. I'm sure it would never occur to you that she's behaving this way because she was the one who found you unconscious, that it was your irresponsible actions and those of your brother that led her to—"

"Stop it," Pearl screamed. "I'm going to do it right now if you don't tell me the truth!"

"But I've told you the truth," Lila's mother said. "What more do you want—"

Pearl's hand was twitching. "Wait," Lila said quickly, "I'll tell you, but your father shouldn't have blamed himself. He was only trying to protect me. And he was very young, your age, fifteen years old." She'd never said this to anyone, but that wasn't why she hesitated. She had to make sure Pearl didn't overreact to the news that her father had done something violent to Harold. Unfortunately, Lila wasn't sure what Billy had done because her brother always said he didn't want her to be involved, in case whatever it was came to light. In the hospital, she'd dreamed or remembered Billy saying he shot him. Was that possible?

"First," she told her niece, "you should know that our stepfather was very abusive. He—"

"This is a total fabrication," her mother said. "There wasn't—"

"He beat you," Pearl said, staring at nothing. "Once he had you lie on your bed without your shirt on, and he beat you on the back with his belt. All you'd done was ask him a question."

Though Lila didn't remember this, Billy had told her about it many times. "Yes," she said, astounded that her niece could rattle it off so quickly. "Did your father talk about this?"

"No, he wrote about it. In a book."

"What book?"

"Clearly it was one of his *stories,*" her mother said. "Billy had an incredible imagination, but Lila knows she was never beaten in her life. She was punished occasionally, yes, but—"

"The book is about a man who can't escape," Pearl said. "That's in the first sentence. And then there's all this true stuff like the guy's name is Billy and he has a twin sister named Lila and he grew up in this house in Pennsylvania. So it's like my dad was writing about himself, but then he starts some chapters with, 'What you are about to read isn't true' or 'Believe the following at your peril.' " Pearl swallowed hard. "I just don't understand it. I tried and tried, but I'm not smart enough."

Her niece had let her arm fall to her side, but she was still holding the gun. If only Lila could convince her to put it down. She heard noises upstairs, meaning William was back inside. She wondered why he hadn't come down yet, but she hoped he stayed safely where he was. "This makes perfect sense," she said to Pearl. "You think if you did understand it, you would understand your dad. Perhaps I could help you. I know your father's—"

"But he says in the book that the guilt he can't escape is because of his twin." Pearl's cheeks grew pink. "Was he like . . . in love with you?"

Her mother started to say something, but Lila cut her off. "No, honey. Of course not." She could feel her mother sneering at her, but she kept her eyes on her niece. "That's what I was trying to tell you before. When our stepfather was beating me one night and wouldn't stop, your father—"

"Shot him," Pearl said. "I know that, it's in the book." She closed her eyes for a second. "But it's in one of those chapters he says isn't true."

"Because it isn't," her mother said. "It's frankly ridiculous that we're having this discussion, as your aunt knows full well that she never even had a stepfather." She crossed her arms. "I never married any of the men I was involved with. I considered it, but at the end of the day, I valued my freedom more."

Lila felt cold even though she knew it was actually a little warm in the room. "Perhaps she didn't marry him," she said, as evenly as she could manage, "but we thought of him as our stepfather and he certainly treated us—"

Pearl shook her head. "His name was Harold Duval, right?"

Lila nodded, and her mother sputtered, "No it wasn't. My boyfriend's name was Harold Tarley. How can any of this—"

Pearl shrugged. "That's what he named the stepfather in the book."

Lila was trying to focus. If there wasn't a Harold Duval and never had been, then the word Billy could never utter without his voice filled with rage was the name their mother had given them. Their *mother*'s last name.

Pearl was looking at her. "Are you saying he did shoot this Harold guy, even though it's in the not-true chapter?"

"I don't know, but your father did something to protect me. Your grandmother knows it, too. She knows something happened the night Billy and I ran away."

"Would you like me to describe that night?" her mother said.

"No," Lila said, glancing at her niece.

"Oh, it won't hurt Pearl, I'm confident of that. Because your brother didn't do anything. Something happened that weekend, though; you're quite right there."

Lila said she didn't want to hear any more, but her mother ignored her. She knew from the thinly disguised glee in her mother's voice that her mother had found an opening to hurt her, though she had no idea how badly.

"On Saturday night, when my boyfriend Harold came home, you tried to attack him with a butcher knife. You claimed that he was going to beat your brother, which was absolutely ludicrous. After that stunt, I had no choice, I had to put you in a hospital."

Lila felt as stunned and disoriented as if she'd smashed into a wall. Her hands were knotted together as though she was literally holding on to what she'd always believed, what her brother had told her a thousand times about their past.

"Is she telling the truth?" Pearl looked at Lila. "There was something in Dad's book about you trying to save him. He even had that page you wrote stuck in the middle of the chapter. Remember? I gave it to you at the cemetery."

I know what my mother did, but I can't hate her for this. It's not her fault that she lacks imagination. But I have to be strong and save my brother. He told me he wished he were dead. I'm really afraid he'll kill himself if we don't get out of here. I'm writing this because I have to do whatever it takes to make sure he's all right. He needs me now so badly. I can't ever be weak again.

Lila had looked at this note Pearl had given her several times, even kept it in her purse, but she'd never guessed it was something she herself had written. The effect on her of this realization was as immediate as it was strange. Her mother was still talking about that night, and she was trying to concentrate, but she was barely able to breathe, much less respond. Something was happening to her; she had to keep blinking to see her niece and the wall of books and the room they were sitting in. For a split second, she wondered if she could be having a seizure for the first time in years, but then the convulsion wracking her mind gave way to a clear vision that was less like a normal memory than like a veil parting in front of her eyes, revealing the past, timeless and all at once.

They were gathered in the front room for the Saturday afternoon debate: her mother, Lila, and Billy. Normally, Lila spent debate time in her room, reading and daydreaming, but today was different. Today, she was worried about her brother.

There was music playing, Bach's concertos, which her mother believed helped clarify the mind. Her mother and Billy were sitting on the white couch; Lila was sitting on the blue chair across from them. The coffee table was new, a massive oak antique that her mother had purchased from a dealer in New York. They were having cakes served on the ivory china they'd had for years, an inheritance from her mother's grandfather, like this house. Lila had broken one of the saucers a few months ago by throwing it against the wall. She didn't remember this, but her mother had mentioned it so many times that simply seeing this china reminded her.

Their mother had just announced today's topic: "Is gratitude an obligation?"

"Taking the affirmative," her mother continued, "I will argue that when extreme sacrifices have been made, the beneficiary has an obligation to be grateful." Her mother nodded at Billy. "You will argue the position you apparently hold: that of the spoiled child."

"Come on," Billy said. "I can't debate this." He sounded hopeless. "You know I don't hold that position. Why are you—"

"I assure you I don't know. I'd told you Friday night was going to be difficult for me." She touched her face with her napkin. "You were well aware that I was going to be alone, without Harold. Apparently, you didn't care."

Her brother had stayed out late on Friday with a friend. But he was a sophomore in high school, and it was normal to have friends; Lila knew that from her books.

"I'm sorry," Billy said. "I've told you that over and over. I don't know what else —"

Her mother pointed at Lila. "And what was she supposed to do while you were out with your quote-unquote *friend*? Even if you forgot about me, surely you didn't forget about your darling twin."

"I was okay," Lila said. She was speaking as softly as possible, trying not to do anything that would make this worse for her brother.

"Don't do this again," Billy said, looking at their mother. "Please."

" 'Oh, don't make me choose,' " her mother said, mocking his voice. " 'I love you both. I love you, Mother, I really do.' "

Lila was trying to concentrate on the conversation, but as it kept going on and on, this became increasingly difficult, especially as she was having one of her fuzzy days, when nothing seemed to make sense and her thoughts jumped around like popcorn kernels in a pan. But she liked listening to Bach; she imagined his fugues like green and gold kites, floating and bobbing across the sky.

She snapped out of her reverie a few minutes later when their mother jumped up and began shaking Billy's shoulders. "After all I've done for you. You evil, evil boy!" She was shrieking. "I've chosen you over everyone in my life, but you couldn't choose me over someone you'd just met!"

Then she stomped out and, a moment later, Billy ran upstairs to his room. Lila followed him. She found him facedown on his bed.

She sat down next to him and rubbed his back. "It'll be all right," she said slowly. "Mother will get over it."

"No, she won't." His voice was muffled against his pillow. "She knows about Jennifer. I don't know how she knows, but she does. Christ, I wish I were dead."

The friend he'd gone out with on Friday was a new girl in his school named Jennifer. And Billy liked Jennifer, Lila knew that, because he smiled whenever he said her name.

Her brother sounded so depressed that Lila begged him for the hundredth time to run away with her. "Is the world, then, so narrow?" she said. "Does the universe lie within the compass of this house?" She was alluding to *The Scarlet Letter,* a book she and Billy had read over and over. After a minute, she added, "We could take Jennifer with us, too, if you want."

"Hester didn't leave," he muttered. "She stayed and took her punishment."

"He's going to punish you? That's not right!" Harold often hit her when he came home, usually for something she'd said to her mother that she'd already forgotten about. Each time, she vowed to control what she said in the future, but then she would feel the angry words bubbling up from her stomach through her esophagus and right out of her mouth. But Billy was different. Even when their mother had screamed he was an evil boy, he hadn't said anything back. He was always in control, and perfectly reasonable; he didn't deserve this.

"I can't stand to have him hurt you, too," she said. "I won't let him!"

Her brother turned over and looked at her. Then he surprised her by reaching up and touching her cheek so gently, as if she were the one about to be punished, not him. She laid her hand on his and tried to figure out what he was thinking. After a moment, maybe more, he pulled away and said he needed to be alone.

By the time she was back in her own room, she'd decided she had to do something to save him. She wrote it down to make sure she wouldn't forget. She even wrote what Billy always said about their mother lacking imagination, which was why Mother didn't see that her complaints about Lila to Harold would invariably lead to him beating Lila with his belt.

While her mother was busy dressing up for Harold's return, Lila snuck into the kitchen and grabbed the butcher knife. She didn't plan on hurting anyone, but she needed something to threaten Harold with if he even approached Billy. She took the knife into her room and sat, trembling, at her desk. She wanted to be strong for her brother but she was so afraid, especially after she heard the front door slam, meaning Harold was home. The only thing that worked to calm her was a passage from the book she was reading, *Moby-Dick.* Captain Ahab wasn't scared of anyone. "I'd strike the sun if it insulted me," Lila said, repeating Ahab's words.

Still, when she heard Harold's heavy footsteps as he climbed the stairs and stopped in front of Billy's room, her heart was skipping like a frightened bird's. She rushed into her twin's room and held the knife pointed out, aimed right at Harold.

Her brother was sitting on the bed. He said, "Lila, no!" and Harold took a step back toward the window that faced the tree in the backyard.

She moved closer, still brandishing the knife at her stepfather. "You're not going to hurt Billy."

"Stay calm," Harold said, holding up his hands. "There's no need to overreact."

Her mother must have heard Billy scream. She came into the doorway. She sounded bored. "Take the knife away from her."

"Put it down," Billy said. "Please, I'm all right." Lila was thinking about doing what he asked until she glanced over and noticed he was crying. Her brother never cried. Harold must have hit him before she got here. She couldn't let him do it again.

Her mother barked at Harold, "Do it now, before she hurts someone!"

Billy hated Harold, but Lila never could, no matter how many times he hit her, and no matter how many times Billy said it was all Harold's fault, the way their mother treated them. She wasn't about to give him the knife, but she couldn't watch it happen, either. So as Harold came closer and closer to her, she shut her eyes, and when she felt him try to grab her arm, she stabbed blindly in what she hoped was the right direction.

She opened her eyes when she heard him groan. She'd only nicked him in the arm, but he stepped back immediately. "That's it," he said. "I'm through with this!"

"What?" her mother said.

"All of this! You tell me every time I get back that Lila has to be punished because she's been hitting you and Billy. This time, you said Billy had to be punished because he hit Lila." He was pressing his fingers against the cut, but Lila saw the blood running down his arm. "If you ask me, everyone in this house is crazy as hell."

He left the room, taking care to stay as far away from Lila as possible. Her mother went after him, and a few minutes later, they heard him yell a curse and then the front door banging shut.

Lila whispered to her brother, "I think I'd better go to the tree house."

It was the one hiding place where their mother never thought to look for her, because her mother still believed the tree house wasn't strong enough to hold a teenager. She didn't know that Billy had reinforced the boards in the floor last spring, to give Lila somewhere to read in peace when he was at school and her mother was in a bad mood.

Billy agreed that she should go because he knew, as Lila did, that this was worse than a bad mood. As she ran up the hill, she wondered if her mother would ever forgive her. But she was proud, too, because she'd kept her brother from being beaten. She'd done the right thing.

When she got to the tree house, she was so tired that she curled up on the floor to rest. At some point she must have fallen asleep, because the next thing she knew, her brother was standing at the base of the tree, telling her she had to come down now. He sounded so sad that she wondered if Harold had come back to threaten him again, and she rushed down to see if she could help. That's when she saw that he wasn't alone. In the light from the moon, she could see their mother standing next to him, and a few feet away, two strange men.

As the men grabbed her, Lila wanted to fight or run away, but she couldn't move. To say her heart was broken would be wrong. She felt like her heart had left her body and there was an empty space where her feelings should be.

"I'll come for you," Billy said right before they took her away, with her hands bound up like a criminal. He was crying, but she didn't shed a tear or even say good-bye.

Lila came out of this memory gripping the arm of the love seat so tightly her knuckles had gone white. It was nothing like at Mrs. Lewis's house, where she'd felt that on some level she'd always known about the night her father died. This day, the day she'd attacked Harold, and everything it meant, had been buried in her mind—and actively hidden from her by her brother, whose version of what happened had been completely at odds with the truth.

Her mother was talking to Pearl as if nothing had changed. "As I've mentioned before, by the time your father and his sister were teenagers . . . well, I won't go into that again, but suffice it to say,

Billy couldn't bear being away from her, so he ran away and managed to sneak her out of the hospital when the nurses weren't paying attention. He showed terrible judgment, given that she needed to be treated, but when the hospital asked me if I agreed to her release, I said yes. Your father had already told me if I didn't agree, he would never speak to me again. As it is, I didn't see him for years, though he let me know that they were staying with their grandmother in North Carolina. I suppose I should have been grateful for small favors."

Pearl was looking at Lila, pleading with her to make sense of this. But how could she, when she was drowning herself? Everything Billy had told her was a lie. Harold had been mean, yes, but he was hardly the villain her brother had created. He wasn't even tall or menacing; he was a guy she'd remembered in one of her dreams, the short bald man who'd given her pennies when she was a little girl. Were there other men, other boyfriends, who'd punished her at her mother's behest? She felt sure there were. But worst of all was discovering that her belief that Billy had always protected her was an utter distortion of reality. He was the one who'd been called evil that night, and not by Harold, by their mother. And Lila had tried to protect him; yet Billy had told her mother and the men from the hospital about her hiding place. He'd led them right to her.

Finally, she found the anger Dr. Kutchins had insisted she must have. Billy had always told her not to be weak; yet he was the one who'd really been weak. He'd never had the courage to tell her the truth. He'd even continued to visit their mother after they'd started their new life. How could he have betrayed her like this?

"What does any of this have to do with you?" she finally said to her niece. She was trying to breathe slowly to keep herself from crying or screaming or running from this house. "Let's say your father hated himself when he was child. What difference does it make now?"

"No need to get snippy," her mother said. She turned to Pearl. "You'll have to forgive your aunt. She's always been too selfish to sympathize when someone is obviously hurting."

For her mother to talk about sympathy was absolutely laughable. Yet Lila knew she'd sounded angry, and she was about to tell her niece she was sorry when Pearl whispered, "Because I hate myself, too. And I'm afraid I'm always going to, like he did."

Tears started rolling down Pearl's cheeks and soon she was sobbing so hard she was hiccupping as she stammered out, "I told him on the phone that Mom was right about him putting William in danger. I just wanted him to understand and change so he could see us again." She collapsed to her knees and hugged herself with her arms. The weapon was still in her hand, dangling like a purse. "It was only two days later when Daddy . . ."

"It wasn't your fault," Lila said as gently as she could manage. "I promise you, that had nothing to do with the reason your father did what he did." She paused. "And you know what? Your mom was right. Your little brother could have been seriously hurt."

"But why did he do it then?" Pearl cried. "I have to know w—"

"Oh, please," her mother said. "How would your aunt know Billy's—"

"All right," Lila said, and inhaled. "I'll tell you what I think. I think he killed himself because he thought he was a coward. Because he didn't protect me. And because . . . I stood up to Harold and he didn't."

"But that can't be true." Pearl was sitting on her heels now, holding the gun with both hands, gingerly, as though it were a newborn baby. She swallowed hard. "My dad always talked about how important it was to be brave. And he meant that. I know he did!"

Lila looked at the mantel of the fireplace covered with photographs of Billy as a child taken at chess tournaments, and a few pictures of the two of them, mostly taken by their father when they were small. Of course Pearl didn't want to believe this about her father. She'd adored Billy since before she could walk.

But all Lila wanted was to get that gun away from her niece. So she took a deep breath and decided to tell Pearl a story. She ignored all her mother's interruptions as she told Pearl about a damaged little girl who'd fallen down the stairs and a brother who tried his best to make her better. The boy gave the girl books to read when she was frightened. He kept her from getting worse, mentally, by helping her to memorize passages from literature. And because she couldn't really remember from day to day what happened, the boy invented a world for her. That world had a clear villain and two heroes: the boy and the girl. And that world held out the promise of a beautiful future, where the two of them could be safe.

But when Lila got to the part of the story about Harold's punishments, she didn't shrink from the boy's failure to protect the girl. She knew the story wouldn't be convincing if she didn't account for this. She repeated that the boy thought he was a coward—but she emphasized that he was wrong. He couldn't see that he was the best part of the girl's childhood. He couldn't see what a great gift he'd given her by making her love stories. In truth, it was the boy and his stories that had protected the girl from despair and might have even saved her life.

Finally, she looked into Pearl's eyes. "He had to be brave to do all that, don't you think? In a sense, you could even say it was worse for him, because he didn't have someone like him to invent a better world. All he had was the painful truth."

"Bravo," her mother said, smirking. "You've outdone yourself, though I suppose—"

"Be quiet!" Pearl said, before turning back to Lila. "I think you're right, you know? Because in his book, Dad talks about the imagination like it's this force for good. In real life, he told me this quote about people not being able to bear too much reality. It sounds like he was trying to help you the only way he knew how."

Lila knew this quote; it was from Billy's favorite poem, Eliot's *Four Quartets*: "Go, said the bird, for the leaves were full of children / Hidden excitedly, containing laughter. / Go, go, go, said the bird: human kind / Cannot bear very much reality."

When her niece not only put down the gun but pushed it away from her, under the couch, Lila was so relieved her body felt limp and exhausted. She wondered what time it was. It was still dark outside, but a lighter dark, more purple than black.

A moment or two later, William appeared in the room, as though he'd been watching all this. She was concerned that it must have upset him, and he looked shaky and frightened, but his voice was confident when he said, "My mom and Uncle Patrick are coming to help us."

"How do you know that?" Lila said.

"I called them on Pearl's cell phone." He handed the phone to his sister. "I've been looking out the window, so I could let them in."

Lila's mother stood up and went into the hall, but before she could do whatever she planned to do—probably call CPS—William ran to the front door and then Patrick and Ashley were in the room, too. Ashley rushed to her daughter, and Patrick came over to Lila. It was so strange to have him in this house, knowing how much she'd wanted to keep all the tragedy of her past away from him.

When her mother returned, she frowned at Ashley. "I could have you arrested for taking the children, but I don't want to traumatize Pearl after the night she's had. I tried my best with them, but you obviously don't appreciate it. Apparently, you've forgotten that I was doing you a favor." She lifted her chin. "Ah, well. I have a hunch they'll be back here before long."

Before her sister-in-law could respond, Lila said, "No, they won't ever be back in this house. And if you try to force the issue with lawyers, I'll fight you." She took her husband's hand; his wide palm was warm and so familiar, it gave her courage. "I'll tell the court what it was like living with you."

Her mother didn't defend herself for a change. It seemed like it was finally over. But when they were all at the door, packed and ready to leave, Pearl suddenly ran off in the direction of the stairs. Ashley was holding William, who was half-asleep, but she started after her until Lila said she would go. "Don't worry," she whispered, looking into her sister-in-law's eyes. "She probably just forgot something."

She found Pearl in her bedroom, standing by the window, with her backpack lying at her feet. When Lila asked what was going on, Pearl said, "I don't know."

Her niece clearly meant that. She sounded like a confused little girl. Then Lila noticed what she was looking at. In the corner, on top of the small dresser, was another framed picture of Billy. He was a teenager about Pearl's age. He was standing in the woods in the snow, wearing a navy blue cap, pointing at something. Lila knew she'd taken this photo, and not only because he was smiling, but also because his body looked relaxed, the way it only did when their mother wasn't there.

She picked up the picture and asked Pearl if she wanted it.

"Can I?" the girl whispered. "I really like thinking of him as happy. I mean, some of the time."

"Of course," Lila said and handed it to Pearl. Her mother had hundreds of photos of Billy as a child; surely his daughter deserved at least one.

As Lila watched Pearl putting the photograph in her backpack, carefully, as though she was trying to avoid bending her right arm, it suddenly struck Lila that she knew what had happened to her niece. "Your grandmother did that to you, didn't she?"

"How did you know?"

"Because she hit me, too." It was hard to admit, but she knew it was true: her mother had hit her and pulled her hair and even whipped her with a belt. She felt like she'd always known this on some level, which was why she'd needed Billy to keep telling her the plot. And maybe why Billy had made up the part about Harold being their stepfather? It was so much easier to accept having been beaten by a stepfather whom your "weak" mother couldn't stand up to, rather than by a boyfriend whom she'd obviously told to punish you. It was so much easier to believe that this stepfather had been cruel to you rather than your own mom.

Lila went to her niece and put her arms around her. At first, Pearl accepted the hug somewhat stiffly, but when Lila said, "I want to help you, honey," the girl relaxed and leaned against Lila, and Lila could feel how worn-out she was. "I'm here for you," she said softly. "And we're going to get through this. I'm not sure how we're going to get through it, but we have to, don't we?"

Pearl looked up. Her eyes were swollen from crying, but she said yes.

Then Lila noticed her mother standing in the doorway.

"I feel I should correct one thing in the tale of woe you told my granddaughter downstairs. Don't worry, it doesn't contradict the central theme of poor, poor Lila, who was always being mistreated."

"Save it, Mother. I know you left me alone for days to travel to chess tournaments with Billy. Even though I had seizures. You should have been arrested for that and—"

"You were not *alone.* The housekeeper was with you, if not all day, then at least part of each day. And your seizures were controlled with medicines."

Lila turned to Pearl. "Go on down to your mom, okay? I'll be there in a minute."

Pearl nodded and Lila waited until she heard her niece's footsteps on the stairs before she hissed, "You hit that poor girl! How dare you?" She clutched her hands together. "And you hit me. I remember that, too, now. You hurt me and you—"

"As I've already said, you were the kind of child who had to be punished. Blame me all you want, but I think you'd sing a different tune if you had the courage to have your own children, rather than judge me for how I raised mine."

Lila was standing near the closet. Though she hadn't thought about it when Pearl was with her, this used to be her bedroom. It had been completely redecorated, but she could feel the ghost of the child she'd been. She could feel the way her mother had been, too, that night when she'd stood in this same doorway and blamed her for her father's death.

"I have to go," she said.

"This won't take long. I just want to tell you about the day you fell down the stairs. The doctor said you might never remember that, because trauma victims often don't. But it was the day of your father's funeral." She sighed. "A difficult time for me, of course. I'd lost the only man I'd ever loved and been left a single mother of twins. I didn't know how I'd—"

Lila felt suddenly nervous, but she said, "It's always about you, isn't it? Nothing else matters but how you feel and what you want."

"I can't believe I raised such a rude child."

"That's it," Lila said, "I'm leaving." She rushed past her mother and into the hall, but her mother followed her.

"You seem to think your brother was a saint," her mother continued, "but the truth is he was a lot like me. He had, shall we say, no patience for fools."

"He wasn't like you," Lila said without turning around. "He made mistakes, but he was capable of loving other people."

"Believe what you wish. I only wanted you to know that you didn't fall down the stairs, Lila. I didn't push you, and you didn't fall. Make of it what you will."

Lila felt like she was falling again, but this time she could hear her brother screaming. She felt immediately that it was true; her mother lied about feelings and minimized the damage, but she rarely lied so blatantly about facts. She didn't need to; she could always present any fact in a way that defended her, while devastating the other person.

But if her mother seriously expected Lila to wonder whether Billy pushed her on purpose, she didn't understand anything about the two of them—or anything about the nature of love. They might have been squabbling, as all children do, but of course he'd never meant to really hurt her. She'd remembered the way they were before she fell: crying when they got stung by bees, reading together in the tree house, rolling down the hill as superheroes, swimming and playing and laughing and talking about his stories. He was a little boy. If only someone had told him that this was not his fault.

She could feel tears welling up, but she heard Patrick's deep voice and the surprising sound of Pearl's laughter. "My family is waiting for me," she said. Then she headed to where they were standing by the front door and told them she was ready to go home.

EPILOGUE

A few days later, early in the morning, Lila was standing at Billy's grave. It was a little after sunrise and the first time she'd seen the headstone. Most of the words Ashley had chosen were traditional: his name and dates, along with the acknowledgment that he was a father, a husband, and a brother, but across the top she'd had them carve: *Step Softly, a Dream Lies Buried Here.* She wasn't sure where Ashley had found this epitaph—maybe the funeral home suggested it—but it seemed simple, sad, and true.

She'd decided to come to the cemetery the night before, when Pearl had given her a blue folder. "It was really supposed to be yours all along," Pearl said. "I'm sorry."

Lila's heart jumped into her throat when she realized what she was holding in her hands. It was Billy's book. On the front was a sticker where he'd written: "For LEC: Truth Comes in with Darkness."

The phrase was from "The Piazza," one of Melville's stories she'd written about in her dissertation. The story is about a man who imagines that a glittering house on a faraway mountain is an enchanted fairyland. Then one day the man journeys to the house and finds that Marianna, the girl who lives there, is not only wretchedly poor, but near despair: an orphan, living alone with a brother who must work constantly and is never home. Yet the one thing that keeps her going is her belief that the house she sees down in the valley is a magical place. She believes if only she could meet the happy person who lives there her sorrow might abate. Of course, the man himself is this person and it is his house that she sees. But he leaves without telling her, and the story ends with him saying that he will not set out for fairyland again.

Billy's manuscript was typed, obviously written years ago; yet it felt as intensely personal as if it were a three-hundred-and-something-page letter he'd written to her. As she'd carefully flipped through the pages, seeing her name and Billy's on nearly every one, she'd begun to grasp what this meant.

Now, as she moved closer to the headstone, she whispered, "I understand." She knelt down in the dewy morning grass. "You wanted me to know. Even if you couldn't tell me yourself, you wanted me to know."

The sun was up but fighting with the clouds. She watched the yellow and pink struggling against the dark sky and remembered the first time she heard "The Piazza." She and Billy were in North Carolina. They were sitting on their back porch, and he read it aloud to her. They were so young, the world was all before them, but her brother's voice was tinged with sadness, as if he already knew the way the story would end.

THE PROMISED WORLD

Lisa Tucker

A Readers Club Guide

Questions and Topics for Discussion

1. Discuss the novel's title (page 75). What is "the promised world" and how does it play into the aspirations of the characters? Does Lila, in the end, attain some form of redemption?

2. Describe the novel's structure. How did you feel about the changing voice of the narrator? How did Lisa Tucker's portrayal of women, men, and children differ?

3. How do the members of the Cole family respond to Billy's suicide? Do they grieve differently?

4. Discuss the role of luck in the novel. How does belief in the "Cole curse" affect the actions of Billy, Ashley, and Lila? How do Billy and Ashley's children view luck and superstition?

5. What does *The Promised World* tell us about the nature of marriage? How does Patrick's relationship with Lila change over the course of the novel? What sacrifices does Ashley make for Billy?

6. Describe the role of literature in the novel. What does it represent? What is the significance of the Cole family's interest in American literature? Are you familiar with the authors they study and discuss? How do they play a larger part in the novel, particularly Melville?

7. Early in the novel, Lila tells us that Billy would probably have considered her therapist a "hack." What is the role of therapy in the novel? Does attending therapy help or hurt Lila?

8. What are the repercussions of the parenting styles presented in the novel? Was William harmed by Billy's "challenges"? Was Ashley a bad or selfish mother? How did Barbara Duval affect both Lila's and Billy's sense of self?

9. On page 124, Lila recalls "Billy said it was not only the central theme of American literature but also the promise of the American dream—that we can reinvent ourselves however we want." Do you think Billy and Lila have reinvented themselves or are they simply hiding part of themselves from their new families?

10. What aspects of Lila's life emerge during her trip to North Carolina? Who does she meet and how do they put together the puzzle of her past?

11. How does Lila's relationship with Billy compare with Pearl's relationship with Billy? Do you see similarities in the different generations of the Cole family?

12. The action of the book revolves largely around the revelation of secrets. What scene in the novel surprised you the most?

13. What does the Duval house represent to Lila? How does the house add to the suspense of the novel?

14. How would you have responded to Pearl's threat at the end of the book?

15. What were you thinking as you read the novel's closing scenes? Which characters had changed the most, along with your impressions of them?

16. What themes are woven throughout this novel? What is unique about the approach the author uses in bringing the Cole family to life? If you've read other novels by Lisa Tucker, do you see similar themes?

Tips to Enhance Your Book Club

1. Read and discuss "The Piazza" by Herman Melville. Does reading this story enhance your experience of *The Promised World*? Do you think this story influenced Lisa Tucker? If yes, how?

2. Explore the works of other American Literature authors mentioned in the book (i.e. Thomas Pynchon, Nathaniel Hawthorne).

Printed in the United States
By Bookmasters